NOT MY FATHER'S HOUSE

A Novel of Old New Mexico

Loretta Miles Tollefson

Palo Flechado Press

Library of Congress Control Number: 2019912438

Palo Flechado Press
Santa Fe, NM

Cover Art by Fresh Stock

Other Books by Loretta Miles Tollefson

Old New Mexico Fiction
Old One Eye Pete (short stories)
Valley of the Eagles (micro fiction)
Not Just Any Man
The Pain and The Sorrow (Sunstone Press)

Other Fiction
The Ticket
The Streets of Seattle

Poetry
But Still My Child
Mary at the Cross, Voices from the New Testament
And Then Moses Was There, Voices from the Old Testament

A Note about Spanish Terms

This novel is set in northern New Mexico and reflects as much as possible the local dialect at that time. Even today, Northern New Mexico Spanish is a unique combination of late 1500s Spanish, indigenous words from the First Peoples of the region and of Mexico, and terms that filtered in with the French and American trappers and traders. I've tried to represent the resulting mixture as faithfully as possible. My primary source of information was Rubén Cobos' excellent books, *Refranes, Southwestern Spanish Proverbs*, (Museum of New Mexico Press, 1985) and *A Dictionary of New Mexico and Southern Colorado Spanish* (Museum of New Mexico Press, 2003). Any errors in spelling, usage, or definition are solely my responsibility.

For my mother, Loretta Dawkins Miles, who always cheered up when spring planting season came around.

CHAPTER 1

There's a man standing on the grassy ridge south of the cabin, and it isn't her husband.

At the bottom of the cabin steps, Suzanna sets her bucket of water on the ground, pushes a tendril of black hair from her forehead, and cups her hands around her eyes to block the sun. The figure at the top of the rise seems to be staring straight at her. A flash of light blinks near its head, then again.

Suzanna squints, trying to make out details. A man's figure, bulky and dark against the sunlit sky. Dread clutches her chest, but she shakes her head against it. Enoch Jones is dead in the Salt River wilderness. Gerald killed him, much to her guilty relief. Yet she still shivers in the bright July sunshine.

She leans down for the water bucket and carries it onto the porch and into the cabin. Ramón is in the lean-to that serves as the kitchen, shelling the new peas she'd brought in an hour before.

Suzanna puts the bucket on the rough wooden counter beside him and forces her voice to sound calm. "Someone's on the ridge to the south."

Ramón looks up. "Señor Gerald?"

Suzanna shakes her head. Ramón's eyes tighten. He drops the pea pods in his hands back into the bowl and moves into the cabin's main room. Suzanna follows him as he lifts the shotgun from its place beside the heavy wooden door and steps onto the porch.

He turns to scan the ridge on the far side of the marsh below the cabin. The rise is empty of everything except long green grass. A single cow grazes at its base.

1

"That cow, she has escaped again," he says absently.

"I saw a man." Suzanna's right hand slips to her belly. "He just stood there, watching."

Ramón nods. His eyes move from the slope to the marsh that lies between the ridge and the hill where the cabin is located. "And there was nothing else? No horse? No pack mule?"

"He was alone. Just standing there. Watching."

"It wasn't el señor?"

Suzanna's lips tighten. "I know what my husband looks like, even from that distance. It wasn't Gerald."

"It may have been a passing hunter who was puzzled to see a house here, so far into the Sangres."

Her jaw clenches. Then she closes her eyes. He's simply trying to relieve her anxiety. She turns to face him. "I'm sorry, Ramón. I didn't intend to speak so sharply. It's just—" She waves a hand. "We're so isolated here. And now, with the child coming—"

He nods and gives her a sympathetic look. "It is many leagues to Don Fernando de Taos. And you have not seen your father in a long time."

"And you have not seen your beloved," Suzanna says contritely. "At least I have mine with me here."

He gives her a small smile and looks toward the mountains on the valley's western edge as if he can see through them to the village of Taos and its spreading farmlands. "Encarnación will be here in due time. We will be married when she has found someone to care for your father." He grins at Suzanna mischievously. "Mí Chonita has very high standards."

Suzanna laughs. "She certainly does." In the bottom of the valley below, movement catches her eye. "There's Gerald now. Is that a deer on the mule?"

Ramón studies the man and laden beast who are moving up the track that threads the center of the valley. "I think it is an elk," he

2

says. "A small one." He hands her the shotgun. "If you will return this to its place, I will see to the arrangements for the butchering."

Suzanna takes the gun. "I'll finish cleaning the peas," she says. "Then what should I do with them?"

He's already at the bottom of the steps. He turns toward her. "They will need to be cooked very quickly." He pauses, then shakes his head slightly. "Place them in water and leave them. I'll attend to them later."

"Because you don't want me to ruin the first good crop we've had," she says drily.

He chuckles and turns to head across the yard to the adobe-and-timber barn. Suzanna smiles ruefully. Her legendary lack of cooking skills is one of the reasons Ramón is with her and Gerald in this remote valley. While she doesn't like admitting her weaknesses, she's glad of his ability in the kitchen. And his company. Between the two men, she's rarely left at the cabin by herself.

But there are still times when loneliness creeps in on her. When she longs for another woman to talk to, other people. Ramón, still just a boy when he became her godfather, is very dear to her, and she has Gerald and her garden. But it would be nice to have other people nearby.

Though not people who remind her of Enoch Jones. She glances toward the ridge south of the cabin. A red-tail hawk circles above it, alone in the empty sky.

Her shoulders tighten. Whatever possessed her to agree to move here, a bride just turned sixteen, so far from her father and Taos?

The hawk calls, a piercing cry to the clouds. Suzanna's shoulders tighten again, but she remains on the porch, gun still in her hands, gazing at the green expanse below.

She knows the answer to her question: She loves a man who loves this valley.

And she must admit that it is pretty. Majestic, even. Even now, with rain clouds gathering in the hills behind the cabin and more massing over the stone-topped Sangre de Cristo peaks to the west. They'll meet in the middle of the valley soon. She grimaces. Probably before Gerald turns off the track below toward the cabin.

She agreed to live here, she reminds herself. Gerald was clear from the beginning that this was where he wanted to settle. And that it was a good three or four day mountain journey east of Taos. But now that she's here, it seems much farther than that. And the valley seems so foreign, so closed in, so restricted, somehow.

She swallows the sudden acid in her throat. She could have fought him, insisted that they live closer to Taos. But Gerald studies this land with such deep satisfaction in his gray eyes, the same look of wonder and joy he gave her the day she said she'd marry him.

Suzanna smiles, thinking of his creamy brown profile, the wavy black hair, the square forehead, the intelligent eagerness in his look, the strong hands that know just how to touch her, and feels herself soften once again. She can't resist either him or his desires. She blushes and glances around the yard self-consciously, glad that Ramón is nowhere in sight. Would he know, just by looking at her, what she's thinking? She takes a deep, steadying breath and tucks a stray black curl behind one ear.

In the valley below, Gerald suddenly lifts his head and looks toward the cabin. Even from here, she can see his face brighten when he realizes she's on the porch. He lifts an arm, acknowledging her, and her heart lurches again. She waves back at him and watches until he and the mule make the turn toward the cabin. Then she moves into the house, returns the gun to its place by the door, and crosses to the kitchen and the abandoned peas.

As her thumb systematically presses into the end of each pod and scoops the small spring-green spheres from their shells, Suzanna's mind wanders to the low row of brush the men have placed around her garden. This morning, the leaves on her squash plants had been ragged on the edges, as if something had been nibbling at them. And some of the pea plants had looked like someone had pruned them. Both clear signs of rabbit encroachment. She's going to have to shore up the fence if she expects to gather more peas this spring.

Or corn, for that matter. She'd also spotted raccoon handprints in the soil between her carefully planted rows of maíz. She grimaces. Those furry gray, stripe-tailed beasts Ramón calls mapaches are as large as a mid-size dog and twice as bulky. And notorious both for their rapacity and their love of corn. The fact that they're already sniffing around, when the slim green plants haven't yet even begun to develop ears, is not a good sign.

Suzanna's hands move quickly over the peas, hurrying to finish up. Gerald will be here soon. And whoever she saw on the ridge this morning isn't as important as her husband or her plants. If she hurries, she'll have time to work on the garden fence before the men finish with the elk.

Besides, Ramón is probably right. It was just some passing stranger, surprised to spot a cabin where there'd been only elk the last time he crossed the valley to the Cimarron and the Eastern plains beyond.

Yet, despite her resolution to focus on her garden and not her fears, Suzanna finds herself telling Gerald about the stranger late that afternoon. They're perched on their favorite boulder on the slope above the cabin, side by side on the sun-warmed rock, gazing out over the valley. "There was something about him that reminded me of Enoch Jones," she says, trying not to shudder.

Gerald nods, his eyes somber. He puts an arm around her shoulders. "But Jones is dead somewhere in the wilderness north-

5

west of the Gila mountains." He pauses. "I knifed him, remember?"

"I know," Suzanna says. "I still feel ashamed at the relief I felt when I learned what had happened." She leans into the warmth of his arm and shoulder. "And I suppose I should be thankful to the man, lout that he was. After all, if he hadn't accosted me that day in Taos, you wouldn't have come to my rescue and we might never have met." She turns her head to smile at him, then sobers. "I never thought I'd be glad for a man's death. But he was such a shadow on my life. Such an ongoing threat." She gazes out over the valley. "Jones was just an ugly man, inside and out. It's hard to imagine how anyone could be so evil-minded. I suppose he was just bone-bad from the beginning."

"Oh, I don't know." Gerald looks south, studying the ridge where the stranger had appeared, then looks beyond it and west, toward Palo Flechado Pass. "Things happen to a man and change him. Get inside his skin. Sometimes the memories and the bad feelings about them just won't let go."

"Or things don't happen to a man. And that also creates bad memories," Suzanna says wryly, remembering a story Encarnación once told her of Jones, of his inability to perform as a man. But she certainly isn't going to explain what she means. Not even to her husband.

Gerald gives her a quizzical look, then lifts a shoulder. "It may be that some people are so confused inside that nothing can heal them." He pulls her closer. "But Jones isn't a danger to anyone now, so there's no need to worry." His hand drifts lower, to her belly. "We should be celebrating, instead." Suzanna chuckles and snuggles closer to him, watching contentedly as the setting light brightens the western peaks.

CHAPTER 2

The man on the ridge grunts in satisfaction and tucks the spyglass into his pocket. It's her, all right. With some greaser. Word in Arroyo Hondo was she married that bastard Locke, but that ain't him. Must be that Mex named Chavez that used to work for her pa. The big man snorts and shoves his dirty-blond hair away from his face. The greaser and Locke, too, probably. Take two men to keep her the way she thinks she needs.

He steps backward down the slope, no longer sky lit on the grassy ridge. Don't want her gettin' too good a look. Just enough to make the little bitch wonder. 'Cuz he's dead. Killed by that interferin' bastard Locke. Left to be tore apart by the Gila Apaches and the wolves after them. He's just a pile of bleached bones, somewhere west of the Zuni villages.

The big man chuckles sardonically. Ain't he?

CHAPTER 3

A month goes by before Suzanna sees another man who isn't her husband. This one is tall and thin, clothed in black, and walking up the trail from Taos beside a well-rounded woman whose head is shrouded in a voluminous shawl. They each lead a donkey, a wooden bench perched precariously above bulging packsaddles. Half a dozen cattle splay out on the trail behind them, raising lazy spurts of dust when they aren't straying into the grass and patches of purple flowers that lie beside the path. A thin young man walks behind the cows, waving a long switch at them when they wander too far off-track.

Suzanna stands in her corn patch below the cabin and gazes at the little caravan, puzzled. Then joy lights her face. It's her father. And Encarnación. Ramón will be so glad! She makes a face at the raccoon tracks in the dirt at her feet and trots up the hills toward the house.

But Ramón has already spotted the travelers. He's watching them from the cabin porch, a basket of eggs in each hand. He smiles at Suzanna as she reaches the steps. "It is Gregorio Garcia with the cattle," he says. "And your father with the mules." His eyes brighten as his smile broadens. "And la Encarnación." He glances down at the eggs, his mind clearly on the evening meal. "It is well that el señor went hunting this morning."

Suzanna nods, then follows him into the cabin and begins straightening the books on the table by the set of four panes of thick mica that form the single window. In the kitchen, Ramón whistles tunelessly. She chuckles at his gladness. Though she has to wonder whether the figure trailing behind the cattle actually is Gregorio Garcia. How can Ramón possibly have recognized him?

But the young man really is Gregorio, as dark eyed and lanky as ever. He drives the reluctant cows into the rough wooden corral at the edge of the hilltop and swings the gate shut behind them just as Gerald and his horse trot in from the hills, a deer carcass slung over the back of the trailing mule. Gregorio follows Gerald into the open-sided shed behind the barn and helps with the butchering while Suzanna and Encarnación supervise the unloading of her father's pack animals.

The two carved and brightly painted benches come off first, followed by Suzanna's big wooden spinning wheel on its stand, three bags crammed with wool, containers of dried maíz, chile, and ground wheat flour, and two rhubarb plants that have been carefully swaddled in straw, then wrapped in rough cotton.

"Rheum rhabarbarum for medicinal or other uses," Jeremiah Peabody says with a small smile as he strokes his black chin beard.

"Thank you for bringing it," Suzanna says. "It should do nicely up here. I had such a time keeping it alive in Don Fernando. The heat was almost too much for it."

Encarnación turns to Ramón. "For medicine or other uses," she says. "It is also called pie plant." She tilts her head, her eyes crinkling. "But perhaps you prefer las natillas."

"Ah, Chonita, I prefer anything that you prefer to make," Ramón says and she rewards him with a brilliant smile. "Come, let me show you the kitchen and how I have arranged it," he says. "It does not seem quite as it should be."

As Encarnación sweeps before him into the cabin, Suzanna turns to her father. "He certainly knows how to please her," she says, smiling.

He looks down at her. "And you?" He glances toward the barn, then peers into her face. "Does your life here please you?"

She looks down at the ground, blushing, knowing that he really wants to ask if her husband pleases her, then looks up. "Yes," she says shyly.

A shadow crosses his face and she puts her hand on his arm. "It is not my father's house," she says. "And I do miss you, papa." She wrinkles her nose. "And the mountains are closer than I would prefer." Then she looks into his eyes. "But my life here is as pleasing as it can be without being in Taos and near you."

He smiles ruefully and gives a little nod as he turns to look out over the valley. "The mountains are very near, but the view is delightful." He tilts his head toward the corn patch at the bottom of the hill. "And I see you've already planted a garden." He smiles at her slyly. "Your husband is a very smart man."

"It's a source of food," Suzanna says defensively. Then she laughs. "And it keeps me occupied. I have peas and spinach and squash and potatoes and maíz, all of which are doing quite nicely, now that the monsoon rains have begun. And as long as I can keep the pernicious raccoons away from them. Though the corn seems slow to develop. We had no rain in June, and it didn't get a good start." She tucks her left hand into her father's elbow. "But come and let me show it all to you."

Her right hand brushes her belly as she leads him down the hill. How will she find a way to tell him? She feels an unexpected shyness toward the man to whom she's always been able to say almost anything.

But there's no need for her to speak. Immediately after the evening meal, Encarnación rises and begins clearing the table. Suzanna stands to help her but the other woman waves her back into her chair beside her father. "Women in your condition should not carry heavy dishes," Encarnación says gaily.

Suzanna reddens as her father's head swivels toward her. Ramón and Gerald, at the other end of the table, both chuckle. Gregorio looks at her with wide eyes.

"Chonita!" Suzanna protests. She slides a glance toward her father and covers her face with her hands. Then she glares at Ramón. "Did you tell her?"

Encarnación laughs and reaches for the serving platter. "There was no need to tell me. I have eyes. A woman sees such things before a man does."

Suzanna looks helplessly at her father. "I was going to tell you this evening." She gives Encarnación a mock glare and glances away from Gregorio's embarrassed face. "In private."

"It may come from a private matter, but there's nothing very private about a child, as you will see!" Encarnación chortles as she turns toward the sink.

"There's no keeping her quiet, when she wishes to speak," Ramón says as he rises and follows her, his hands full of plates.

Suzanna, Gerald, and Jeremiah exchange bemused glances. Jeremiah chuckles and shakes his head. He turns to Suzanna. "I am delighted, of course. When do you expect to be confined?"

"As nearly as I can tell, at the end of the year," Suzanna says.

"We may give you a grandchild as a Christmas gift," Gerald adds.

Jeremiah's thin face works under his beard. There's a long silence, then the unemotional New Englander lifts his palms and stares down at them. He reaches blindly for Suzanna's hand and turns to Gerald, tears welling in his eyes. "You have made me quite happy," he says simply. Then he releases Suzanna's hand, gives it a sharp pat, rises, and leaves the kitchen.

As the door to the porch thuds closed behind her father, Suzanna looks at Gerald. "He is quite speechless. I have never known words to fail him."

11

Gerald chuckles. "His baby has grown up and is about to become a mother. I'm sure it will be a shock to us when it happens."

She laughs in sudden delight. "It is something miraculous, isn't it?"

He pushes back his chair, moves to stand behind her, and bends to kiss her the top of her head. Encarnación turns from the sink and flaps her wet hands at them. "Go, go," she says, beaming. "The kitchen is not a place for such activity."

When Suzanna wakes the next morning, Gerald's side of their attic pallet is already empty. Encarnación moves around the room below, shaking out blankets and pushing furniture back into place. Suzanna smiles drowsily. It will be good when the other woman is here permanently. She's missed Chonita's bustling energy.

Then the image of the man on the ridge rises unbidden in her mind. Suzanna frowns. Should she tell Encarnación what she saw? If Enoch Jones is still alive, Encarnación certainly has a right to know. After all, the dirty-haired mountain man harassed her, too.

Suzanna gives herself a little shake. Jones is dead. Gerald killed him. The man she saw on the ridge was simply someone passing through, someone built like Jones. Those hunched and strangely massive shoulders, that angry bull-like tilt of the head. Or perhaps she simply imagined the whole thing. Ramón didn't see anything and he has exceptional eyesight. He knew Gregorio was Gregorio when the young man was still well down the valley and behind a haze of dust kicked up by half a dozen cattle.

And, if she tells Encarnación that she thinks she saw Jones, her father is certain to hear of it. And then he will worry. Besides, Jones is dead. Gerald killed him. Well, knifed him in the chest, a wound that would kill most men. Though after Jones fled into the wilderness, the searching trappers never did find his body, never actually confirmed he was dead.

12

Suzanna closes her eyes, fighting the bile in her throat. Her hand wanders to her belly and she takes a deep breath. Worrying about such things is bad for the child. She will think about pleasant things and not let her imagination run away with her.

In the room below, Encarnación throws open the door to the porch. A broom swishes vigorously across the plank floor. Suzanna chuckles and sits up. At this rate, Chonita will be whitewashing the rafters before the day is half over. Suzanna stretches, lifts herself from the sleeping pallet, pulls on her clothes, twists her hair into its usual loose bun at the nape of her neck, and heads to the ladder.

Their visitors stay a week, her father walking the land with Gerald and Ramón, Encarnación organizing the kitchen for maximum efficiency, Gregorio hoeing the corn patch and devising ways to stave off raccoon depredations. Then they head back down the valley to Palo Flechado Pass and on to Taos.

Suzanna watches them disappear over the first long rise that bisects the valley, then turns back to the cabin. The men are in the barn, harnessing the mules for a wood cutting trip up the slope behind the cabin. She gazes around the empty cabin. It's so quiet without Encarnación's bustling, her father sitting by the fire holding a book, Gregorio in the corner mending mule harness. So empty.

She takes a deep breath, gives herself a little shake, and heads out to her corn patch to see whether the rascally raccoons have succeeded in breaching Gregorio's barrier of brush.

CHAPTER 4

The emptiness has just begun to feel normal again when a band of Ute Indians rides into the cabin yard.

Suzanna is on a bench on the porch, shelling peas, enjoying the mid-August warmth, and congratulating herself that the rabbits seem to be leaving the plants alone. Plants that are still producing. In Taos, their leaves would be turning yellow by now, the stalks withering in the heat.

She just wishes the pestiferous raccoons would stop snooping around her corn. This morning, she found a stalk bent to the ground, as if the furry black-masked lumps of mischief have been inspecting the ears to see if they're ready to eat.

Her head is bent over the bowl of peas, fingers running appreciatively through the small orbs of damp greenness, when an unshod horse hoof thuds on the hardened-clay soil between the corral and the barn.

Suzanna lifts her head. A tall Indian man, his black hair chopped off at his chin in Ute fashion, watches her from the back of a brown gelding with white spots. Four horseback men and three boys on ponies cluster behind him.

Suzanna rises, clutching her bowl.

Then Ramón is behind her in the doorway, shotgun in the crook of his elbow. "Ah, Stands Alone," he says. "Buenos días." He steps onto the porch and waves Suzanna toward the cabin door as he nods at the men behind the Ute leader. "Many Eagles. Little Squirrel."

"We have met before," the man called Stands Alone says. He's looking at Ramón, but his words are clearly for the benefit of the men behind him. "In this valley in the season of many snows." He waves a hand at the grassland below. "We shared meat and bread in this place." He nods at Ramón's gun, his face inscrutable. "And now you have returned. In the place of Señor Locke?"

"El señor and I have returned together." Ramón motions toward Suzanna, in the doorway now, holding her bowl of peas. "With his woman."

Stands Alone studies Suzanna for a long moment. "It is well." He turns to address the group behind him. "I have agreed to this thing." He turns back to Ramón, whose shotgun still lies in the crook of his arm.

"You are safe here," Stands Alone says. "My people listen to me."

From the doorway, Suzanna sees a shadow cross the face of the man Ramón called Many Eagles, the man with a thin, prominent nose and one brow higher than the other. He doesn't look as if he listens to anyone. Or answers to anyone but himself.

Ramón makes a welcoming gesture with his free hand. "You are welcome."

"You are here as Señor Locke's servant?"

"Señor Chávez is my partner." Gerald says from the end of the cabin. He steps into the yard. "His welcome is my welcome." He turns toward the porch. "And this is my wife, Suzanna, the daughter of Señor Jeremiah Peabody of Don Fernando de Taos."

Stands Alone gazes at Suzanna for a long moment, then looks at Gerald. "Your woman is the daughter of the French Navajo girl and the New Englander? The woman called She Who Does Not Cook?"

Ramón chuckles. Gerald throws back his head and laughs. Suzanna shakes her head in embarrassment.

"We prefer to say She Who Plants," Gerald says.

Stands Alone's eyes twinkle. "I have heard that it is so." Behind him, Many Eagles' stallion moves impatiently. Stands Alone turns and gestures to one of the boys, who moves forward and smiles shyly at Suzanna. Stands Alone says something in Ute and the boy slides from his pony.

"This is my son, Little Squirrel," Stands Alone says. He turns to Gerald. "I was told of your cabin and that there is maíz growing now in this valley. We have brought you a gift to keep the grazers and the mapache from the crops of your woman."

A woven pannier with tied-down lids lies across the rump of Little Squirrel's pony. At a signal from his father, the boy unties the nearest cover and reaches into the space below. He pulls out a bundle of brown and black fur and sets it on the ground. As the bundle resolves itself into a fat puppy, Little Squirrel places another one, this one more yellow than brown, beside it. "Un perro y una perra, a male and a female," he says shyly.

Suzanna clutches her bowl of peas and eyes the puppies warily. She isn't sure she wants a dog. Or two of them. They'll simply be one more thing to see to. She has a baby coming and crops to tend to. That's enough to worry about.

"They will be grown before the child can walk," Stands Alone says. Suzanna glances up in surprise. Is her ambivalence that apparent? But the man is looking at Gerald. He nods toward the field below, where the corn plants stand in neat rows, leaves flowing in the sunlight. "They will protect el maíz. If it bears fruit."

Suzanna's lips tighten. "The cobs are forming well," she says. "I see no reason to expect the crop to fail, if I can keep the raccoons out of it." She glances at the puppies. They seem unlikely to be much use against grown raccoons. Then she looks at the Ute's impassive face and softens. The young dogs are a goodwill offering, no matter how unhelpful they may turn out to be. "Perhaps the smell of them will be enough to keep the raccoons away." She gives him a little nod. "I thank you."

A glimmer of a smile crosses Stands Alone's face. He nods back at her, then glances at Little Squirrel, who leaps back onto his pony. The boy maneuvers his mount away from the pups and toward the group by the barn.

Suzanna opens her mouth to invite the Utes to a meal, but Stands Alone speaks first. "Los mapaches will leave when the deer come, and they will be here soon. The snow in the hills will push them into the valley." He looks toward the western slopes, which show no signs of yellow, though the aspens seem brighter than they were in July. "The leaves will drop early this year," he says. "We go to Taos for winter blankets." He nods abruptly to Gerald and Ramón and wheels his white-spotted horse toward the barn. He speaks a single word to his men, and then they're out of the yard and moving due west across the valley.

Suzanna turns to Gerald. "Is there a more direct way to Taos than through Palo Flechado Pass?"

Gerald shrugs but Ramón nods. "There is a way there, past the sacred lake of the Taos Pueblo," he says. "The trail is rugged, but it is more direct for those wishing to trade at the pueblo. It is also good for travel to the settlements north of Don Fernando, those of Arroyo Hondo and such. But one must go softly there and only in peace. The Taoseños set a watch there that is never broken. They have many sacred places in the mountains."

The yellow-brown puppy has nosed its way across the yard and is sniffing at Ramón's boots. He reaches down and lifts it by the scruff of its neck. "This is the female." He sets the puppy back on its feet and looks at Suzanna. "What will you call them?"

She shrugs. "Perro and Perra? Boy and girl?"

Gerald chuckles. "Surely we can do better than that!"

"I don't plan on being friends with them," she says. "I have enough to do."

Gerald and Ramón trade a look which Suzanna chooses to ignore.

"Spot and Brownie?" Gerald suggests.

"That's not very original," she replies.

Ramón grins. "Negro y Amarilla?"

"Black and Gold?" Suzanna chuckles. "That's just as bad."

Both dogs are now sniffling busily along the edge of the porch.

"Uno y Dos," Ramón says.

Suzanna laughs. The two men grin at her. "One and Two," she says. "Sure. Why not?" Then she grins. "But the yellow-brown female is Uno, not Dos."

CHAPTER 5

Stands Alone's prediction that fall will arrive early holds true, and Suzanna realizes irritably that he also correctly predicted that her corn won't ripen in time. The September afternoons are chilly, but the ears of maíz are still so thin that the raccoons have stopped monitoring them.

The scarecrow she erected to keep the ravens away isn't necessary, either. The big croaking corvines are too busy playing tag with the red-winged blackbirds in the clear sunlight. Two eagles circle endlessly above the smaller birds, seemingly indifferent to everything but each other.

As she stands in the middle of her corn patch, the Ute puppies playing at her feet, Suzanna rubs the sore spot under her ribs and turns slowly, studying the mountain slopes north and west. They're gradually turning yellow, the patches of aspen getting brighter each day.

She turns back to her half-formed ears of corn. Tarnation. She planted as soon as she was able. There'd been so much to do when they arrived in mid-May. Although it's unlikely that planting any earlier would have done any good. It had been too cold to expect corn to sprout.

Suzanna's cheeks redden. It hadn't been too cold for other things. The little lean-to she and Gerald had slept in those first few nights before Ramón arrived and the men started work on the cabin had never really felt chilly.

She smiles and rubs the sore spot just below her rib cage again. She has to admit she was a little preoccupied when they first arrived in the valley and not terribly concerned with getting the planting underway. She chuckles. As a result, she's going to be preoccupied next spring, too. She'll have a baby to care for.

But surely that won't take all her time. And surely this last spring was colder than usual. Suzanna studies the anemic rows of corn. "This child had better like to garden," she mutters. "Because next year I need to get seed into the ground a good month earlier than I did this season."

She shakes her head at the maíz and turns away. There isn't a blessed thing she can do to speed it to harvest. She moves on to her produce garden, which lies closer to the marsh. At least the squash is doing nicely.

When she returns to the house, she's dragging a half-full bushel basket of fat green-striped squash behind her. The kitchen is empty. Ramón and Gerald are in the hayfield in the valley bottom, turning the windrows they'd scythed that morning.

Suzanna sets aside the squash she thinks Ramón will need for the evening meal, wraps an apron over her dress, and begins washing and slicing the remaining vegetables into strips for drying. "At least I can do this much," she mutters.

When she's filled the largest of Ramón's wooden bowls, she carries it to the ramada that shelters the woodpile behind the house. There's just enough space beside the stacked wood for the woven-twig drying racks Gerald constructed for her. She arranges the strips of squash on the racks, covers them with a light cotton cloth to discourage the flies, and returns to the kitchen.

It's almost noon. Suzanna's feeling both hungry and restless. She pokes in the cupboard to see if she can tell what Ramón has planned for the midday meal. A cloth-wrapped stack of corn tortillas and a bowl of mashed beans. A plate containing the small tomatoes she harvested yesterday. The few that were ripe. She shakes her head in disgust. She'll be drying green tomatoes before long.

She studies the tortillas, lifts them from the shelf, and turns to the fireplace. The coals are carefully banked, conserving their heat until a fire is needed again. She can at least get it going, ready for Ramón when he and Gerald come in. She sets the tortillas on the table and crouches beside the hearth.

Her father did her no favors when he banned her from her mother's kitchen, she reflects as she scrapes ash from the live coals and feeds the resulting glow with thin strips of juniper bark. Regardless of what he thought of her mother's morals and the value of a girl learning Latin, her father's choices definitely stunted her development in wifely duties.

The baby kicks just then, jabbing a foot into Suzanna's ribs, and she dimples self-consciously and pats her belly. Well, not all wifely duties. And she certainly knows how to sew, though it isn't her favorite task.

She sits back on her haunches and studies the kitchen's hand-hewn work table and food cupboards. She learned to sew by observing a neighbor woman and then asking Encarnación for occasional advice. Surely she could lean the rudiments of cookery the same way. Her lack of ability here makes her so dependent.

It's also hard on the men. Ramón never seems to sit down. And his kitchen duties reduce his ability to assist Gerald outdoors. Assistance Suzanna can't give, especially now that she's pregnant.

In the fireplace, tiny flames lick at the narrow strands of juniper bark. Suzanna adds a few pieces of kindling, then layers thicker pieces over them. At least she can build a fire. She looks around the room. The water bucket is nearly empty. She adjusts a piece of wood to better catch the flames and pushes herself to her feet.

As she crosses the yard to the well, she sees the men in the field below, heading toward the house, the wooden windrow rakes over their shoulders. Gerald's hat is pushed back on his head, his long stride shortened to keep pace with Ramón, who waves a hand at the remaining grassland and turns his head to say something to the taller man. Gerald laughs, then places his hand companionably on Ramón's shoulder. They stop and turn to look back at their handiwork.

Suzanna lowers her bucket into the well. As she hauls it up again, her stomach rumbles. The men are certainly taking their time. Once they get their tools put away, they'll still need to clean up. She turns toward the cabin. In the meantime, she might be able to warm the tortillas without burning them. And heat the mashed beans.

Back in the kitchen, she finds the smallest of the cooking pots, scrapes the beans into it, and sets it to heat at the edge of the fire. Then she positions the cast-iron skillet and its three-footed supporting grate over the flames and goes to the cupboard for a small pot of lard.

She drops a spoonful of the grease into the skillet and watches it slowly begin to soften. Suzanna yawns. The fat looks as if it'll sit there all day, doing nothing. This is why she dislikes cooking. There's so much sitting and waiting. She pokes at the fire with a stick and repositions a burning log so it's more fully under the grate and the pan.

Finally the fat heats and liquefies. It sizzles busily and Suzanna nods in satisfaction and drops a tortilla into the black skillet. But the extra flame has made the pan hotter than she realized. The flat yellow tortilla buckles sharply in response and the fat pops furiously, then turns into a smoky haze.

Suzanna jumps up, grabs a wet towel from the counter, and darts back to the fire. Smoke fills the room. She leans down, tosses the towel over the skillet handle, and yanks it away from the flames. As she pulls, heat sears through the wet towel, stabbing her palm.

"I swear!" she yelps, jerking away. The skillet clatters to the floor and the charcoaled tortilla tumbles out beside it. Suzanna is doubled over, gasping in pain, when the men come through the door from the main room.

Gerald leaps toward her. "Are you all right? Let me see."

Suzanna collapses onto the floor. "How stupid of me," she gasps. "I know heat goes right through a wet towel."

Gerald reaches gently for her hand. Two red welts bisect her palm. Ramón appears at Gerald's elbow with a dripping cloth. Gerald wraps it around Suzanna's hand, then lifts her to her feet and guides her to a bench beside the table. "Just sit," he says soothingly. "I don't think it's very bad."

She nods, ashamed of her outburst, embarrassed by her stupidity. "I know to use a dry towel," she says again.

"We all make mistakes," Gerald says soothingly.

"Not in the kitchen." She raises her head, her mouth trembling. "I'm the only woman I know who makes mistakes in the kitchen."

Ramón has placed the skillet and tortilla on the work counter and is now crouched over the fire, moving the pot of beans away from the licking flames. He half turns as he wraps a dry towel around the pot. "I almost killed my brothers and myself once," he says. "I had no sisters at that time. My parents were called away and I was assigned to cook while they were gone. I used a haunch of pork that had gone bad." He rises, places the pot on the wooden counter, and stirs it gently. "These are nicely warmed."

He returns to the fire and uses a thick piece of kindling to maneuver the three-legged grate away from the center of the flames. Over his shoulder he says, "I decided the meat simply needed more seasoning to cover the bad taste." He rises and lifts the skillet from the counter. As he wipes it out with a small towel, he shakes his head. "I didn't want to take the time to check the rabbit snares or go fishing."

He leans to place the skillet on the grate. "We were all sick as dogs when my parents returned." He chuckles. "And soon after they returned, I was also sore on my backside. My father was very angry and he was a firm believer in the dicho that says la letra con sangre entra."

Gerald raises an eyebrow. "The word enters better with blood?"

Ramón grins. "The parents' words. There seems to be some truth to that saying. Never since then have I forgotten to throw out bad meat."

Suzanna chuckles and rearranges the cloth over her palm. Her fingertips tingle with incipient blisters. She winces. "My hand will certainly remember to reach for a dry towel when I need to lift something hot from the fire."

CHAPTER 6

Her hand is still wrapped in bandages several mornings later. She's sitting on the front porch, watching the Ute puppies play and studying the pattern of gold on the western slopes, when a scrawny mountain man, his long red hair clumped in rough braids, rides into the yard. He's hunched forward over his sorrel mare, his shoulders almost touching his knees, which are level with the horse's withers. A pack mule trails behind him on a leather lead.

Suzanna smiles. "Well, Mr. Old Bill Williams," she says. "It's good to see you again. How long has it been? Since last fall? I see you've found a horse to match your hair."

"Well now, you know what they say," the mountain man says. "Caballo alazán tostado, primero muerto que cansado. A sorrel-colored horse would rather die than show fatigue." He pats a long red braid. "I figured I'd get me a horse that could righteously match me for stamina."

Suzanna laughs and stands up. "I'm sure even a horse with her endurance must need rest and sustenance. Let me show you where to house her."

He glances over his shoulder toward the barn. "Oh, I can find my way," he says. "You just set there and rest yourself."

"I've been resting all morning and I'm about ready to go out of my mind." She lifts her bandaged hand. "I can't clean, I can't sew, and I can't garden."

Old Bill laughs. "Now that is a trial. Are you tellin' me that your pa sent you into the mountains without a righteously sufficient supply of reading material?"

"Even turning pages is difficult," Suzanna says. She steps off the porch. "Come, I'll show you where to store your tack."

If Suzanna wants someone to talk to her, then Old Bill Williams is the man. He has plenty to tell her. "You know I went huntin' beaver with Sylvester Pratte and his bunch up in South Park last season," he says as he settles onto a porch bench with a tin cup of water in his hand. He glances down at the cup, its sides sweating with moisture. "This is righteously tasty well water, but you don't happen to have anything stronger, do you now?"

Suzanna shakes her head. "But I can make you some tea," she says. "I'm not completely incapacitated."

He grins. "Well, now, tea isn't quite what I had in mind."

She chuckles. "I didn't think for a moment that it was." She tilts her head. "We heard a rumor that Pratte took fifty men with him to South Park. Is that true?"

Williams snorts. "More like thirty. Which was still too many. Pratte always did have ideas that were too big for actual implementation."

Suzanna frowns. "Did have? Has something happened to him?"

"Got bit by a dog and died. Your old friend St. Vrain up and took over for him and we brought back a righteously good catch, in spite of all the commotion." Williams salutes her with his cup and takes a long drink. He shakes his head. "Well, it most certainly isn't whisky, but it's dandy well water." He leans forward and studies the well in the center of the yard, the adobe bricks that form the lower half of the log barn, the rows of corn and the hayfields in the vega below, the men at work with their scythes. "You all have been keepin' yourselves occupied."

"Gerald and Ramón have worked diligently to get us situated for winter," Suzanna says. She lifts her bandaged hand. "I was trying to do my part when this happened."

"Burnt it, did you? Tryin' to do kitchen work?"

She nods ruefully and Old Bill snorts self-righteously. "Your pa keepin' you out of that kitchen was a sure-enough mistake, to my way of thinkin'. But he was settin' you up for bigger things. Better than what your ma ever had. Or was."

His eyes rake the snow-topped mountains to the west. "Yes sir, and then you went and married a—" He slides her a look, then shifts on his bench, adjusting himself. "Married a farmer," he says. He tilts his head back. "Hah! And one that's hell-bent on settlin' just about as far away as he can get from any kind of righteous civilization."

He shakes his head and studies the mountain slopes on the other side of the valley. "You seen any Injuns yet?" He turns and looks at the cabin door. "You do have a firearm close enough for grabbin', don't you?"

Just then Gerald and Ramón top the path from the valley. They cross the yard to the porch, tools over their shoulders. "Well, that's the last of the hay," Gerald says. "Hello, Bill! Where'd you drop in from?"

"You got a firearm she can use while you're down in the fields?" Williams demands.

"It's right inside the door," Gerald answers mildly. He turns to Suzanna. "How's the hand?"

She grimaces. "Still aching. I wish I had a prickly pear pad to put on it."

"I haven't seen any prickly pear up here." He glances toward the hill behind the house. A few yucca plants are scattered on the drier parts of the slope. Their pointed pale-green spines contrast

27

sharply with the dark-green ponderosa clustered at the top of the hill. "Will yucca do?"

"No, it's not the same. I wish I'd asked Encarnación to bring me some prickly pear pads to plant."

"That would be a good food source, if they will grow up here," Ramón says. "We should send word."

Suzanna nods and shifts her hand to her shoulder, an old trick Encarnación has always said will speed healing. "In the meantime, I wait," she says, trying to keep the frustration out of her voice. She turns to Old Bill with a smile. "But Mr. Williams has been keeping me entertained."

Gerald and Ramón lean their tools against the cabin wall and move forward to clasp the older man's hand, then go inside to dip their own cups of water from the bucket in the kitchen. When they come back, they settle on the porch benches, and Suzanna turns to Williams. "So tell us what happened to Sylvester Pratte."

"Well, you know he rounded up a bunch of us to go huntin' in South Park and along the Platte River last fall. Right before we headed out, he was visitin' some woman with one of those little yap-hammering dogs and it bit him."

Ramón chuckles and Williams laughs. "Yep, nobody seems to know who the dog belonged to or why it decided Pratte needed bitin', poor devil," he says. "I figure the woman's true man put a spell on the dog to keep Pratte away." He grins. "Or maybe Pratte's wife back there in St. Louis did a little voodoo." He turns to Suzanna. "Anyhow, the bite got righteously infected and the poison seeped into his blood." Williams grimaces. "I'd rather get caught by Comanche than die all swelled up like that."

Gerald glances at Suzanna, then gives Williams a warning look and changes the subject. "Pratte had half that group under contract, didn't he? What happened with those agreements?"

"Oh, they all got together and talked St. Vrain into takin' over." Williams shakes his red head. "I'm not saying it was smart of St. Vrain to agree to do it. It's risky enough to run your own outfit, much less somebody else's, with contracts you didn't set up. But it does say something about the youngster that they asked him to do it. Says he can do more useful things than what he's been doin', with his smugglin' goods in across the mountains and undersellin' those who don't.'"

"My father believes Ceran will go far," Suzanna says. "Despite the smuggling rumors, men seem to just naturally trust him, even if he is only in his mid-twenties."

"He does seem sensible enough," Williams agrees. "More'n that fool Smith."

"Smith was with that expedition to the Gila and Colorado that I joined a couple seasons ago," Gerald says. "That group William Wolfskill and Ewing Young put together. Smith had an opinion about just about everything. Half-way up the Colorado, he and a few of the others split off and headed out on their own." He shakes his head. "He was so opinionated, I think Young was glad to be rid of him."

Williams snorts. "That's Smith, sure enough. I heard he and that little bunch of his had a hell of a time before they made it back to the settlements. Served 'em right." He stretches his legs into the patch of sunlight that's moving across the wooden porch. "He was as opinionated this last season as he's ever been, and now he's a big hero for cuttin' off his own foot."

They all stare at him. Williams grins, flips his braids behind his back, and leans back against the cabin wall.

"Cómo fué eso?" Ramón asks.

Williams chuckles. "How indeed," he says with a satisfied air. He looks at Suzanna. "You should of seen it. We got in a right-eous bit of a scuffle with some Rocky Mountain natives and Smith took an arrow in his left leg." He gestures toward his ankle. "Right about there. It shattered the bone. There was blood spoutin' everywhere—" He looks at Suzanna. His gaze rests lightly on her midsection, then flicks away. "It's a righteously bad thing to be tellin' a woman."

"My imagination will probably make it worse than it actually was," Suzanna says.

"I wouldn't be too sure about that," Williams says. He looks away and studies the mountains as he speaks, choosing his words. "An arrow got him in the left ankle." He waves toward his leg again. "Well, just above. It was quite a sight. He kept his head though, and tied it off quick, so the bleeding stopped soon enough. But the bones were sticking—" He glances at Suzanna apologetically, then turns his eyes back toward the mountains. "He decided it was too mangled to save, so he took a butcher knife to it." He glances at the two men. "Did it himself."

Suzanna's bandaged hand goes to her mouth and Gerald growls, "I think that's enough."

Williams scowls. "She wanted to know."

"I did," Suzanna says. "Poor Mr. Smith! Is he all right now?"

"He and Milt Sublette got the foot and ankle off clean enough and tied up the leg. It appears to be healin' well enough. There's talk of making him a wood stump." Williams shakes his head. "The man's all mouth and fire, but he's got gumption, I'll say that for him."

Suzanna shudders. "What a horrible thing. He'll never be able to trap again."

"Knowing Smith, I doubt a missing foot will stop him," Gerald says. He looks at Old Bill. "Do you have anything less graphic and more pleasant to tell us?"

"Well, let's see." Williams scratches his head. "St. Vrain's back in Taos, selling goods and prosperin' well." He grins. "Of course, no one he's sellin' to is demanding to know if any customs duty was paid on the goods." He turns to Suzanna. "I saw your Pa as I passed through. He says to tell you hello and that he and that girl cook of his'll be here for Christmas."

Suzanna smiles in delight, then shakes her head at him in mock disgust. "That should have been the first thing you told me."

Gerald laughs. "If you'd told her that first, she wouldn't have even heard the rest."

"But thank you for the message," Suzanna says. She stands and moves into the cabin's main room and toward the ladder to the loft. "I'll just toss down some blankets and we can make up a pallet for you by the fire."

The men move to follow her inside and Ramón heads to the kitchen. Suzanna, halfway up the ladder, suddenly gasps and stops, her bandaged hand in mid-air.

"Are you all right?" Gerald asks.

"I just put too much pressure on my hand." She turns her head so he can't see her face. The hand throbs and her stomach churns. She fights to keep her voice steady. "I just need a moment."

"What're you puttin' on that burn?" Williams asks.

"I made an ointment from some dried prickly pear, but it's not the same as fresh," Suzanna says. She begins climbing again, careful to grip the ladder with her left hand and use her right forearm for balance. She maneuvers carefully into the loft, but the right hand has to accept some pressure no matter how she positions herself.

She bites her lip and drops onto the floorboards, waiting for the throbbing to lessen. Then she takes a deep breath and goes to the chest for the blankets Williams will need. As she tosses them down with her left hand, a wave of shaky nausea hits her. She takes a deep breath, pushing the acid away, steadying herself. Pain bites her hand and she gasps against it. She gulps hard, blinks the tears away, then peers around the ladder into the room below. "I'm going to remain up here," she says, trying to keep her voice steady. "It's too rough on my hand to go back down and then come up again."

"I can fold my own blankets," Williams tells her with a grin.

"I'll bring a plate up to you," Gerald says.

She nods gratefully to him and moves backward to sit on the pallet. The pain stabs again. As she bends over her hand, biting back the pain, Williams say, "She needs some fresh prickly pear on that."

"It's healing, but very slowly," Gerald says. "Which is making her impatient, of course."

Williams chuckles. "Suzanna Peabody impatient? That's just righteously difficult for me to believe!"

Suzanna grins, in spite of the pain. "I heard that!" she calls and the men chuckle and move into the kitchen. "By the way, I hear your Pa's gone north to the Yellowstone," Williams says as the door closes behind them.

The red-headed mountain man's blankets are empty when the others rise the next morning. Gerald returns from the barn to report that the trapper's packs and mule are still there, but Williams and the sorrel are missing. "So there's little doubt he'll be back," he says as they gather around the breakfast table.

Sure enough, the red horse and rider clop into the yard late that afternoon, a lumpy cloth bag tied behind Williams' saddle.

"I've been down Cimarron canyon," Williams says as he dismounts. He unties the bag and turns to Suzanna. "This here is what that hand of yours is needin'."

She takes the bag with her left hand, shakes it slightly open and peers into it. She looks up with a blazing smile. "That is exactly what I need!" She turns to Gerald and tilts the top of the bag toward him. "Prickly pear pads."

A few minutes later, she's sitting at the kitchen table and Gerald is removing her bandages while Ramón gingerly disengages a thick pale-green oval pad covered with two-inch spines from Williams' bag. As Williams hovers in the doorway, Ramón rinses the pad in water, singes it over the fire, then deftly scrapes the remaining needles off with a sharp knife. He fillets the green slab into two half-inch pieces and crosses the room to the table.

Gerald dabs at the wound with a damp cloth, then Ramón places a prickly pear pad, cut-side down on Suzanna's palm and holds it in place while Gerald secures it with a fresh bandage.

"My palm feels better already," Suzanna tells Williams. She nods at the lumpy bag on the work table. "And it appears that you've collected enough for me to plant some, as well."

"That's what I had in mind, all right," Williams says. "Since there's yucca on the gravel spots on these hillsides, I'm bettin' pear cactus will grow up here too, if it's given half a chance."

Gerald straightens. "Once more I'm indebted to you."

"Ah, it ain't nothin'," the mountain man says. "You'd of done it yourself, if you'd known where to look."

Gerald nods, then frowns. "I don't remember seeing prickly pear in the canyon."

"It's further down," Williams says. "Where I found it really wasn't canyon anymore." He grins at Suzanna. "We've got to get those hands of yours righteously back in shape so you can take care of that baby that's coming. That and plantin' your plants. I saw you had maíz at the bottom of the hill. Are you gettin' it to grow proper-like up here?"

"What I've been able to keep those rapacious raccoons out of has been growing, but it doesn't seem to want to ripen," Suzanna says. She moves her hand and winces. It still hurts, though not as much. "The growing season up here is remarkably shorter than it is at Don Fernando. We had snow showers off and on and the ground was half-frozen all through May, so I wasn't able to plant until early June. Then keeping it watered was a challenge, since we had no rain until the July monsoons began." Her eyes darken. "I lost a quarter of my plants. When the corn finally did start to form, the raccoons were more than inquisitive, the pernicious beasts. Nothing seems to slow them down much, not even Indian puppies." She lifts her hands in disgust. "And the deer will be descending pretty soon. I'll be surprised if there's anything left to harvest at all."

There's a small silence, the men glancing toward the walls and the floors, carefully avoiding Suzanna's eyes. Then Ramón turns to Williams. "How far north did you all travel this past season, Señor Bill? Did Señor Pratte's party clean out the Platte River region completely?"

Two weeks later, Bill Williams has gone on his way, Suzanna's hand is healing nicely, and the little corn that has matured is safely harvested and dried for planting the following season. It and the peas for next year are stored in the root cellar beside the strips of dried squash and ropes of garlic.

At least the squash and garlic crops were good, Suzanna thinks ruefully as she lifts her lantern over the cellar bins and shelves to see the results of her first season in the valley. The potatoes still need to be harvested, but they're well covered with meadow hay and she hopes to winter them in the ground.

And now she has nothing to do. She hates the end of the growing season. The baby kicks just then and Suzanna chuckles in spite of her low spirits. She rubs her belly. "Yes, I know," she says. "You're going to keep me occupied soon enough." She turns, looking again at the nicely-crowded cellar, then heads toward the door. "But in the meantime, I have nothing to do but clean and sew. How righteously enjoyable, as Old Bill would say."

As she fastens the root cellar door and moves across the twilight-filled yard, Suzanna reflects that, if she were in Taos, her father would be creating a reading plan for the coming months and deciding which Latin texts she's ready to tackle.

She could create her own reading and study plan. But somehow she doesn't feel up to it. She's just too restless. And bored at the same time. She needs to find something active to do while she still can. Before winter sets in completely.

CHAPTER 7

Suzanna stands in the middle of the field of harvested corn-stalks, her hands on her hips, her belly bulging, a machete on the ground at her feet. Although it didn't yield much in the way of food, the maíz patch contains plenty of dead stalks that now need to be dealt with.

She could leave them standing until spring. The elk and deer would probably find them useful as winter forage. Certainly, the raccoons would enjoy the remnants of the corn that was too small to pick. Not that she wants the pestilential beasts to get any ideas about coming back next season for ripe corn. They don't need to be encouraged.

She scowls at Dos and Uno, who are chasing each other through the rattling stalks. Perhaps next year they'll make themselves useful. They certainly didn't protect anything this season.

She bends awkwardly to pick up the machete and hefts its smooth cottonwood handle in her right hand, then swings it experimentally in a long sideways circle. The long flat metal blade makes a hissing sound in the crisp fall air. If nothing else, chopping stalks will make her feel better. They won't be visible anymore from the cabin porch, taunting her inability to make them produce or to protect the little they cared to yield. And she needs the exercise.

In Don Fernando, there's always someone to hire for this type of work. Gregorio Garcia or one of his cousins. But here there are no young men eager for a few coins. And Gerald and Ramón are busy with their own winter-preparation chores: hand-hewing sections of board to partition the cows from the hay in the barn, hauling and splitting more firewood, placing yet more rocks at the base of the chicken run to guard from predators. Raccoons, those furry vexations, love eggs even more than corn.

Suzanna scowls at the thought of the pesky raccoons. Her grip tightens on the machete. The resulting pressure on her still-tender palm reminds her to pinch her thumb and forefinger around the machete handle, the way Ramón showed her. She repositions her hand and flicks her wrist forward and down. The blade swings smoothly. Her raccoon-chopping fantasy may even be plausible.

Suzanna chuckles and sets to work, cutting steadily down the first row of dead stalks. At the end, she turns and nods in satisfaction. Severed stalks scatter the ground, their long dead leaves stabbing in every direction. The half-grown Ute puppies run among them, chasing each other and their own tails.

As she watches them she feels a sudden pressure under her bottom left rib, shoving outward. She takes a slow deep breath, then massages the spot with her left hand. The pressure shifts toward her abdomen. Suzanna grins. This isn't the first time this had happened. This baby seems to crave activity. Little feet and elbows poke outward the minute Suzanna stops moving.

"You want more action, little one?" she asks. "Shall we cut some more cornstalks?" The brown and black puppy yips as if in answer and Suzanna laughs, then goes back to work.

The baby may like movement, but Suzanna finds that she can't chop as many stalks as she would like to in any one work session. It takes her almost a week to get to the last row of maíz. She's moving up the row, her back to the western mountains, when the weather shifts, the air suddenly colder. A haze of damp stings her cheeks. But vigorous movement and her heavy wool coat have made her so warm that the bite of the air merely feels invigorating. She keeps chopping.

Suddenly a voice behind her says, "You may want to wait to finish that."

Suzanna turns to see Gerald. Beyond him, a mass of gray cloud blocks any view of the western peaks. "I don't think you have time to cut the rest of the row," he tells her. He gestures toward the clouds. "This snowstorm's coming in pretty quickly. "

Suzanna frowns. "It's too early for snow. Not a heavy snow, anyway. It's only the middle of October!"

"You're not in Don Fernando anymore, wife," he says gently.

"So I've been told," she says. She looks back at her row of cornstalks. "I just want to finish this."

He glances up the hill toward the barn. "I can get the other machete. We can finish it together."

"I know you're busy—"

"The barn is well enough. And the wood can wait." He steps forward to kiss her forehead. "I'll be back in a minute."

She watches him head toward the barn with his long easy stride, and smiles. He's interrupted his own work to help her with something that isn't essential, but is important to her. He's a good man and she loves him dearly. Even if he does think this desolate mountain valley is the best possible place to live.

Together they quickly finish leveling the row of dead cornstalks. Then Suzanna heads toward the cabin, the dogs at her heels, while Gerald returns the machetes to the barn. The clouds have dropped into the valley now and the wind is pushing them steadily toward the cabin. The air is bitterly cold.

When she reaches the porch, Suzanna turns to gaze at the approaching storm. She can't see the western peaks, but she knows they're there. A patch of blue sky has opened directly above the almost-black clouds that cover them. The blue is a glorious contrast to the ominous billows below. Even in its foreboding iciness, the scene is majestic.

She squints at the foothills farther down, where a gray screen of moisture slants toward the grassy brown slopes. The mist half obscures the hills, but she can see movement at the top of the one on the right. A lone elk?

No. A thick-set man on a black horse. Facing the cabin across the valley. And Suzanna.

There's something menacing about the stillness of both beast and man. And familiar. Those sloping yet bulky shoulders. The shapeless mass below. Suzanna's stomach twists. It's the same figure she saw south of the cabin in July. And it still reminds her of Enoch Jones.

Suzanna shudders, blinks, and shakes her head. Surely she's imagining it. When she looks again, the gray screen of mist has thickened and dropped. The hilltop is gone. There's nothing to see. And the screen of snow is moving steadily toward the cabin. She shivers again and the half-grown dogs slink up the porch steps and edge toward her feet.

Gerald crosses the yard and follows Uno and Dos onto the porch. "Aren't you cold?" he asks. He circles the animals to move behind Suzanna and wrap his arms around her waist. His cold cheek touches hers as he looks past her at the oncoming storm. "I can keep you warmer than the dogs can," he murmurs. "And we're all set for winter, so I can do plenty of this."

She smiles, tilts her head toward his, and nestles back into his arms. Whatever she thought she saw, it isn't there now. And he is.

CHAPTER 8

The man in the bulky bearskin poncho yanks the gelding's reins, forcing the big black backward and down the snow-driven hilltop and out of sight. He's seen what he came for and with no risk of sunlight sparking from the spyglass.

He reaches under the poncho. The glass is still in his coat pocket. Only good thing he got out of that damn desert. When he'd finally stopped bleeding and had moved away from the river caves to the dry lands above, he'd stumbled on the picked-over skeleton of a man less hardy than himself. The dented spyglass beside him was the one thing the buzzards hadn't wanted. It's right handy for watching the Peabody bitch and her men.

He squints up at the Sangres. Ice-bound snow stings his face. Storm came in faster'n he expected. Horse'll need to move quick if he's gonna get back to camp before it starts driftin'.

But he got a good head-on look at the shanty Locke and the bitch are living in. His tongue runs over his lips. Girl's tasty, in that Mexican way of hers. Well, French Navajo. Not that there's much difference. All foreigners. And her New England pa with his high'n mighty ways.

Her men don't keep her real close. She was down there choppin' corn a good hour or more, no one else in sight. His pale blue eyes gleam. They're gettin' lazy already. Or tired of her and her airs. Be willing to have him take care of her. He grins. He'll do that, all right. When the time comes.

At the bottom of the ice-slicked hill, he saws on the reins and gives the gelding a sharp kick, jabbing it into a trot against the on-coming snow, toward the ravine where he's stashed his gear. Not much danger of anyone spotting him in this weather. He can af-ford a fire tonight.

CHAPTER 9

Suzanna hums a little tune as she sweeps the cabin floor. These planks are quite different from the hard-beaten and oxblood-sealed earth floors of the Taos casa she grew up in, with their smooth surfaces, their soft indentations. The cabin's wood floors are rougher and give more underfoot. They've taken some getting used to.

But they don't show the dust in the same way, and she appreciates that. She dips the tip of her broom into the bucket of water beside the open door, shakes the excess moisture onto the porch, and goes back to her sweeping.

When the broom straw begins to clog with dirt, she carries it to the porch and shakes it out in the cold mid-November light. The chickens have escaped from their pen in the barn and are pecking around the edge of the corral. Dos lies nearby, watching them wistfully. The rooster will happily attack half-grown dogs if they get too close to the hens. The puppy has already experienced his wrath.

Suzanna chuckles. As she gives her broom a final shake, her eye catches movement in the valley below. She squints and shades her eyes with her hand. A man riding what looks to be a mule. A slender man who seems vaguely familiar. Ramón will probably know who he is.

But Ramón is in the kitchen and there's no sense in disturbing him. Besides, her growing belly is weighing her down. Suzanna leans her broom beside the door and drops heavily onto the nearest bench. The rider could just be a hunter passing through. There's no guarantee he's coming from Taos and has word from her father and Encarnación.

Though he may. The thought keeps her on the porch in spite of the cold. When the rider turns the gray mule's head toward the cabin, a surge of gladness rushes through her. It's Gregorio Garcia. Perhaps he'll have a letter from her father. Perhaps Encarnación has sent word to Ramón to set a marriage date.

But when Gregorio reins in beside the corral, he doesn't look as if he carries good news. In fact, his eyes seem to avoid the porch, where Suzanna has pushed herself up from her seat. And he doesn't dismount. He just sits there, staring dully at the pole corral and the valley beyond.

Suzanna frowns. Does the slant of the November sun shade the porch so thoroughly that Gregorio can't see her from where he sits? Does he think no one is home? She suppresses a surge of anxiety and waddles down the steps and across the yard.

"Gregorio!" She smiles up at him. "How good to see you! How is your mother? Is everyone well? You're riding a mule! Have you come into money?" She reaches to pat his mount's gray shoulder.

Gregorio shakes his head somberly "It is Señor Beaubien's mule. He leant it to me."

There's a tension in his voice that makes her look sharply into his face. Her smile fades. "You bring news." Her chest tightens. "My father?"

Gregorio seems to shake himself out of a deep fog. "Forgive me," he says. "No. El señor, he is well."

"Then what is it?"

He looks toward the cabin. "Señor Ramón? He is here?"

She nods, then steps back. "But I'm keeping you out here when you must be tired and cold from your journey. Please come inside. Would you like some tea?"

He nods wearily. "But the mule first."

"You'll find Gerald in the barn." She turns toward the house. "I'll tell Ramón that you're here."

"Por favor," he says. She turns back to him, and he hesitates. "Please do not speak to mí primo of possible danger or sorrow."

Her eyes widen in alarm.

"I must tell him myself." His shoulders straighten. "I promised my mother I would speak to him myself."

Her forehead wrinkles in confusion, but she only says. "I will tell him only that you are here."

He nods without looking at her, clucks at the mule, and reins it toward the barn. Suzanna watches him silently, afraid to ask what news he brings, afraid that Ramón will know there's bad news by the very look on her surely-anxious face. She turns toward the cabin.

"Gregorio just rode in," she says when she enters the kitchen.

Ramón straightens from the fire with a puzzled frown. "He rode in? He didn't walk? There is news of your father? He is well?"

She shakes her head. "He says the news is for you."

Ramón's face brightens. "Perhaps Encarnación is ready for me."

Suzanna looks away, and he sobers. "Or perhaps she has decided to marry another."

She laughs and shakes her head. "You know she won't do that."

He shrugs. "Anything is possible. Nothing is certain."

"He took his mule to the barn," she says. "Well, Charles Beaubien's mule, which he apparently borrowed for the occasion. He'll be in soon. Would you prefer to speak to him privately?"

Ramón shakes his head, smiling slightly, and she smiles ruefully back at him. There's no place truly private here, unless Ramón

44

wishes to hear his message on the icy porch or in the barn. Even then, Suzanna and Gerald would have to carefully remove themselves from hearing range.

"I thank you, but there is no need," Ramón says. "Undoubtedly, he comes to tell me my mother's fourth cousin has died and there are debts the family must pay."

Suzanna chuckles but neither of them are truly amused. They move silently into the cabin's main room and stand waiting. When Gregorio and Gerald come in, Suzanna gives Gerald a questioning look. He shakes his head. Whatever message Gregorio has brought, he hasn't spoken it yet.

Gregorio goes straight to Ramón and stops directly in front of him. He moves his feet apart, bracing himself, and takes off his hat. He fingers its worn brim as he looks into Ramón's face, then at the floor.

"You are well, my cousin?" Ramón asks.

Gregorio nods.

"And your mother? She is well?"

He nods again.

"You have a message for me?" Ramón asks.

Gregorio glances toward Suzanna and Gerald, who stand together on the other side of the room.

"You may speak freely here," Ramón says.

The teenager gulps and looks into the older man's face, then away. "My cousin—," he croaks. He takes a deep breath. "Su novia—"

"My sweetheart? Encarnación?" Ramón's face stiffens. He blinks, then his lips twist, as if he's forcing himself to speak. "Yes, what of her?"

"Ella murió."

"Died!" Suzanna gasps. Her knees buckle and Gerald's arm grips her waist. On the other side of the room, neither man stirs.

"Murió?" Ramón chokes.

Gregorio nods. His lips move soundlessly and he stares at the floor. "Killed," he says softly.

Ramón shakes his head and moves backward, toward the wall and some kind of support. "It is not possible," he mutters. He closes his eyes, then opens them, locking onto Gregorio's face. "You know this for a fact?"

Gregorio nods miserably. "I saw it." He shudders. "The wounds from the knife." He turns his head. "The tears in her clothing."

"She was molested?"

He looks away, his face twisting, then back at Ramón. "Sí," he whispers.

There's a long silence, broken only by Suzanna's soft sobs.

"It cannot be true!" Ramón says.

"I wish that it were not so." Gregorio takes a deep breath. "But it is most true."

"Who did this thing?"

Gregorio shakes his head. "No one knows."

Ramón gropes blindly to a chair. Gregorio sinks onto the color-ful flat-topped chest by the fire and Suzanna drops into her own chair. Gerald stands behind her, holding her shoulder. The room has grown dark while Gregorio delivered his news, the sun slip-ping remorselessly behind the black-shadowed Sangre de Cristos.

The men's hands dangle helplessly, their eyes everywhere but on each other's stunned faces. Suzanna sobs quietly, her face in her hands. "Encarnación dead!" she whispers. "Chonita, of all people! So full of life! It seems impossible!" She lifts her head. "What happened?"

"No one knows for certain." Gregorio spreads his hands. "Clearly, she had been to the potato field to gather more food. There were las patatas on the path beside her. And the basket." He turns his face toward the wall. "And blood everywhere." There's a long silence, then he gulps and faces the others. His eyes flick from face to face. "She had been knifed in the chest and the face," he says flatly. "Potatoes were flung everywhere, as she if used the basket as a protection at first, but the killer flung it aside."

"Where did this happen?" Gerald asks.

"On the path from the garden plot back to the town, the one that follows the acequia."

Gerald and Suzanna look at each other. The path that had been so dear to them, where they first declared their love. Those memories will be tainted now. The bit of land that brought them together has become the instrument of Encarnación's death.

Suzanna bends forward, covering her face with her hands.

Ramón clears his throat. "And no one was nearby?"

"No one heard anything or saw anyone."

Suzanna shudders. "My poor Chonita. To die so horribly." She looks at Ramón. "And when she had so much to look forward to." The tears start again, silent this time, and she makes no move to wipe them away.

Ramón braces his elbows on his knees and drops his face into his hands. His shoulders shake with suppressed grief.

"She spoke to my mother of her marriage only the day before," Gregorio says. "She said the woman she hired to serve el señor was learning quickly. She had purchased new blankets and was sewing linens in preparation."

Abruptly, Ramón stands up, his face averted. "Forgive me," he mutters. He crosses to the kitchen door. They can hear him moving restlessly around the room. In the kitchen fire, a log drops into the flames and sparks snap.

Suzanna takes a deep breath. The baby kicks in response. Suzanna places her palm on her belly and rubs in slow circles. The

47

child Encarnación will never hold, will never spoil with her famous natillas.

Gerald turns to Gregorio. "No one has come forward with information?"

Gregorio shakes his head. "No one heard or saw anything. I— I was on my way into the village—."

They look at him in horror. "You found her?" Gerald asks.

Gregorio nods.

Suzanna closes her eyes, picturing his shock, the potatoes scattered across the path, the blood.

"She was already quite dead," Gregorio says, almost defensively. "The wounds were from a knife." He looks at Gerald. "They were very deep and there was blood—."

"Yes," Gerald says.

Suzanna opens her eyes to find them both looking at her anxiously. Gerald's eyes flick to her abdomen.

"You need not worry for me." Suzanna shifts in her chair. Her fingers touch her belly and the child kicks again. "The little one is strong and healthy." She takes a deep breath. "Every child must learn of evil and pain. It is not something that can be avoided."

Gerald studies her. "I've never heard you speak so sadly."

"I've never been so sad." She closes her eyes, willing her lips not to tremble. "Encarnación was a good friend to me and to my father. My potato patch killed her."

Ramón steps in from the kitchen just then, a tray of tea things between his hands, his face slack with grief. "Please do not speak so," he says as he crosses the room.

He places the tray on a small table near the window and turns to Suzanna. "Encarnación loved the goodness of the things you grow. All food was of value and a pleasure to her. Your potatoes did not kill my love. Some man did."

His face twists again and he makes a visible effort to control himself. "For jealousy. For lack of protection." His voice trembles and he looks away, his fists clenching and unclenching. "I should have insisted that she come with us. I should not have left her alone." He turns and hurries back into the kitchen. The door to his sleeping room beyond shuts with a thud.

There's a long silence, then Suzanna rises and goes to the little table. "Tea?" she asks Gregorio.

He nods as if ashamed of needing sustenance, but drinks the hot liquid greedily.

"Thank you for coming so quickly to tell us," Gerald says.

"De nada," Gregorio says. "Ellos son mí familia."

"You will stay a few days before you return?"

"I must go back tomorrow at first light," Gregorio says. "My mother needs me. Especially now, when all the women of the town feel vulnerable to attack." He glances at the mica-covered window. "The weather is uncertain and she will be anxious for me." He looks at Suzanna. "I would not have her anxious."

49

CHAPTER 10

The next morning, Suzanna wakes in the cabin loft with a headache and a pain in her chest. She rubs her hands over her face. Why does she feel so miserable? So exhausted? Then she remembers. Encarnación. Dead.

Suzanna closes her eyes against the hopeless tears. They won't do any good. Her friend is gone. Never to join her here in these mountains. Nausea grips her and she fights it down, then gingerly pushes herself from the sleeping pallet. The only thing that might help is to move, to get outside, to breathe the fresh outdoor air.

She dresses, climbs clumsily down the ladder, and retrieves the egg basket from the kitchen. Ramón nods to her somberly but she can't meet his eye. She slips out of the house to the barn.

There's a small door at the end nearest the corral, there to provide foot access when they're not leading animals in and out. The door is partly open, though it provides little light to the interior. Suzanna steps inside and stops to let her eyes adjust to the dimness. She can hear Gerald and Gregorio in the far stall, preparing the mule for Gregorio's return to Taos. As she crosses the straw-covered earth floor toward them, Gregorio says, "A knife was found."

Suzanna freezes. He has clearly waited until now to tell Gerald about the knife. There must be a reason he didn't mention it yesterday. She swallows against a sudden surge of anxiety and closes her eyes, listening.

"It was that big horn-handled one Enoch Jones used to carry."

Suzanna's throat tightens. Her fingers are cold on the basket's woven handle.

"Jones is dead," Gerald says, his voice stiff.

"So we believed."

"No man could survive that wilderness with those wounds. If nothing else, the wolves would trail his blood and finish him off."

The mule moves impatiently. Gregorio speaks to it softly.

Gerald clears his throat. "Someone must have found Jones' body and stolen the knife."

There's a pause, then Gregorio's reluctant voice. "There have been stories."

Suzanna starts to move forward, then thinks better of it. They'll stop talking the moment they know she's here.

"Encarnación laughed and called them ghost stories," Gregorio says. "Tales of a man shaped like Jones in the mountains." There's another pause. "Between here and Don Fernando," he adds, his voice dropping. Suzanna has to strain to hear him.

"I did not wish to alarm la señora," he adds. "Especially with the child coming."

"I appreciate that," Gerald says. "They may just be stories."

"Sí, they may just be stories."

Suzanna opens her mouth and steps forward, then stops. They're only trying to protect her. And there's no point in worrying them about worrying her. She moves quietly back to the door and the cold sunshine. She waits a long moment, then shoves the door open all the way and reenters the barn.

"Hola!" she calls. "Gregorio, are you leaving so early?" The two men turn toward her almost eagerly, as if they don't want to think about what Gregorio has just said.

After Gregorio returns to Taos, a pall falls on the cabin, a haze of pain that refuses to lift. Gerald seems anxious and unwilling to stray far from the hillside. Suzanna watches him impatiently, sud-

51

denly refusing to believe her own fears about the man she saw on the ridge. Somewhere deep in her belly, she knows she's being unreasonable. That the stories being told in Taos and the presence of the knife beside Chonita's dead body mean that it's likely Jones did somehow survive that terrible knife fight and has returned from the wilderness.

But surely that's impossible. It must be someone else who's haunting the mountains between the valley and Taos. She simply cannot allow herself to live in terror of any other possibility.

Besides, if Gerald believed that Jones had returned, he would have told her so. He's said nothing about the Taos rumors or Jones' bone-handled knife. He's staying close to the cabin solely out of concern for both her and Ramón's emotional state. There's also her physical condition. The baby is due soon and Suzanna is increasingly uncomfortable.

The shock of Encarnación's death has hit Ramón hard. The realization that she lay dead while he happily anticipated their marriage has left him in a kind of stupor. He still cooks and tends the animals, chops wood and hauls water, but he goes about his tasks in a sort of daze, eyes glazed with pain.

Suzanna herself finds that she's sitting for long stretches, hands empty in her lap, staring blindly at the windows, glowing yellow with afternoon light. It's hard to imagine a world without Chonita's vital laugh, those knowing eyes, that gift for las natillas. Even the mica windowpanes remind her of the other woman. Suzanna smiles, remembering the arguments between her father and the cook about the need for sunlight and fresh air through the old-fashioned kitchen windows with their carved wooden grills, the ones her father wanted to replace with mica.

Ramón enters the room carrying an armload of firewood. Suzanna looks up at him. "You know, I think Encarnación was right," she says. "The clear light from an open window aperture is so much brighter and truer than sunlight filtered through mica."

Ramón kneels to add the wood to the small stack at the far end of the fireplace. "It is so," he says. "She—" Then he stops, a piece of juniper still in his hand. He shakes his head, carefully positions the chunk of wood on top of the stack, then stands and moves toward the kitchen without looking back.

She closes her eyes. She shouldn't have spoken. It only deepens his pain. And yet, how can she not speak, when everything seems to remind her of her dead friend? She sighs and sorrowfully rubs her belly. She had assumed Encarnación would come for the child's birth, to assist her through it and perhaps stay on with Ramón.

Grief overwhelms her again, and Suzanna creeps across the room and climbs clumsily up the ladder to the loft. Out of the way, where she can't do anything else to increase Ramón's pain.

When the tears finally wear out, Suzanna lies limp on the blanket-covered pallet and stares at the bare rafters overhead. The weeping will erupt again. She hasn't completed grieving for her friend. But the pressure in her head and chest has subsided a little. She wonders if Ramón has wept at all, if he's found an outlet for his grief. But he's a man. Men learn early to suppress their emotions. Perhaps speaking of his loss to another man will be all he can manage.

But when she asks Gerald that night if Ramón has spoken to him of Encarnación's death. Her husband shakes his head.

"It will fester in him if he doesn't express it." Suzanna pushes another pillow behind her back, trying to get comfortable on the thin bed. "It isn't good to hold in that kind of pain."

"You don't know that he's not expressing it," Gerald says. "We each have our own way of dealing with grief." He leans down to give her a kiss and pokes at the pillows behind her. "Are you comfortable yet?"

"Not until this child decides to be born," she says, exaggerating her grumbling tone, glad to have something else to think about. "Ouch!" She presses a hand against her lower chest. "That foot just jabbed my rib and now it's pushing straight out."

"Pushy little thing, isn't it?" Gerald grins and he stretches out beside her. "Must be a girl."

She gives him a slit-eyed look. "You certainly are in a good mood tonight." Guilt wells up in her and she turns her head away. How can she be happy when Encarnación is dead and Ramón so bent with grief? Tears brim into her eyes. "When my father arrives for Christmas, Chonita won't be with him." She gives Gerald a bleak look. "If I can't bear the thought of that, how must Ramón feel?"

Gerald lifts himself onto one elbow and gently strokes her dark hair. "I don't mean to be hard hearted. I know your heart weeps for her and that Ramón is burdened with grief and self-reproach."

"Self-reproach?"

"He believes that if he'd insisted that they marry when we did, she would have been here and safe, instead of on that acequia path."

Suzanna's eyes fill again. "On that path with potatoes from my patch, so far away from the village." She shakes her head. "And I was so willing for her to stay in Don Fernando, so quick to leave her with all the work while I took what I wanted. When I left, she remained to arrange everything, to take all the responsibility for my father. And to have none of my joy." She turns her head away from his sympathetic eyes. Her voice shakes. "I'm more to blame than Ramón!"

"Neither of you are to blame," Gerald says firmly. "Encarnación insisted, remember? She decided what she wanted to do and that was it." He chuckles. "Did you ever know her to change her mind once she had decided a thing?"

"No, not that I can remember." She manages a small smile. "In fact, it was never clear whether she or my father was the first to decide that she would be our cook and housekeeper. I've always suspected it was Chonita's idea before it was his, even though she was only fourteen at the time."

Gerald grins. "She set you a good example."

She narrows her eyes. "Now what exactly is that supposed to mean?"

He laughs. "Only that you and she both know how to get what you most want." He leans forward and kisses her forehead. "Now please relax and let that baby finish its last bit of growth so it can arrive soon." He reaches for her hand. "Ramón and I expect to have a surprise for you tomorrow morning, but if it's to truly be a surprise, you'll need to stay up here until we're ready to show it to you. Can you do that?"

She grimaces. "Since I now need help to get down the ladder, I suppose I don't have much choice, do I?"

He laughs and squeezes her hand. "I suppose not." He looks around the loft. "You have the lamp and your books. The chamber pot's empty and the wash basin has clean water in it. Is there anything else you need?"

"Chonita to be alive and this child to be born," she says, closing her eyes. She can feel the grief pulling at her again.

Gerald touches her hair. "I wish I could make both those things happen," he says. "I didn't know Encarnación well, but I also feel her loss."

Suzanna reaches for his hand. "I don't mean to be such a weepy woman about it. I suppose it's as much the weight of the child as grief for Chonita. If my time doesn't come soon, I may dissolve in a lake of tears."

"When the baby does arrive, it will be a comfort to all of us." He looks up at the rafters. "Though I dread the process of its coming."

"I'll be fine." Suzanna puts more courage into her voice than she actually feels at the moment. "We both know what to expect. After all, cows aren't much different from humans."

"Still, I wish you could be in your father's house." He turns his head, eyes dark with concern. "I shouldn't have taken you from Taos."

"It's too late for that now," she says. "I'll be fine. I'm sure of it."

He rolls toward her. "I'll certainly be glad when it's over," he says, his face against her shoulder.

Suzanna turns her head to kiss him gently, then turns back to stare at the rafters herself. She can sleep only on her back now. Every other position is uncomfortable. As she stares into the darkness, Gerald's body relaxes into sleep.

She can't let go that easily. Despite Gerald's reassurances, she still regrets her eagerness to hasten her own marriage and delay Encarnación's. One of them needed to stay in Taos with her father and arrange for and train a new housekeeper. She had selfishly let that person be Chonita. Who is now dead. The tears slip silently down Suzanna's face.

Finally, she sleeps. She wakes to a muttered curse in the room below and a muffled thud on the plank floor. "Are you two moving furniture?" she calls, but the only response is the scuff of boots across the floor and the thud of the front door shutting.

Suzanna frowns. What are those two up to? Oh, yes. The surprise. Well, if it distracts Ramón a little from his pain, it's a good thing.

She closes her eyes against her own grief, then sits up. Her bladder is full to bursting. Or at least it feels like it. It could just be

56

that the baby is pushing against it again. That nothing much will happen when she uses the chamber pot.

She gets up anyway, then slips back onto the thin pallet. She shifts impatiently, trying to get comfortable. The loft's floor boards seem especially hard this morning, the pallet especially thin. It's no use. She'll read for a while, until they're ready to show her the surprise.

She pushes herself into a sitting position. As she reaches to light the lamp, the door below thuds open again. "Shhh!" Gerald hisses. "Careful now! She'll hear us!"

Suzanna pulls her hand away from the lamp and lies down again, a small smile playing on her lips. Let them think she's still sleeping.

She's actually dozed off again when Gerald's head appears at the top of the ladder. "Wife?" he says.

"Ummm?"

"Your surprise is ready." He sounds so pleased with himself.

She sits up and stretches her hand to him.

"Well, almost ready," he says. "You have to see it before it can be completed."

She chuckles. "Now I'm really curious."

"Don't look over the edge of the loft," he warns. "And you'll need to close your eyes on the way down."

"Isn't that's rather dangerous?"

He laughs. "You haven't been able to see your feet on the ladder rungs for the last month," he reminds her. "I'll stay right below you just like I've been doing, and you'll be perfectly safe."

"I put myself in your hands," she says, smiling. She wraps a shawl around her shoulders and ties it firmly in place. "All right, I'm ready."

Gerald guides her carefully down the ladder, then places his hands on her shoulders and turns her, eyes still closed, toward the fireplace. "Here it is!" he says.

Suzanna opens her eyes. A bed stands between the fireplace and the window. A real bed, large enough for two people, with a sturdy pale-gold wooden post at each corner and thinner pieces forming the frame. Strips of rawhide have been woven together and attached to the frame to create a mattress support.

"It isn't quite ready," Gerald says apologetically. He slips his arm around her waist. "We'll bring the pallet and blankets down and make it up properly."

Ramón stands on the far side of the bed, watching her. His face holds the glimmer of a smile, the first she's seen since Gregorio arrived with his news. "It is for you and the little one," Ramón says. He glances at the ladder to the loft. "You will be safer here."

"It's beautiful." Suzanna leans against her husband and smiles at Ramón, both hands on her protruding belly. She looks at the bed. "The wood is such a beautiful soft yellow. Is it aspen?"

"Sí," Ramón says eagerly. "And we have coated it with a thin layer of resin, to preserve it. It should last all your days—" He stops suddenly and looks away.

Suzanna's throat catches. She turns to Gerald. "I want to try it right away," she says. She moves to her chair and eases herself into it. She looks at Ramón, her eyes twinkling. "I'm afraid you've made more work for yourself, because I'll also need the lamp and my books."

The men move up the ladder to do her bidding and the cabin is filled with activity, pushing the loss of Encarnación into the shadows, at least for a little while.

CHAPTER 11

The hill's western slope is coated with a thin layer of icy snow. The big man grimaces, then drops awkwardly to his knees. The mangy bearskin poncho has twisted as he knelt. He yanks it flat over his chest and drops belly-first onto the freezing slope. Then he pushes himself up onto his elbows, fumbles for his spyglass, peers over the top of the hill.

Not much chance the men in the cabin yard will notice a flash of light from this direction. They're hell bent on whatever it is they're doing, hauling timber and armloads of leather binding from the half-mud barn to the shanty.

The sun's coming up over the Cimarrons behind the cabin, it's making his eyes water. He pulls the spyglass away and swipes the lens with a dirty sleeve. Even without it he can see that Locke and the greaser are moving between the barn and the cabin again. They're lugging some kind of gate-like wooden contraption between 'em. The wood's got that pale mealy look aspen gets when it been pealed.

What're they gonna do with a gate inside the house? A few minutes later, they return to the barn and haul the same kind of thing across the yard. The big man grunts. A bed, maybe. Or somethin' to help with the birthing.

He swings the glass, studying the little farmstead. The little bitch must be about ready to whelp. She's made no effort to hide her belly. Standing in the middle of the corn patch, rubbin' at her stomach like a damn cow. She sure ain't no lady, for all her airs and her father's pamperin'.

He grunts. Can't cook, but she does seem to know how to breed. Bound to happen. Two men, and one of them with a dead sweetheart.

He scratches his scraggly beard. "Wonder which of 'em the brat belongs to?" Then he chuckles. "Bet she don't even know."

His groin twitches and he rolls over and sits up. He reaches under the poncho and yanks his buckskin trousers into a more comfortable position. Baby'll keep her closer to home. And her men can't always be watchin' for passing strangers. He grins, then pushes himself to his feet and moves down the slope, careful to stay out of sight of the cabin.

Give it a little more time, after the brat comes, and she'll be easy enough to take.

Just like that piece in Taos. He chuckles, remembering the pleasure of that thrust, the satisfaction of giving that devil-tongued little whore what she deserved.

CHAPTER 12

As Suzanna's time grows closer, Gerald finds excuses to stay in the cabin with her, springing to her side whenever she grimaces in discomfort, looking for reasons to keep her indoors and away from any icy patches on the ground outside.

At first, Suzanna finds all the attention endearing, but then it begins to be aggravating. When Gerald offers to screen off part of the porch so she can use the chamber pot there instead of going to the outhouse, she puts her foot down.

She's just opened the front door of the cabin when he makes the suggestion. She closes it against the cold and turns back into the room, trying to keep the exasperation out of her voice. "I am perfectly capable of making the short trip out the door and around back to the outhouse."

"Then tell me when you need to visit it and I'll go with you." He moves toward her and lifts his coat from the peg on the wall.

She puts her hands on her hips. "I don't need an escort. I am not a child."

"But you're with child and I don't want anything to happen."

"Nothing's going to happen."

"You don't know that."

"Gerald—" She gives him a long look, then crosses the room and sinks into her chair, her coat billowing around her. "I know you love me, but this anxiety seems out of proportion to the event."

He puts his hat on his head. "I think it's exactly proportionate. You're going to have a child any day now."

"Women have children every day of the year," she says. "It's not an abnormal occurrence."

"You don't."

"I would hope not. It's a good deal of work. " She shifts in her chair and grimaces. "Ouch." She unbuttons the heavy wool coat and massages the top of her belly.

Gerald frowns anxiously, but Suzanna only chuckles. "Baby just wants to let you know that he's almost as anxious to get this over with as you are."

Gerald grins. "She is, is she?"

"I'm not getting into a discussion about whether it's a boy or a girl." Suzanna shifts slightly in her seat. "I'll even put off going to the outhouse to find out why you're so anxious." She crosses her hands over her belly. "Is there something you're not telling me?"

He turns his head away.

"Gerald?"

"My mother had a rough time."

"With you?"

"With my brother."

"I didn't know you have a—"

"I don't." He gives her a bleak look, then turns back to the fire. "They both died."

She leans forward, her hand reaching for him, but he shakes his head as if the memory is still too fresh for comfort. "She also had no woman to help her," he says.

"But you were in Missouri."

"There was no one nearby." He looks at the bed, then the window. "No one to help an Irish servant girl who'd made decisions of which they didn't approve."

62

She opens her mouth to ask for more details, but there's something about the set of his shoulders that says he isn't going to discuss it, no matter how hard she probes.

He turns back to her. "So I worry." He shakes his head. "Part of me is sure that you and the child will be fine." Mischief glints in his eyes. "Whatever its gender." Then he grimaces. "But another part of me is gripped with fear. Especially—" He looks toward the window again. "Especially since the news about Encarnación. Her death reminds me just how fragile life is, how quickly we can lose those we love." His shoulders tighten. The hat brim shades his eyes. "I couldn't bear it the way Ramón does. So quietly. I think I'd go mad."

Suzanna's hand rubs her belly. "It does make you realize how tenuous life can be." She takes a deep breath. "I wish Encarnación was here. It would be less daunting to face childbirth with her at my side." Her voice trembles. "And I miss her so much." There's a long silence, then she takes a shaky breath and steadies her voice. "But I have you here. And Ramón is here to help you. And I'm young and strong."

Gerald nods reluctantly. "My mother was in her late thirties," he admits. "She was really too old to have a child. And she was worn down with work and—"

Suzanna waits for more, but he's silent again, staring at the window.

"I am young," she repeats. "And strong. I don't anticipate any problems." She reaches for him again, and this time he leans forward and takes her hand. "You shouldn't either," she says gently.

He shifts and nods reluctantly. "I'll try. But I still think I should accompany you to the outhouse." His gray eyes brighten. "And I could put ashes on the path to soften the ice."

She makes a small face. "Well, I suppose you going with me is better than using the chamber pot on the porch," she says drily.

"Though you may be sorry you offered when you realize just how often I need to go outside these days!"

He laughs and squeezes her hand.

"Speaking of whether it's a boy or a girl—" she says.

"Yes?"

"If it's a girl, I'd like to name her after my father's mother, Alma."

Gerald nods.

Suzanna glances toward the kitchen, where Ramón is rattling dishes, and tugs on Gerald's hand, to move him closer. He kneels beside her and pushes his hat off his forehead to look into her face. "Yes?"

"And Encarnación," she says.

"Alma Encarnación Locke." He smiles as he nods. "It's a good name."

"You don't mind that there will be no name from your family's side?"

He shakes his head. "We'll save my family names for the next child," he says. "Or if it's a boy. But if it's a girl, then her name will honor a woman who's part of our family in spirit, if not in blood."

Tears well in Suzanna's eyes. "It's hard for me to think of her as gone. It seems as if she's still there in Taos, training someone to run my father's house. Preparing to join us." She takes a deep, shuddering breath. "And yet, when I remember that she is gone, the pain seems unbearable."

He squeezes her hand and stands up. "I know," he says. "There are times when I think of my own mother, who I saw on her deathbed, and I still can't believe that she's not waiting for me somewhere in Missouri, ready to tell me to wash my hands and wipe the mud off my feet before I step through the door."

"As Encarnación did me, although she was only a few years older than I." Suzanna chuckles as she brushes the wetness from her cheeks. She pushes herself out of her seat. "And now I really need to use the outhouse."

He grins, flattens his hat on his head, and crooks an elbow in her direction. "At your service, madam," he says.

CHAPTER 13

Even with Gerald's attentiveness, the increasingly-shorter winter days begin to seem very long to Suzanna. As her belly expands, housework becomes more uncomfortable. She can barely manage to even sew. And she's prepared everything she needs to for the child. There's really nothing to do but sit and wait, feeling as if the child will never arrive. It's almost a relief when her pains begin.

Then time stretches again, into a black tunnel of contraction and fear, Gerald's hand gripping hers, his brown face fighting to remain calm, but his gray eyes dark with anxiety. Suzanna focuses instead on the comfort of his hands on hers, then Ramón's solid grip as Gerald does what is needed between her bent knees.

They've brought her a piece of buckskin to bite down on when the pain becomes too intense. The gamy taste of it mixes with the salt on her lips, the saliva in her mouth. The taste seems to get stronger as the pain intensifies, nausea sweeps over her in waves, in time with the contractions. Then Gerald cries "I see it!" as a searing pain cuts across her belly.

"Push now!" Ramón says in her ear. He reaches across her and grips her other hand. "Push!"

"Here it comes!" Gerald says. "There's the head!"

Suzanna gulps back her terror, grinds her teeth into the now-slimy leather, and pushes into her hips as hard as she can. Ramón's palms are tight under her fingernails and there's an enormous pressure between her legs. A buzzing haze fills her head.

"Push!" Ramón says again. "That's it, push!"

Then the dam between her legs seems to burst and the pressure is gone. Gerald laughs exultantly. Suzanna lowers her shaking thighs and Ramón's hands flex slightly under her fingers.

Suzanna turns her head to look up at him and Ramón chuckles. "You have a strong grip."

She makes an apologetic sound and releases his hands. He flexes them gingerly and grins at her. "Next time I will give you a piece of wood to hold," he jokes.

"Ramón, I need the scissors," Gerald says anxiously, and Ramón drops Suzanna's hand.

As the two men cut the umbilical cord and clean the baby, Suzanna lets herself sink into the pillow. She's so tired.

Then Gerald appears, and she forces her eyes open. He's holding a small cloth-covered bundle awkwardly in his hands. "It's a girl," he says as he slips the baby into Suzanna's arms. When he straightens, he gives her a smile that's both proud and relieved. "Our little girl."

That afternoon, Ramón goes out to look after the cattle, leaving the new parents alone with their new infant. "Look at this!" Suzanna says as the baby nuzzles her breast. "She has a heart-shaped freckle!"

Gerald moves closer. The baby's face is splotched with dark freckles that seem large on her tiny brown face.

Suzanna points to her tiny left cheek. "See here?"

Gerald chuckles. "I think it's more heart-shaped from where you're looking."

Suzanna smiles contentedly as the tiny fingers wrap around her own and the baby burrows its face into her breast. "Alma

Encarnación Locke," she says wonderingly. She looks up. "Have you told Ramón?"

The outer door opens and Ramón appears, carrying a pail of fresh milk. "There will be another storm in the next several days," he says. "I can feel it in the wind." He turns to close the door behind him, then looks at Suzanna. "How is la nena?"

She smiles at him. "She is well." She looks at Gerald. "We have decided on her name."

Gerald hesitates, then looks at Ramón. "She will be called Alma Encarnación Locke," he says. He glances at Suzanna apologetically, then turns back to Ramón. "That is, if you agree."

The milk in the pail sloshes slightly as Gerald speaks. Ramón leans to place the bucket on the floor. When he straightens, there are tears in his eyes. "I agree," he says softly. "You do Encarnación a great honor."

Suzanna smiles at the baby still latched to her breast. "She will be honored to bear the name of such a woman." She looks up at Ramón. "If she becomes half the woman Encarnación was—" She swallows hard, then starts again. "If she is like Encarnación in any way, then I will be satisfied."

"Do you know what 'alma' means en español?" Ramón asks.

Suzanna shakes her head.

"It means 'soul.'"

Her eyes widen and they stare at each other for a long moment. Then Suzanna closes her eyes and tightens her grip on her child. "My soul," she whispers.

Gerald crosses the room to Ramón, touches his forearm, and reaches for the pail of milk as Suzanna lifts the baby away from her breast and covers herself. She looks up at Ramón. "Come and say hello to her," she says. "See her freckles?"

Gerald carries the milk into the kitchen as Ramón crosses to the bed. Two tiny black eyes open and gaze at him solemnly. "She is so tiny," he says. "Smaller than you were, I think." He reaches to touch the baby's cheek. "Hola, nita."

"Little sister?" Suzanna asks in amusement. "Hopefully, she will be a big sister someday."

Ramón laughs. "You are already prepared for another?"

"Well, perhaps not quite yet!"

He sobers. "Today is Sunday," he observes.

"Is it? I've lost track of the days."

"It is a good sign, to be born on a Sunday. A good omen."

She gives him a quizzical look. "I didn't think you believed in omens."

He chuckles and shrugs. "I do when it is convenient." He reaches out again to touch Alma's cheek. "To be born on a Sunday and to be named Encarnación. La nita is doubly blessed." A shadow crosses his face, then he gives his head a little shake and turns abruptly toward the kitchen door. "I must strain the milk."

Two days after Alma's birth, the storm Ramón predicted arrives with a vengeance. Snow and wind beat across the valley, obscuring the mountain peaks in both directions and making travel to or from Don Fernando impossible.

In spite of the weather, Suzanna continues to hope her father will somehow arrive in time for at least part of the holiday, but the year changes and he still doesn't come.

With the disappointment comes an overwhelming exhaustion compounded by the demands of motherhood. The baby seems to tug at her constantly. Suzanna's attitude toward her veers between tenderness, exasperation, and sheer exhaustion. Motherhood seems to consist of sleeping in fits and starts, waking in a gray haze to let the ever-hungry mouth latch onto her breast, and listlessly sitting up just enough to feed herself. The men slip in and out of the house as if afraid to disturb her, as if her only function is to feed and clean the child.

She's a beautiful baby, Suzanna tells herself. Yet, all she really wants to do is push Alma to the other side of the big wooden bed in the cabin's main room and curl into an oblivious ball. Exhaustion weighs her down like a pile of heavy blankets. She feels Chonita's loss even more now. And guilt for feeling that way. For wishing for the other woman's presence most when it would be beneficial to herself. But Suzanna is too tired to sort out her emotions. All she wants to do is sleep.

Except at night. Gerald, thinking it will help Suzanna recover, has taken to sleeping in the loft so that she and the baby can rest undisturbed. But after he climbs the ladder each night, Suzanna finds herself wide awake, staring at the dying fire. Her mind wanders to Taos and her father, then back to the baby beside her. She should be happy. But she feels only a blankness that borders on despair.

During the daylight hours—what she can see of them, given the limited light from the mica-covered windows—Suzanna finds it impossible to stay awake, except when Alma's fussing at her. Then she comes unwillingly out of her daze.

If the baby isn't hungry again, she smells like an outhouse. When this happens, Suzanna rolls away, breathing through her mouth, trying to block the stench. Eventually, footsteps will cross the floor from the kitchen and she'll hear Ramón murmur "Pobre nita!" and feel him lift the infant from the other side of the bed.

As he crosses back to the kitchen, baby in his arms, Suzanna is crushed with guilt. She's a bad mother. She can't even bring herself to care that her child is dirty. A man who isn't even related to her is caring for her infant. Suzanna turns her head and sobs into her pillow, but she still can't work up the desire to rise and take care of Alma's needs herself. If only her Chonita were here. Or her father.

Though why her father's presence would make her feel better, Suzanna doesn't know. The thought of him fills her with terror. There's been no word from Taos. No one passes through the valley when the snow is this deep and the weather so uncertain. Perhaps he also is dead. Whoever killed Encarnación has come for him, too. And this person Chonita hired to be his housekeeper. Does she know how to provide the meals her father likes? To keep his clothes well aired? To make sure he drinks strawberry-leaf tea to ward off his winter cough? Can she talk to him about the books he's reading or his conversations with Padre Martínez? Suzanna is filled with longing for the warm fireside of her father's book-filled parlor.

"I should be there, not here." She struggles to sit up and pushes her disheveled hair from her face. "Taking care of my father and studying with him, not chained to a child who constantly demands to be fed and cleaned. Who I can't even bring myself to feel pity for, much less affection. Even Ramón cares for her more than I do."

She leans back against her pillows and the tears come again. She's so far from everything here. Her father. Other women. How she misses Encarnación's warm kitchen and the camaraderie there.

She wipes at her tear-stained cheeks with the back of her hand. It would have been better if she'd never married, never come to these mountains, never had a child. She should have stayed in Don Fernando with her father and been nice to Ceran St. Vrain. He wouldn't have dragged her into these god-forsaken hills. She closes her eyes, her body limp against the pillows.

There's a rustle of sound in the kitchen doorway. Suzanna opens her eyes. Ramón is in the door, Alma in his arms. He gazes at Suzanna sympathetically. "It is bad, the pain?" he asks.

She shakes her head. "There is no pain." She looks at the window. "That is, there's no physical pain."

"It is a pain of the heart." He moves toward the bed, then veers off and settles himself onto the brightly-painted storage chest by the fire, Alma still in his arms. He looks down at the infant and croons something in Spanish. "She is a good baby." He looks up at Suzanna. "She does not cry like some I have heard."

"She cries enough." Suzanna bites her lips against the petulant sound of her voice and looks away. "I don't know what's wrong with me," she mutters.

"Qué?"

Suzanna lifts her hand as if to brush her words away. Her throat tightens, making it difficult to speak. "I want to be a good mother," she croaks.

"But you are a good mother," Ramón says.

Suzanna closes her eyes. "I don't feel very good."

His eyes widen in alarm. "You are unwell?"

She shakes her head. "I suppose I am well enough physically. But not inside myself. I feel—" She frowns, trying to define the turmoil inside her. "I feel sad, I suppose."

"Because your father isn't here?"

She nods unwillingly.

"But there is more."

She nods again.

"Chonita?"

She raises a limp hand. "That is always with me. This is more, if that's possible."

"It is natural, I think," Ramón says. Alma grunts and he moves slightly, shifting her in his arms. "Among my sisters and cousins, there have been women who suffer from a great sadness after a child is born." His brow wrinkles. "Sometimes it can lead to madness."

72

Suzanna's head twists toward him. "Madness!"

He dips his head. "I have never known it to lead to such a thing. It is only something I have heard spoken of."

Suzanna stares at him. "What happens to a woman who goes mad after a child is born?"

He looks at her reluctantly, then shifts Alma again, snuggling her into his chest. "La madre weeps uncontrollably. She becomes restless and angry with her child. Sometimes she injures the child."

Suzanna stiffens, then wets her lips with her tongue. "And is there a way to prevent this madness?"

He stares into the fire. "They say that too much rest can be harmful," he says reluctantly.

"Gerald thinks I should rest as much as possible."

Ramón nods unhappily. "It is only what they say. I don't know that it is true."

Something that Suzanna recognizes as amusement glimmers inside her. "I thought you believed the old sayings."

He chuckles and pats the baby's back. "Only when it is convenient."

Suzanna frowns. "Perhaps I should try to be more active."

He shrugs without looking at her.

"I can try," she says doubtfully. "I certainly don't enjoy feeling like this."

The door to the porch opens and Gerald comes in. He gives her a delighted smile. "You're sitting up!" he says. "How are you feeling?"

She feels a sudden stab of anger. Of course she's sitting up. She has to sit up to feed the ever-hungry child, doesn't she? But she pushes the fierceness away and smiles at him instead. "I think that staying in bed isn't really helping me feel better," she says. "Could you bring me my shawl?"

A few days later, she's kneeling beside the pallet Gerald has made for himself in the loft, straightening the bedding. It really needs to be aired. But heavy gray clouds are hanging once again over the peaks to the west. More snow is about to descend on the valley, on top of the eighteen inches already on the ground. It's clearly not a good time to try to air blankets.

Her back twinges as she sits back on her heels and pulls the pallet blankets straight. She grimaces and twists, trying to stretch the tightness. She's not sore as much as she is tense. A good walk in a spring meadow would do her a world of good. But that isn't going to happen anytime soon. Not in this weather. She eases grimly into a standing position in the center of the room and moves toward the ladder.

As she reaches to brace herself for the climb down, Gerald and Ramón come through the front door. "I swear I saw someone," Gerald says. She can hear the frown in his voice. "Just by the corner of the barn." His voice drops and Suzanna hears a low rumble, then "Jones."

Ramón makes a noncommittal grunt. A boot thuds on the wood planks.

"But you didn't see anything?"

"Nada," Ramón says.

"I must have imagined it." Gerald's voice drops into a stubborn growl. "Jones is dead. I'm sure of it."

In the loft, Suzanna shakes her head. And the knife that was found by Encarnación's body? What of it? She isn't sure why, but she doesn't lean forward to let the men know she's there or to question Gerald's assertion.

"It is probably nothing," Ramón says.

"Or it's a lone trapper, trying to decide whether or not to ask for shelter." Gerald's voice lifts, his relief palpable. "But we should check the barn, just to be on the safe side. If there is someone out there, they'll need more protection than the barn can offer in this weather. I'll go. You already have your boots off."

Above them, Suzanna crouches by the ladder and listens to Ramón cross in his stocking feet to the kitchen. Behind him, Alma begins to fuss in her cradle. Suzanna moves her aching legs into position on the ladder rungs and slips into the room below. She lifts the baby into her arms and goes to sit pensively by the fire. The image of a man on the ridge south of the cabin rises unbidden and she shivers and hugs Alma closer to her chest.

CHAPTER 14

Hell, he edged too close. It ain't time yet. The man in the bear-skin poncho turns away from the wind-driven snow and scowls at the cabin on the slope below. Sneakin' around that sorry excuse for a barn was plain stupid. What was he after, anyway? Warm smoke from a chimney? Smell of bread bakin'?

He adjusts his filthy gray wool scarf over his mouth and snorts in disgust. He's gettin' soft. Livin' wild long as he has, that chimney smoke comin' up through the pines smelled good. Sharp-sweet smell. Campfire, but warmer.

He shakes his head at his own foolishness, hefts his rifle, and positions his feet sideways, making it easier to maneuver up the snow-slicked dead grass and into the trees above, where Locke and Chavez have been cutting firewood. What'd he expect? Open door? Wide-arm welcome? From that nigger and his wench? From their hanger-on greaser?

Not that they're doin' all that well. He chuckles and shakes his shaggy head. North end of that barn roof's caved in. That flimsy stretch of canvas over the cut meadow grass they're usin' for hay ain't gonna protect it much from the snow.

He grins and stops to peer down at the mud-and-log barn. Or cow shit. He got a good double handful into the loose hay before the door rattled and he ducked out the other side. Cows eat that, they'll be sicker'n dogs before spring.

He snorts. They got plenty of time to get sick in. Spring comes late here. And wet. That canvas'll be no protection at all. April rains'll pour across it like a funnel, right into that hay. And that's before it soaks through and damps the whole lot. He grins. Then that shit poison'll spread even faster. He chuckles, pleased with his work.

When he reaches the top of the hill, he turns again. Smoke rises from the cabin chimney, a plume of white that merges with the falling snow. Not like his own sorry lean-to, fire spitting with random flakes, wind burning the smoke into his eyes.

Then he snorts derisively. Those two tenderfeet'll be thinkin' they can turn those beeves out to pasture come early March. Valley grass don't come in that early. They'll be lucky to have any stock left by late May. Even without his little gift in their hay pile. He grins and spits at the icy snow at his feet.

Those cows'll be dry as the Arizona desert and that girl'll be thinner than she was before she got hitched. His lips twist and he adjusts the gray scarf to cover them. Feed gets scarce enough, she'll be ripe for a change.

His hands move toward his crotch, then he catches himself and scowls. Too cold for even a little self-pleasuring. Hell of a place. He eyes the western mountains. Another, denser wave of snow is working its way down slope. A steel-gray mass of clouds hides the peaks. Storm's not slowin' down anytime soon. The air's heavy with damp.

And there's more snow-bound months ahead, damn it all. That tiny valley to the west where he's stashed his mule and goods is even more apt for snow than down here. But it is out of sight. And on a well-traveled game trail. He can sit at his campfire and kill what he needs with an easy shot. Ease out from the lean-to and bring it in, no work at all. To bad his hut ain't as snow-tight as the cabin behind him.

Snow-tight and crowded, what with two men, a girl, and a baby. He grins, pale blue eyes icy above the stinking wool scarf. They'll be hatin' each other by spring. He'll make his move then.

He settles his shoulders under the big coat, twitches his poncho straight over his belly, and plods uphill through the snow, visions of next spring keeping him warm.

CHAPTER 15

The activity Suzanna has forced on herself makes her feel better, if not truly well. Much of the dull grayness has lifted, but now she's restless during the day and her sleep is troubled by dreams of being lost in the woods, unsure which direction will lead her home; of Ceran St. Vrain reaching out to touch her, her breath quickening; of her father sitting blank-eyed by a cold fire.

Although they haven't resumed marital relations, Gerald is sleeping beside her again in the big wooden bed, which they've moved to the loft. He doesn't stir when Suzanna jerks awake in the midnight darkness, gasping for breath, heart pounding in her chest.

She's unable to go back to sleep unless she takes Alma into the blankets with them. As aggravating as the child can be during the day, only her arms slung across Suzanna's chest, the confident warmth at the baby's core, can soothe her mother into some semblance of rest.

She knows that a long walk or two in the fields would cure her restlessness and probably her troubled dreams, too. But walking is difficult in the snow-bound valley and its late-January winds. When she does venture out, the icy air chaps any uncovered skin, leaving her face and hands with tiny cuts that refuse to heal.

All she can do is try to keep herself busy with Alma and the mending that piled up while she waited for the child to come and then afterwards, when she was so bound by her sadness. Now, she feels more irritable than sad, and the sewing threads tangle when she least expects it.

And the light in the cabin is so inadequate. She's standing by the window, trying to distinguish between black and dark blue thread, when Gerald comes through the front door with an armload of firewood. "It looks like we're going to get hit with another storm," he says cheerfully. "That breeze out there is feeling mighty brisk and damp."

Suzanna looks up. "How exciting and unusual."

He raises an eyebrow at her, crosses to the wood bin beside the fireplace, and begins stacking the firewood into it. "Spring will come eventually," he says.

"How long is 'eventually'?" she asks. She lifts the thread, each wound on a separate bit of paper, closer to the window and peers at them, then drops her hands. "This is just impossible. I can't see the difference at all." She sets the papers on the sill, grabs her shawl, then reaches for the thread and heads to the door.

"Where are you going?" Gerald asks. "You'll need more than a shawl."

Suzanna turns, her hand on the latch. "What I need is dark blue thread to mend your shirt with. The light from that so-called window is so inadequate that I can't tell if I'm using blue or black thread."

"Does it really matter?"

"Of course it does!" She flings the door open. A gust of wind shoves her back, pushing her into the center of the room, and sending a flurry of snow after her. "I swear!" The thread falls to the floor as she grabs the door with both hands, trying to push it against the wind.

"I'll get it." Gerald moves across the room, places both palms flat on the back of the door and leans in, shutting out the cold.

As he lifts the latch into place, Suzanna looks at her hands. "Now I've lost both the black and the blue," she grumbles. "Curse it!"

Gerald chuckles. "I don't think I've ever heard you swear that much in any given two minutes."

She glares at him. "I have never been provoked as much as I am at this minute." She turns her attention to the floor. "I must have dropped them. But who knows where they are?" She lifts her hands helplessly. "That was the last of my thread in either of those colors."

He looks around the room. "I doubt the wind took them outside."

"No, they're probably in the kitchen." She scowls at him. "I thought you said it was breezy out. That's a good deal stronger than a mere breeze."

He grins. "It's risen a little since I came in. At the level it is now, I'd call that a wind. Just a little one."

She shakes her head and begins pacing the floor, scanning for the dropped thread. Gerald goes to the fire, holds a sliver of wood to the flames, then uses the burning stick to light the lamp on the side table. He carries the lamp to the center of the room and leans down to place it on the floor. As the light flares across the floor boards, Suzanna says "Aha!" and bends to retrieve both papers of thread, which are lying side by side, a foot away from the lamp.

"Thank you." She looks down at the thread. "But I still don't know which is black and which is blue."

"Perhaps you can read instead. Can't that piece of mending wait?"

She looks up. "Until when? Until I finally get the glass windows you promised me?"

A shadow crosses his face and he turns away. "Well, until the snow stops and the sun comes out again, at any rate."

"You mean 'eventually'?"

He moves to the fireplace and looks into it for a long moment. Then his shoulders straighten and he turns to face her. "Why are you so angry with me? I can't control the weather."

In the corner, the baby begins to wail. Suzanna crosses to the cradle and lifts Alma to her shoulder. "I just want the wind to stop. And the snow that comes with it." She settles herself and the child on the storage chest by the fire. "I had no idea winter here could be this long or that it was possible for a snowstorm to block every last bit of sunlight."

"It snows in Don Fernando, too."

"Not like this." A gust of wind thuds against the cabin logs and they both wince as the shovel on the porch slams into a bench. "Taos snow doesn't continue for days at a time," Suzanna says. "And the wind isn't this strong."

"The wind here is powerful," Gerald admits. "It's torn part of the barn roof off, but there's nothing we can do about it until the weather clears. Ramón put a piece of canvas over the hay to protect it from getting completely soaked before we can get up on the roof and patch it."

"Eventually," Suzanna says drily. She looks down at the baby and shakes her head. "And you need to be changed again, don't you, my soul?"

When Suzanna looks up again, Gerald is gone. Alma mewls impatiently and Suzanna unfastens her chemise. What have I done? she wonders wearily. I try not to be sad, but it's difficult sometimes. I'm not yet seventeen and I'm caught in this valley like a beaver in one of Gerald's hunting traps. She chuckles bitterly. It's a good simile. Like the beaver, she can't escape. However, unlike the beaver, she's in a vise of her own making.

She shakes her head. The essence of her problem is that she married too young. She should have listened to her father. He'd been willing to accept Ceran St. Vrain as a son-in-law. He'd even suggested Christopher Carson, who's no older than herself.

Alma's head turns slightly, latching more firmly onto Suzanna's nipple, and Suzanna gasps at the knife-like pain. She puts a finger under Alma's chin, trying to ease the connection, but the infant ignores her and sucks fiercely on.

Suzanna takes a deep breath and impatiently blows air through her nostrils. She looks at the window and the little light coming through it, and fights back the tears. She's being unjust. Her father did approve of Gerald. The questions about St. Vrain and Chris Carson were more to test her attachment to him than to suggest the others were better men.

"And I do love him, I do," she murmurs. She strokes Alma's face. "And this sweet girl. But I'm so tired and the days are so long and so cold and so dark. All I want is some light and some movement."

She closes her eyes and sucks in her cheeks, willing the tears to stop, trying not to think of Taos and sunshine glinting on brown adobe walls, her father's book-lined parlor. She looks around, at the fire-shadowed log walls, the single bookcase with its three small shelves. "It's certainly not my father's house," she mutters.

Alma's arm moves and Suzanna looks down. The baby's fist waves in the air, batting at Suzanna's chest. Suzanna chuckles in spite of herself. "All, right, all right. I know I'm being dissatisfied and it won't do any good," she says. "Do you think you can cheer up your cantankerous mama?"

CHAPTER 16

Gerald's 'eventually' turns out to be almost a month. When the winds finally stop blowing in mid-February, Suzanna breaths a sigh of relief. The winter was bad, but now it's over. On both sides of the valley, the mountaintops are still blanketed in snow and the air has a definite bite to it, but the pale tan of last year's grass is visible again on the low ridges that finger their way from the slopes toward the valley's center.

Tiny silver streams thread down the ridges to the bottom lands, where they wind through the snow-patched grass to the marsh below the cabin. From there, water will seep into the first of the beaver ponds in the canyon below, then overtop the curved dams and begin working its way east through the canyon to the grassy llano beyond, becoming the Cimarron River along the way.

As Suzanna stands on the porch listening, the sun breaks through the puffy white clouds overhead. The sky is a brilliant blue. In the cabin yard, the ground is patchy with mud and half-frozen slush. But under the eaves, snowmelt from the roof has created a long thin line of damp soil. Tentative green shoots edge into the light. Her two pie plants are unfurling crinkly red-veined leaves. On the corral fence, a blue bird flitters its wings as if testing the air for warmth. A hawk swoops over the grassland below, hunting unwary prairie dogs.

Her garden lies waiting. Suzanna ducks into the cabin to make sure Alma is sleeping. She hesitates over the crib. What if the baby wakes? The men are in the barn, dealing with the livestock and the weather-exposed hay. But it's not warm enough out there for an infant.

The thought of staying indoors, tied to this crib, this semi-lit room, squeezes Suzanna's chest so hard she can hardly breathe. She scowls at the sleeping child, defiantly hitches up her skirts, and heads to the door to pull on her boots.

As she moves down the porch steps and across the mud-sticky yard toward the barn, Suzanna laughs out loud. Even the mud delights her. It clings to the soles of her boots and she's gained at least an inch in height before she reaches the barn. She says hello to the men, who are hauling out the aspen-pole ladder so they can get onto the roof for a closer look, then rummages among the tools for the shovel and hoe, and heads down the hill.

At the near end of the garden, she drops the tools on the ground and studies the oblong plot, hands on her hips. There's a good deal of work to be done before she can actually plant. Her lips twist. In Taos, she'd be planting early peas, spinach, and lettuce by now. But it can't be helped. And, if she starts preparing the ground now, she won't be too far behind her normal planting schedule.

She tucks up her skirts, steps into the plot, and walks up its length, studying the ground. It slants slightly, draining toward the valley floor, so the soil at the lower end is mucky with moisture. The heavy clay mud sticks to her boots. Suzanna grins. She's now a good three inches taller than when she left the cabin. It's so good to see wet, unfrozen dirt again.

She clumps back to her tools, tucks her skirts up more thoroughly, then grabs the shovel and moves back to the bottom of the plot. As she wedges the shovel blade between two ridges of mud, positioning it for the first cut, she glances up the hill. Ramón stands on the cabin porch, watching her. She waves at him happily and he lifts a hand in return.

Suzanna places her right foot on top of the shovel blade. Her sole is so thick with muck it slides off the shovel. She chuckles, stands on one foot, and uses the blade to scrape as much mud as she can from the other. When she's cleaned both boots, she repositions her shovel and feet and presses firmly down. But the blade doesn't budge. She frowns and stomps more sharply on the shovel.

Nothing. It won't cut into the soil. There must be a rock just here. She twists the shovel sideways and uses the side of the blade to scrape at the mud. But there's no rock underneath the dirt. Just a milky white layer of what looks almost like ice.

She pokes at it with her toe. It's as solid as caliche, that salt-impregnated hardpan below the surface that tortures the farmers and gardeners on the other side of the mountains. Suzanna frowns. She turned over the whole garden early last spring before she planted. And grew peas and maíz and other fairly deep-rooting plants in it. There's no caliche in this plot. In fact, Ramón told her the nasty stuff probably doesn't exist anywhere in the valley.

So what's blocking her shovel? Surely the soil can't still be frozen. The sun's been shining for three days now and snowmelt is saturating the entire valley.

She'll try the hoe. That might be more effective than the shovel. She clumps up the garden, collecting yet more mud on the soles of her boots, and switches out her tools. Then she goes back to where she's been digging, raises the hoe high over her head and swings the blade sharply down.

The metal blade hits the ground with a clicking sound and bounces in her hands. The wooden handle jerks painfully. "Tarnation!" she yelps. "What was that?"

"It is too soon," a voice behind her says.

Suzanna looks up. Ramón is standing near the shovel at the edge of the garden. He lifts his hands, palms up in a helpless gesture. "The ground, it is still frozen."

She scrapes at the dirt with her hoe. A layer of mud skims off, revealing a dirt-streaked icy surface below. "Perhaps I can use the mattock," she says. "Surely it can't be this frozen all the way down."

A small smile crosses Ramón's face. He looks up at the western mountains. "It is not frozen as far down as the deepest roots of the trees up there," he agrees. When he turns back to her, his face is rueful. "But for the grasses and the small plants here, it is frozen enough." He gives her a sympathetic look. "I cannot say for how long."

"But it's been so warm," Suzanna protests. "Surely the sun will soften it quickly. In Don Fernando, I would be planting the first peas by now."

"But even in Taos, this is the month of the false spring," he says gently.

She looks up at the white-topped mountains and nods unwillingly. It's true. By the time she was twelve she'd known what it was to plant the corn too early, that only lettuce and peas can survive the late spring frosts and the occasional fast-moving snows that descend as late as early May.

But those snows always melt quickly because the ground is already warm. That's apparently not going to happen here. Suzanna's shoulders drop. She lifts her hoe and plods toward Ramón. The mud weighs down her feet and makes walking awkward.

"It's so discouraging," she says. She turns her face, so Ramón can't see the tears trying to form, and stiffens her shoulders. She will not weep. She will not. She's a married woman now. Grown, even if she won't be seventeen until next month. A mother. Too old to cry. She steps out of the garden, bends her head, and stands for a long minute before she leans down to pick up the shovel.

When she turns back to Ramón, he's gazing at the mountains again. "It is possible that the soil will soften sooner than I think," he says. "I do not know for certain what the weather here will do."

"Does anyone know for certain what the weather here will do?" Suzanna asks bitterly. Then she looks at him apologetically. It isn't his fault. "What do you think it will do?"

He looks up at the blue sky. The white clouds are mere wisps now, moving in a breeze Suzanna can't feel.

"I think—" Ramón shakes his head. "I have seen this valley green in summers when all others are brown." He pauses, considering. "I think it will be warm for a short time, as it would be in Don Fernando, and then it will rain, and possibly snow again. And then the spring and the summer will come." He chuckles and grins at her. "And then fall and winter."

Suzanna chuckles. "Yes, I'm sure spring and summer will come eventually. I just wish I knew when eventually will be."

He shrugs again. "It is as God wills."

"I suppose so." She hefts the shovel and hoe, one in each hand, and he takes them from her.

As they move toward the barn he says, "The ground, when it thaws, will be rich with moisture."

"I certainly hope so," Suzanna replies. "It's my one consolation." She looks up at the sky. "At least there's enough sunlight now to allow me to tell black thread from blue. And enough warmth to allow me to do so outside, where I can actually see."

Ramón smiles noncommittally and carries her equipment into the barn. "Will you stay and collect eggs?" he asks as she follows him. "Mí nita is still sleeping and I need to turn the hay." He frowns. "Cow manure seems to have been tracked into it."

Gerald's head appears from the hole in the roof. He braces his gloved hand on the beam beside him. "If this wind stays down, I think we can replace the missing portions of this pretty quickly," he says.

"What do you mean, if the wind stays down?" Suzanna asks. "Haven't we seen the worst of it?"

"It is as God wills," Ramón says again.

Suzanna shakes her head and moves to the chicken pen. The hens cluck at her from their nests and ease aside only slightly as she reaches for their eggs. They seem to know that it's not time yet to venture out into the mud. They know more than she does. Will it ever truly be spring in this valley?

But when she returns to the cabin she notices again that there are green shoots edging out of the mud along the drip line. She stops at the bottom of the steps and studies the plants, then crouches down and pokes a finger into the dirt. It's softer here. And there doesn't seem to be a layer of ice underneath the top half inch of soil.

She moves onto the porch, scrapes mud off her boots, and hurries into the kitchen, where she puts the basket of eggs on the counter and hunts through the wood box for a thin kindling stick.

On her way back outside, she pauses beside Alma's cradle. The baby's head is turned, showing the heart-shaped mark on her left cheek. Suzanna smiles slightly and uses her free hand to adjust the blanket over Alma's shoulder, then heads outdoors.

The stick goes into the soil a good six inches. There's hope after all. She wiggles the piece of wood out of the dirt and turns slightly, studying the landscape. The cabin faces west. Once the sun is well up, this side of the house gets light until sundown. And warmth, as the sunlight bounces off the cabin logs.

She turns back to the strip of dirt and leans forward to look more closely at the sprouts of grass. There's no sign that rabbits

89

have been nibbling them. The smell of Dos and Uno must be keeping the browsers from coming right up to the house.

Suzanna rocks back on her heels. Her smile broadens. She can plant lettuce and peas here. An early crop that could be producing before the garden soil below is even ready to be turned.

Inside the cabin, Alma begins to fuss. Suzanna tosses the stick aside and heads indoors. "We'll beat this valley and its cold yet," she says as she lifts the baby from her cradle. "Won't Ramón and your daddy be surprised!" She settles into her chair and opens her bodice. As Alma begins to suckle, Suzanna chuckles. She feels more rested now than she has in weeks.

CHAPTER 17

Over the next few days, Suzanna widens the strip of thawed soil in front of the cabin, coaxing the water from the dripping roof to soak and soften a broader path area. She plants both lettuce and peas and is adding a few green-and-white striped squash seeds near the front steps the afternoon Stands Alone rides into the yard.

Suzanna stands to welcome him.

Stands Alone studies her. "You are She Who Plants."

Suzanna grins. "I can also boil water and slice bread. Would you like some tea?"

He chuckles and swings from his horse. "I would speak with your men."

She nods toward the barn. "They are there, cleaning out the old hay."

He looks at the low adobe and timber building. "The roof is newly patched."

"The winds were quite strong this past winter."

His lips twitch as he nods, his eyes still on the barn. Gerald and Ramón appear at the open door and cross the yard to them. "Stands Alone," Gerald says. "It's a pleasure."

The Indian grimaces. "You may not think so when I tell you my news."

"Please come inside," Suzanna says. "We have new bread."

After the meal, there's a long silence. Suzanna looks from Stands Alone to her husband and Ramón. The men are silent, avoiding her eyes, clearly wishing she'd leave the room but unwilling to ask her to go.

Men. Well, let them have their talk. She'll find out soon enough. She rises abruptly. "It's time to feed Alma," she says. She nods stiffly to Stands Alone and goes out, leaving the door slightly ajar behind her. At the table, someone chuckles.

Suzanna stops in mid-step and narrows her eyes. If they think she's going to go quietly to the other end of the cabin or the loft so she can't hear what Stands Alone has to say, they are sadly mistaken. Her chin lifts defiantly. She was never sent from the room in her father's house. If the men had something to say, they said it in front of her or not at all. She's not going to be left out now.

Gerald's voice rumbles. Suzanna tilts her head. "She doesn't appreciate being left out of discussions," he says.

"That is for you to decide." Stands Alone lowers his voice and Suzanna takes a quiet step back toward the kitchen. "There is news," he says.

"Yes?"

"An americano is trapping our waters."

Suzanna can hear the frown in Gerald's voice. "I have set no traps this spring."

"I know it. If you wish to do so, we have no objection. This is another man. A big man with broad shoulders and dirty hair."

"Have you asked him to leave?"

"He has not come into the camp. And the beaver do not come often to his traps."

"Yet you are concerned."

"He is hunting our women."

A bench scrapes the floor. "Hunting?"

"Yesterday morning he attacked my cousin Little Bear's daughter while she was out gathering wood."

Another bench scrapes. "Attacked her?" Ramón asks. "Does she live?"

"She is a brave one, that woman. She cut him on his hand and then she ran. She is unhurt."

A dish moves on the rough wooden table. Ramón clearing the plates.

"This thing happened at the beaver pond where the canyon widens and turns," Stands Alone says. "The signs say he remains nearby."

"That's over three miles from here." Though his words deny the idea of danger, Gerald's anxiety is palpable.

Stands Alone's voice is grim. "He is a big man with dirty yellow-white hair and thick shoulders."

Thick shoulders. Suzanna's stomach clenches. The man on the ridge.

There's a long silence, then Stands Alone speaks again. "I believe he is that Jones."

"Jones is dead," Gerald says stubbornly. "In the wilderness of the Salt River far to the west and south of here."

"They say it is so," the Ute concedes. "The name he is called is of little importance. His size and his deeds speak for him."

"Yes." There's a long silence, then Gerald says, "I appreciate the information." He pauses. "And that you chose to speak only to me and to Señor Chávez."

"Although She Who Plants will know of it before my horse reaches the valley." The Ute sounds amused and Suzanna's jaw clenches.

"Perhaps." There's a long pause, then Gerald speaks again, his voice grim. "In any case, we will be watching for a strange American with big shoulders."

"That is certain," Ramón says, his voice rough.

The kitchen benches scrape the floor again, more sharply this time, moving away from the table, and Suzanna turns and crosses the room to Alma's cradle. When the men enter, she has the child cupped over her shoulder.

Stands Alone nods to her as he passes to the door. Gerald and Ramón follow him into the yard. She's in her chair, nursing the baby, when Gerald comes back inside. "So what's the big secret?" she asks lightly.

Gerald shakes his head. "Just man talk. Nothing to worry you."

She narrows her eyes at him and opens her mouth. At her breast, Alma clamps down impatiently, sucking in the last drops of milk. Pain stabs Suzanna's breast. "I swear, I wish she would stop doing that!" she exclaims. She pokes her finger under the baby's chin. "That hurt!"

When she lifts her head, Gerald is gone. Suzanna's lips tighten. He doesn't want to repeat Stands Alone's news. To admit that Jones is still alive.

She shifts in her seat, easing the baby's weight on her arms. The uncouth trapper was such a menace, shadowing Taos' narrow streets, appearing unexpectedly at odd moments, leering at her from across the plaza. She'd never told Gerald or her father just how much his attentions worried her. Or repeated to them the stories the other women told about the big man.

She shudders a little, remembering that time and that fear, and shifts Alma to her other breast. She'd been so relieved when she learned that Gerald had mortally wounded Jones during that knife fight on the Salt River. Guilty about feeling relieved, but still relieved. And perhaps the wound was truly mortal. Perhaps the injury from Gerald's knife did actually end Jones' life. Gerald certainly believed it did. And Gregorio was there. He thought so, too.

94

Then she remembers the knife Gregorio found by Chonita's body. A big horn-handled blade. Like the one Jones carried. Suzanna shudders.

And Gerald wants to keep all this from her. Her jaw tightens. He won't tell her what Stands Alone said because he doesn't want to hear her response. He knows she'll point out that there'd be nothing to worry about if they were in Don Fernando instead of this god-forsaken valley. Where strangers roam at will and attack women who dare to gather firewood on their own. If she'd stayed in Taos, in her father's casa, they'd all be safe. And Encarnación wouldn't be dead.

Suzanna's chin trembles. Even if Gerald's right and the man who attacked Stands Alone's relative isn't Jones, there's still danger. But Gerald won't budge from here. There's no use in even trying to persuade him.

A wave of despair sweeps over her just as Alma clamps down on her nipple again. "Tarnation!" Suzanna exclaims. She gives the child's cheek a sharp tap and glares down at her. "How can you do that to me?"

Alma's little mouth puckers and she begins to whimper. Suzanna's grief overwhelms her. She pulls the baby against her chest and begins to weep along with her. Taos isn't the answer. If Jones is truly still alive, he'll just follow them there. After all, Chonita was in Taos when— But it doesn't bear thinking of. None of it bears thinking of. She and the child weep in unison.

CHAPTER 18

But as the days go by, there's no sign of a stranger in the valley and Stands Alone doesn't reappear with more news. The weather is unpredictable: sunny one day, snow flurries the next. Suzanna piles straw over the rhubarb and alongside the other plants coming up in the cabin's drip line.

But even this isn't enough. One gray and drizzly morning, she steps off the porch to find the dogs sniffing along the edge of the cabin. Her heart sinks. There's no longer any green peeking through the pale straw. Only miniscule black dots where she planted the peas and squash. A spot of black slime marks the location of each lettuce plant.

"Curse it!" Suzanna says as she straightens. "Hell and tarnation!" The words don't ease her. She turns and glares at the western mountains, their peaks hidden by the blanket of gray clouds that reaches toward her across the valley.

She turns back to what's left of her plants. "The weather was so balmy," she mourns. "And they were protected by the cabin wall. I was so confident they'd do well." She twists to scowl at the mountains again. "And they actually were doing well!"

She stomps onto the porch, drops onto a bench, and grabs the piece of wood left there for scraping mud. As Suzanna begins working the wet soil from her boots, Alma begins to fuss inside the cabin.

Suzanna drops the stick and closes her eyes. She leans back against the cabin logs and tries to swallow her tears. It's just too much. No matter what she does, it's not enough. Her plants die and Alma is continually hungry and the weather refuses to warm up. The baby begins to wail and Suzanna wants to wail with her, to scream all her frustrations out.

She takes a deep shuddering breath and pushes herself from the bench. Suddenly, Alma's cries stop. Suzanna hears Ramón say, "Yes, little sister. What is it, mí nita?"

Suzanna sinks back onto the porch bench and wipes at her cheeks with the back of her hands, grateful for the reprieve. But then the tears start again. She's a bad mother. Even a man with no children of his own, no experience with babies, is a better mother than she is. As she stares out over the dreary snow-splotched valley, a dull steady rain begins falling again.

Two weeks later, the rain is still coming down and the ground is still too frozen to plant. Suzanna alternates between days curled up in the bed in the loft, trying to ignore the baby beside her, or hours of frenzied cleaning. The cabin is spotless from top to bottom.

"Es una casa limpia como un oro fino," Ramón says, but Suzanna only scowls and turns away. He may think the house is clean as pure gold, but she can't give the bedding a proper airing because she never knows when the rain or another snowstorm will descend. She has nothing to do and it's driving her insane.

She's completed all the mending, after carefully labeling her black and dark blue threads so she can tell them apart. Spring may have arrived, but there's still not enough light from the window to distinguish between the colors. Nor is there enough light to read by. Both the glow of the oil lamp and the fire make her eyes itch with fatigue.

She's moving restlessly around the cabin, stopping to peer out the door at a misty-gray rain, the morning Gerald cheerfully announces that he's going hunting.

Suzanna turns away from the door. "It must be pleasant to be able to escape into the forest."

He's sitting on the carved wooden storage chest, oiling his rifle. He doesn't look up. "We need meat. I shouldn't be gone more than a few days."

"It will be a respite for you," she says. "Away from a cantankerous wife and a fussy baby."

He glances at Alma, asleep in her cradle. "The baby's not fussy."

"But I'm cantankerous," Suzanna says.

Gerald chuckles. "You said it, I didn't." He begins sweeping a soft cloth across the rifle's stock.

"Very amusing!" She slams the door shut and flounces across the room to the ladder.

As she puts her foot on the first rung, he sets the rifle on the floor, crosses the room, and touches her arm. "Suzanna— Why are you so angry with me?"

She turns her head away. "I'm not angry with you. I'm simply angry."

"That explains it," he says drily. He drops his hand and turns away.

Suzanna sets both feet on the floor, leans her forehead against the ladder, and closes her eyes. "I just feel so restless. There's nothing to do but wait for the weather to clear and tend the baby." She glances at the cradle. "And she's either screaming to be fed or she's a boring lump. All she does is smile or cry. It's not as if I can talk to her." Suzanna shrugs. "There's really not anything for me to do."

Gerald turns back to her and touches her arm again, more firmly this time, his fingers caressing her. "We could make another one." His eyes twinkle. "Two ought to keep you busy enough."

Suzanna snorts and twitches away from his hand. She turns, leans her back against the ladder, and gazes toward the window.

Gerald looks at the fire. "You say you're not angry with me, but it certainly feels as if you are. And less than enthusiastic about the marriage bed."

"I'm still sore."

He turns, his eyes anxious. "After all this time? It's been four months! Is that usual?"

"How would I know? There's no woman nearby to ask, is there? No one at all to talk to, for that matter. Except you and Ramón."

His shoulders slump. "You're clearly unhappy with me," he says wearily. "Our situation. This valley. I'm sorry I brought you here."

She wants to say, "So am I," but instead finds herself raising her hands helplessly. "I don't know what I am." She turns back to the ladder. "Please just go hunting. Leave me alone."

And he does. Suzanna lies in the loft and listens to him tramp back and forth across the room below as he gathers what he needs, then moves into the kitchen to speak to Ramón. Of course he can leave her here and go off and hunt in peace. Ramón will be here. Let him deal with the angry and frustrated wife.

Suzanna balls her hands into fists. He doesn't need to go hunting. He's just finding reasons to escape her and her pain. The coward. Hiding in the hills and the canyon of the Cimarron while she's cooped up in this cabin with nothing to do but feed an ever-hungry infant and wait for the pernicious weather to change.

She turns her back to the edge of the loft and pretends to be asleep when he climbs the ladder to say goodbye. She feels him lean over her. There's a long pause while she steels herself not to respond to his kiss. But he doesn't bend down to kiss her. Instead he moves silently backward and retreats down the ladder to the main room. A few minutes later the outer door closes with a thud.

"Curse him!" she whispers.

CHAPTER 19

The man with the thick shoulders studies the cabin through his spyglass and grunts in satisfaction. Logs cold and black, wet with March rain. Mud-filled yard. In the pasture below, a man slogs toward the cattle whose flanks are splattered with mud.

The watching man snorts disapprovingly. That fool Locke went off hunting, left the farm work to the Mexican. Left the girl to him, too.

Maybe they all like it that way. They all get their fill. He chuckles, lowers the glass, and pushes his long, dirty-blond hair out of his face. He knows what he'd do with that little señora, if he had her to himself. He chuckles, then scowls. Teach her some manners, for one thing. Thinks she can order grown men around, making 'em carry her tools, workin' that machete last fall like she knew what she was doin'.

Then he grins. Though she's been gettin' some lessons about not knowin' everything there is to know. The arm wavin' and head shakin' when those plants next to the cabin froze made for some mighty fine watchin'. Even from here he could tell she was one angry gal.

He chuckles. Dealin' with her then would of been fun. He likes a woman in a temper. Like that gal in Taos, that Chonita. That one was sure a fiery-tempered greaser bitch. He licks his lips, feeling himself harden, remembering the ditch path, the scattering potatoes, the big basket toppled in the dirt, just out of reach of her hand. Her skirts all sideways-like, wantin' more.

He grins and rubs himself through his britches. Those potatoes sure came in handy. Specially that long skinny one. He throws his head back and barks with laughter. Then he clamps his mouth shut and stares at the cabin. Sounds travel farther in this valley than a body might think and they say that Mexican of Locke's has some kind of sixth sense about who people are even when he can't rightly see 'em.

He raises the glass again. The greaser is headin' back up the hill, toward the ramshackle barn with its patched roof. The big man snorts contemptuously. They'll be back up there soon, patchin' again. Hell of a windy spot, this valley.

He was smart to build his own shelter in that tiny hill-bound meadow west of here. It might get cold in that hollow, but the wind don't hit it like it would out here on the flat. He glasses the cabin, but there's no sign of the woman. Too busy feelin' sorry for herself to come out of doors, get what little sunshine might be offerin'.

Or maybe she's gettin' herself ready for a night with the greaser. His eyes narrow and he grins malevolently. When those two idiots finally come to blows over that woman, he'll be waitin. Ready to move in and take care of her. And whichever man is left standin'.

His tongue flicks against his lips. Hope it's Locke. Won't kill him right away though. Make him watch while he has a little fun with the girl. The big man's groin trembles, and he squirms impatiently. Keep Locke alive, long as he can. Make him bleed, right in the chest. Let him feel what it's like. Then he'll finish him off, one thrust, right in the heart. Show him how to do it right. Won't that bastard be surprised to find out he ain't as big a man as he thinks.

The dirty-haired man's eyes narrow. Locke and his woman won't be surprised if they already know he's watchin' 'em.

What'd that damn Injun tell 'em when he showed up? He was inside that cabin a good stretch. Long enough for a meal and a chat. Must speak American.

He turns his head and spits thoughtfully. Ute, more'n likely. From the same band as that Indian bitch who knifed him. Her men haven't come lookin' for him, so she must not be worth a whole lot to 'em. Not a real looker, even if she does have breedin' hips. He'll go huntin' her again when he gets a chance. Teach her to cut him. It was just a scratch, already healed. But the thought of it still rancors.

That no one came huntin' for him is a puzzle. 'Less they think it was Locke or his Mexican that was after her. Maybe the Injun visit was to warn 'em off.

Now wouldn't that be somethin'? He chuckles and scratches his hair-covered chin. If he finds another squaw loose, those two greenhorns will be in serious trouble. Blamed for what he done.

Then he shakes his head. It's a bad idea. The Utes'd get their revenge and he'd be out his.

"Better stay away from that Injun camp," he mutters. "Keep my sights on this one." He lifts the spyglass and aims it again at the cabin on the other side of the valley.

CHAPTER 20

The day after Gerald leaves for his hunt, the rain stops. The sun shows fitfully through the clouds, but there's enough additional bit of light at the window to lift Suzanna's spirits with hope.

Until she goes out to stand on the porch. The yard and fields below are bog-wet, not only from the rain that's been falling but from the thawing ground. The hillsides behind the cabin are warming up and releasing the moisture that's been captured underground all winter. Water seeps past the cabin and pools in every flat space available.

Suzanna's shoulders slump. All she wants is some small change of scenery, a long brisk walk across ground that won't suck the boots from her feet. A flicker of movement on the valley floor catches her eye. She shades her eyes with her hand. A group of horsemen rides up the valley. Light flashes from a spear point. Indians? Stands Alone's people don't carry spears.

She bites her lower lip. She's alone at the moment. Ramón is on the hill above with the mules, fetching wood. And Gerald, of course, is off hunting. She should go inside, out of sight until the horsemen pass. Instead she moves to the edge of the porch and studies them.

There are perhaps half a dozen, all well-mounted, moving steadily and in good order up the muddy track from Palo Flechado Pass. The one in front is holding a pole upright in front of him. There's a banner of some kind attached to it. These men are definitely not Stands Alone and his band.

Perhaps they'll just keep moving north, toward the smaller valley above. Then a flash of light bounces from the top of a head and she realizes it's a troop of Mexican soldiers. One of them is wearing an old but well-polished conquistador helmet. Sunlight flashes on it again as the little band wheels to the east and begins moving toward the cabin. Suzanna hurries inside to prepare for them.

She has the tea water ready and Ramón's latest tortillas and a pot of his soft cheese on the table by the time the little cavalcade enters the yard. Suzanna positions herself on the porch steps as their leader reins his mud-splattered horse to a halt beside the corral. The man's eyes narrow when he sees her, but his tone is polite enough.

"Señorita?" he asks.

"Señora," she replies. "I am Señora Suzanna Locke."

"Forgive me, Señora," he says, though his tone isn't apologetic. His eyes flick across the front of the cabin, as if looking for her man. "I am Lieutenant María Jesús Gabaldón de Anaya. I was unaware that anyone resides in this valley."

"As you can see, my husband and I live here." There's an arrogance in the man that's unappealing, but she feels herself bound to observe the proprieties. "Please come in," she says. "If you would like to rest your horses, there is feed in the barn."

He considers her for a long moment, then dismounts and gestures at his men to do likewise. His boots sink into the mud and he looks down in disgust, then turns and barks an order. Three of his men lead the horses toward the barn while the lieutenant and two others, one quite short and thin and the other quite tall and fat, leave their boots on the porch and follow Suzanna into the cabin.

"An americano house," the lieutenant says disapprovingly as they enter. "No mud walls here."

Suzanna chuckles. "There's enough mud in the yard," she says ruefully. In her cradle, Alma makes a fussing sound. Suzanna crosses the room, picks her up, and carries her into the kitchen ahead of the men. The men stop at the sight of the food on the table.

"I'm afraid I don't have much to offer you," Suzanna says apologetically. She moves Alma onto her hip. "There is tea, if you'd like."

"Americano tea?" the lieutenant asks a little sarcastically. "No aguardiente? No vino?"

Suzanna bites her tongue. He's a guest. She will be patient. "There is no Taos Lightning in this house," she says evenly. "Nor wine, for that matter." She smiles apologetically at the lieutenant's men.

The thin man smiles back at her as the lieutenant says, "No vino. You must put great faith in la agua." He sits down at the table with a thud, crosses himself, and reaches for the tortillas and cheese. The other men follow his example.

"It is good," the fat man says to Suzanna as she seats herself on the bench opposite him. He glances at his leader. "We have been eating our own food for five days. It is good to eat a woman's cooking again."

It's Ramón's cooking, of course. Suzanna smiles but doesn't correct him. She turns to the lieutenant. "You have come from Don Fernando?"

The lieutenant nods reluctantly.

"Perhaps you know of my father." She looks at the fat man, who's scooping more cheese onto a tortilla. "Señor Jeremiah Peabody."

"The americano." The lieutenant gives her a sharp look. "The one who married the French girl."

"Half French," Suzanna says. "Her mother was Navajo."

106

"Not Spanish." He says it as if he is saying 'not human.'

"No," Suzanna acknowledges. "Not Spanish."

"Americano y tu esposo es americano. And now he is taking our land."

Alma gurgles and twists impatiently. Suzanna turns her around and seats her on her lap, so she's facing the men. The lieutenant regards the child balefully. "She has marks on her face."

This man is the rudest person Suzanna has ever encountered. She purses her lips and looks down at Alma. "They are freckles," Suzanna says. She touches the baby's cheek, forcing herself to look pleased with her child, as a good mother ought. "This one is shaped like a heart."

The thin man leans forward and peers at the child's face. He chuckles. "Yes, I see it." He reaches out to touch Alma's curly black hair. "Ella está muy bonita."

Suzanna smiles at him as the lieutenant applies himself disapprovingly to his food. When he's finished, he grudgingly mutters "Gracias," then demands, "And where is your man?"

"He is hunting," Suzanna says. She nods at what's left of the food and smiles a little. "As you can see, we have only cheese to eat at the moment."

"Humph." He leans back in his chair and stares at her. "And he leaves you alone here. It is very foolish of him."

How she wishes Ramón would return. But all she can do is look the man in the eye and say calmly, "I have nothing to fear."

"Apaches, Comanches, Utes," he says. "These are all to be feared." Then his eyes narrow. "But not contrabandistas, heh?"

"Contrabandistas?" she asks.

He leans forward suddenly. "Sí. Smugglers. You know what it is? To smuggle? To deal in contraband goods?"

"Of course I know what it is." She allows a slight smile to cross her face. "After all, I grew up in Don Fernando." She looks squarely into the lieutenant's face. "But we are not smugglers here. You saw the fields below. And the barn. We are farmers."

"Americanos pretending to be farmers!" he spits. He makes a visible effort to control himself, then leans back, looks down at his legs as he straightens them under the table, then looks up at her with a sneer. "It is entirely likely tu esposo is hunting the furs he has hidden in a cache, or goods carried by others across the plains from Los Estados Unidos to be brought into Don Fernando by night." His eyes narrow. "You are acquainted with Sanvran? The man Joaquin?"

St. Vrain and Ewing Young. Suzanna's stomach tightens, but she manages to only look puzzled. "I don't understand."

The lieutenant pulls his feet back. He leans toward her as if ready to pounce. "I have been in Don Fernando de Taos only a short while," he says. "But I know of these men who visit your father's house. This Sanvran. This Joaquin who your man hunted with not so many seasons ago. These men trade in many furs and have much merchandise but pay few fees to the comisario of the Santa Fe custom house." He sits back again and gives her a self-satisfied smile. "It is a great mystery."

So he knew who she was before he left Taos. And he knows of the rumors of St. Vrain's activities. And Gerald's association with Ewing Young. Young, whose methods for getting his furs out of New Mexico and to Missouri haven't endeared him to Santa Fe officials. Especially the Governor.

Suzanna puts on her mildest voice. "I know nothing of such things."

"Perhaps we will wait until your husband comes home from his hunting to discover the truth of these matters," the lieutenant says. "And then perhaps we will take him away with us to Santa Fe and learn there what he knows of such things." He smiles, his lips thin. "Then you will be all alone in this deserted valley with your americano baby." His smile widens. "Until the wild tribes find you here. The Comanches and the Apaches, too."

Suzanna forgets herself then. And her good intentions. She straightens, eyes blazing. she exclaims. "How dare you speak to me in such a way! You think you can bully me because I have no protection!"

He chuckles, his eyes amused for the first time. Then the outer door opens. Ramón enters the kitchen, taking off his hat as he moves through the door. The lieutenant jerks in his seat and his bench scrapes the floor.

Ramón's eyes sweep the room. Then he nods to Suzanna and turns to the lieutenant. "Hola, mí amigo," he says. "How are you? And how is your good father and your lovely mama, mí primo?"

Ramón's cousin. Or the son of his cousin. Suzanna bends to kiss Alma's head and keep herself from laughing at the stunned look on the lieutenant's face. The fat man and the thin man glance at each other, then at the table, and reach simultaneously for the plate of tortillas.

The soldiers head back to Taos that afternoon with assurances from Ramón that any evidence of smuggling will be promptly reported. He also sends messages of greeting to the lieutenant's mother, father, and various siblings.

"I've known you all my life, but you continue to surprise me," Suzanna says as they settle into the kitchen after the little cavalcade has trotted out of the yard. "I declare, I think you truly are related to every family in New Mexico."

Ramón chuckles and lifts himself from the table to pull out the mixing bowl and begin preparing more masa for tortillas. "I am not related to everyone in the province," he says. "But I have enough relations for convenience's sake."

"He threatened me with Apaches and Comanches," Suzanna says soberly.

Ramón shakes his head. "That one has no manners. But we have seen no wild tribes, no gentiles here. And if they do appear, Señor Gerald will deal with them respectfully, as he did with the Utes. For that matter, Stands Alone is likely to bring us word if Apaches or Comanches come in from the plains. And he will assist el señor to know how to speak with them." He shrugs. "They may wish to hunt. But the land we use is a small part of the valley. There is enough here for all."

"I hope so," Suzanna says. "And I certainly hope they will think so." She snuggles Alma to her chest. The Sangre de Cristos are so vast. There are so many miles between this tiny cabin and Taos. And Alma is so tiny, so fragile. So able to irritate Suzanna and yet pull on her heartstrings.

Suzanna shakes her head. Everything is so much more complicated here than it was in her father's house. Whatever possessed her to agree to live here?

She's still thinking about wild Indians, the tribes that Ramón calls gentiles, when Gerald returns two days later. He's on foot, a gutted mule deer slung across both the pack mule and horse. Suzanna greets him quietly. In bed that night, she accepts his attentions but feels no great rise of passion in response. When it's over, she lies back, staring into the darkness.

"Did you miss me at all?" Gerald asks. "You seem very— Thoughtful."

She turns her head to face him, though its too dark to make out more than a dark shape on his pillow. "We had visitors."

"So Ramón told me." He rolls toward her, onto his side. "He said they were here with you when he came back with the firewood." He pushes himself up onto his elbow. "You didn't say anything, so I assumed there was no problem. They didn't insult you, did they?"

110

"No, no." She waves a hand, brushing away his concerns. Then she shrugs. "Well, the lieutenant was rude, but they offered no physical harm. It was his intimations about the wild tribes that concerns me."

"Intimations?"

"He said I'd be in great danger if the Apaches or Comanches found me here alone with no man to protect me."

He lays back down, elbows out, his hands under his head. "These are the same wild tribes that, when we were courting, you assured me posed no danger to you," he says. "You said they knew your father and besides, you carried a knife."

"That was different," she responds stiffly. "I was living in Taos. There was little danger. And now there's a child to think of."

"There's no land for me near Don Fernando," Gerald says patiently. "Even if there was, it's doubtful anyone would sell to a stranger. They all want to leave land to their children, and that's understandable. I'd do the same myself. But it means that there's just no land available there anymore."

"You could trap."

"And leave you and Alma for months at a time? I won't do that. Besides, you were upset that I went hunting for just a few days."

"I could go to my father while you were gone. It would be the sensible thing to do."

There's a long pause, then he says, "Trapping is an uncertain business. Especially now, with the Mexican government stance toward Americans and the suspicion that any furs a man is found with are contraband. Besides, I'm not really a trapper at heart, Suzanna. You know that. I'm a farmer. Just as you need dirt under your fingernails, so I also need to watch plants growing, tend cattle." He stops, then makes an impatient gesture. "Please don't ask me to do something I'd hate."

"You've asked me to do something I hate." Her voice thickens with unshed tears. "I should be planting by now, and all I can do is wait for that pernicious mud to warm up."

"Oh, wife." He reaches for her, his hands warm on her shoulders, and she doesn't pull away. Somewhere deep inside, she wants to be comforted almost as much as she wants to go home to Taos. But she doesn't move toward him, either.

"Spring will come," Gerald says gently. "The ground will thaw. And then you'll see again what this valley can produce for you. Remember last year? How beautiful the garden was? How well that green and white striped squash did? How prolific the peas and onions were? How long the lettuce produced before it bolted? And you'll get an earlier start this year, because the corn and garden plots are already cleared."

Suzanna swallows. Her throat feels as if it's on fire. "I'm so sick of waiting," she whispers. "So tired of the lack of activity. It's driving me crazy." She turns toward him and props herself onto her elbow, the words pouring out of her. "I wasn't meant to be a housewife, cleaning and taking care of a baby and waiting passively for something to happen. I was meant to be busy and doing and moving around in the fresh air. Planting."

He kisses her forehead. "I know." His lips move down her face and she finds herself responding in spite of her anger. "I know," he whispers again and then she pushes her frustration away and lets herself respond to the comfort of his embrace, feeling an urgency she hadn't allowed herself when he touched her an hour before.

CHAPTER 21

It's warm enough that he don't need the bearskin poncho. He moves quickly for a big man, moving east across the greening valley south of the cabin, keeping well behind the ridges that jut out from the foothills. The cabin's out of sight, but that Peabody bitch's men don't stay close to her no more. Never tellin' when they might show up somewhere else.

He's aiming for the little valley that parallels the big one on its eastern side. It's got some good-size beaver ponds, that ain't likely to be trapped yet this season. The warmth's makin' him restless and a little beaver tail'd be a change from rabbit, elk, and venison.

And from there it's a straight shot north through the hills to the Ute camp. He grins and pushes his dirty blond hair from his face. Maybe he'll get lucky and scare up that squaw what drew blood last time.

Wasn't plannin' too, but he's hungry for a woman. Even that ugly Ute squaw'd be better than nothin'. Give her a taste of her own medicine, and then some. A little blood'd go a long way toward helping the old sword stay up. Not that it's old or needs any help. But a little excitement never hurt.

He glances toward the grass-covered ridge between him and the cabin. A steady plume of chimney smoke rises above it, shimmering a pale gray against the blue sky.

The big man scowls. A coyote, trotting west across the greening slope, gives him an indifferent look. "Damn varmint!" the man mutters. "I'd shoot you just for the hell of it if I was ready to rouse that cabin!"

But not yet. He refocuses on the stone outcropping that marks the entrance to the little valley to the east. Beaver tail, Injun tail, then high tail it back t' camp and keep watchin' 'til it's time. He grins, pleased at his play on words. His tongue runs over his lips. All three anticipations make him hungry. What comes after the last one, most of all. But for now, he'll settle for beaver tail.

CHAPTER 22

By late April, the ground has thawed enough to allow Suzanna to plant peas and spinach in the garden plot. But she remembers the February freeze, as well as the way her corn crop behaved the previous spring, and manages to wait for truly warm weather before she plants anything else. How she wishes for glass windows, so she can start something indoors! But all she can do is wait. Surely it won't be long now.

Then, the morning of May 10th, snow falls. Suzanna cracks the door open and peers out in disbelief. "This is the most intractable weather I have ever seen or heard tell of!"

Gerald is sitting on a bench near the fire, mending harness. Alma is on the floor, her back against his legs and playing with the leather scraps from his work. "There's nothing we can do about the weather but find something to keep us occupied indoors," he says. "And this snow is likely to melt quickly enough, once it stops falling."

"Well, it certainly doesn't look likely to stop any time soon." Suzanna pulls the door farther open. Snow swirls into the room. "Just look at it!" She slams the door shut and leans her back against it, facing the room.

Gerald lifts his brown face, sparked by the fire, and grins at her.

"There is nothing funny about this!" She flounces across the room to the fire and bends to pry a piece of saliva-wet leather from Alma's hand. "Don't eat that! Who knows where it's been?"

The baby pouts up at her mother, then leans forward to search the floor for more scraps. Suzanna scowls, grabs her up, and carries her to a bench on the other side of the room. Alma frowns at her mother, opens her mouth to protest, then seems to think better of it. She sticks her fist in her mouth and turns her head to gaze at her father.

"I can find some clean scraps to give her," he says. "She seems to like the feel of them on her gums."

"She's too young to be getting teeth."

Gerald raises an eyebrow and goes back to his work.

"If this snow kills my peas and spinach, I'm going to be really and truly aggravated."

Gerald nods but doesn't answer.

"I simply cannot understand how it can be snowing in May."

"The ground's been warming up fairly well," Gerald says, peering at his work. "The grass in the lower pasture has been coming in nicely. I don't think this storm will do your plants any real damage."

"It had better not!"

"That's farming." Gerald leans toward the fire and tilts the leather in his hands toward the light. "If the crops die, you replant. That's all you can do." He glances up at her. "At least we're not hauling water to keep them alive."

Suzanna nods unwillingly. "That's true enough," she says begrudgingly. "Or cleaning out acequia ditches and praying there's enough mountain snowmelt to fill them." She sighs and looks wearily at the condensation dripping down the sheets of mica and onto the windowsill. "I suppose this is the water the farmers in the Taos Valley are praying for."

Alma gurgles and reaches for her mother's finger. Suzanna lets her take it. The baby pulls it to her face and into her mouth, her gums slimy with saliva. "Ouch!" Suzanna exclaims. She turns

116

Alma on her lap and pushes an exploratory finger between the child's lips.

When she looks up, Gerald's watching her warily. "Why, I didn't think it possible!" Suzanna says. "It feels as if she has a tooth about to burst!"

"Could be," Gerald says. "She did seem to be enjoying that piece of leather."

Suzanna's eyes narrow. "Just make sure anything you give her is fit to go into her mouth."

It's late May before Suzanna feels it's safe to plant. When she does, the seeds seem to sprout overnight. There's more rain in June than there was the year before, and the valley is bright with wildflowers. Paper-thin blue petals of wild flax wave in the lightest of morning breezes, and each afternoon the hillsides glow with yellow swathes of golden pea. Masses of purple mountain iris spread in the low spots between them, along the impromptu streams and seeps.

It's enough to take a woman's breath away and send her, knife in hand, to heap her basket with flax for cordage or, digging knife tucked into her belt, to collect iris root for future medicinal purposes. As Suzanna threads her way toward the flowers, the scent of wild onion tempts her, and these also go into the basket, for Ramón and the kitchen.

She returns to the cabin flushed and smiling, to a child who gazes at her in wonder, then raises her arms to be fed, more for the comfort of her mother's body than to satisfy her hunger. Ramón has taken to giving Alma small sips of cornmeal broth at every meal.

There's also plenty of work to be done in the garden. The men dig narrow irrigation ditches from the creek and Suzanna creates smaller furrows to place the water precisely where she wants it. While the adults work, Alma sits on a small blanket on the grass beside the garden and pokes at the ground with a small stick. The men construct what they hope will be a more rabbit-proof fence around the garden, and the cattle grow fat on the dark green sedge and meadow grasses in the fields beyond.

The rhubarb Suzanna's father brought the spring before produces enough stalks for two pies and some dried cubes for winter use, but the plants aren't quite as healthy as she'd like. And the raccoons are still investigating the corn on a nightly basis, although Uno and Dos seem to be keeping them from doing any major damage.

Suzanna goes to bed each night pleasantly relaxed from a good day's work and rises the next morning with the anticipation of more activity. As her mood brightens, Gerald seems to grow more relaxed, too.

But eventually the rest of the world intrudes on their lives and tension returns. Ewing Young arrives in late July. Suzanna is glad to see him at first: He brings a letter and a small parcel of books from her father. But he also brings unwelcome news.

"Bill Williams was in St. Vrain's store last week, purchasing whiskey for yet another of his sprees," Young says. He stretches his long legs toward the fireplace and glances at the flames. "You all actually need an evening fire in these parts, even in spring, don't you?" He shakes his long head. "This valley is certainly a different place from Don Fernando." He nods at Gerald, who's seated on the painted storage chest at the other end of the fireplace. "Williams says he saw our old friend up on the Platte. He sent me a message asking me to let you know."

Gerald frowns. "Which old friend?"

"That Jones fellow."

Suzanna looks up from her letter.

Young keeps his eyes on Gerald. "I reckon he wasn't as dead as we all assumed. That knife thrust didn't go quite as deep as you thought."

Suzanna looks at Gerald, who's looking at Ramón. All the anger she'd felt last fall when she'd overheard Gregorio and Gerald in the barn, comes flooding back to her. But now it's out in the open. Now she can speak. "But of course, you knew this," she says flatly.

"Gregorio said something when he was here," Gerald admits reluctantly. "There had been rumors." Suzanna notes that he says nothing about Gregorio finding Jones' knife beside Encarnación's body. Or the stranger in the barn. But if she says anything about either event, he'll know she was eavesdropping. Her lips tighten, waiting.

"I didn't credit it," Gerald says. He frowns down at his hands, then meets Ewing Young's eyes. "Did Williams actually see the man? See him to speak to?"

"He says he saw him, but they didn't speak. Jones was on the ridge above and when he caught sight of Williams, he faded back into the trees. That's what Bill's sayin'."

"So he may have been mistaken."

Young glances at Suzanna, letter clutched in her hand, glaring at Gerald. "Might have been."

Suzanna's chin lifts. She's through being protected. "Mr. Williams has excellent eyesight." She turns to Young. "And I strongly suspect that you don't truly believe he was mistaken."

Young shrugs, his eyes on Gerald again. "Any man can be mistaken." He grins slightly. "Even Old Bill Williams isn't always right."

Ramón chuckles. "I wouldn't say such a thing to el hombre himself."

Young turns to Suzanna, eyes steady. "Williams didn't say he was absolutely sure it was Jones, just that it looked like him. He said it made him righteously believe the rumors were true."

He grins at the quote, then sobers. "It wouldn't be the first time someone was thought to be dead and it turned out they somehow survived. Got picked up by Indians and nursed back to health, or were just too cussed strong and stubborn to give out when another man might have succumbed."

He glances at Gerald apologetically. "But I don't know for certain it was Jones who Old Bill saw. It could have been someone else. And it was up on the Platte. That's a good deal of distance from here."

Suzanna nods and lifts her letter, closing the subject. There's a long silence, then the men's conversation drifts to other topics: the price of beaver, news from the States, the latest changes in administration in Santa Fe, Gerald's father's plans to try his luck in California. It doesn't seem likely that he'll be back in New Mexico any time soon.

Suzanna doesn't really hear any of it. She's looking blindly at her father's elegant yet spidery handwriting, but seeing a man built like Jones watching the cabin, a big bone-handled knife lying on the acequia path beside Encarnación's body, Gerald glimpsing a dark shape at the corner of the barn. And Stands Alone's face as he described the attack on his cousin's daughter.

She shudders. And farther back: a narrow Taos street, Jones' sharp breath in her face, arms out, blocking her way. Thank God Gerald happened by and intervened. And that he'd stepped in again, all those months later on the Salt River in Gregorio Garcia's defense. The knife fight which he'd never described to her in any detail. They'd all thought the thing ended there, with Jones bleeding to death in the dry, empty lands above the Salt. Surely, no one could survive a chest wound like that.

And yet— She drops her father's letter into her lap and lets herself feel the potential danger for the first time. It doesn't matter where Old Bill saw him, how far away it was. Jones is still alive. He may very well be here, somewhere in the hills. Watching. Waiting for her the way he must have waited for Chonita.

She shudders and takes a deep trembling breath. In the cradle on the other side of the room, Alma whimpers in her sleep and Suzanna slips around the men to collect her. There's a strange comfort in the sturdy little body. Suzanna carries the baby across the room and settles back into her seat to listen to the men chatting, doing their best to ignore the implications of Ewing Young's news.

Young stays a week, hunting with Ramón, touring the valley pastures with Gerald. On the third afternoon, he and Gerald head into the Cimarron canyon to scout beaver. When they return, Suzanna's on the porch shelling peas. Alma sits at her feet carefully picking up, examining, and then chewing on a small set of blocks Ramón has carved for her.

"I'll think on it," Gerald says to Young as they reach the steps.

Suzanna looks up. "What is it you're going to be thinking on?" she asks. She glances at the voluminous gray and white clouds that tower over the mountains on the opposite side of the valley, and shakes her head. "I'm thinking we're going to get rain this afternoon."

Young, at the bottom of the steps, turns to study the clouds. Gerald moves onto the porch, scoops Alma into his arms, and carries her to the bench under the window. Alma wiggles impatiently. "Young is putting together a group to trap the Salt River area this fall," Gerald says as he stands the baby beside the bench, where she braces her chubby hands against the wood.

Suzanna's hands stop moving. "The Salt? Northwest of the Gila?"

Both men avoid her eyes.

"The Gila wilderness?"

"More or less," Gerald says. He holds out a finger to Alma and she grabs it and gurgles happily.

Young turns his head. "That's one quiet baby," he says.

Gerald chuckles. "She is quiet a good deal of the time," he agrees. "Though when she decides to make noise, she lets her presence be felt."

Suzanna's face darkens as she watches the men try to distract her with the child. "That's where you had the run-in with the Apaches." She looks at Young. "Where Thomas Smith's horse was wounded."

"That general area." His eyes are still on the baby.

"And where you had another run-in with the same group when you went back two months later," Suzanna adds. "That time, four Apaches were killed, including their chief." She shakes her head. "They won't have forgotten that. They'll still be looking for revenge. Why would you go back there, of all places?"

"It's good hunting," Gerald says. He holds another finger out to Alma, who grabs it. "The beaver was thick when we were there. Word has it that they've come back stronger than before." He turns Alma slightly, to face her mother, and the baby laughs in delight.

But Suzanna isn't so easily deflected. "That is simply ridiculous," she says flatly. She reaches into her bowl of peas. "Any man going back there will be hunting trouble, not beaver."

Then she looks at Gerald, whose eyes are still firmly on the child. "You aren't thinking of going with him, are you?"

He glances up at her, then back to Alma. "We could use the money."

Suzanna glares at him, then at Young, who's now studying the fields below the cabin. She stands up abruptly, the bowl of peas against her chest, opens her mouth, glares at Young again, then closes her mouth and turns and stalks into the cabin. She pauses just inside the door, listening.

"You gonna let a woman tell you what to do?" Young asks mildly.

Suzanna's eyes snap and her jaw tightens, but she stays where she is.

"She's going to have some mighty powerful arguments at her disposal," Gerald says. Alma fusses and Gerald's bench scrapes against the porch. He seems to be lifting the baby into his lap. "Especially since you just brought word that Enoch Jones seems to have come back from the dead."

"If the man Williams saw is actually Jones," Young points out. "And if Jones is truly gunnin' for you all, which seems unlikely. Jones didn't like anyone. I don't know why he'd be coming this direction in particular. Or that he'd know to look for you up here, of all places."

Inside the cabin, Suzanna's lips tighten. The man is certainly full of arguments.

But she has time to marshal her objections and she takes full advantage of that fact. When she and Gerald are alone in bed that night, she's ready. "I don't know why Jones wouldn't know where we are," she says. "After all, everyone in Taos knows we're here. And he certainly has reason to hate us. I spurned him. You intervened. Then you intervened again when he was persecuting Gregorio. If you didn't kill him in that knife fight, you almost did. In fact, we had every reason to believe he was dead. And to be glad of it."

She sighs. "I suppose we shouldn't have been glad, but we were. And I was glad as much for Encarnación's sake as my own. After all, he'd been after her, too."

Encarnación. Suzanna's eyes close against the threatening tears. She turns her head, trying to make out his profile in the dark. "Please don't go with Young on this trapping trip."

"It would be a way to get the money for those glass windows you want so badly."

Suzanna exhales breath she hasn't realized she was holding. If that's his only reason for going— "I do want glass windowpanes," she says. "But I want to be safe, and safe here with you, more than I want glass windows."

He turns toward her. "Are you certain?"

The very doubt in his voice makes her sure. "I'm certain." As she says it, she realizes it's more true than she'd known. That she truly will endure almost any sacrifice to keep him with her.

"All right then," he says.

A wave of gratitude sweeps over her. "Thank you," she whispers.

He leans toward her in the dark and kisses her hair, and she turns to thank him more fully.

CHAPTER 23

Outside, the two dogs are barking wildly. Apaches? Comanche? Jones? Suzanna's breath catches as she jams her knitting into its basket beside her chair. She's alone at the moment. The men are in the hills gathering firewood.

Suzanna glances at Alma, who's sitting quietly in her cradle, then takes a deep steadying breath and crosses the room to the shotgun beside the door. She grabs it up and retreats to the window, where she stands to one side and leans cautiously forward, just enough to peek out without being seen.

But of course she can't see a thing. The mica is too thick, too wavy. It distorts even the light filtering into the room. She tilts her head, listening. The barking is coming from below the hill. She moves to the door, opens it a crack, and peers cautiously out. Nothing in the yard. She stands on the tips of her toes and leans forward, trying to see more clearly. There's movement near the garden. Large brown shapes larger than the barking dogs, who seem to be dancing excitedly at the edge of the corn patch.

Shapes bigger than raccoons. Suzanna drops the gun and flings the door wide. Alma's startled by the noise and starts to cry, but Suzanna doesn't turn back to her. Instead, she runs wildly across the yard and down the hill, tugging at her apron strings as she goes. There are deer everywhere, trotting through her peas and potatoes toward the knee-high corn, standing in the patch itself, teeth reaching daintily for fresh green foliage. Suzanna charges toward them, waving her apron and yelling "Shoo! Shoo!"

Dos and Uno plunge after her, rampaging through the corn-stalks, and the deer flee, crashing through the plants as they go.

Chest heaving, Suzanna stands in the center of the field and surveys the damage. Some of corn is completely uprooted. It's hard to tell who wreaked the most havoc, the deer or the dogs. She glares down at the dogs, who are now lying panting at her feet. "You certainly weren't much help!" she snaps. "You may be some protection against raccoons, but you're completely useless against deer!"

She turns, surveying the field more carefully. Her jaw tightens. The thorny fence around the vegetable garden was no barrier at all. The deer simply hopped over it. Something larger is clearly needed.

Her shoulders slump. She worked hard to get this corn growing and it's done fairly well so far this year. She's hoed and weeded diligently. Rearranged countless irrigation paths to get moisture to each and every stalk. And now the deer are hell-bent on eating it all.

Her chin lifts. She isn't about to let those pernicious beasts get it now. She needs a strong and high fence, and she needs it imme-diately.

But when she tells Gerald this, he's less than amenable. He studies the damaged cornfield and shakes his head. "The ears probably wouldn't have ripened before the first snow, anyway," he says. Beside him, Ramón nods sympathetically.

"A few ears ripened last year," Suzanna points out. "Those are the ones I used for seed this spring. After a few seasons of saving the earliest crop, I'll be on track to a consistent, early-ripening strain. You're a farmer. You know that's how it's done."

Gerald nods, acknowledging her plan but still doubtful. "It'll take years to get a strain that will grow at this altitude."

126

Her chin lifts. "Then it will take years. You want to stay in this God-forsaken valley, don't you?"

He keeps his eyes on the damaged field. "I doubt a fence will keep the deer out for long. They can jump just about anything you put in front of them."

"Then what would you suggest? Those mongrel dogs have proven themselves worse than useless." Her voice rises. "They didn't keep the deer out of the patch. Instead, they danced around the edge like the foolish curs they are. And when I came running and they finally got the courage to give chase, they caused as much or more damage than did the deer!"

Gerald shakes his head, still contemplating the cornfield. Suzanna sets her jaw, takes a deep breath, and prepares to launch another tirade.

But Ramón interrupts her. "There is a man at Arroyo Hondo who has dogs called masteef," he says. He lifts a hand, palm down and waist high. "They are this big and used for hunting."

Gerald turns his eyes from the corn. "Do you think he would sell?"

Ramón shrugs. "We could go for a visit and ask him. He is a relation of my mother's."

Gerald grins. "Who are you not related to in this country?" he asks affectionately. Then he sobers. "Arroyo Hondo, you say? North of Taos. That's a long trip, and we don't know if he'll sell or if a mastiff will be more effective than Dos and Uno have been."

"It's certainly worth a try," Suzanna says.

But her preparations for the trip to Arroyo Hondo are interrupted two days later by the sound of men's voices in the yard.

She drops the blankets she's folding, lifts Alma from her cradle, and moves to the porch. Gerald is standing beside the corral watching a band of young Ute men haze a herd of ponies onto the grassy foothills north of the barn. He turns east and gazes at the slope above the cabin, then sees Suzanna and waves a hand toward the hill. "It appears that we're about to have visitors."

Suzanna moves into the yard to stand beside him. A band of Utes rides down the hill. Stands Alone is in the lead on his brown and white gelding. Women and children trail the men, lodge poles dragging the ground behind their mounts. They lead ponies laden with packs of fine deerskin.

The Utes disappear around the back of the barn, then reappear at its near end. Stands Alone moves into the yard and reins in beside Gerald and Suzanna.

"It is good to see you again," Gerald says.

The other man nods. "All is well?"

"All is well."

"We have come to trade."

Gerald lifts an eyebrow. "I have little to offer."

"More will come," Stands Alone says. "Apache and others." He gestures to the west. "Taoseños y quizás Americanos."

"Ah," Gerald says. "A trade fair."

Stands Alone turns in his saddle and studies the valley, then points south and a little west. "There," he says. "Where the stream comes in from the Taos land."

Suzanna follows the men's gaze. It's far enough from the cabin pastures to limit damage to the hay and cattle. And the stream from the mountains is steady enough to provide for a good-size group of folks. The site is also within walking distance of the cabin.

"It is a good location," Gerald says.

Stands Alone tilts his head to study the position of the sun, then glances toward his band. "We will be ready tomorrow at the midday meal," he says. "Join us then."

It isn't an invitation so much as a command. Gerald's eyes glint in amusement. He smiles slightly and nods. "With pleasure."

The Ute reins his horse toward his people and Gerald and Suzanna cross the yard to the porch. "It looks like we're going to have to postpone our little visit to Arroyo Hondo," Gerald says. "It's hard to say how long this trade fair might last. A week or two, I'd guess. If you have any produce to spare, there's likely to be a market for it."

She nods, considering. Then she smiles at him. "I haven't seen that many people in a long time. This will be fun."

He grins back at her. "You can find a woman or two and have a gab fest just like the old days with Encarnación."

"Nobody can replace Chonita," Suzanna says sadly.

He reaches toward her. "I'm sorry. I didn't mean—"

But she shakes her head. "It's all right." Then she brightens. "I hope Stands Alone's wife is with him. I'd like to meet her."

But when Suzanna is introduced to Stands Alone's wife the next day, there's little they can say to each other. Sings Quietly doesn't speak English or Spanish, and Suzanna knows no Ute. They smile at each other, the short middle-aged Ute woman with her kindly round face, the tall thin mixed-race woman with her black hair and eyes, and shrug companionably. They'll make do somehow. The older woman's fingers move in a questioning way, and Suzanna chuckles and nods. She knows a little sign. They can communicate what they need to.

Sings Quietly seems to know that Suzanna's cooking skills are limited. She gives Suzanna a questioning look as she gestures toward a pot bubbling over the fire and makes stirring motions with her hand. Suzanna grins and nods. She can stir, at least.

"I didn't know she only speaks Ute," Gerald says apologetically as he and Suzanna make their way home that night. Gerald's lantern wraps them in its yellow sphere of light.

129

"Oh, we managed," Suzanna says. "It's nice to have so many people around." She looks back at the campsite, the fires dying down as everyone settles into their blankets. "I suppose the runners have already gone to Taos and returned. I expect there'll be considerably more here tomorrow."

"And possibly a mastiff," Gerald says. "I asked Little Squirrel to take a message to Ramón's relative in Arroyo Hondo, requesting the loan of a dog." He shrugs. "The man may be unwilling to send an animal that way, but you never can tell. Ramón wrote him a short note."

"Oh," Suzanna says. She had harbored a secret hope that the journey to Arroyo Hondo might include a side visit to Taos and her father. But this new development means she won't be seeing him any time soon.

"Is that all right?" Gerald asks. "It's not a short distance across the mountains to Hondo. This will save you and Alma the wear of a journey by horseback."

"It would be nice if there was a wagon road to Taos," she answers.

"There's likely to be one eventually," Gerald says.

In spite of her disappointment, she chuckles. Eventually. It seems to be becoming his favorite word.

CHAPTER 24

"Gonna all have the clap an' french pox besides," the big man mutters as he scans the Indian trade camp with his glass. "Utes, 'Pache, Taos, those greasers." On the hillside to his right, a young woman moves down the slope. A blanket is draped over her back and tied in a knot on her upper chest. The bulge on her back is filled with branches for the cooking fires. She's bent slightly forward to balance the weight. Her doeskin dress is tight over her large firm breasts.

The man pushes his long, pale hair away from his face. His tongue flicks across his lips. Then he's distracted by movement on the faint path from the cabin on the Cimarron side of the valley. Two men and a woman.

His face twists. Even in this wilderness, they got friends. If you can be friends with an Injun. But then, they ain't none of them white, now are they?

They been carousing for three days now, Injuns and Mexicans up and down the valley, Locke and his crew back and forth from the cabin. Yesterday, half a dozen Taos braves comin' direct from the pueblo almost stumbled on his hideaway.

Didn't spot him, though. He snorts derisively. Better woodsman than all of 'em together. Had his rifle trained on 'em all the way down his little valley. Could of wiped out the whole bunch if he wanted to.

The Peabody bitch is hanging back from her men. Haulin' the kid is slowin' her down. Cub's gettin' heavy. His lip curls. It's a wonder Locke or Chavez ain't haulin' the papoose, instead of her.

Then a Ute woman approaches the men, nods slightly, and moves on to the girl and baby. He grunts approvingly. Maybe the Injuns'll teach the bitch some manners, how to act proper toward her man. A little instruction now'll save him some time in the long run. He grins, anticipating next fall.

He's decided that's when he'll do it. Sweep in while the men are off huntin' meat for the coming season. Smash the black curly head of that varmint-child and carry its mother off to the woods. Teach her a few tricks even the Injuns don't know.

His groin tightens and he moves restlessly, then lifts the glass again, to distract himself. More Mexicans are trudging up the valley from the direction of Palo Flechado. He pivots and peers north, where the valley pinches down and then widens again below the west slopes of the Cimarrons.

The Indian bucks have moved their little herd farther that direction, driving them out of sight. Gives them the chance to talk the horses up to potential buyers without havin' the animals close enough for anyone to get a good look at. And the men guardin' the herd can play a little, no one watchin'. Good bet they got girls from the camp slippin' up the valley after dark.

His eyes narrow. When those bucks are liquored up and distracted enough, that herd'll be ripe for the pickin'. Then he shakes his head impatiently and turns his attention back to the trading camp. If any of those horses go missing, the Utes'll be combin' the hills for whoever done it. He don't need anyone findin' his little valley and his gear. Not yet.

His tongue darts out, wetting his chapped lips. Not yet.

Below, there's a cluster of people at the edge of the camp. While Locke and the greaser listen to the Utes talk, the Peabody slut and the Injun woman bend their heads over the black-haired baby. Suzanna pulls the little varmint's wrappings off and the other woman reaches for the kid. The big man scowls. He wouldn't let no Ute woman touch any offspring of his. But then, Locke's different.

Different all right. Ugh. The big man turns his head and spits into the green grass beside him. Dark-skinned runt. "Knew him fer what he was, minute I saw him," the man mutters. "Nothin' but trouble ever since."

Makin' him look a fool when those Pawnee spawn started that shovin' match there alongside the wagon train. And spookin' those mules in the mountains east of Taos so's to get his foot crooked up like that. The big man flexes his ankle. Winter cold'll be twingin' it again in a few months. He scowls. Damn that Locke and all belongin' to him.

That little bitch down there, that señora with her mincin' ways and her don't know how to cook. She'd be his by now, if it weren't for Locke. She'd know how to cook, too, damn her, or he'd know why not.

He'd been so close, that day in Taos. That narrow street, those nooks where the adobe house walls don't match up straight. His tongue flicks over his lips. Plenty of spots there to make her his, permanent-like. Her daddy done it. Knocked' up that Navajo girl, kept her for a cook the rest of her days. And got himself a little one of his own in the bargain.

The big man snorts in disgust. Ain't lookin' for a daughter. Just a spitfire to keep him warm, use up proper 'til he's done with her. He smiles slowly. His tongue touches his lips again. Those breasts. That sharp look she gets in her face. She'll take a while to tame. Keep him good and hard in the meantime. He's gettin' horny, just thinking on it.

Then he scowls. He would of had her by now if that bastard Locke hadn't got in the way. Locke sure is some kind of interferin' nigger. Interrupted his fun with the greaser boy, too. There by the Salt. The big man's tongue flicks against his lips. Boy like a willow, movin' around the camp. Askin' for some educatin'. Just askin' for it.

He feels himself harden. Boys can do that to him, sometimes even more'n a girl. Then he scowls. Ain't nothin' wrong with it. Just a tool for teachin' an upstart cub a thing or two. Keep him in line. And that Garcia was a pretty one. But Locke had to go and get in the middle of that, too.

"Damn bastard can't mind his own business," the big man growls. His left hand moves to the left side of his chest. Even through his coat, he can feel the scar. Just beside the heart, the puckered skin a long twisted gash that pulls across his torso. He'll be feeling that, too, come winter. "Damn whoremonger," he mutters.

Left him for dead. Locke and all those others. Didn't even bother comin' after him. His jaw tightens. He laid up in that cave a long while, sure he was goin' to die, braced for the moment the searching men's shadows fell across the cave's narrow mouth. He'd of got his revenge then. The broken-off piece of juniper he'd been using for a crutch would of done some damage before they finished him off. He'd of taken at least some of them with him. Given them all what they deserved. But they never came.

His eyes move east toward the cabin. Revenge is still comin'. And it'll be sweeter for the waiting. The urge for it has grown with every sign of activity and companionship in the tiny log house.

"Locke!" the big man spits again, as if Gerald Locke, Jr. embodies every wrong ever done him, every slight he's received from Ewing Young, Old Bill Williams, Ceran St. Vrain, Suzanna

Peabody and her female friends, and all the rest of nuevomexico. "Damn foreigners!" he mutters.

CHAPTER 25

The man from Arroyo Hondo hasn't yet arrived with the mastiff when the trade fair ends. In less than a week, the pony herd has melted away, a few more animals departing each afternoon. By the time the horses are gone, there's little else to trade. The men from Taos Pueblo and the plains around it head back home and the bands of Ute and Apache take down their teepees and drift in various directions. The valley feels curiously blank.

During the fair, Suzanna exchanged a basket of eggs for a cleverly-carved wooden horse rattle. She's demonstrating the toy to Alma a few mornings later, tilting it this way and that to make the pebbles inside fall dramatically, when Uno and Dos begin yipping anxiously in the yard.

Suzanna carries Alma to the open door. Ramón is beside the well shaking hands with a man who could be his twin. Both are short and dark, with the same narrow build and slightly bemused eyes. A massive black and tan dog stands beside the stranger, its broad forehead level with the man's waist. The mastiff is gazing at Dos and Uno, who are huddled together next to the corral, their tails tucked under their bodies and their ears laid submissively against their heads, but still yipping.

Suzanna shifts the baby to her hip and studies the tall, thick-bodied dog as she moves off the porch. The animal is very calm. It doesn't look at all threatening. Though it certainly is large. Can it really keep the deer from her cornfield? Beside the corral, the other dogs have subsided, but they're still huddled together with anxious eyes.

The men nod as she approaches. Ramón introduces his mother's cousin-in-law, then bends to stroke the mastiff's black-muzzled head. "His name is Duc," Ramón says. The dog studies Suzanna with sleepy brown eyes, then slowly wags its tail.

"He seems very docile," she says doubtfully.

"They are bred to hunt and are very protective," the man from Arroyo Hondo says.

"There's only one way to find out," Gerald says from the barn door. He crosses the yard and shakes the visitor's hand. "I am grateful to you, señor."

The other man shrugs. "To come this way was convenient for me." He waves his hand toward the blue-tinged mountains at the valley's southern end. "I have business with the Martínez shepherds there in the valley of the little coyotes."

"Shepherds?" Suzanna asks.

"The Martínez family of Taos grazes their sheep and goats there each spring," the man explains. "My son has arranged to purchase a small bunch, to begin his own herd."

"Please, come inside," Gerald urges. "There is fresh venison, traded from the Utes."

"Sí, word came to us regarding la feria," the man says. "I hope it was a good one for all concerned."

"Stands Alone seemed content," Gerald says.

As they reach the porch, the mastiff's owner looks down at the dog and points toward the ground. The animal turns to face the yard and drops obediently into a sitting position at the bottom of the steps.

Next to the corral, Dos and Uno lift their heads. Suzanna pauses to see what they'll do. They separate cautiously and slink behind the well and toward the end of house. The mastiff turns his head to watch them, then lies down, his head on his black paws, and closes his eyes. Suzanna chuckles as she turns toward the door. The big dog is certainly confident.

After the meal, the men and mastiff head toward the corn patch. The other dogs romp alongside but the mastiff pays no attention. Suzanna's lips twitch in sympathy, then she lifts Alma onto her hip and follows them all down the hill.

Gerald walks the mastiff around the perimeter of the cornfield, the big dog stopping periodically to lift his leg.

This is going to take a while. Suzanna turns and carries Alma back up to the cabin. "I certainly hope that dog is meaner than he looks," she tells the child. "Old Bill would say he has Uno and Dos righteously hornswoggled." She chuckles and shakes her head. "But then, they're likely to be considerably easier to frighten than a herd of grown deer."

Alma shakes her head, imitating her mother, and giggles up at her, then snuggles her curly dark head into Suzanna's side.

"We'll see," Suzanna says. She bends her head to kiss Alma's forehead. "I have my doubts about Duc's effectiveness, but we'll see."

The barking begins at daylight. High yips from the mongrels and a deeper, steadier sound an octave below them. Gerald sits up to pull on his boots and Suzanna scrambles down the ladder and darts to the door.

She grabs a shawl from the row of pegs and throws it over her nightdress as she crosses the porch on bare feet. At the edge of the field below, Dos and Uno prance in circles, yipping at the sky and dancing around each other. She can't see the mastiff, but she can hear deep-throated barking beyond the rows of corn. Then he appears at the far end of the field and trots steadily past the other dogs, his big black and tan head focused on the rows of corn, barking as he goes.

Suzanna moves down the steps and across the yard to the top of the hill, where she can see the entire field. There don't seem to be any deer among the plants. The dirt is cold under her bare feet and she shivers a little as she watches the mastiff circle the field again. This time he stops every few paces to mark the boundary, then looks up at the hill behind the cabin and barks menacingly.

Suzanna moves to the corral, steps onto the lowest rung, and twists around to scan the hillside behind the cabin. A dozen or more deer leap up the slope, bounding steadily toward the pines at the top.

This might just work. Suzanna grins, no longer aware of her cold feet. She nods briskly and jumps down from the corral.

Gerald is standing on the porch watching her.

"How long would it take a mastiff puppy to grow to Duke's size?" she asks as she approaches.

Gerald chuckles triumphantly, but Suzanna shakes her head at him. "You may still need to build a fence. If I get enough seed from this crop, I'll want to plant a larger area next spring."

When she reaches the top of the steps, he puts his arms around her. "Aren't you cold?"

"Not now," she says. "Not now that my corn has a chance of surviving this valley and its pernicious deer."

He chuckles again as he draws her into the house.

With September and the first traces of gold on the valley slopes, the men go into a frenzy of hay cutting and windrow turning. The days are crisp and clear, made for outdoor activity. Alma is nine months old now. Suzanna seats her on a blanket at the end of the corn patch, gives her the Ute horse rattle to play with, and begins harvesting. Duc settles down beside the baby and watches Suzanna work.

The few ears that have ripened are still whole, thanks to the mastiff, who not only keeps the deer and raccoons under control, but also seems to intimidate ravens and crows. They circle overhead, making mocking sounds, but they don't descend into the cornfield. Above them, two eagles wheel, seeming to ignore everything below.

Suzanna picks every ear on the stalks, both green and ripe, and hauls four basketfuls to the woodshed behind the kitchen. She leaves them there for husking, confident Ramón will find a way to use the green as well as yellow, knowing he'll set aside the best of the cobs for her to dry for seed.

As she heads back to the corn, Suzanna sees that Alma has dropped her rattle and scooted herself to the edge of the blanket. She has one hand on Duc's neck and is leaning forward to draw her fingers through the dirt at the edge of the field. Suzanna chuckles. Alma is definitely her daughter. And she's so comfortable with the big dog.

Of course, Duc is easy to be comfortable with. He's certainly more peaceful than the year-old Uno and Dos. They're romping through the windrows in the hayfield beyond, scattering the carefully raked rows of grass and staying just out of reach of the men's wooden hay rakes. When Gerald and Ramón finally shoo them away, the dogs dash off to tease the cows.

Suzanna turns back to her corn. Duc is so much easier to have around.

But the mastiff isn't hers and a week later Ramón takes time from the haying to return Duc to Arroyo Hondo. Gerald and Suzanna are too busy with the harvest to go with him.

Suzanna braces herself to deal with the meals while Ramón is away. He's left plenty of tortillas and enough meat for two days, but on the third day she's forced to cook. She stands in the kitchen late that morning and looks anxiously at the fire. Gerald has brought her a rabbit, gutted and dismembered. All she has to do is cut it into chunks and stew it.

Alma is napping. Suzanna can work undisturbed. She chops the meat into pieces, then takes a deep breath, lifts the largest of the cast iron pots onto the iron rod that extends from the fireplace, and swings the pot closer to the flames. Well, at least she's able to do that much successfully.

She dumps a spoonful of lard into the pot, adjusts the rod to position the pot over the flames, and watches impatiently. The fat softens slowly, then finally begins to melt. When it starts to sizzle, Suzanna grabs a handful of meat from the counter and tosses it into the oil.

Fat splatters back at her. She jerks away. "Tarnation, that's hot!" she grumbles. She rummages on the counter for Ramón's longest carved-cottonwood spoon, then stands well back from the pot and gingerly stirs the meat. She's seen Ramón do this. It helps the meat brown evenly.

She moves the chunks more vigorously. They don't seem to be browning at all. She nudges the pot a little closer to the flames, to hurry the cooking. The fire is hot on her face. She turns to one side, tilting her head to keep the heat from her skin, slewing her eyes sideways to see what she's doing.

When most of the pieces of meat finally seem to be brown on all sides, Suzanna crosses the room to the water bucket. She pours water from the bucket into the tea kettle, then carries the kettle to the fire, swings the pot away from the flames and pours the water in. The liquid swirls around the meat and almost immediately turns a rich brown.

Suzanna smiles triumphantly. Very good, so far. This isn't so difficult, after all.

Remembering Ramón's instructions, she sprinkles a pinch of salt into the water and repositions the pot over the flames. It should take a while to start simmering. She turns to tackle the vegetables. Ramón has suggested wild onion, a clove of garlic,

141

potatoes, and carrots. And some of the corn, as well, if she wants to include it.

Suzanna's shoulders straighten confidently as she washes, scrapes, and chops, then carefully drops her results into the hot liquid. She adds more water until it's about an inch below the brim, gives it all a good stir, places the lid on the pot, adds wood to the fire, and is taking off her apron when Alma begins fussing in the next room.

Suzanna moves through the door. "You're becoming too big for this cradle," she tells the baby as she lifts her out. "Someone's going to need to make you a larger bed." Alma gurgles and kicks her legs, making walking motions with her feet.

Suzanna laughs. "And we'll need something with sides on it, to keep you from climbing out at night!" She jiggles the baby up and down, and Alma laughs happily. "Let's go outside and talk to the chickens," Suzanna says. "It's time to gather the eggs."

She closes her eyes against a stab of sorrow. Eggs always make her think of Encarnación and her natillas, that wonderful egg custard she made so well and Suzanna's father liked so much. The thought makes her miss her father almost as much as her dead friend.

Her chin lifts. She'll think of something happy instead. She smiles. How surprised her father will be to hear that his kitchen-hapless daughter has successfully made rabbit stew! "Perhaps one day I can even learn to make natillas," she tells the baby.

Alma laughs again. Suzanna chuckles. Perhaps. Eventually, as Gerald would say. She puts Alma on her hip, collects her basket, and heads to the barn.

Gerald is there, standing in the bed of the hay-filled wagon, forking the fragrant dried grass into the section reserved for winter feed. He pauses as they enter. "Hola," he says with a smile.

Alma waves her arms at him. "'Ola!" she squeals.

Suzanna stops in mid-stride and looks down at her, then up at Gerald. "Did you hear that?"

Gerald drops the hayfork into the wagon bed and swings down onto the hard-packed dirt floor. "I did," he says. "Or I think I did." He mops his brown brow with his handkerchief. "Do you think she meant to say it?" He moves closer, bending toward the baby. "Hola, Alma. Hello."

Alma giggles, turns her head away, and rubs her face on her mother's shoulder. Gerald chuckles, shakes his head, and straightens. He leans in to kiss Suzanna on the cheek. "You look very domestic, standing there with your baby and basket."

"I feel very domestic," Suzanna says complacently. "There's a rabbit stew cooking over the kitchen fire."

"Congratulations!" He kisses her again, then turns back to his work.

Gathering eggs with Alma on her hip is a little awkward, but Suzanna collects all she can, then returns to the house. The stew is bubbling nicely. She gives it a stir, then carries Alma down the hill to the potato patch.

The two dogs follow them down the hill and nose through the plants while Alma sits on a small patch of browning grass, batting at it and making babbling sounds. Suzanna leaves her there while she goes to the barn for the rake, then returns to draw straw and dirt over the plants she's going to winter in place.

The fall sun is lightly warm on her shoulders and the cottonwood handle of the rake is soft and almost silky in her hands. Suzanna smiles at the baby. This is nice. Raising a child isn't so difficult, after all. She tilts her face toward the sun. If the weather would stay like this all year, this valley would be a delightful place to live.

But winter is on its way. She grimaces, then shrugs. At least the weather is decent today. The sun is shining and Alma is playing contentedly while she works. She'll enjoy the pleasantness while she has it.

She works about an hour, enjoying the sunshine and the activity. Then a breeze springs up. When she lifts the straw with her rake, the wind grabs it and whirls it away to locations she hadn't intended it to go. Suzanna drops the tool in disgust, next to the plant she wanted to cover next, gathers Alma up, calls Dos and Uno, and returns to the cabin.

A scorched smell meets her at the doorway. She plops the baby into her cradle and rushes toward the kitchen. When she opens the door, smoke billows toward her from the stew pot.

Suzanna grabs a thick dry towel, wads it around the iron rod, and swings the pot off the flames. When she lifts the lid, oily, smoky steam slaps her face.

She pulls back, eyes smarting. "Tarnation!" she exclaims. She pulls the iron arm, swinging the pot off the fire, and crouches beside it. The meat and vegetables are clearly cooked through. Nicely softened, in fact. Except where they're stuck to the bottom. Not a drop of liquid remains.

Suzanna groans. "All that water boiled away." She rocks back on her heels. "And I filled it almost to the top!" She closes her eyes. She's a grown woman. She's too old to cry. "Curse it!" she mutters. "I should have stayed in the house. Watched it more closely. I should have just sat here and stared at it all afternoon, blame it!" She leans forward to peer into the pot again. "It's completely ruined."

"What's the matter?" Gerald asks from the doorway. He's holding Alma, who has her fist in her mouth and is looking at her mother with worried eyes.

"I burned it!" Suzanna wails. She pulls herself to her feet and waves a hand in the general direction of the potato patch. "I went down to cover the potatoes while it cooked and all the water boiled away!"

Gerald crosses the room and leans to look into the pot. Alma makes a fussing sound and wrinkles her nose. Suzanna scowls at her.

"It's not black on top," Gerald says. "Can't you just add more water? It may not be as burnt as you think."

Suzanna sniffs. "It certainly smells burnt." She looks at Alma, who's now rubbing her nose against her father's shoulder. "Even a baby can tell it's not fit to eat."

Gerald chuckles and moves toward the back door. "We'll just open this to create a draft and get the smell out. Then it'll seem more edible."

Suzanna nods, wipes at her wet cheeks with the back of her hands, and moves to the water bucket to fill the kettle again. Gerald jiggles Alma in his arms as he goes into the main room to open the front door, and she squeals with delight.

Suzanna smiles in spite of herself, gratitude mixing with her frustration. Every woman on the face of the earth can cook, except her. But he only makes light of her ineptitude. What a kind man he is.

A rush of guilt floods her. She's so cross with him sometimes, so quick to speak angrily, so impatient. Yet he quietly endures her cooking—or lack of it—and never criticizes. As she pours water into the still-sizzling pot and watches the larger pieces of vegetable lift off the cast iron bottom, she vows to be kinder and more patient with her man.

CHAPTER 26

Ramón returns from Arroyo Hondo two days later. He brings a three-month-old mastiff pup with him. When he places the bundle of black fur in Suzanna's arms, her knees buckle. "He weighs more than Alma does!" she exclaims.

"He is a big one," Ramón agrees. "Claramente, he will be a big dog."

Gerald is standing on the porch. Alma is perched in his arms, face out. "So he had a puppy available?" he asks. "One he was willing to sell?"

"He gave him to me." A shadow crosses Ramón's face. "He was a second cousin to my Chonita. He gave the puppy in memory of her."

The three adults exchange a somber look. Suzanna hugs the dog to her chest and closes her eyes. When she opens them again, Gerald is bending his head to touch Alma's curly black hair with his lips. Then he looks up at Suzanna. "Well, let's see him."

Suzanna places the puppy on the ground. He sniffs the edge of her skirt, then turns and heads straight toward Gerald. The dog pulls himself awkwardly up the steps, then sits abruptly down, looks into Gerald's face, and lets out a single yip. Gerald laughs and Alma chortles and tilts forward for a closer look.

Suzanna shakes her head. "It's hard to believe that such a friendly bundle of fur will grow up into a useful guard dog."

"Let him get the feeling the corn patch belongs to him, and I think you'll be surprised." Gerald grins at her. "As I recall, you didn't think Duc looked very protective, either." He nudges the puppy's belly with his toe, and the dog rolls onto his back and tries to grab Gerald's boot between his teeth and front paws. Alma crows with delight.

Suzanna grins in spite of herself. The baby mastiff looks too soft and good-tempered to guard anything. But it is very sweet. Large. But sweet.

Early the next afternoon she puts Alma down for a nap, shuts the other dogs into the barn, where Ramón and Gerald are butchering a young bull who's not needed for breeding purposes, and leads the puppy to the corn patch. She needs to clean the field anyway, so she won't have to just stand there while the dog gets used to its territory. Suzanna moves down the field with her machete, systematically toppling dead stalks, while the puppy noses through the already-cut pieces.

At the end of the second row, Suzanna stops for a breath, drops the machete, and puts her hands on her hips. The mountainsides are brilliant with gold. As she looks at them, a ground squirrel pops up from a set of crisscrossed stalks. The puppy yips in excitement and races toward it.

Suzanna laughs and shakes her head. "I certainly hope you develop a true bark," she says. "Or we're going to have to call you Yip." She pauses, considering. "I suppose we do need to find a name for you. At the moment, Chaser seems appropriate."

She glances toward the house. She should probably head back. Alma will be waking soon. Reluctantly, she leans down for the machete. She straightens and looks at the remaining cornstalks. If the cold sets in as quickly as Ramón says it will, she may not get to the rest of the patch before next spring. Damnable weather.

She turns and heads up the path to the cabin. "Come, Chaser!" she calls, trying out the name. The puppy stops in his tracks, looks at her quizzically, then trots obediently to her side. "Hmm," Suzanna says. "Well, if you'll answer to it, then I suppose we'd better make it official. Chaser, it is."

The puppy has acquainted itself with the house, the rest of the yard, and the other dogs within a week. It's quickly housebroken, which is a good thing, because winter is definitely setting in. Clouds blanket the western peaks each morning, then slowly spread toward the cabin and disappear into the Cimarron range behind it. There's little moisture, but the air carries a chill that wasn't there a month ago. It's certainly too cold to finish cleaning up the cornfield.

The clouds create fascinating light patterns. In the late afternoons, a flat layer hides the stony mountaintops, but not the sky above them, which glows with reflected sunlight. In the mornings, the slopes below the clouds shine pink light in the sun rising on the opposite side of the valley.

Returning to the cabin from the morning milking, Suzanna stops to take it in. It's beautiful, but she's distracted by the way the wind whips her skirt around her legs and ruffles the warm liquid in the milk buckets. Winter will be here far too quickly.

A raven lifts from the corral and flies diagonally over her head toward the far end of the cabin. Its wings huff in the breeze. Suzanna watches it disappear toward the marsh below and turns to study the mountain directly north of the cabin. The aspens on the foothills below its peak are a shining gold, but its cone-shaped top is dusted with snow.

Ramón says the winter will be a cold one. How he knows these things she can't fathom, but she trusts his predictions. Suzanna grimaces. Although they can change quickly enough. Two and a half weeks ago, he said they'd have a dry spell before winter arrives.

Based on that forecast, Gerald headed into the Cimarron canyon a few days later for a quick round of trapping before the freeze sets in. But this morning, Ramón told her gravely that the signs have changed. The valley is likely to see snow before nightfall. And more by tomorrow.

Suzanna sighs. It's been a long and beautiful fall. But now the nastiness is settling in. The discomfort that is winter here in the Valley. Just thinking about it makes her shiver. The cold and the never-ending potential for snow that will keep her cabin-bound for the next six months. Her only strategy for coping will be milking the cows and gathering eggs, just to escape the cabin's four walls for a spell. To breathe a moment of fresh air between house and barn, even if it does make her lungs ache from the icy cold of it.

Her throat aches at the thought. She gulps back the threatening tears, stubbornly straightens her shoulders, and carries the milk into the cabin, then returns to the barn with the egg basket and food for the dogs.

They're huddled in a heap in a corner of the hay pile, just as the chickens are huddled in their nest boxes. Suzanna lifts a skim of ice from the chickens' water pan, pours grain into the hollowed-out chunk of aspen that serves as their food dish, and checks to make sure their entry door is pinned open. They're unlikely to want to venture outside, but you never know.

She carries a shovel back to the cabin with her, in preparation for tomorrow's path-clearing, and leans it beside the benches on the porch.

"All I need now is some assurance that Gerald is safe and dry," she mutters as she bolts the cabin door behind her. "Wherever he is. Of all the times to go trapping, this is not it."

She turns as Ramón comes in from the kitchen.

"He has not returned?" he asks.

She shakes her head.

"It will be soon, I think."

"I certainly hope so," Suzanna says. "He's been out two weeks. Surely there aren't that many beaver ponds to investigate in that canyon. He should be home by now."

He doesn't answer. Just stands and watches as she crosses to the fire and pokes at it with a stick. A log tumbles onto the cabin floor and she gives it a sharp kick, jamming it back into the fireplace. "Tarnation!" she says.

Ramón turns and goes back to the kitchen.

Suzanna moves to the window. In her cradle, Alma sighs and flings out an arm, bumping it against the wooden side.

Suzanna turns at the sound, then studies the room, lit as it is by the dancing flames and the bit of sunlight lighting the windowpanes with gold. It is a pretty space. Quite cozy, with the bright cushions on the painted storage chests and benches. But the cushions remind her of Encarnación. Who would be here now, for this winter, if— She stops, not wanting to end the sentence, knowing she will anyway.

Then she closes her eyes and lets the thoughts take her where they always do. If Encarnación hadn't been returning to Taos from the patch of potatoes Suzanna planted so far from the village, she wouldn't have been attacked. She would be here now.

Suzanna gives herself a little shake. It's a hopeless progression of thoughts, an endless ladder of pain. If Gerald hadn't found the small field for Suzanna's potatoes, she wouldn't have planted them there. If Charles Beaubien hadn't brought her those first few seed potatoes, there would have been none to plant. If Gregorio Garcia's mother hadn't allowed pigs to root in her patch of ground by the acequia the previous fall, it wouldn't have been any good for potatoes. Suzanna raises her hands helplessly. If she continues this line of thinking, Antonia Garcia is going to be responsible for Encarnación's death. "It's just that I miss her," she whispers. "And Gerald should be home by now."

Then Alma stirs fully awake and pushes herself up to peer at her mother over the side of the cradle. "I'll be glad when you can talk," Suzanna says as she lifts her out. "Then I can complain to you about your crazy father and his trapping ideas."

She tends to the child, then seats her on the floor near the fire with her rattle and blocks. Suzanna rummages through her mending box for Gerald's torn shirt, pulls the small table closer to the fire, and lights the lamp. With it on her left and the fire on her right, she has just enough illumination to see what she's doing.

Gerald still hasn't returned when Ramón comes in to say that dinner is ready. Suzanna eats silently as Ramón takes Alma into his lap and feeds her bits of tortilla softened in milk.

Suzanna is amused to see how the quiet Mexican man brightens whenever he holds the child and how confidently Alma leans against him. She wonders sadly if Ramón would feel the same way toward the baby if he'd had one of his own by now. She shakes herself. She's being morbid tonight, a combination of the weather and the fact that Gerald still hasn't returned. "She didn't wake me last night," Suzanna tells Ramón. "Your food is replacing me."

He looks up at her, eyes dark with concern. "I will not feed her the tortillas if you wish it."

"No, no. It's all right. It was nice to sleep until dawn for a change." Suzanna smiles. "In fact, it was wonderful." She looks at the baby, who stretches her hands toward the tortilla between Ramón's fingers and babbles incoherently. "I'm glad you thought of the tortillas. She seems to like it more than the corn gruel."

He chuckles, looks down at Alma, and moves the tortilla closer to her face, then pulls it away as she grabs at for it. He moves it toward her again and she leans forward. Her fingers close over a corner of the food and she laughs triumphantly. When she leans back, a bit of the tortilla stays in her hand. She looks at it in sur-

151

prise, then puts it cautiously to her mouth. Her brown eyes widen and she sucks on the tortilla, swallows wonderingly, and leans to reach for more.

"Greedy girl!" Suzanna laughs.

"Slowly, nita, slowly," Ramón says.

Outside, the wind gusts against the shutters and the shovel falls with a clatter. The adults both straighten and turn toward the cabin's main room. "I must tighten the latches on those shutters," Ramón says. "Their noise is confusing."

"I should have brought that shovel inside," Suzanna says absently. She pokes at the food on her plate, suddenly not hungry. "Blame it, I wish he hadn't gone!" she exclaims. "We don't need those furs so very much."

Ramón bends his head over the child.

"I think he just wanted to get away for a while."

Ramón clucks at the baby. "More, mí nita?"

"When he begins feeling cooped up, he can just go," Suzanna grumbles. "It hardly seems fair."

Ramón lifts the baby from his lap and leans to set her on the floor, another piece of tortilla in her fist. He rises and crosses to the fire, where he removes the simmering tea kettle from the flames. He carries it to the work bench and begins pouring the hot water into the wash basin.

Suzanna's lips tighten. Ramón can be so aggravating sometimes. He simply refuses to listen or respond to her complaints. The bench scrapes the floor as she rises from the table and begins clearing the dishes.

But once the dinner things are washed and put away, there's nothing to do. Suzanna returns to her sewing, but before long it's too dark to properly see the shirt she's mending. It's also too dark to read.

On the chest at the other end of the fireplace, Ramón is braiding long thin strips of elk rawhide into rope. His brown hands flash in the light.

Suzanna drops her work into her lap and stares at the fire, vacillating between irritation with Gerald and concern for him. Twice, the wind gusts jostle the porch benches against the side of the house and she rises to open the front door.

But there's no one there. Only the wind and the snow. Large flat flakes whirl across the yard, filling in the rutted path to the barn and making the ground deceptively smooth. She moves to the far end of the porch and peers down the hill toward the marsh and the mouth of the canyon beyond.

When she comes back inside, Ramón looks up. "If he comes tonight, I think it will not be by way of the marsh. The ice there is too thin to be safe and the snow will make the way treacherous."

Suzanna returns to her seat. "Coming through the hills from the canyon will also be risky. The snow will have drifted over the path and into the ravines." She shudders, thinking what a fall into a snow-obscured ravine could mean for man and mule, the sharp edges of upturned sandstone hidden underneath the thick drifts. "I suppose he'll find somewhere to camp and then try to get through in the morning."

"It is likely." He says it so apologetically that she feels a spasm of guilt for her earlier irritation. The man has a difficult enough task, keeping her company when Gerald is away. He probably wishes he'd gone, too. Anything to escape her anxiety and grumbling.

If they were all in Don Fernando, she'd have her father to talk with. Her father, who would give her a study assignment. She glances toward the small bookshelf in the corner. But she doesn't feel like studying and there isn't enough light, anyway. She shivers. Even with the fire roaring, she still feels cold. And the winter has only just begun, she thinks wearily. She's exhausted by it already.

"There will be more light tomorrow, I think," Ramón says. "This storm will blow over and the sun will come out for a few days."

"A few days." Suzanna closes her eyes. "But not longer than that. Then the next storm will roll in."

"It is the way of the mountains," he says, his eyes on his rope.

She shakes her head and crosses the room to gather Alma up. "I'm going to bed. There's absolutely nothing to keep me awake."

CHAPTER 27

But when she and the baby are settled into the big bed in the loft, Suzanna finds herself unable to sleep. Where is Gerald? Is he warm? Dry? Or has he met with an accident? A cougar? A hidden slab of rock, slick under the treacherous snow. A terrified mule dragging him down the boulder-ridden canyon, plunging him into a beaver pond, half covered with ice. Her breath tightens.

Then her fists clench. Why does he have to do this, this wandering into the wilderness? He says he simply wants to be a farmer, but he can't seem to stay away from the forest. Or is he just so exasperated with her complaints that he will do anything to escape them?

Fury fills her heart. Legitimate complaints she has every right to make. Then her anger turns to dread. What if he doesn't come back? What if he's injured?

But she'll go mad if she lets herself imagine what might be happening to him down there in that canyon. An angry determination sets in. She lifts her chin. If he thinks she's just going to sit here and wait, not knowing if and when he'll return, he is very much mistaken. She doesn't need Ramón to sit with her as if she were a child. Tomorrow, she'll convince him to venture into the canyon himself. He'll go if she asks him to. It isn't as if she's in danger of anyone turning up here anyway. Not in this weather.

Having a plan of action soothes her nerves a little and she finally drifts off to sleep.

She wakes to yet more snow. The storm has exceeded Ramón's predictions and continues unabated. Suzanna doesn't say anything. Just grimly ties her red shawl over her head and slogs down the narrow path Ramón has dug through the snow to the barn.

She hurriedly milks the cows and gathers the few puny eggs. The animals are also responding poorly to the cold. The single milk bucket is only half full this morning, and the chickens have virtually stopped laying.

"You don't think much of this weather either, do you?" she asks the black hen, who peers at her accusingly, as if Suzanna is responsible for the lack of sunlight.

Snow stings her face as she trudges back to the house, milk bucket in one hand, egg basket in the other. The flakes are smaller now. Inexplicably, the weather has turned colder.

Her shawl is white with snow. Suzanna sets the basket and bucket on the porch bench nearest the door and works at the knot under her chin with frozen fingers.

Ramón opens the door and peers out. Suzanna wordlessly hands him the bucket and basket. She yanks the shawl off her head and shakes the snow from it, then follows him into the cabin. Alma looks up from the fireplace, where she's playing with her blocks.

Clumps of snow drop onto the wooden planks from Suzanna's skirt. Pieces of straw, swept up by her skirt in the barn, are embedded along the edge of the icy lumps. She looks grimly at the floor. "Well, I wanted something to do."

"It is a very cold snow," Ramón says. "The lumps will melt slowly."

"That's a comfort." She pulls off her coat, hangs it and the shawl on the pegs by the door and goes to the kitchen for the broom.

By the time she returns, Alma has crawled across the room to the chunks of frozen snow. She's sitting beside them, one hand on a particularly large piece, the other in her mouth.

"No!" Suzanna cries. "Tarnation!" She drops the broom and darts toward the child. Alma looks up in surprise, hand still in her mouth, and begins to wail. Suzanna grabs her up and slaps at the hand still clutching the clump of ice. "No!" she snaps.

Alma shrieks defiantly and tightens her fist. The melting snow slips through her fingers to the floor. A piece of wet straw sticks to her small palm.

Suzanna flicks the straw onto the floor. "Now it will be even more difficult to clean up, curse it!"

She turns to return the crying child to the hearth. Ramón is standing in the kitchen doorway, watching. The sympathy on his face is clearly more for Alma than her mother.

Suzanna scowls at him, then looks down at Alma. "That snow is filthy!"

Ramón turns and disappears into the kitchen. Suzanna plunks the whimpering baby next to the fire and goes back to her broom. An angry silence fills the cabin. The only sound is the swoosh of Suzanna' broom and an occasional hiccup from Alma.

"Curse it, I wish he'd come home!" Suzanna mutters. She gathers the straw and ice into a cloth, crosses to the door, moves gingerly across the icy porch, and flings the mess into the yard. When she reenters the cabin, she realizes she's tracked snow from the porch in behind her. She shoves the plank door shut with a thud. "Blame it! How I do despise winter in this valley!"

It's a long day. Snow continues to fall from a sullen gray sky. Suzanna wipes the melted snow up with another cloth, reads a little, sews some, and then sits glumly staring at the fire, trying not to imagine where Gerald is or what might be happening to him.

She rouses only when Alma fusses or Ramón enters to say the midday meal is ready.

As darkness begins to fall, a wind comes up and eases the snow clouds toward the southern end of the valley. The moon rises in an almost-clear sky. Surely Gerald will come now. Surely there's enough light for travelling. But Ramón is doubtlessly right. The marsh at the head of the canyon will be too icy, too unpredictable. Even if Gerald's willing to risk it for the sake of getting home to a warm cabin, the mule will have more sense.

It's possible he'll choose instead to move into the hills behind the cabin, try to locate the track he and Ramón use to bring in firewood from above. But he'll be as aware as she is that the snow drifts will obscure even the deepest of the ruts the dragging logs have worn into the slope. No matter what route he chooses, it will be too dangerous to travel at night. Surely he'll wait until morning.

Yet she can't stay away from the kitchen and the door to the woodshed, which faces the hills behind the cabin. If Gerald does come tonight, that's where he'll first appear, either moving up from the marsh in the fold that lies between the cabin hill and the one beyond, or down from the trees on the crest of the hill above.

She looks out again after dinner, on the pretense that she's examining the amount of snow that's blown onto the woodpile in the open-sided shed behind the cabin. When she turns back into the kitchen, she catches a glimpse of amused compassion on Ramón's face. She lifts her chin and busies herself with the dishes. But once they're cleaned and arranged on their shelves, she finds herself at the door again.

"The moon is almost full," she tells Ramón over her shoulder. She squints at the hill behind the cabin. "And the wind seems to have died down."

"A good night for wolves," Ramón says absently as he wipes down the hand-hewn plank counter.

She turns sharply. "Wolves? There are no wolves here!"

He glances at her, then looks away and scrubs at a spot in the wood. "It's only a dicho. An old saying of my grandmother's. You are right. We have had no problems with wolves."

She opens her mouth, sure he's prevaricating just to placate her, then turns back to the door. "Well, at any rate, the snow has stopped falling." She looks up at the rising moon. Light glints from the snowy hilltop. Is there something moving there farther up? But it's only a shadow from a passing cloud. "Although it is certainly cold," she adds as she shuts the door.

She goes into the other room and sits on the cushioned bench nearest the fire. If only she had something to do, something to move her thoughts beyond Gerald, the darkness, and the snow.

"Alma, can you play pat-a-cake?" she asks. But the baby is crawling purposefully across the floor toward her wooden blocks and doesn't turn around. Suzanna stares into the fire. Its flames flick shadows around the room, making her eyes ache at the mere thought of sewing or knitting.

When Ramón comes in a few minutes later, she says, "I wonder if I could learn to braid rope. The firelight would be sufficient for that, wouldn't it?"

He crosses the room to the wooden box where the long coils of thin rawhide are stored and opens the lid. He studies its contents, then turns to her. "I also have hair for a rope. I was planning to use a spindle to create the threads, but if you are willing—" He glances toward the spinning wheel in the far corner. Suzanna hasn't used it since her father brought it the previous spring. It reminds her too much of Encarnación.

"Hair?" she says doubtfully.

"From the mules' manes and some from the cows' tails." He pulls a cloth bag from the box. It's bulging with thin strands of hair, both soft and coarse. "I've been collecting it all spring." He reaches into the box again and pulls out a spindle carved from a single piece of cottonwood. "It was my father's." He grins at her. "But it is used only for making rope."

She chuckles in spite of her anxiety. "Not yarn or thread for clothing, I suppose. Because that's women's work."

He grins. "The spindle doesn't produce as smooth a result as does the spinning wheel. The hair is really too fine to be spun on a spindle."

She frowns slightly, but there's a sense of relief in her chest. At last, something to do. "I'm rather out of practice, but I'm willing to try."

They rearrange the furniture and maneuver the spinning wheel closer to the firelight, and Suzanna experiments with the hair in the bag, moistening her fingers to twist the first bits into place. The strands stick together almost as well as wool, and she soon gets the feel of it. Her foot pumps the pedal rhythmically and she feels her breath steady. She'd forgotten just how relaxing spinning can be.

She feels a little disappointed when the bag is empty. Ramón chuckles at how quickly she's accomplished a task that would have taken him days and sets her to braiding the resulting strands into rope. But this task doesn't require as much concentration. Her mind wanders into the Cimarron Canyon. Where is Gerald? Is he cold? Wet? Dry? He should have been back two days ago!

The door at the back of the cabin exerts an almost magnetic pull. He won't come inside from there, of course. He'll circle around the cabin and stable the mule before he takes care of his own needs. Or hers, to know he's back. But she still finds herself listening for the creak of the back door.

Finally she gives in, drops the half-finished rope to the floor, and stands up. "I think I'll check just one more time and then head to bed. I can finish this tomorrow."

Ramón nods. She can feel his eyes follow her into the kitchen. She knows she's being irrational, but she opens the back door anyway.

And there, coming down the slope of the hill behind the cabin, are Gerald and the mule, breaking their way through knee-high snow. As she watches, Gerald raises his head. He stops, lifts his free arm, and waves at her, then points toward the barn.

Suzanna nods vigorously, though she knows he probably can't see anything but the black shape of her against the fire-lit room. She watches as he turns to angle down the slope toward the barn, forcing his way through the snow, breaking a path for the pack-loaded mule. Then she closes the door and leans against it for a long moment, her eyes closed. He's home.

Then she straightens. He'll be hungry, as well as cold. A warm blanket for his shoulders, a cup of tea. Food. "Ramón!" she calls as she moves across the room. "He's back!"

CHAPTER 28

"Sure cozy down there," the man on the ridge growls as he peers down at the snowbound cabin. A dim light glows through the thick panes of the single window. Just a piss-ant shanty. Little one, too. Must be gettin' on her nerves by now.

He stands shrouded by the falling snow. The bearskin poncho and the crude beaver-plew cap are coated white. Against the white mound of the hillside, there's little danger of anyone spotting him, even if they're looking in this direction.

Which they ain't. The girl hasn't been outside since Locke came back from his trapping.

The big man grins. Bet they got no idea how much he knows of their goings-on. The greaser doin' the cooking, the girl actin' like she's queen of the world. Little princess spent all spring standin' around watching the men dig ditches to get water to her damned plants, puttin' up fences to keep the grazers out of what's rightfully theirs.

And bringin' her another dog to play with while they worked. His teeth grind in disgust. Three of the beasts now and all apt to bark at the slightest movement. Rabbit. Deer. Coyote. Man.

He did a scout before the snow set in. East of the cabin from his campsite and across the upper valley where the Ute bucks pastured their horses during their little trade fair. Then he cut across-slope and worked his way along the long sugarloaf ridge south of it. Trip wasn't nothin'. Just had to stay below the tree line. Between the aspen and pine, there was cover enough.

But then he'd reached the hill above the cabin and the cover all but disappeared. What with the logs for the cabin and the firewood they'd hauled off it, Locke and the greaser have that hilltop thinned out so it's more like a park than a forest. No cover to speak of.

No cover for man, but plenty of grass for the deer, come next spring. He snickers. Nice view of the little bitch's cornfield, too. A plain invitation to the grazers to come on down and pay it a visit.

He'd been tempted to visit himself, right then and there. She'd been alone enough. Locke off on his trappin' jaunt, the Mexican busy in the barn. Greaser spent plenty of time there while the other one was gone.

Can't blame him. The big man spits into the snow. After he gets that female to himself and right tamed, he'll be wantin' to get away from her, too. Her an' her cub. Even if he's the pa.

That cub that she's got now, can't tell if it's a boy or a gal. Sure can tell its ma's got mixed feelings about it, though. The way she's snuggling all over it one minute and the next leavin' it plopped in the dirt, payin' it no mind at all while she messes with her plants.

Or leavin' the thing in that ramshackle house for hours at a time while she wanders in the fields. Did it all spring. He shakes his head. Her wanderin'll stop short once he gets his hands on her. No traipsin' around for his woman. She'll just get herself in trouble, like that bitch in Don Fernando.

He grins and rubs at his crotch. Just thinkin' about it can get him goin'. This one he'll keep alive. Keep her too busy takin' care of him to be wanderin'.

A squall of high-pitched barking erupts near the cabin. The big man scowls. Damn those dogs. He'd tried slipping down from the trees, even with no cover, but the dogs set up such a ruckus, they pulled that damn greaser out of the barn. Peerin' around, rifle in hand, watchin' the slope above the house.

He grunts in disgust. All he'd wanted was to poke around a bit, give her a scare, let her know what was comin'. See if he could have a little fun. Wasn't gonna haul her off just yet. Too cold. Could of had a look at the cub, too. See if it's worth keepin'.

But the dogs spotted him. Or smelled him, more likely. He hadn't even got to the edge of the trees before they started carryin' on.

His cold blue eyes narrow. Three of 'em. If he wants to get any closer to that cabin without them lettin' on, he's gonna need to shut them up permanent. Poison of some kind. Which means a trip into that damn Don Fernando and the risk of bein' spotted. More'n likely, that damned Williams'll be there, swilling Taos Lightning, gambling and whoring all his money away.

The big man grunts. It's fur trappin' season. Williams might be out huntin' plews. Maybe even up in here. Damn fool likes to trap by himself, just like Locke. His thin lips curve, pondering this. Up in these hills, it'd be easy enough to give Williams what he deserves. Locke, too. Now that's an idea.

But it ain't the plan. He wants Locke alive when he takes the little bitch for the first time. Wants him watchin'. He chuckles and refocuses on the cabin. And Williams ain't likely to be up here in this kind of weather. That opinionated bastard likes his comforts. If he was up here, he'd of high-tailed it back to Taos and the tabernas by now, figurin' to head back into the hills when it warmed up some.

Only Locke's fool enough to try to winter up here. The big man's face twists and he stomps his booted feet in the snow and hunches his shoulders. Even the heavy wool coat and the bearskin together ain't enough. The cold's seeping in anyway, fingering its way to his skin. Damn that Locke. Only way to keep track of him is to stay up here watchin'. Not that there's much chance of gettin' out now, anyway. Every pass to Taos is snowed in and likely to stay that way from now until spring.

And then he can slip into Taos and buy him some dog treats. His lips curve in anticipation. Treats for those mangy Injun dogs and that big pup, whatever it is. Probably the best food they ever had. Shut 'em right up. He'll watch for when both the men are gone. Get good and close and slip those curs some nice juicy rabbit. All bloody-like to cover the smell of what's inside. Put in plenty of that poison to make sure it knocks 'em out good and solid.

He grins, planning it out. Dogs done for, he'll smash down that cabin door and take what should of been his right from the start. Little Navajo bitch. Thought she was too good for him. When he's done with her, he'll rope her up tight an' wait for her men.

His lips twist. When he gets hold of them bastards, they're gonna pay for what Locke done there on the Salt. First, he'll break a bone or two in each of 'em. Just enough to keep 'em quiet and payin' attention while he takes her again. And maybe some more.

Then he'll make her shoot 'em. His throat gurgles at the thought. Those pretty brown eyes will go wide with shock. Shoot your men or I shoot your cub, that papoose you thought you didn't care nothin' about.

"Hah!" the laugh barks out of him and he bites it off. Not now. He can make all the noise he wants then. But, for now, he's best quiet. Waiting. In the dark.

He scowls as he peers toward the cabin again and yanks at the bearskin, trying to block out the cold. He'll make them pay for this waitin' of his. The longer he waits, the more payin' they're gonna do.

CHAPTER 29

The two dozen beaver plews Gerald collected on his trapping trip aren't likely to bring him much. At least, that's what Ceran St. Vrain says when he shows up in early December. He's fought his way through yet another snowstorm up Taos Canyon and over Palo Flechado Pass, then swung north to the cabin on his way to the Santa Fe Trail and St. Louis.

"Things are quiet in Don Fernando at the moment, so I thought I'd slip through before winter really sets in. I want to spend some time with my St. Louis relatives and then be in place to bring trade goods back early next year, as soon as it's warm enough," he explains from the carved bench by the fire. His tall broad forehead gleams in the light.

Suzanna hands him a hot cup of tea and he smiles up at her. "This certainly brings back memories." He frowns slightly, sets the teacup beside him on the bench, and begins patting his pockets. "I came your way partly because I saw your father right before I left and he asked me to bring you this." He pulls out a carefully folded and sealed packet of paper.

"Oh! Thank you!" Suzanna gives him a brilliant smile and carries the lamp to the corner so she can read her letter while the men talk by the fire.

Gerald swings Alma onto his knee. "Are you taking furs with you to St. Louis?" he asks St. Vrain. "I picked up a few plews recently, if you'd like to make me an offer."

166

The big merchant shakes his head regretfully. "It wouldn't do either of us much good. The news from St. Louis is that beaver prices have dropped off a cliff. The Hudson's Bay Company has been busy in the Northeast and they're unloading everything they take in New York. The merchants there have more furs than they have warehouse space."

Alma twists from her father's knee and he stands her on the floor. He holds her hands, steadying her, while she thumps her feet up and down, pretending to walk. Gerald glances up at St. Vrain. "So Hudson's Bay is flooding the market?"

"Trying to push us all out of business," St. Vrain says grimly. He shrugs. "I'm wagering that it'll pass. The best thing for you would be to hold those plews until things get back to normal and Rocky Mountain beaver is king again." He leans back on the bench. "For my part, I'm seriously considering the potential for moving out of the fur trade altogether and putting my money into calico and other female geegaws instead." He twists to grin at Suzanna. "And maybe glass windows."

She looks up from her letter and smiles at him. "Set some aside for me when you bring them back."

Gerald's head is bent over Alma, coaxing her to move her feet forward instead of just up and down, but Suzanna sees his face tighten. "Even just one or two panes would be lovely," she adds wistfully.

Gerald looks up at St. Vrain. "But unlikely, if the price of beaver is as low as you're saying." He moves his hands, pulling Alma gently forward, and she takes a hesitant step. Gerald turns to Suzanna. "Look at that!"

It's the first time Alma has tried to walk. Suzanna bites back a comment about distractions from glass windows and puts her letter aside. She moves across the room, drops onto the floor a few feet from Gerald, and holds her hands out to the baby. "Come to Mama," she coaxes.

Alma crows with delight but stays where she is, her chubby legs pumping energetically up and down but not moving forward.

St. Vrain chuckles and looks at Gerald. "Will you have a good beef herd, come spring?"

Gerald hands Alma off to Suzanna as he nods. "I don't know if I'll be wanting to sell just yet, though. We need to build the herd up. It'll depend on how many calves are born next spring and what Ramón thinks we can feasibly carry through the following winter."

The other man nods. "This here's a nice section of land." There's a wistful note in his voice. "The only better place I've seen is the country around Mora. Now that's a valley rich with grain. If I ever get the wherewithal, I'm going to find some acreage in that vicinity I can call my own."

"I would imagine the weather's a little warmer there," Suzanna says. She has her hands under the baby's armpits and is bouncing her gently up and down, bending and straightening Alma's chubby legs. She glances at Gerald. "It's probably far enough south that you can grow a decent corn crop without worrying about the frost."

As St. Vrain chuckles, Gerald shakes his head. "We already have a cabin and barn constructed here," he says. "And no one crowding us for land."

"There is that," St. Vrain says. "The land in the Mora Valley is already fairly well divided up. I'm sure I'll have to pay for the privilege of farming there."

Suzanna's lips tighten. First no glass windows, now the high price of land. But it's not a discussion she intends to have in front of Ceran St. Vrain. She swoops Alma into her arms and moves toward the kitchen.

"So has anything of interest occurred in Santa Fe lately?" Gerald asks as she reaches the kitchen door.

Suzanna lets the door close behind her with a thump. "Baby's hungry," she tells Ramón. "Are there any tortillas left from this morning?"

Before St. Vrain heads into the snow-bound Cimarron Canyon the next day, Suzanna makes sure he's supplied with a batch of Ramón's fresh tortillas wrapped in a clean cloth and a cube of compressed black tea.

When the merchant is out of sight beyond the marsh, Gerald and Suzanna turn back toward the house. He raises an eyebrow at her. "That tea is precious," he says. "I'm surprised you were willing to let some of it go."

"He brought me a letter from my father," Suzanna says. "Besides, I know he likes it." She chuckles. "He used to drink five cups to everyone else's two."

Gerald touches her elbow, aiding her across the icy yard. He glances sideways at her. "You have fond memories of that time, don't you? The trappers and merchants crowding your father's parlor."

"They were primarily trappers then," she says. "When they were in town, we had someone to tea almost every day. There was always something new to hear and the men's stories could be quite entertaining." Her lips curve mischievously. "Especially if they forgot I was in the room."

"You miss it." It's a statement, not a question. There's a tinge of sadness in his voice.

She keeps her head down, watching her steps, not quite knowing how to respond. Yes, she does miss it. But it will hurt him if she says so. They've reached the porch steps and he's moved ahead of her before she speaks again. "It's just that everything is so different here."

He turns to look down at her, his gray eyes shadowed with sorrow.

"And I miss the company." Suzanna makes a small apologetic gesture with her hands. "I do try to be content, but sometimes—"

He gives her a bleak look, then waves a hand at the snow-covered landscape behind her. "This is the best a man like me can expect to do." He looks toward the barn. "I came here with virtually nothing. No family or connections like Ceran de Hault de Lassus de St. Vrain, with his St. Louis relatives and their money and friends."

He looks down at his brown hands and turns them over. There are calluses on his palms. "When I arrived here I had my two hands and what little learning I'd been able to scrabble together." He stares at the fields below. "This land isn't even rightfully mine. But I don't have the money to buy any. Since the Mexican government doesn't seem to care about this valley and no one else has laid claim to it, I figure we'll use it as long as we can. The Utes and Apaches are willing enough to let us be, as long as we don't drive out their game."

He turns his head, his eyes traveling the valley from one end to the other. "It's a beautiful land, even if it is harsh at times. Its very harshness means no one else is likely to push us out. Even the Indians don't want to camp here year-round."

He looks down at her again. There's a kind of sorrowful weariness in his eyes. "This is the best I can do. And if the price for beaver is as low as St. Vrain says, it's going to be a good while before I can buy you your glass windows."

"And I'm unwilling to make the sacrifices that might have made it possible," she acknowledges ruefully. "To have you go hunting an entire season with Ewing Young."

"With prices that low, Young's hunt isn't likely to give him much of a profit," Gerald says. "If St. Vrain is right, Young's likely to bring back a stack of furs that won't cover the cost of his ammunition, let alone food."

"But he'll still have to pay out something to his men," Suzanna says, not knowing if this is actually true. "And at least you wouldn't have been in the wilderness alone." She shivers, reliving her anxiety during his recent trip into the canyon. She crosses her arms and her shoulders with her hands. "It's when you're out there alone that I get truly anxious."

"I can take care of myself."

"I know that. But anyone can get caught in a storm, have a horse go lame, be exposed to dangers I haven't even thought of." She shivers again.

He grins at her. "I suspect you've thought of some that are beyond the realm of possibility."

Her back stiffens and her eyes narrow. "It is not a laughing matter."

He reaches to put his hands on her shoulders, but she pulls away.

"You have no idea what the waiting is like," Suzanna says. A gust of icy wind blows from the yard, lifting her hair. She shoves it back and turns to glare at the frozen mud on the ground, the stony mountains. Snow clouds are massing behind the western peaks.

"The wind's coming up and snow's coming in. Again." She gives Gerald a bitter look. "At least I'll always have them to keep me company." She pushes past him, up the steps and across the porch.

The door shuts with an angry thud behind her and she moves to the window, expecting him to follow. Instead, he turns and heads down the steps and across the yard to the barn.

Guilt fingers her heart, but she hardens her thoughts against it. He can apologize all he likes, rationalize his decision to remain in the valley as much as he's able to. But the fact remains that she's left here with little or no sunshine, in a house with no real windows, at the beginning of a winter that she knows from experience will be heartlessly long. All the apologies in the world can't alleviate her pain.

Though there is some comfort in knowing she was right to object to Gerald's plan to go trapping with Ewing Young, even if she was arguing for it a few minutes before. She tucks this knowledge away into her arsenal of arguments, for the next time he wants to do something that leaves her here virtually alone. She sniffs, lifts her chin, wipes a tear from her cheek, and crosses the room to the fire.

However, knowing she was right to resist Gerald's desire to join Ewing Young's trapping expedition doesn't make Christmas any more pleasant for Suzanna. The weather is too bitter for travel to Don Fernando or for her father to join them.

As the year turns, the cold becomes even more bitter, the howling winds stronger and more dangerous. The men spend much of their time in the fields and the barn, fighting to keep the cattle alive. There isn't room for them all inside, except during the worst conditions, so there's a good deal of discussion about how low the temperatures are likely to drop and how much snow they can expect to cover the little grass that remains in the pastures.

When conditions do plummet, the men plow through the snow drifts, searching for cattle too stiff with cold to want to move from where they're currently standing. Even the barn doesn't tempt them, though when they're finally driven inside they balk at leaving, despite the crowded conditions. Gerald spends hours each day with the stock, coming in each evening looking grim and exhausted.

Only the seven-month-old mastiff and the thirteen-month child are happily occupied. Chaser is learning what to chew on and not to. Alma is toddling everywhere and discovering just how far her hands can reach. Between them, Suzanna is kept busy saying "Leave that be!"

But that's about all she can do. The feeble light from the mica-covered windows make sewing, knitting, or reading impractical for any stretch of time. She's already spun every bit of wool from the bags her father and Encarnación brought two summers before, and there's no more hair in Ramón's bag to spin or turn into rope. She's restless and strangely tired at the same time, a combination that frays at her nerves. Alma and the puppy bear the brunt of her aggravation.

Finally, Suzanna decides to combat her listlessness by assigning herself one household chore each day. She's dusting the bookshelf the morning Chaser decides Alma's cradle might be the cure for his itching teeth.

At the sound of teeth scraping on wood, Suzanna looks up. Alma's standing over the dog, watching in fascination. Suzanna darts across the room, pushes the toddler aside with one hand and slaps at the dog's hind end with the other. "No!" Suzanna shouts. Her voice rises. "Leave that be!"

Alma drops to the floor and begins to wail. Suzanna turns on her in a fury. "Stop it!" she snaps. "Just stop it!"

Alma's cries double. Chaser turns and noses her. Suzanna shoves him away with the side of her foot and swings the screaming baby from the floor. As she straightens, Ramón appears in kitchen doorway, looking anxious. Suzanna glares at him, and he turns and disappears into the kitchen.

Suzanna shoves her foot into the dog's side again and sends him sliding across the floor. She carries Alma, still crying, to the mica-covered window and glares at the yard outside. It's snowing again.

Tiny icy flakes ping against the windowpanes. If you can call them panes. Suzanna scowls at the milky-white squares, growing even whiter with condensation as the heat from the cabin fire interacts with the temperature outside.

Alma's cries subside into a low snuffle. Suzanna jiggles her a little and the baby hiccups and leans against her mother's chest, exhausted from her tears. Suzanna looks down at her and sighs. When she's quiet, the child is very sweet. But even here there's no real comfort. She should be glad of this little girl, with her heart-shaped freckle and her solemn brown gaze. Instead, she feels only a wave of almost-hysterical despair and the exhaustion and tears that come with it.

It's just so perpetually dark. She's never going to be able to see out of this cave of a house. Not with the price of beaver what it is. Even when the skies are clear, the winter sunlight never truly enters the house. It remain in a state of semi-dusk, lit only by a flickering fire and an uncertain circle of yellow light wherever the lamp happens to be placed.

Even during the spring, when she can open the door without fear of freezing to death, she can't see the entire room in one glance. There are always shadows playing tricks in the corners, beams of light straying in to highlight the dancing motes of dust.

It's as impossible then as it is now to determine if the place is truly clean. There's simply no conceivable way to get enough light into the room to reveal all the corners at once. How she wishes she was back in Taos, where sunlight floods every niche of the house almost every day of the year.

She knows this isn't really true. Adobe walls are so thick that light has to angle in, seek each corner at odd hours.

But the light there is different. Brighter, somehow. Not so blocked by gray clouds overhead. Blame it, how she hates this valley.

Her throat burns with the effort to hold back her sobs. "Tarnation!" she whispers. She tucks Alma's drooping head against her chest, retreats to her chair, and gives in to the pain. Tears stream silently down her face.

Chaser creeps to Suzanna's feet and she pokes at him with her toe. "Stupid dog!" she growls. "You'd best leave that cradle alone or you won't be on this earth very much longer!" She sniffs and feels the pain lighten slightly. It feels good to snarl at something outside of herself.

In the kitchen, the door to the hillside opens and shuts. When it doesn't reopen immediately, she knows that Ramón hasn't gone out to get firewood. He's breaking a path to the barn from the back of the cabin, rather than coming through the main room and using the already-cleared path from the porch.

Suzanna scowls. He's clearly avoiding her. Doesn't want to deal with her and her pain. No one wants to come near her except the dog, whose only purpose in life is to find something else to chew. Preferably a piece of furniture.

Suzanna wipes at her wet cheeks with the back of her hand. "It's just too much!" she whispers into Alma's curly black hair. "It's just too much!"

The baby's right arm lifts and her thumb blindly finds its way to her mouth. "I wish I was so easily comforted," her mother sighs. The puppy sits up, looks into Suzanna's face, and whines softly. She closes her eyes and the dog slips across the room and settles himself on the hearth.

CHAPTER 30

When Gerald and Ramón open the front door two hours later, Chaser is still dozing on the fireplace, Alma is asleep on her mother's chest, and Suzanna sits and stares bleakly into the dying fire.

As the men begin quietly unwrapping themselves, Suzanna stirs and looks up. She doesn't speak. She should ask about the condition of the cattle and other animals, but she can't find it in herself to care.

Ramón goes to the kitchen as Gerald hangs his coat, scarf, and hat on the wooden pegs by the door. He crosses the room, bends to kiss the top of Suzanna's head, and reaches for Alma, then pulls back. "My hands are too cold," he says. He moves to the fire and places a log on the hot coals. "This is about to go out." He smiles at Suzanna. "I see you were otherwise occupied."

She nods slightly, to indicate she heard him, and stares blankly toward the window. Gerald gives her a long look, adds another log to the licking flames, then pats the dog's head and extends his hands over the fire. "It's bitter out there!" he says.

Suzanna turns her head. "And that makes you happy?"

He glances at her and leans to scratch behind the mastiff's ears. The dog moans with pleasure. "A little contrast is nice sometimes," Gerald says mildly.

"This valley is just one big contrast."

"Hmm."

She straightens and glares at him. "You think I'm just being an emotional female. That I have no reason for my discontent."

"I didn't say that."

"You didn't need to. All you have to do is go outside to the animals, you and Ramón both, and stay out there as long as possible. You'd rather endure any amount of cold than be shut up inside this cabin with me." She can feel the tears threatening again. She looks away, then jerks her chin at him. "And then when you do come inside, you look so happy with yourself, so contented with your life. As if you've just spent three hours out in the woods hunting instead of digging through snow drifts and forcing icebound cattle into the barn. Cattle too stupid to know what's best for them." She wipes at her cheeks with the back of her hand. "Anything is preferable to being here, listening to me!"

Gerald lifts his head, his gray eyes hooded, then turns and crosses to the bench that stands by the wall nearest the kitchen.

"Even when you're here, you stay as far away from me as possible!" Suzanna says.

"It seems safer," he says. "Nothing I say or do is going to make you happy. I've said I'm sorry. But there's nothing I can do about conditions right now. I'd take you to Taos if I could."

"And I'd gladly go!" She twists to glare at him. "However, it's a little late to make that offer now, isn't it? When it was possible, when the roads were still clear, you didn't suggest such a thing!"

"When the roads were still clear, you weren't as upset as you are now." He drops his gaze to his hands. "But then, St. Vrain hadn't been here."

"Ceran St. Vrain has nothing to do with this!"

Gerald looks up. "Doesn't he?"

Suzanna glares at him, then turns toward the fire. "No, he does not." She closes her eyes. After a long silence, she hears Gerald stand and move to the ladder. Its rungs creak slightly as he climbs it, then there's a small thud as he lies down on the bed in the loft.

She opens her mouth to remind him to take off his boots so they won't dirty the blanket. Then her lips close. What does it matter?

She stares at the fire. Alma shifts in her arms and Suzanna adjusts to accommodate her. Slowly, her body relaxes in response to the child's sleeping weight and her mind softens with it. Gerald's right, as much as she doesn't want to admit it. Ceran St. Vrain's visit has reminded her of everything she left behind. The dim but cheerful parlor. The men scattered around the room, following her every move with admiring yet respectful glances. The comfort of tea and Encarnación's white bread.

The complacency of St. Vrain's broad face and the knowing twinkle in his eyes, as if he has a wonderful secret he'll tell only if you ask. The sheer bulky self-satisfied confidence of the man. Suzanna closes her eyes. He would have pursued her if she'd made the right gestures. The unspoken offer was there, but she hadn't turned toward it. She'd been so certain the womanizing St. Vrain wasn't for her, that Gerald was the man she wanted.

She hardly remembered now why she'd chosen as she had. If she'd permitted St. Vrain to court her, she'd be living in Taos now. Near her father, with sunny skies overhead and a mere dusting of snow on the ground. Snow which melts quickly after it falls. The temperatures there aren't anything like they are here. And the wind—

She snorts at herself. When she was a girl, she hated Don Fernando's spring winds, the way they poured down from the mountains and seemed intent on ripping every newly-sprung flower to shreds. Raised the dirt from the streets and flung it everywhere. Now, those winds would seem like mere breezes to her compared to the incessant howling of these winter gales. These storms that push ever more snow down from the cloud-shrouded mountains.

She has to admit that when the sun comes out here, it's glorious. But winter is interminable. Any glimpse of sun will simply be followed by yet another gray mass on the western slopes, preparing to dump yet another blanket of snow on the frozen ground, making even a trip to the outhouse a thing of torture.

But here she is. Her throat tightens. She made her choice. There's no going back. At least not now, with every route west completely blocked. How St. Vrain got through is a mystery. He must have a sixth sense for when to travel, when to stay home.

Of course, this trip to St. Louis is his own strategy for avoiding the mountain winter. Perhaps it's just something men do: find it impossible to stay in one place, have to be constantly pursuing the next big chance to earn another dollar or two. After all, St. Vrain has a wife. Well, a woman. Who has borne him at least one child. Suzanna smiles ruefully, remembering why she hadn't been interested in his interest in her. The man has a wandering eye. And probably would even if he were formally married. Gerald, at any rate, saw only her.

A hand touches her shoulder and she jumps. Alma's head jerks and Suzanna reaches to steady it.

"I'm sorry," Gerald says. "I didn't mean to startle you."

"I didn't hear you come down the ladder."

"You did look lost in thought." He moves to the fire, adds another log, and angles a bench so he's sitting directly opposite her. He looks into her eyes. "I know this is a hard time for you."

Her chin trembles a little, but she catches her upper lip between her teeth and forces it still. She nods wordlessly.

"I wish I knew how to make life easier for you." He leans toward her slightly. "I would do anything to make you happy."

"Except move," she says, trying to make the words light, trying not to sound bitter.

He spreads his hands. "Where would we go? There's no land for me anywhere near Don Fernando. It's all owned by people with families of their own to provide for."

"I know it." All the available land is taken, either by the Pueblan natives, the Mexicans and their families, or the few trappers or merchants like Ewing Young who've managed to rent a house and small pasture from a local. No one leases the amount of land necessary for a farming operation.

Suzanna gestures hopelessly toward the window. "It's just that it's so dark all the time. The lack of light is overwhelming." A blast of icy snow slaps the milky windowpanes and she flinches. "And the wind." She closes her eyes. "The everlasting, infernal, pernicious wind."

"The wind is a bit much." He rubs his chin ruefully. "I don't think I've ever seen anything like it." He shakes his head. "But there's nothing I can do about it, wife. And it doesn't do any good to complain."

"At least complaining keeps me aware that I don't have to simply succumb to it!" She straightens in her seat. "If I didn't complain, I'd just waste away under the pressure of it all, the way the pie plants disappear in the fall."

"But the rhubarb does come back in the spring."

Her mouth twists. "I'm not so sure about that. They seemed weaker this last spring, not stronger."

"Did you put down some chicken manure for them?"

"Of course I did. I know how to care for them." She forces herself back into some semblance of calm. "I just don't know if what I did will be enough."

"It may be that you need another plant or two." Gerald shifts, stretching his legs toward the fire. "We'll take a trip into Taos this spring and you can see your father and get more plants from him. He didn't bring you all he had, did he?"

"No, what he brought is a division of the plants he's had since 1822." She chuckles. "It was the first thing he ordered when the Santa Fe Trail opened and the Missouri merchants started showing up in Taos."

"And I thought you were the one with the green thumb."

His voice is lighter now, palpably relieved that they're on a safe subject. A wisp of annoyance crosses Suzanna's mind, but she pushes it away, glad for a respite from the intensity of her emotions. "I suppose it is something I inherited from him," she says. "Certainly he encouraged my interest. In fact, in some ways, those rhubarb plants became mine more than his."

She frowns. "I hope he's spending more time with them, now that I'm gone. More time out of doors, I mean. Walks across the village to debate with Padre Martínez hardly constitute a true physical regimen."

"I'm sure he's doing well," Gerald says soothingly.

She shoots him an irritated look. She doesn't need to be soothed, she needs real conversation. But his face is turned toward the fire again. The flames dance in his gray eyes and across his square brown face.

In her arms, Alma twists and makes a mewing sound. Gerald looks up. "Is she still making demands on you? I haven't heard her in the night."

Suzanna gives him a sharp look, then decides to accept the change of subject. "No, she prefers Ramón's cooking to anything I can give her." She stands the baby on her lap. "She's wet."

"I'll take her." Gerald rises and holds out his arms.

Alma looks up at him with a brilliant smile and flaps her hands. "Pa Pa!" she crows.

It's the first time she's tried to say the word. Suzanna and Gerald exchange a smile of wondering delight.

CHAPTER 31

"Waste a time," the man in the bearskin cape and crude beaver cap mutters. But he remains crouched in the snow behind the ridge, watching the cabin below. The windswept ridge top is clear of snow, so the rock in the niche where he's positioned himself is dry enough. But the stone is cold as ice and the black gelding behind him is moving impatiently. Damn thing'll start snortin' and who knows what all if he don't get movin' soon. Back into the hills and the cone-shaped mountain, then west across the northern valley to his lean-to.

Ain't much to see, anyhow. Locke and the greaser driving unwilling cows in and out of froze-over pasture. Cattle gettin' scrawnier every day. And fewer. End of fall, there was fourteen head, maybe fifteen. Now they're only movin' nine or ten to the fields when the snow lets up enough to let them. Either they lost a third of their herd or the stock's too weak to get to pasture and back. He chuckles. At this rate, there'll be nothing to keep 'em here, come spring.

A growl rises in his throat and he lowers the spyglass. If they leave, it'll be harder to track 'em. All the time he's spent settin' up his campsite and scoutin' game trails through the hills will be wasted.

His eyes narrow. Gonna have to watch closer, once spring comes. If they start lookin' like they're gonna hightail it, he'll need to make his move whether he's ready or not.

He growls again, grinding his teeth. The bitch is his and he'll have her, by God. They look like they're packing up, he'll ease in the night before, toss those hellhound mutts some poison meat, then slip into the barn. Chickens'll be asleep then. Cows and mules won't even notice him. There'll be wire there somewheres. When the men come out for the cattle in the morning, he'll garrot 'em. His fingers twitch.

They generally go to their work separate-like. First Locke, then Chavez.

The big man smiles, his eyes slitting in anticipation. He'll be ready behind the door, pounce on 'em with the wire, twist it round their scrawny necks before they even know he's there. His fingers twitch again, feeling what it'll be like. The struggle, the sharp twist, the sudden release of tension.

And she won't even know what's happenin'. Little cabin'll be sittin' there all calm and still, smoke comin' out the chimney all cozy-like, and he'll be stalking across her yard. He'll be in charge then. Taking what he wants, no one to stop him.

His mouth opens in a whole-hearted grin, revealing his rotten teeth. He licks his lips. The look on her face when he opens that cabin door and she lifts her head from feedin' the brat. The terror in her eyes. He chuckles and feels his groin twitch. Now that'll be a thing to see.

Then his eyes narrow, considering. She's been lettin' the black mutt that looks like an overgrown puppy sleep in the house.

Then he shrugs. A blast of shotgun will take care of that thing, whatever it is.

He grins again. And put the fear of God in the woman. Before he puts the fear of man in her. He chuckles. Won't that be a surprise. She'll find out what a real man is like. Learn her place, once and all.

Behind him, the gelding stomps impatiently. "All right, damn you," the man says. He keeps an eye on the cabin as he backs down the slope toward the horse. "We'll be goin' for now. But don't you worry. We'll be back."

CHAPTER 32

Finally, the February thaw arrives, that blessed period of false spring which at least gives Suzanna hope, if not the ability to plant. The sun is out and the wind's died down. She feels as if she can breath again. She busies herself with chopping down the cornstalks that haven't yet been broken down by browsing elk and deer. Alma toddles between the rows of uncut stalks while Chaser noses the broken pieces, runs imaginary hoofed beasts out of the field, or roughhouses with the other dogs.

They're in the field the morning the next visitor arrives. Suzanna glances up from her work to see a boy on a chestnut-brown mule veer from the north-south road and head straight across the fields toward the corn patch.

Her stomach tightens. More bad news? Her father— The boy reins in at the edge of the corn patch and takes off his battered leather hat, and she realizes that the person looking down at her is actually a small and wiry young man. He looks friendly enough, but her anxiety has already hardened her grip on the machete's wooden handle. She glances around to confirm that Alma is playing quietly two rows away.

"Buenos días, señora." The rider says. "Is this the place where Juan Ramón Chávez is working?"

"Yes, Ramón Chávez lives here." She flicks the tip of the machete toward the pines on the hilltop behind the house. "You will find him there, cutting wood."

He nods his thanks and nudges the mule with his heels. The animal plunges up the path to the cabin, then, instead of veering toward the barn and the worn track behind it, heads straight past the cabin to the slope beyond.

Suzanna's lips twitch in amusement. He certainly is a straightforward sort of person. Not a man to waste words. Something about the set of his jaw reminds her of Ramón. He's probably a relative of some kind. She chuckles and turns back to her work. Is there anyone in New Mexico who isn't related to Ramón?

But there isn't much time to ponder this question. An hour later, Old Bill Williams reins in beside the cornfield. Two loaded pack mules trail behind him.

Suzanna pushes her hair from her forehead and smiles up at him. "Well, Mr. Bill Williams," she says. "How have you been?"

"Could be better." He gazes at the corn patch and the nearby fields, scowls, and flips his red braids onto his back. He jerks his head toward Alma. "That your'n?"

Suzanna nods. "It's been a while since we've seen you," she says. "She's fourteen months old now."

He nods toward the cabin. "Anyone up there?"

Alma waves her machete at the hill behind the cabin. "The men are cutting firewood back behind."

His scowl deepens as he looks down at her. "You got a gun handy?"

"No." She lifts the machete slightly. "Although I do have this."

He glances at the cornstalks that litter the ground behind her. "And can use it," he says grudgingly. "You ought to have a shotgun with you, though." He glares at the hillside behind the cabin.

She studies him. "I hear you saw a man up on the Platte that looks like Enoch Jones."

His head jerks toward her. "I saw Jones," he snaps. "No 'looks like' about it. In fact, I talked to the damned bastard. Didn't St.

187

Vrain tell you that?" His voice rises. "I sent word for him to warn you!" His blue eyes snap at her, then at the hilltop. "Those men have no business leavin' you alone down here."

She opens her mouth, shuts it, then decides it's unfair to lay the blame on Gerald and Ramón. "They think I'm in the cabin, with the shotgun by the door."

Williams' eyes blaze at her. "And why ain't you, then? You tryin' to get you and this baby of yours killed?"

Suzanna's chin lifts. The man presumes too much. "I will not be held prisoner by a man who may be five hundred miles away." She waves the machete at the still-standing cornstalks. "And I have work to do. I can't sit inside all day sewing and knitting and dusting and waiting for my man to come home."

He snorts. "Can't or won't."

"I'd go stir crazy!" She peers up at him. There's more to his aggravation than finding her alone in the field. "Did you have a good hunt?"

"Oh yes, I had an righteously spectacular hunt," he says bitterly. He jerks his chin toward the pack mules, who've taken advantage of the halt to nibble at the new grass coming up at the edge of the cornfield. "Got me the best batch of furs I've had in a coon's age," Williams grumbles. "And I can't find a buyer who'll pay more than a pittance of what they're righteously worth!"

"Ah." Suzanna drops her machete to the ground and crosses the patch to Alma. She places the toddler on her hip, then returns to the machete and crouches down to retrieve it. As she rises, she looks up at Williams. "If you'd like to put your animals in the barn, I'll go see about making some tea. And I think there may be stew left from the noon meal." Her eyes twinkle. "I didn't cook it, but I think I can get it warm without burning the house down."

The mountain man chuckles unwillingly and leans forward over his horse's withers as if he's a jockey in a race. "See you there." He turns his head. "Come on, mules."

She doesn't need to heat water or stew after all, because Gerald, Ramón, and the small stranger are already in the kitchen. They've come down the hill behind the cabin while Williams and she were talking.

As Suzanna had suspected, the young man with the leather hat is indeed related to Ramón: a distant connection named Jesús Ruperto Valdez Archuleta, better known as Pepe, who's in his early twenties and who knows who Old Bill Williams is. The look of admiration on Archuleta's face when the red-haired trapper comes through the door makes that clear.

Williams' bad temper softens a little under the young man's gaze and the influence of Ramón's cooking. When the venison and tortillas are followed by natillas, the trapper stares down at his plate for a long moment, then looks wistfully at Suzanna. "Your Encarnación used to make this." He turns to Ramón. "Or I should say your Encarnación." His eyes darken sympathetically. "I heard what happened to her. That was a righteously terrible thing."

Ramón nods soberly and turns away. Pepe Archuleta looks as if he wants to ask a question. Suzanna stands abruptly. "Would anyone like tea?"

In the other room, Alma begins to fuss. Suzanna leaves the tea things to tend to her. When she carries the baby back into the room, Ramón is filling the pot and Williams is telling Pepe about his plans for the coming year.

"I ain't stickin' around here, that's for righteously sure," Williams says. "I aim to head north towards South Park and the Platte. Then I'm gonna swing eastward and find out for myself what in tarnation is happenin' with these fur prices. I'll go as far as Fort Osage if I have to. Got family there I should visit, anyway. I'll go to St. Louis itself, if I have to."

"Ceran St. Vrain says it's bad all over," Gerald observes.

Williams scowls. "And he may be tellin' God's righteous truth about the price of plews, but then he's a sharp trader. St. Vrain may just be tryin' to get what he can as cheap as I'll sell 'em. He has all the traders in Taos and Santa Fe believing every word out of his mouth. Claims he knows all that can be told about what's goin' on in St. Louis. New York too, for that matter."

"So you'll be taking the furs you have now and gathering more?" Gerald asks as Suzanna and Alma slide in beside him. He takes the baby from her mother and places her on his lap, facing the table. "Or is this just an information-collecting expedition?"

Alma reaches toward Gerald's plate and he tears off a small piece of tortilla, dips it into the natilla custard, and places it in her open mouth. "Tilla," she gurgles happily.

The men laugh and Suzanna shakes her head. "She needs meat as well as natillas."

"Tilla!" Alma crows.

Suzanna knows a lost cause when she sees one. She turns to Bill Williams. "If you're planning on caching your furs up here, you should know there were soldiers up here last spring, looking for smugglers."

"Humph," he snorts. "Those politicos in Santa Fe are a right-eously anxious bunch of bureaucrats, ain't they? They're inclined to think everyone in the world is hell bent on cheating 'em, even when they've got no evidence otherwise."

Suzanna glances at Gerald, who's looking down at the baby, his lips twitching.

Pepe leans toward Williams. "What will you do?" he asks anx-iously. "I know that lieutenant in Taos, that Lieutenant María Jesús Gabaldón de Anaya. I am related to him on my mother's father's side." His lips twist disparagingly. "Él está un hombre muy inteligente, but he has a great anger toward all americanos and those dealing with them."

Williams barks with laughter. "If that's so, he must be perpetually and righteously angry with the great majority of his people!"

Pepe chuckles. "I believe that is the truth."

Williams gives him a sharp look. "I take it you ain't necessarily in agreement with this relative of yours?"

"No señor. Nuevomexico has been isolated too long, I think. I believe this new commerce and knowledge you americanos bring is a good thing." He lifts his hands, palms up. "I only wish I could learn more of it."

Williams' eyes sharpen. "You know how t' read?"

"No señor. Unfortunately, I do not."

Williams shrugs and turns back to his plate. He uses the edge of a tortilla to swipe at the last bit of his natillas, and grins at Suzanna. "Only thing missin' is Encarnación's white rolls."

Suzanna nods. Pain shivers through her, but she pushes it away. Now isn't the time. "I'm afraid no one will ever be able to duplicate Chonita's rolls."

"Or herself," Ramón says from the counter, which he's wiping for the third time.

Williams' hand stops halfway to his mouth. He looks down at the dripping tortilla, then up at Ramón. "I surely didn't mean to pain you."

Ramón turns to face him. "It is no more pain than I already bear." He shakes his head. "The burden of not knowing who killed her, of not being able to avenge her death, is almost greater than her loss." His fist tightens on the cloth in his hand. "If I knew who did this thing, I would not be wiping this counter so calmly."

Williams drops the piece of tortilla onto his plate and leans back, away from the table. He gives Suzanna, and then Gerald, a long look, and turns to Ramón. "I know who did it," he says. He glances at Suzanna. "That's why I sent St. Vrain to say that I'd seen the bastard."

Ramón stares at him. "Jones," he says flatly.

The room goes silent. Alma twists around to look up at her father.

"Yeah, it was Jones. He told me so himself." Williams' eyes harden. "The damned bastard bragged about it. He seemed to think it was funny that we all thought he was dead, and then he came back and got to Peabody's cook."

Williams' eyes flick toward Suzanna, then focus on Gerald. "He said he'd be back. Bragged right righteously about how he wasn't finished with you all. He knew you were married. And he seemed to know where you were." He looks around the room. "Where you are."

Suzanna stares at him, her mouth dry. Old Bill is only saying what she already believed to be true, but hearing him say it somehow makes it more real. More terrible. Too terrible for her to be angry with Gerald for not believing her in the first place. She turns to him. "The man on the ridge."

He nods unwillingly.

Alma whimpers. Suzanna lifts her from Gerald's lap and absently places her on the floor.

"You sayin' you've seen him?" Williams demands.

Suzanna nods. "I believe so."

"It was a while back," Gerald says. "The spring we settled here."

"And again that fall." Gerald's face swings toward her and she gives him an impatient look. There's no use pretending anymore. "The man you saw in the barn. The one you didn't tell me about."

He opens his mouth then closes it again. Suzanna looks at Williams. "A big bulky man on a black horse. Staring down from the ridge." She closes her eyes. "If only I'd insisted that we get word to Chonita. She might be alive now." She looks at Ramón, tears threatening. "She might be sitting here with us now."

Ramón turns back to the counter and begins wiping it again.

"Or you both might be dead," Williams growls. "He would of righteously enjoyed comin' for you both in the same cabin." He scowls at Gerald. "You ought not to be lettin' her out of your sight."

Gerald nods grimly.

Suzanna shudders and Gerald wraps an arm around her shoulders. "I should go home," she says. "Back to Don Fernando, where there are more people."

"Where Encarnación was knifed on an acequia path," Williams says grimly.

Suzanna stares at him, shudders again, and closes her eyes.

"You know how to use that shotgun?"

Suzanna nods.

"And will be putting in more practice time," Gerald says.

Williams nods and pushes himself away from the table. "Well, now that I've spoiled your dinner, I should be checkin' my gear in preparation for heading into the hills tomorrow." He cocks an eyebrow at Pepe. "What say you come and give me a hand?"

As the outside door shuts behind the trapper and the young man, Ramón turns from the counter. "Old Bill Williams is a man who likes to embroider a tale."

Suzanna shakes her head. "I've known Bill Williams since I was a tiny girl. He wouldn't concoct a story for the purpose of upsetting me."

Gerald's arm tightens around her shoulders. "His concern for you might cause him to exaggerate a little, in order to make you pay attention to what he says. Or to make me do so."

"He apparently thinks you should guard me like a sheepdog," Suzanna says. "But none of us will get much accomplished if one of you has to stand guard every time I need to chop cornstalks or dig potatoes."

At the counter, Ramón chuckles ruefully. Gerald makes a hopeless gesture with his free hand. "I guess all we can do is make sure you have a loaded shotgun with you at all times." He swings himself from the bench and bends to lift Alma from the floor. As he straightens, he looks down at Suzanna, his face somber. "I'll set up a target first thing tomorrow."

Williams rides out early the next day, Pepe Archuleta behind him with the two pack mules. They'll cache Williams' plews, then proceed north, with the younger man as apprentice camp follower.

Ramón watches them go with a wry smile on his lips. "El joven will learn much from the old man if he listens carefully," he says. "How much of it will be true may be another question."

Gerald laughs and claps Ramón on the shoulder. "You don't wish you were going with them?"

Ramón chuckles and shakes his head. "No, I don't think so. Although Señor Williams is an interesting hombre. He is a man of many stories and much information."

"Too much information," Gerald says grimly.

Suzanna is standing at the end of the cabin porch with Alma on her hip, watching the travelers angle down the fold between the cabin and the hill beyond, toward the marsh and the Cimarron.

"I could wish he spoke of Jones without the señora's presence," Ramón says.

Gerald glances at Suzanna. "As do I. On the other hand, he wishes her to be cautious."

Suzanna turns. "Bill Williams has always been very protective of me. Perhaps too much so."

"To be cautious is one thing," Ramón says. "To live in fear is another." He shakes his head. "It is not well for a woman to live in fear."

Suzanna lifts her chin. "I'm not afraid."

A smile glimmers across Gerald's face. "Or you won't admit that you are."

She scowls at him and opens her mouth, but then Ramón says, "Encarnación was the same." He stops, his face stricken. "I am beginning to become used to saying 'was' when I speak of her, instead of 'is.'" He looks at Suzanna bleakly. "It pains my heart to speak of her in that way."

"Yes," Suzanna whispers. She glances at Gerald, whose smile has faded.

He steps toward his friend, claps him on the shoulder, then turns away and crosses the half-frozen yard toward the barn. Ramón follows him.

Suzanna moves into the cabin. Words are such inadequate things, she muses. There's simply no adequate way to express one's sorrow at another person's pain. All she can do is try not to remind Ramón of his loss. Or her own danger. And complaining about being here. Speaking about Don Fernando as if she would be safer there is yet another way of reminding him—reminding them all—of Encarnación.

Surely Williams is exaggerating. Surely there's nothing for her to truly fear. After all, Williams saw Jones on the Platte river, of all places. That's hundreds of miles to the north. And they don't know for certain that the man she saw was Jones. Even if she did, that was almost two years ago.

But she isn't surprised when Gerald comes for her later in the day, shotgun in one hand, box of ammunition in the other.

CHAPTER 33

Although Suzanna tells herself firmly that Old Bill was probably exaggerating the potential danger from Enoch Jones and reminds herself that there's been no sight of anyone resembling the hulking mountain man for at least a year, she can't quite forget the sharpness in the trapper's voice, the tightness around his eyes. Anxiety pokes at her in spite of her best efforts.

The wintery weather settles in again and there's little time for target practice. But there's also little reason for Gerald to stray far from the cabin. Suzanna is restless, but she somehow manages to get through the month of March without too many flares of temper.

This is partly due to Alma. The baby is walking more confidently now and beginning to talk. Her mother finds her a good deal more engaging that she did a few months before.

Which is a good thing, because Ramón has become disengaged from all of them. He spends all his free time in his lean-to bedroom off the kitchen. Old Bill's news has re-opened the wound of his slowly-healing pain. There's a darkness about him now, a brooding quality Suzanna's never seen before. He moves through his duties in a kind of abstracted daze.

He does notice, however, when Suzanna begins planting in early April.

The spring has been warmer than usual, and the melting snow and the rain have furrowed deep ruts of mud across the pastures and garden plots. Suzanna doesn't care. She's desperate to get outside and moving again.

She pulls on a pair of boots, tucks up her skirts, and goes to work piling a low brush fence around the section she plans to sow with onions, peas, and lettuce. When she finishes, she moves to the cornfield and begins clearing what remains of the dead stalks.

She's left Alma in the house, but she isn't surprised when she sees Ramón coming down the hill with her in one arm and a jug of hot tea in the other. He's looking off to the right. She follows his gaze. Gerald is approaching from the pasture.

They all meet at the edge of the muddy field, where Suzanna gratefully accepts a drink of tea. "You are planting the corn so soon?" Ramón asks indifferently as he hands Gerald the jug.

"It does seem rather early," Gerald says. He takes a long drink and grins at Suzanna. "But you just can't wait, can you?"

"The weather is warmer now than it was at this time last year," Suzanna says defensively. "And I'm not planting all my seed. It's an experiment." This elicits a laugh from Gerald and a small smile from Ramón. Suzanna takes Alma from him and smoothes the child's black curls. "Next year, you can help me plant the corn and the peas," she says. She mock-frowns at Gerald. "Even if your father thinks it's too soon."

Gerald laughs again and shakes his head.

Ramón is gazing abstractly at the mountains. He jerks his head, as if waking himself, and says, "It is true the weather is warmer now than it was last April." There's a long pause, as if he's gone a long ways from them, then he adds, "But only for the moment, perhaps."

"Perhaps," Suzanna agrees. "But then again, perhaps not."

"Perhaps," Gerald says.

Suzanna's chin lifts. "Well, I'm going to try, anyway. If I want to harvest a decent crop, the seed needs to be in the ground as early as possible."

As she speaks, the three dogs appear from the edge of the marsh. They bound along the far edge of the field, throwing up sprays of mud as they go. "And I hope to have some real help keeping the raccoons and deer out of the field out this season," Suzanna adds. "If Chaser lives up to his name."

When the corn begins sprouting later that month, Suzanna's work seems vindicated. She's very proud of herself and delighted to see the bright green shoots glimmering against the dark soil.

But then icy black clouds move in from the west. She wakes one morning to two feet of snow.

She peers out the door at the heavy white blanket that covers the yard and turns to the men, who are hurrying into their outer clothes to see to the animals. "My poor corn."

Ramón gives her a commiserating look as he pulls on his coat. "It is unlikely—"

"You don't know that!"

His eyes drop. He bends down to reach for his boots.

"Now, wife," Gerald says.

She turns on him. "The weather was so warm! How was I to know it would snow again? And like this!" She waves her hand toward the still-open door.

"Ramón told you—"

"He said 'perhaps'!"

Ramón glances at her, then turns away and begins searching through his pockets for his knitted cap.

Gerald gives Suzanna a wry smile.

"Don't you dare laugh at me!" she snaps.

"I'm not laughing." He pushes the door shut and puts his hands in his pockets. "I know this is upsetting."

"That's one way to put it. This valley of yours—"

"The weather is unpredictable everywhere. That's the nature of farming."

"I've never known any weather as unpredictable as it is here!"

"But you'll keep trying. Planting as early as possible."

Her chin lifts. "Of course I will. I'm not going to let a little weather stop me!"

Gerald's eyes crinkle with laughter, but she's still scowling. He sobers. "It's possible that some of your sprouts will survive."

"You never can tell," Ramón agrees. He pulls his hat onto his head. "I just hope that new calf made it through the night."

Gerald reaches for the door. "We'd better go see." He turns to Suzanna. "If you'll bring me the basket, I'll fetch the eggs this morning."

When she comes back into the room with the basket, the men have their heads together.

"She just may succeed," she hears Gerald say. "She's a stubborn one, my Suzanna."

"It is a great strength," Ramón says as she reaches them.

Suzanna gives him a startled look and hands Gerald the basket. He leans in to kiss her cheek, then turns toward the door. She watches them down the icy steps, then withdraws to the fire, sinks into her chair, and stares at the flames.

Strong? She's never thought of herself in that way. Intelligent, yes. Moody, sometimes. Impatient, certainly. She chuckles. Gerald would certainly agree with that.

But a great strength? She shakes her head. Ramón has mistaken stubbornness for strength. A stubborn resistance to anything she doesn't like.

Including the thought of Jones being alive. A shiver runs down her spine and she shifts in her chair. Now where did that thought come from? She forces her mind back to her plants. Surely some of the corn sprouts have survived.

But when she investigates her field two days later, the tiny sprigs of corn have all disappeared. Oddly, most of the pea plants are still standing. She returns to the cabin. As she mounts the steps, she sees that the pie plants, tucked under the eaves on the sunny side of the cabin, are pushing through the wet soil like crinkled red and green fists.

Suzanna touches them gratefully, adds a little fertilizer from the pile outside the barn, and a few days later begins replanting the corn.

But even in the pleasure of planting, Williams' warnings intrude. She tries to talk herself into ignoring the trapper's words, but fingers of anxiety still brush her mind. Her shoulders itch with the sensation that someone is watching. She finds herself turning to study the greening ridges, the foothills that stretch toward the mountains that surround her. Is Jones there somewhere? Is he watching?

She lowers her gaze, looking closer to home. Alma plays at the edge of the corn patch. The men move across the far pasture, assessing the new grasses, discussing which fields to use as pasture, what to leave for hay. They each carry a rifle, a precaution they've never taken before.

They've both encouraged her to stay closer to the cabin. But she's not sure she's truly safer there either, if they aren't with her. Jones could be on the hillside behind the house. Or in the marsh, waiting to slip up through the fold between the cabin and the hill behind it. He'd reach her before they even knew he was there.

She forces herself to breathe. She must stop this. If she continues thinking about all the ways Jones might approach the cabin without being seen, she'll become unable to think about anything else.

She takes another deep breath and her chin lifts. Curse him, she isn't going to let the mere thought of that filthy mountain man affect her like this. And if he is indeed watching, she certainly isn't going to let him think she's afraid. Even if she is.

She makes a mental note to talk to Gerald about more shooting practice and goes back to work, punching the pointed end of her planting stick into the wet soil, bending to drop her precious seed corn into the dirt.

But Jones isn't the only danger to the spring peace. Suzanna and Gerald are amending the soil in the potato patch when soldiers appear again, cantering steadily up the still-muddy north/south track in the valley's center. There are only four of them this time, their apparent leader slightly ahead on a tightly-reined gray-spotted white horse.

Gerald, shoveling aged cow manure out of the wagon bed, sees them first. He looks down at Suzanna. "I wonder if that's the officer who gave you such a bad time last spring," he says. "They'll wear those horses out, galloping through the mud at that speed. The prairie dogs have been active all along the road. It'll be a matter of pure luck if none of those men gets thrown by a tripping horse. Or a horse doesn't break a leg."

Suzanna raises a dirty hand to her forehead and peers at the tiny cluster of men. "It's hard to say if it's the same officer. Though Ramón would probably know."

"I expect we'll find out soon enough." Gerald tosses another shovelful of manure to the ground. "At the rate they're travelling, they'll be here before we finish with this. If they're actually headed this way."

Suzanna nods and goes back to work. As she turns the manure into the soil, she glances occasionally toward the road. The riders have dropped into single file down the center of the track, where prairie dogs are least likely to dig, but they're maintaining their rapid pace.

They don't slow until they turn onto the track that breaks toward the cabin. Then they move into a trot, up the hill and into the cabin yard without so much as a glance toward the potato patch. The little band halts beside the pole corral and sits stiffly, as if waiting for someone to announce its presence.

Suzanna jams her shovel upright into the dirt, puts her hands on her hips, and peers up at the yard. The man positioned in front of the others does seem to be the lieutenant who's related to Ramón. She chuckles. "I wonder just how long they'll sit there without deigning to acknowledge our presence down here."

Gerald leans his shovel against the side of the wagon. "I suppose we should go and greet them."

"I wonder if he'll be more polite to you than he was to me."

Gerald swings down from the wagon and grins at her. "Now that he knows we're connected with Ramón, I'm sure he'll be more accommodating to both of us."

Their visitor is indeed Lieutenant María Jesús Gabaldón de Anaya, but he doesn't seem to have changed his attitude. The lieutenant turns his head as Suzanna and Gerald crest the hill. He's wearing the same suspicious scowl that greeted Suzanna the first time she met him.

"Welcome," Gerald says. "Lieutenant Gabaldón de Anaya, I believe?"

The lieutenant nods. His horse moves restlessly.

"I am Gerald Locke Jr.," Gerald says. "Welcome to my home. I believe you've met my wife."

The lieutenant nods again.

"Would you care to rest yourself?" Gerald asks evenly.

The lieutenant vaults from his horse, strips off his gloves, and slaps them across his palm as if to keep them in order. "I require lodging this night and tomorrow," he says.

Gerald's eyes glint with amusement, but he only nods politely. He turns toward the lieutenant's men. "You will find fodder for the horses in the barn." He glances toward the cabin porch, where Ramón has suddenly appeared, Alma in his arms. "We will be happy to welcome you to our table."

Ramón comes down the steps and hands Alma to Suzanna. "Mí primo," he says to the lieutenant. "Qué tal? How goes it?"

The lieutenant's scowl deepens. "It does not go well at all, mí primo." He makes a sweeping gesture that takes in the entire valley. "There are men in these mountains who evade the law."

Ramón frowns. "Bandidos? We have seen no such men."

"Contrabandistas! As I told you before!"

"Ah," Ramón says. "But there will be time I think to speak of such things. Come inside and rest yourself and take some food." He turns toward the cabin, motioning the lieutenant to move ahead of him. "I have just prepared a venison stew and there are fresh tortillas. And what of su padre y su madre? They are well? And your sister, the pretty one, María Concepción? I have heard she is soon to be married."

The man's face softens slightly. "Sí, her marriage brings us great honor," he says as he moves forward. Gerald and Suzanna follow them into the house.

CHAPTER 34

But the discussion about potential smugglers and their smuggled goods isn't over. The lieutenant waits until the following morning, when he, Gerald, and Ramón are standing on the porch and gazing over the fields and meadows below the house.

Suzanna has been in the barn gathering eggs. Anaya glances at her dismissively as she approaches the cabin steps, then looks disapprovingly at the cows in the greening pastures below. "It is not a work to keep a man occupied," he says abruptly.

Suzanna halts halfway up the steps. She looks at Gerald, who raises an eyebrow at the western peaks.

A smile twitches Ramón's lips, but he doesn't respond to the lieutenant. Instead, he nods toward the cattle in the nearest pasture and glances at Gerald. "I think that spotted one has an injury," he says. "Do you see the far back leg, how she favors it?"

Gerald's gaze moves to the field. He nods thoughtfully.

"It is work for boys," the lieutenant says. "Cows and sheep. Surely you find other work to occupy yourselves."

Gerald continues to study the cattle. "Such as trapping?"

Anaya glances at him. "It is an americano task, is it not?" He turns his head to study the cone-shaped mountain to the north, looming over the roof of the barn. "Of course, you are not truly americano. Tú eres moreno."

Gerald and Ramón look at each other. Gerald glances at Suzanna, who rolls her eyes and shakes her head. The man is an idiot.

Gerald's jaw tightens. "You know nothing about me," he says calmly. "Just as I know nothing of smuggling or smugglers. Threats and insinuations will not produce information I do not have to give you."

The lieutenant looks at Suzanna, a little smile playing on his lips. She frowns back at him. What is he trying to do?

"It can be dangerous to make accusations, mí primo," Ramón says quietly. "Words are arrows that can be made to fly in both directions. No one knows what damage they might cause."

The lieutenant glares at him and brushes past Suzanna, down the steps. He stalks toward the barn, his back stiff with disapproval.

Suzanna raises an eyebrow at Ramón, who grins and shrugs. "Those listed on one's baptism record as one's parents may not actually be one's parents," he observes mildly.

Suzanna laughs. "And a thing doesn't need to be true to make life uncomfortable." She moves up the remaining steps and crosses the porch.

As she goes through the door, Gerald says, "Thank you," and Ramón answers "De nada." Suzanna shakes her head. What a fuss about nothing. So the man called Gerald a name. Are men really that sensitive? Even if Gerald were moreno—part negro—there are plenty of people here in New Mexico with African blood in their veins. What would it matter? Not that he has any, of course. He's no darker than anyone else here in nuevomexico. She's always wondered if he has a little Cherokee or another Eastern tribe in his veins. But it's never mattered enough for her to ask him.

She's washing the eggs when Gerald enters the kitchen. "We have more company," he says. "It looks like Stands Alone is also traveling today. He's coming in from the north valley."

Suzanna chuckles and half-turns from the sink. "I wonder what he and the lieutenant will think of each other."

"He's Ute," Gerald says drily. "I'm guessing that will be all the lieutenant will see."

She nods ruefully and goes back to washing the eggs.

Lieutenant Anaya's attitude toward the Utes is made clear by the positions he and his men take up in the yard well before Stands Alone and his men ride in. The officer stands on the porch. There's a soldier at either corner of the cabin and a third just inside the barn door. All four have their hands on their weapons.

Stands Alone reins in next to the corral. His eyes sweep the well-placed soldiers, then he nods to Gerald, Suzanna, and Alma, who are standing in the center of the yard, Alma clinging precariously to her mother's skirts.

"Ah, this is the little one," Stands Alone says. Alma smiles shyly up at him. He looks at Suzanna. "And the dogs, they have proved themselves useful?"

As if on cue, Dos, Uno, and the mastiff round the corner of the cabin and stop to stare at the men and horses.

"I see you have added to your collection," Stands Alone says.

"Just a little," Gerald says. He makes a gesture of welcome. "Please, come in and eat with us."

On the porch, the lieutenant snorts derisively. Gerald and Stands Alone ignore him. The Ute leader dismounts and says something to his men, who rein their horses toward the corral.

Anaya's disapproval doesn't keep him and his men from eating at the same table with the Ute leader. After the meal, the men move to the porch and Suzanna puts an unwilling Alma down for a nap. After the child has finally settled, Suzanna slips out the door.

She shoos the mastiff off the porch to lie at the bottom of the steps with the other dogs, then moves to stand behind Gerald, her hand on his shoulder. He smiles at her, then turns back to Stands Alone. "How many were there?"

"The Pawnee? Perhaps fifty."

The lieutenant scowls. "And how many of los pobladores were killed?"

"One man," Stands Alone says. "For a stupid man, he fought bravely. The others hid in their storehouses."

Gerald's eyes stray to the pasture below. "I suppose they were after the cattle."

"There have been few buffalo this season," Stands Alone says. "Hunger stalks their camps."

"And you?" Gerald asks. "Have you found sufficient game?"

"We have enough to feed ourselves. Our bellies are satisfied."

"But when they are not, then you also will raid," the lieutenant says.

Stands Alone's eyes flicker over him and focus on the valley. "We will find a way to survive."

"At the expense of others!"

The Ute turns and studies the lieutenant for a long moment. Then he looks at Gerald.

"I will keep my commitment to you," Gerald says. "I will not block the grazers from this valley."

Stands Alone's gaze strays to the mastiff.

"This Pawnee raid," Suzanna interjects. "Where and when did it happen?"

"Three nights ago in the valley the Mexicans call the Mora," Stands Alone says.

"And where did the Pawnee go from there?"

"North and east. Back to their camp."

"As far as the Cimarron? This valley?"

"It is possible. They will be hunting meat to dry for the coming cold."

Suzanna looks at the cattle below, then farther west. Browsing elk are scattered across the grassy foothills. "They will want elk if they haven't found enough buffalo. And beef, if they can't find the elk." Her stomach clenches. "A man was killed."

Gerald reaches up to pat her hand. "Stands Alone says the man didn't acknowledge the Pawnees' rights."

"What rights would those be?" Anaya growls. "They are Pawnee. Gentiles. Wild Indians without religion. They were raiding, as they always do. Stealing what others have gathered. And they killed a man. They ought to be found and punished for these actions! A lance through each heart!"

"And then they would feel the need to revenge the Pawnee lives which are taken and will have even more reason to attack," Gerald says. "They were only trying to feed their families. Surely there's enough for us all."

"You speak well," Stands Alone says.

"And when they come for your cattle and your family, what will you say then?" the lieutenant demands.

"I would hope to speak words of peace." Gerald is watching the cattle again. "Enough to keep my family from harm and my herd large enough to provide us with food."

"They are wild Indians!" the lieutenant insists. "Unbaptized gentiles with no Christian training!"

Gerald glances at Stands Alone, but the Ute is gazing at two white-headed eagles high overhead, wheeling endlessly against the clear blue sky.

"This is a good place," Stands Alone says. He looks at Suzanna. "A place of great beauty."

"Though a place of little corn," she says drily. "The winter comes quickly and lasts a very long time."

He chuckles. "You must go farther east to find land that is not taken and that will produce the amount of corn you desire." He gestures toward the end of the porch and the marsh below. "You must follow the Cimarron."

"A river which will take me even farther from my father's house," Suzanna says.

Gerald tilts his head to look up at her. She ignores him and smiles beseechingly at Stands Alone, but keeps her voice light. "Please don't convince him to move farther east from Don Fernando."

"The valley of the Utes, it is very green and has a longer season of warmth," Stands Alone observes.

Suzanna's lips narrow.

The Ute's eyes glint mischievously. "You must go where your man goes."

Gerald laughs. "Now please don't go getting her riled up," he says. "She's aggravated enough about living up here."

"And now we have Pawnees to worry about," Suzanna says. She gives him a dark look. "At least in Don Fernando there would be more men to watch for them."

"You have two good men to watch for you, and your man will speak to them with quietness," Stands Alone says. "I believe there is little to fear." He permits himself a small smile and nods toward the mastiff. "And you have the large dog."

"He's useful for chasing deer and elk from the corn patch," Suzanna says. "I doubt he'd be much protection against a Pawnee warrior."

Ramón turns to the lieutenant. "This looking for smugglers. Will it keep you in the mountains a long time? Long enough to warn away the Pawnee?"

Anaya snorts. "You can be sure that those heathen gentiles will return immediately upon our departure."

Ramón glances at Suzanna, then nods reluctantly. "They will prowl where they can," he acknowledges. "We must take our chances." Then his face brightens a little. He gestures toward the western slopes. "But we have seen a man we believe to be americano. He appears to wish to not be seen."

The lieutenant's head jerks toward him. "A contrabandista?"

Ramón shrugs. "That I do not know. Certainly it is a man who lives alone, who watches us but does not come within hailing distance."

Anaya shrugs. "It may be that he has other business here not related to contraband. Business of a personal nature."

Suzanna's eyes narrow. "And if he comes here seeking to do us harm? Will you be concerned about him then?"

The lieutenant glances at her, then lifts his eyes to gaze at the mountain peaks. "Your esposo has made a decision to live on this land without first receiving permission. I have no instructions to protect americanos who flout our laws."

Suzanna opens her mouth, but Ramón interrupts her. "I am not americano."

Anaya nods. "This is true. But you have chosen to live here on the fringes of civilization. You must take your chances with loco americanos as well as the Pawnee."

Suzanna's jaw tightens, but she doesn't contradict him. In fact, she's remarkably quiet until early the next afternoon, when the soldiers head into the canyon to scout for smugglers and their caches and the Utes move north into the upper valley. Stands Alone says they need meat for their lodges.

"They aren't really hunting, are they?" Suzanna asks as she and Gerald watch the Indians ride north. "If they were truly here with a view to replenishing their food supply, their families would be with them. Or at least enough of the women to slice and dry the meat."

"Stands Alone says they're hunting."

A narrow wooded passage between the hills links the upper and lower valleys. The Utes don't take it. Instead, they urge their mounts onto the rock-strewn grassy slopes above the trees.

"They're staying out of the valley bottom," Suzanna says. "As if they're concerned about both what's ahead and what's above them. I think they're scouting for Pawnee."

She frowns and puts her hands on her hips. "Or at least making their own presence known, so the Pawnee won't think they can move this far into Ute territory without repercussions. Also, I suspect they've ventured farther north than Stands Alone told us." She looks at Gerald out of the corner of her eye. "Or than he told you when I was listening, at any rate."

Gerald reaches for her arm. "And I think you worry too much."

She doesn't pull away, but she doesn't lean into him, either. "I have reason to worry," she says. "As much as I don't want to think about it, Jones is out there somewhere. He's probably watching us this moment."

She shivers. "And now Pawnee are roaming the mountains. Men who've killed once and will be happy to kill again. And our only option is to offer them cattle."

"We won't be offering Jones cattle." His eyes scan the western foothills. "If he's really there. And if he actually shows up here."

Her eyes follow his gaze. Maybe she's wrong. Jones may have never been watching them in the first place. Even if he was, surely he's become weary of them by now. But she can't keep herself from asking the question. "Do you really think he's out there?"

"I don't know," Gerald says. "It seems unlikely that anyone would hold a grudge that long. It's been over two years. Or go to the trouble of living out here with no protection from the weather, for the sole purpose of monitoring our activity."

"But then, we thought it was unlikely that he was even alive. And you did try to kill him. He may be holding more than a mere grudge against you."

A shadow crosses Gerald's face. "I didn't try to kill him. I stabbed him and thought he died as a result."

"I'm not sure that's a distinction Enoch Jones is capable of making."

He nods reluctantly. "That's probably true. But why track me here and then lie in wait, if that's what he's doing? Any other man would have walked into the yard the minute he realized I lived here and bellowed a challenge. Or simply started shooting. If he's truly out there watching, it doesn't make much sense."

"Remember who you're speaking of. Enoch Jones is not a sensible man."

"What you saw was probably just someone passing through."

Suzanna purses her lips. What about the figure he saw at the edge of the barn? The bone-handled knife Gregorio Garcia found next to Encarnación's body?

But she's suddenly exhausted from thinking about it. It's just too frightening. And there's nothing she can do about Jones, anyway, even if he is out there. So she only says "I hope so," and turns toward the cabin. "I'm going inside. All this company has left the cabin in disarray, to put it mildly."

But she can't keep her mind from Jones and the warring Pawnee. When Gerald comes down from the loft the next morning, he finds her beside the door, hefting the shotgun in her hands. "I need more practice with this," she tells him flatly.

As he comes toward her and lifts the gun from her hands, his gray eyes are dark with pain. "I'm sorry you feel so vulnerable here."

She looks past him into the room. "I would feel vulnerable anywhere, knowing Enoch Jones is still alive." She gives him a sideways look. "But those Pawnee wouldn't trouble me if we were closer to Don Fernando."

"They hit Mora," he points out. "That's an established settlement with a good collection of stalwart men."

"Mora is on a major route between the eastern plains and Taos, and it's a new settlement," Suzanna says. "Of course they hit it. Those settlers are moving into Pawnee hunting range and will be on the plains soon enough, hunting buffalo for their own needs. The Pawnee will do their best to push out anyone they think is infringing on their hunting grounds. And Stands Alone seems to think this valley is part of the space they hope to claim for that purpose. That's what worries me."

She frowns and reaches for the shotgun. "I need more practice with this thing."

"I'm sorry," he says again.

Her shoulders sag with the futility of his apologies. Then she lifts her chin and turns away. "I agreed to come here." She sights the double barrels at the fireplace. "I came willingly enough."

She feels rather then sees Gerald open his mouth, then shut it again. She wills herself to focus on the shotgun. She doesn't want his apologies. She wants to go home to Don Fernando. But it's the one thing he can't or won't do. So there's no point in even talking about it.

But she does need to practice shooting. She lowers the gun and turns to the door. "Are you coming with me?"

CHAPTER 35

The days pass. Suzanna improves her shooting skills and her plants begin to sprout. There's no more word about Pawnee or other Indian raids, and life in and around the cabin settles onto an even keel.

Alma is a year and a half old now and curious about everything. The mastiff is a bundle of drooling awkwardness, but eager to please. He soon learns not to get too close to the standing toddler, because he'll inevitably knock her down and elicit ear-piercing wails from Alma and a reprimand from Suzanna. However, when both puppy and child are on the floor, he's amazingly patient with the toddler's need to explore his coat, eyes, and tail.

June is dry this year and Suzanna is kept busy adjusting the narrow irrigation ditch from Willow Creek to her vegetable garden, potato patch, and cornfield. A certain amount of this work is created by the dogs, who persist in playing in the mud along the little rivulet. Their clumsy paws break down the irrigation channel's banks and divert precious liquid away from its destination.

Even though they're creating more work for her, Suzanna can't bring herself to be too exasperated with the dogs. It feels so good to be out in the sun, its warmth on her back as she scrapes the soil with her hoe. She looks across the rows of young corn at Alma, who's sitting on a flat rock that's almost level with the ground and leaning sideways to poke the dirt beside her with a small stick.

Suzanna smiles and glances up the hill toward the cabin. Gerald stands on the slope below the corral, his rifle in his hand as he surveys the fields, the cattle, and the valley beyond. In the bright sunlight and green plants, the rifle and his watchfulness don't seem as necessary as they did a month ago. Suzanna waves up at him cheerfully and goes back to work.

Suzanna expects her irrigation efforts to slow in early July, when the monsoon rains will water her plants and also replenish Willow Creek. But the sky remains a clear stubborn blue, no clouds in sight. And the water in Willow Creek drops steadily.

"First too much rain and now not enough," Suzanna mutters as she studies the thread of damp at the bottom of her irrigation ditch. There's no point in deepening the little channel. There's no water to flow into it.

She moves to the edge of the corn patch and puts her hands on her hips. Sickly yellowish stripes run down the drooping green leaves, whose tips are the color of dead oak leaves. The brown breaks off with a crackle when she touches it.

Suzanna looks up at the hard blue sky. "I never thought I'd wish so hard for rain." She raises her hands helplessly. The plants look so sad. So hopeless. Tears flood into her eyes and she wipes at them impatiently. Weeping won't help her corn grow. She smiles bitterly. Unless she can cry enough to water the entire patch and the peas, lettuce, onions, and squash as well.

She sniffs and straightens her shoulders. There's no use in standing here wishing for an event that isn't likely to happen. She might as well go find something else to do. Maybe she can ask Gerald to pull water from the well, fill a cask, and haul it down the hill so she can water at least a few of her plants. Enough to produce seed for next year.

The thought of no harvest to speak of makes her shoulders sag again. She turns and trudges up the path to the cabin. As she climbs, her feet kick up small puffs of dust, shrouding the lower third of her skirts. Ramón will be preparing the midday meal. She should be hungry, but the very thought of food makes her slightly queasy.

She frowns, puzzled by the way her stomach is churning, and then stops in the middle of the path as realization washes over her. Her breasts have seemed unusually tender lately, too. She closes her eyes and silently counts backward. It's been twelve weeks since her last flow. Then she counts the months forward and groans aloud. A baby in January.

"Well, at least now I know what to expect when the child comes," she mutters grimly. She moves slowly toward the cabin through the July dust. Somehow, knowing what's coming doesn't comfort her. Another winter of misery while she waits for the child to decide to appear.

Suzanna closes her eyes. And the pain. Not so much during, as after. Bile rises in her throat. She stops, puts her clenched hand to her mouth, then pulls it away and takes deep breaths of air, fighting the nausea. January. Of all the times to have a child. Dark and cold and miserable.

She turns her back on the cabin and looks longingly at the western mountains. Beyond that stubborn range of green blackness is her father and home. But she'd have to leave soon if she were to have the child there. And then all her plants would die. There'd be no chance at all of any of them pulling through.

She sighs and begins trudging again toward the cabin. It's so small. And will seem even smaller with another child in it. It's certainly not her father's house.

But when she tells Gerald she's with child, he doesn't seem at all concerned about the difficulties of a January birth or the size of the cabin. He grabs her by the shoulders and gives her a big kiss. "That's wonderful news!" he says.

He turns toward the kitchen door. "Ramón, did you hear that? Another child!" He crosses the room, lifts Alma from her blocks, and swings her into the air. "You're going to have a brother!"

Ramón appears in the doorway and gives Suzanna a questioning look. She nods and turns to Gerald, her anxiety giving way to amusement in the face of his enthusiasm. "Just how do you know that it's going to be a boy?"

Gerald grins at her over Alma's head. "I just have a feeling." He looks down at Alma. "I'm glad to have a daughter. But it would be nice to have one of each." His face grows quiet as he studies Suzanna's face. "Not that it truly matters. I'll be just as delighted to have another girl."

"Humph," she says. "But you would be even more delighted to have a boy." There's a tartness in her voice that she hadn't meant to put there, but she doesn't try to soften it with a smile.

Ramón fades back into the kitchen as Gerald opens his lips, but Suzanna turns her head, looking around the room. "This cabin is going to start feeling very small."

"Oh, I think it will be all right for another few years." Gerald returns Alma to her blocks and gestures toward Suzanna's belly. "When there's yet another one coming, we'll need to start thinking about adding a room."

"Another one after this? Let me get through this blessed event first!"

He crosses the room and reaches for her. "We know what to expect now," he says gently. "I don't think this time will be so bad."

She closes her eyes and leans into him in spite of her irritation. "It'll be January. Unless it comes early. Though early will still be in winter." She shudders and straightens, pushing away from him. She shoves a tendril of hair away from her face. "January is bad enough up here, without a new baby to deal with."

"We know what to expect this time," Gerald repeats. "I really don't think it will be so bad."

She turns her head, despair rising beside the nausea. He just doesn't understand. Or doesn't want to. He thinks her dark moods after Alma's birth were the result of her adjustments to motherhood and her grief at Chonita's death. But something in her knows differently, knows that the blackness will be just as bad this time. If not worse.

She opens her mouth to try to express this, to break through his optimism, but then Ramón appears in the kitchen doorway. "The meal, it is ready," he says. He looks at Suzanna, eyes dark with concern. "If you are able to eat it."

"I can't promise you anything," Suzanna says. "But I'll try."

CHAPTER 36

The monsoons arrive the next morning. Suzanna's morning sickness seems to ease as the clouds gather each afternoon and slam the earth with moisture, then retreat into the mountains. The ground dries overnight and each morning Suzanna moves eagerly down the hill to monitor her various patches of growing food. She's so involved with her plants that she forgets to watch the ridge tops for bulky strangers.

Old Bill Williams and the other mountain men seem to be busy with their summer trading activities or their Taos sprees, because the cabin has no more visitors until mid-August. Suzanna is shelling peas on the porch one afternoon when she looks up and sees Lieutenant Anaya trotting up the valley, six men behind him. She bites her lip in irritation. She's alone in the house and is in no mood to listen to the man's accusations and insinuations.

She places the bowl of peas on the bench and moves into the house. Alma looks up from her task of pulling on Chaser's ears and the mastiff continues to chew on Alma's largest block.

Suzanna pulls the slobber-wet wood from the dog's mouth and lifts Alma to her feet. "Let's go find Papa," she says.

"An' Amón?" the child asks.

"Yes, and Ramón."

Alma claps her hands and toddles to the kitchen. Suzanna chuckles as she follows her. "He isn't here." She glances at the counter. "Although his biscuits are. Don't they smell good?" She crosses the room to the outer door. "We can find him out here."

Alma clutches Chaser's neck as she and the dog go out the door together, then stand staring at the woodpile. "Not here!" she announces.

Suzanna closes the kitchen door behind her and points to the top of the hill behind the house. "Up there."

Alma tilts her head at the hill. "Papa?"

"We'll go and find him." Suzanna holds out her hand. "Come now. We don't have much time."

A quarter of the way up the hill, the child's legs give out and Suzanna lifts her onto her hip. "Hiya!" a man's voice calls from the far side of a cluster of juniper. A mule neighs in response and Suzanna heads toward the sound.

As she tops a small knoll, a man calls, "There she goes!"

Suzanna looks up. Thirty feet away, a thick-barked ponderosa creaks and tilts, then gains speed as it crashes to the ground, narrowly missing the trees beside it. Alma's fingers dig into Suzanna's shoulder. "Ouch!" the little girl cries.

Suzanna chuckles and moves forward. Gerald scrambles around the tree and comes toward her. "Is everything all right?"

"It appears that Lieutenant Anaya is about to pay us another visit," Suzanna says, trying to keep her voice light. "I thought it would be helpful if you're at the cabin when he arrives."

Gerald grins. "If I'm not there, he might think I'm out caching furs again."

Suzanna chuckles. "Something like that." She looks at the tree and breathes in the toffee scent of its bark. "It smells so lovely. It always seems like such a shame to cut them down."

He nods. "Ponderosas, especially. But we need the wood and this one is half-dead anyway." He gestures toward the far side of the tree. "See the dead branches?"

She nods and moves closer to the downed tree. Ramón is working steadily down the other side with his axe, lopping off branch-

220

es. Pieces of bark flew from the tree as the branches drop to the ground. Suzanna bends down to pick up a piece of bark and holds it out to Alma. "Smell!" she says.

The baby leans in and sniffs. "Ummm," she says, grabbing at the bark.

"It smells like butter and vanilla," Gerald says.

"No, don't chew it," Suzanna tells Alma. "It won't taste good." She glances toward Ramón, at the far end of the tree, then looks at Gerald. She lowers her voice. "The smell reminds me of Encarnación."

Gerald gives her elbow a gentle squeeze. She leans into him and they stay that way for a long moment until he says regretfully, "We'd best get down the hill if we're going to be there when Anaya arrives."

Ramón moves toward them, his axe over this shoulder, and Gerald tells him the news. They all head down the hill, the mastiff cavorting through the grass, Alma on her father's shoulders and still clutching the piece of bark, Ramón slightly behind them with the axe still over his shoulder, and Suzanna farther back, pausing now and then to gather the narrow-petaled yellow sunflowers that bloom wherever there's a slight dip in the ground.

Ramón studies the southern sky. Fluffy white clouds are forming over the ridge tops. "There will be a monsoon this afternoon," he says as Suzanna catches up with him.

"Good," Suzanna says. "Willow Creek is starting to run again. It's such a relief."

Gerald turns. "Your attitude about rain has certainly changed," he teases.

She grins. "Monsoons, unlike spring rains, don't last forever."

Even the sour moods of certain lieutenants don't seem to last forever. The little band of soldiers has reached the yard before they do. The lieutenant's face breaks into a smile as the three adults and the child round the corner of the cabin.

"Hola," Anaya says. He vaults from his horse and gives Suzanna a little bow. "Señora." He turns to Gerald and Ramón. "Señors."

Suzanna has to struggle to keep the bemused look from her face. He certainly seems pleased with himself. "Please come inside," she says. She looks toward the lieutenant's men. "You must be weary from your travels."

Anaya shakes his head. "Alas, I am afraid we cannot stop. We must arrive on the eastern plains before nightfall."

Gerald raises an eyebrow. "That's still a good distance."

"Sí. Which is why we must move on from here quickly." The lieutenant's eyes slide across Suzanna's belly and focus on Gerald and Ramón. "I bring news which I believe you will be glad to hear."

"Beaver prices are up," Gerald says, grinning.

The lieutenant gives him a reproachful look.

"Forgive me," Gerald says. "It is a joke."

Anaya waves a hand, brushing the comment aside. "This is news of value to you," he says, a little stiffly now. "That man Jones, he is said to have been seen in Chihuahua."

Suzanna's breath catches as Gerald's eyebrows rise. He exchanges a look with Ramón.

"He was seen in the province of Chihuahua? Or in the city itself?" Ramón asks.

The lieutenant raises his hands, palms up. "I was not informed of the specifics. But I was told that he is there, not in nuevomexico. And certainly not in the Sangre de Cristos or this valley." He turns to Gerald, the stiffness returning to his voice. "It is news I believed you would be glad to hear."

"I am very glad to hear it," Gerald assures him. "It is news of great value to us. I very much appreciate that you stopped to share it with us. Muchas gracias."

The lieutenant's face softens. He gives Gerald a little nod. "Then I will be on my way."

As he turns to remount, Suzanna moves forward impulsively. "Can you wait un momento?" She gestures toward the cabin. "There's something I'd like to send with you."

The lieutenant nods, trying not to look impatient. Suzanna hurries through the cabin into the kitchen, wraps the most recent batch of Ramón's biscuits into a square of unbleached muslin, and carries it outside. The lieutenant's stallion twists impatiently toward the men and horses clustered behind him.

Suzanna lifts the bundle toward the lieutenant. "For your dinner," she says. He gestures toward the nearest solder, who leans down to grab the muslin and sniff appreciatively.

"Muchas gracias," Anaya says. He nods to Ramón and Gerald, then wheels away and canters out of the yard, his men following close behind.

"I hope those biscuits don't fall out of that cloth," Suzanna says. She turns to Ramón. "And I hope you don't mind. He did bring us good news."

"It is well to give him them in exchange for such news." Ramón grins. "And there's little danger of them being lost. That soldier will guard them as if they are his newborn child."

Gerald chuckles. "Though woe betide him if he tries to steal one before the others have a chance at them." Alma squirms on his shoulders and he swings her off and sets her on the ground. She toddles toward the corral with Chaser beside her.

Gerald puts an arm around Suzanna's shoulder. "I would willingly give much more than a batch of biscuits to the man who brings us such news."

"Yes," Suzanna says. "It is good news. I can hardly believe it." A series of sharp jabs dance across her abdomen. "Ouch!" She claps a hand to her waist. "Someone else is celebrating. That's the first time I've felt him kick."

"So it is a boy," Gerald says.

Suzanna laughs. "Until he's born and you discover it was a girl all along!"

At the corral, Chaser suddenly stiffens and turns to stare down at the cornfield. He barks once, then twice, and a coyote slinks from between the rows and into the pasture beyond.

Gerald grins. "That dog is certainly protective, isn't he?" Then he sobers and turns to Suzanna. "I'm glad you had him with you earlier. We saw mountain lion tracks this morning."

"Mountain lion? This close to the cabin?"

"The catamount, they travel far," Ramón says. "This one has discovered there are cattle here. And calves."

Suzanna frowns at him. "But the calves are larger now. Surely they'll be safe enough."

He shrugs. "It is probably so. But mountain lions are not predictable. We will need to watch more closely until this one decides to move on its way."

Chaser is still watching the cornfield. "He's developing quite a ferocious-sounding bark," Suzanna says. "That should help to scare any predator off."

"I certainly hope so," Gerald says. "After all the work we had getting those cattle through the winter, it would be a shame to lose them to a mountain cat."

Suzanna opens her mouth to point out that mountain lions aren't much of a problem for people raising cattle around Don Fernando, then stops herself. It's been a pleasant day. Why spoil it by complaining about things that aren't going to change, anyway?

CHAPTER 37

Enoch Jones kneels in the grass behind the granite outcropping and glasses the cabin on the other side of the valley. The Peabody bitch is in the garden by herself, no gun in sight. The papoose is toddling around in the grass like she's in Taos Plaza on market day with twenty sets of eyes on her. He grunts with satisfaction. The fools have taken the bait.

He eases backward down the slope until he's well out of sight, then straightens and heads to the waiting gelding. He grabs the horse's dangling reins and yanks its head downhill. If he mounts now, he'll be visible from the cabin. Though he'd rather ride than walk. Crawlin' around on the backside of these hills ain't his idea of fun.

His eyes narrow. That bitch'll pay for all the misery he's been through, waitin' for her. And now it's time.

He chuckles. They sure got relaxed after that lieutenant showed up. Bunch of fools. He's outsmarted 'em all. A single sentence in a taberna well south of Taos and they're wanderin' off, not watchin' nothin', like lambs without their mamas.

And now he can move in and finish this thing, before another hellish valley winter sets in. His tongue flicks his lips, anticipating the taste of her. Then he brings himself firmly back to the present and his plans. He's got the poison. And rabbits are easy enough to snare. Now all he needs to do is get himself into position.

At the foot of the ridge he mounts the gelding and heads north through the hills, then drops into the northern valley. He camps

225

that night in a rock-strewn ravine on the western flank of the bare-topped peak. The next morning he moves up the gulch and onto a muddy flat halfway up the mountain.

He reins in the black and studies the flat. Water has drained down the slopes above into a muddy seep edged with willow brush. The ground's soft, but not impassable. Here and there, shallow depressions have trapped liquid that's surprisingly clear. The grass between the puddles is thick and green in spite of the late season. Those damn monsoon rains were good for something, after all. The grass is short, too. Deer or other browsers have been keeping it down.

Jones hauls himself off the gelding, flops belly-down onto the grass beside the largest of the puddles, and plunges his face into the water. The horse reaches past him and Jones grunts impatiently and slaps it away.

When he's had enough, Jones pulls himself up, sits on his haunches, and looks more carefully at the flat. There are tracks in the mud wherever the grass hasn't come up yet. Most of the marks are rabbit: the long ear-shaped indents from their hind legs, the dots like two eyes below them. He grins sardonically. Talk about sign.

The black has moved off to snuffle at a puddle three feet away. Jones' head swivels toward the horse and his smile fades. There's sign there, too, but it ain't rabbit. It's catamount track as wide as his hand. Mountain cat. A big one. And recent.

Jones turns slowly, studying the flat, the willows, the mix of aspen and pine on the slopes above. The mountain lion's not hunting him. It's after game it's sure of. Mule deer and the like.

Or the cattle in that valley farmyard. Jones grins. When he's finished down below, that catamount'll have easy pickins. There'll be no one left to tend those cows. The lion can have 'em all. Man flesh, too.

He grins again. It's all gonna work out just fine. All he needs now is a rabbit, and it looks like there's plenty of those around here. By the time anyone happens by that empty cabin, the catamount will have cleaned up his leavings. He barks a satisfied laugh, gathers up the gelding, and moves off the flat to find a campsite for the night.

The next morning he collects his rabbit, then moves stealthily through the foothills, working south toward the cabin until he's got a good view of the hill directly behind it.

The top of the hill is silent and empty as death. Locke and the greaser have wiped it clean of trees and it's got nothing on it but long, browning grass and a rutted turnaround where the mules have dragged logs into position on the track that angles down toward the cabin.

Jones' nostrils flare and his head turns. There's wood smoke at the cabin site. But not from the chimney. That's an outside fire and a good-size one.

He knees the gelding to the hilltop, then eases it to the backside of the hill and a cluster of tangled scrub oak. Healthy stuff, it's a good thirty feet high. He tethers the horse, lifts his rifle from its saddle scabbard, and slips around the hill to an upthrust slab of sandstone that's well above the cabin and big enough to shadow him.

He angles around the grainy brown rock until he has a clear view of the yard behind the house. There's a fire burning in the middle of the space. A black metal tripod is set up over it and a big cast iron pot hangs from the tripod. A rough wooden table stands between the fire and the stacked firewood in an open-sided shed. The shed's between the backside of the cabin and a kind of ravine that drops down toward the marsh where the Cimarron heads.

227

As he watches, the Peabody bitch comes out the door lugging a basket full of clothing. Chavez follows her with an armload of what looks like bed linens. The brat follows him, trailing a small red-and-gray blanket in the dirt.

The Mex drops the linens onto the table and the woman puts her basket on the ground, turns to the child, grabs its blanket, and says something to the man. He nods, swings the kid onto his shoulders and disappears around the corner of the cabin, toward the barn. The Peabody bitch drops the blanket onto the end of the table and moves to the fire.

Jones stretches upward, trying to see beyond the cabin to the field below. The damned roof is in the way. But there's movement farther out. Locke's doin' something with a cow. Chavez, still carrying the kid, is moving toward him.

Jones chuckles sardonically. The woman's washin' clothes and they're stayin' out of her way. Smarter'n he thought they were. No woman in her right mind likes t' wash clothes. Makes her bitchier than ever.

Nice view though. She's bending over the pot, using a small pan to dip water out of it into a big hollowed-out piece of log that's half full of clothes. She kneels on the dirt beside the trough, leans forward, and scrubs at the clothes with a thick-handled brush. Water splashes up and wets her bodice, outlining her breasts.

Jones' tongue touches his lips. Even that bit of a belly she's got on her looks good from here. Time to start movin'.

But as he pushes away from the sandstone, the dogs show up. Jones moves back into the shadows.

The mutts romp across the yard and tag each other a couple times around the woodpile. The big brown dog and the yellow-spotted one rough house their way closer to the working woman, but the black-spotted mutt heads to the table and starts jumping up and down, trying to grab the kid's blanket.

On his third attempt, the dog knocks the rag into the dirt. He dances around it for a minute, then grabs one end in his teeth and shakes it wildly. The big dog turns, dives in, and catches the other end of the blanket in his mouth. The spotted dog pulls away, circling as he goes, and backs right into Suzanna's rear end.

She jerks around, drops the shirt she's been scrubbing, and heaves herself to her feet. "Tarnation!" she yells. "Give me that!"

Jones chuckles. He does like a nice-riled woman.

She puts her hands on her hips. "Chaser!" she yells. "Drop it!" The big dog stops like she's shot him. He releases the rag and turns toward her, muzzle and tail drooping.

She shakes her head and turns to say something to the spotted dog. He drops the blanket, then lays down on it and lifts his head beseechingly.

She shoves the dog's belly with her foot, grabs the blanket, tosses it onto the table, then turns to glare at the two dogs. She puts her hands on her hips, twists toward the outhouse at the north end of the cabin, and yells something. The yellow-spotted dog slinks into view and nuzzles the woman's skirt. She scowls at it, then turns and marches down the hill toward the barn, waving the dogs after her. They follow reluctantly.

When she comes back, she's alone. Jones grins. She's locked them up. He ain't gonna need the rabbit he's got lashed to the gelding's saddle. And he can make his move now, not have to wait. His tongue flicks against his lips again as the woman below returns to her work.

But then she heaves herself to her feet and disappears into the cabin. When she comes back, she's wearing a calico apron with pockets that drag like she's put rocks in them, and she's carrying a shotgun. She leans it against the chopping block at the end of the woodshed.

Jones' smile fades. Then he shrugs. Won't do her much good. Women never can shoot worth a hog's turd. The gun's too heavy and they're scared of the kick.

His thumb caresses his rifle stock as he studies the layout below. The outhouse has some good-length grass around it, but not enough to cover a man his size. But that grass-sided arroyo that cuts between the cabin hill and the one he's on comes in nice and tight behind the woodshed.

He eyes the hill he's on. If he moves back a mite, he can angle down through the trees, out of sight of the cabin. Then he can work around the base of the hill and slip up the arroyo to the shed. Those stacks of firewood'll give him enough cover.

He grins. Won't she be surprised, what with him bein' in Chihuahua and all?

He raises up and looks at the valley again. The men are still there, the brat now on Locke's shoulders. Jones' lip curls. Tendin' kids is women's work. He pushes away from the sandstone slab and moves back and down the slope, toward the marsh.

As Jones reaches the bottom of the hill, a mountain cat eases through the grass at its top. Behind the tangle of oak, the gelding catches its scent and stiffens, ears up.

But the lion doesn't pick up the horse's scent. She slinks down the hill. She's well camouflaged. The autumn-brown grass, the sun-dried clay soil, and the chunks of tan sandstone scattered across the slope are all as tawny-gold as she is. From a distance, the big cat is merely a shadow from a passing cloud.

As the mountain lion moves forward, Jones edges along the base of the hill to the ravine. At its mouth, he stops and studies the rise to the woodshed. It's almost straight up, steeper than it looked from above.

But it's studded with chunks of rock large enough for a big man's foot. In fact, they almost create a stairway to the top. He grasps his rifle with both hands, flat across his chest, licks his lips, and begins climbing.

He's breathing hard by the time he reaches the top. The damn slope is steeper than it looked. He drops behind the nearest stack of wood and forces his breath through his nose, quieter. Even in the hands of a woman, a shotgun can do serious damage.

But he can hear water splashing in the wooden trough, the rasp of a scrub brush on heavy work clothes. She hasn't heard him.

Jones' hands move over his rifle, checking its load. Then he loosens the knife at his belt. That's the way he really wants it. Same as he used on that Mexican bitch. Two of a kind, should get the same treatment. Too bad he won't get to play with her while her men watch. But he'll be sure to tell 'em what he's done to her.

He grins. That'll be a pleasure in itself, wiping that smug Locke's face clean of its self-righteousness. An inadvertent growl escapes his lips. He stops it just in time.

But there's no sign from the woman. Just the crackle of the fire, the water sloshing, the scrape of her brush against heavy work clothes. He pushes himself from the ground and carefully crabwalks his way forward between the rows of piled firewood.

When he reaches the stack closest to the fire, he settles on his haunches and studies the top row of logs. Whoever stacked them left the most misbegotten pieces on top. The nearest one is Y-shaped and twisted around like a piece of taffy. A thick broken-off branch below the Y sticks straight into the air. Good cover for the top part of a man's head. Jones eases upward and peers through the Y toward the fire.

He's just in time for the show. Suzanna Peabody pushes herself to her feet, stretches her arms toward the sky, and twists her shoulders, easing out the kinks. Jones licks his lips.

231

Then she suddenly drops her hands and half-turns toward the outhouse. "That's odd," she says. She turns abruptly and moves toward the woodshed.

Jones ducks out of sight just in time, then eases up again, just enough to see.

Suzanna lifts the shotgun from the chopping block and carries it to the table. She props the gun against the end closest to the fire, then chuckles and leans forward to grab the baby's blanket. "You're next," she says, smiling.

And then there's a snarling growl behind her and the smile is dropping from her face and she's grabbing the shotgun, leveling as she turns. The gun roars and buckshot slams the outhouse door, tearing into the wood.

The gun roars again and she's scrabbling at her apron pockets for more ammunition. Jones can hear her breath, sharp and ragged and scared.

In the field below, a man yells a question. The dogs in the barn howl in terror and one of them bays furiously. Suzanna's hand comes empty out of the apron and she moves backward toward the woodshed, her breath hard and gasping. She clutches the shotgun against her heaving wet breasts.

Jones stretches to see more clearly and reaches to brace himself on the woodpile. A chunk of ponderosa slips out from under his hand and hits the ground with a thud.

Suzanna stiffens and whirls, shotgun ready, eyes wide with terror, but steely just the same, her hand reaching for her apron pocket again.

As Jones drops into a low crouch, Gerald rounds the corner of the cabin, rifle barrel ready for action.

Suzanna whirls toward him, then gasps with relief and drops the shotgun next to the chopping block. She covers her face with her hands.

Gerald stops where he is, turning slowly, rifle steady, taking in the battered outhouse door, the fire, the table. And what lies between them. "By God!" he says.

A six-foot-long blood-stained mountain lion is stretched in the dirt, its mouth open in a silent snarl, its chest torn with buckshot.

Suzanna drops onto the chopping block and puts her hands to her stomach. "I think I'm going to be sick."

CHAPTER 38

It's over a month before Suzanna recovers from the shock of what she's done. She isn't sure if she should be proud of her shooting ability or not. She wants to be, but she doubts she could repeat those shots, those moments of sheer instinct. She's just grateful she had the gun close. And that she heard the big cat.

Of course, if the dogs hadn't been locked up in the barn, the beast wouldn't have prowled as close as it did. She shudders and goes about her business, but the shotgun stays a little closer to hand than it has in the past, even when the dogs are nearby.

Gerald and Ramón gut the cat and tack up its skin in the barn to dry. The chest section is pretty torn up from the shotgun pellets, but Gerald says the rest of it might be useful for something. A small rug, perhaps.

"You can put it on the floor on your side of the bed," he suggests one morning as they're getting dressed. "A symbol of your prowess."

She pushes her hair away from her face and gives him a bemused look. "As an example of how I can tread on my enemies?"

He grins at her. "Just don't tread on me."

She sighs. "You're not my enemy. I just get frustrated sometimes."

He crosses the loft and leans to kiss her cheek. "I was just joking."

As she opens her mouth to answer him, the baby jabs her ribs. "Ouch!" she says. She rubs her side. "This one doesn't kick often, but when he does, I can certainly feel it."

"Quiet but opinionated, like his Daddy."

She glances up at him. "You certainly are in a silly mood this morning."

"Maybe it's because we're about to have company."

"Hmmm?" She pulls a clean chemise over her head.

"It's been six weeks since Little Squirrel came through with news of the fair."

"News of what fair?" She crosses to the clothes chest and picks up her hairbrush.

"You were so preoccupied with laundry and then the mountain cat that you've forgotten," Gerald says. "Stands Alone and his band arranged with the Taos Indians and a band of Sioux to hold another trade fair here in the valley. And they set it for right about now."

She runs the brush through her hair. "I don't remember anything about it. When is this supposed to happen?"

"Little Squirrel said it was set for mid-September. When the moon is just past full."

"So any day now." Suzanna frowns. "I wish you'd reminded me earlier. Are we going to have enough food?"

"They'll bring some and Ramón says he has plenty of flour. The question is whether you want to harvest anything for trade."

"I wonder if anyone will bring pumpkin seed. I'd like to try growing it here."

He chuckles. "You and your seed." He turns away as he buttons his trousers. "We may get Kiowa and Pawnee, as well."

Her hand stops in mid-brush. "Pawnee!"

He shrugs and turns back to her. "Probably not. They weren't invited, as far as I know. But it's always possible that they'll show up anyway."

She begins twisting her hair into its usual knot at the base of her neck. "I hope not, or you're going to be mighty busy trying to keep the peace."

"Oh, that'll be Stands Alone's task," Gerald says easily. "He's the one who invited them all."

When the Indian bands begin riding in a few days later, there doesn't seem to be any need for peacekeeping. The Sioux arrive first, look uneasily at the cabin and its outbuildings, then pitch their long-poled lodges well into the valley, alongside a stream that flows from the western slopes.

Then Stands Alone and his band show up. Many Eagles is with them. His eyes narrow at the sight of the cattle Ramón and Gerald have pulled through the winter, and he sneers openly at the fields of carefully stacked meadow hay.

Finally, the Taos Pueblo Indians arrive. It's almost as if they've waited until everyone else is present before deciding whether to risk carrying their fired earthenware pots across the mountains to the fair.

Stands Alone hosts a feast the night after the Taoseños come in — a fresh mule deer and corn from the fields his people cultivate on the edge of the eastern plains. Suzanna offers garlic and fat onions to cook with the corn and Sings Quietly accepts them with a smile. "It's all I have to share," Suzanna tells Stands Alone apologetically. She waves her hand at her cornfield. "Our corn is still green."

He smiles noncommittally.

"I know," she says. "You told me they wouldn't grow." She looks ruefully at her plot, green and bright in the sunlight. "But they certainly look healthy." She gives him a small smile. "And

236

the dogs have been helpful in keeping the raccoons and the deer and elk out."

"They help the big dog."

Suzanna grins. "The big dog has a big bark, at any rate. Now that he's grown so large." She nods toward Little Squirrel, who's approaching his father from behind. "And this one has also grown larger."

Little Squirrel smiles at her as he reaches his father's side. He's almost as tall as Stands Alone and his shoulders have broadened over the last year. His smile has changed too. It's more confident, somehow. His adolescent shyness has been replaced by an almost insolent confidence. Some girl must have told him he's handsome and he's believed her wholeheartedly.

Suzanna looks at Stands Alone, who gives her a small knowing smile.

Little Squirrel turns to his father and jerks his chin toward the western mountains. "The Sioux will arrive for the feast as the sun drops."

"It is well," Stands Alone says.

"The women will come dancing," the boy adds.

There's something about the way he says it that pulls Suzanna's attention. Is the girl who's told him he's good-looking among the band of Sioux? She glances at Stands Alone, but he's looking at Little Squirrel. The Ute leader nods impassively.

Suzanna turns toward Stands Alone's lodge. Little Squirrel's mother is at the cook fire, watching her son. She glances at Suzanna and the two women exchange bemused looks. Sings Quietly shrugs slightly and goes back to her work.

She's still looking bemused that evening when Suzanna slips beside her into the watching circle around the hard-packed dancing space. The Sioux women are already performing. Sings Quietly taps her fingers against her thighs, in time to the drums and the soft thump of mocassined feet. The dancers' multi-faceted colored beads and silver jewelry flash in the firelight as they circle the flames and each other in intricate patterns.

Suzanna turns her head, looking for Little Squirrel. The direction of his gaze will satisfy her curiosity about the girl he's interested in. Then she glimpses Gerald, deep in conversation with a man who doesn't look either Sioux or Ute. His front hair is swept up in an impossible stiff pompadour.

Gerald turns, catches her eye, and gestures her to join them. Suzanna pats Sings Quietly on the arm and nods toward her husband. The other woman smiles and nods companionably, then turns back to the dancers.

When Suzanna reaches Gerald, he draws her hand through his arm. "I find that I have an old friend in the Sioux camp," he tells her. "Some Kiowa are travelling with them." He half-turns toward the young warrior on his other side. "This is He Who Sees. I met him on my way out to New Mexico, shortly after I joined Ewing Young's merchant train."

The other man gives him a small smile. "You did not know my name then."

"Ah, but I remember you." The two men share a conspiratorial glance. "I wondered what became of you."

"And the cross one?" He Who Sees asks. "The one who wanted to shoot me? Do you know what became of him?"

Suzanna gives Gerald a quizzical look.

He holds out his other hand, his palm at chest height. "He Who Sees was just a boy then, perhaps this tall, and mischievous as most boys are."

"And almost killed for my mischief," the Kiowa man says.

Suzanna raises an eyebrow at Gerald.

"He tried to get into the liquor wagon, but Jones caught him."

"Ah," she says.

"Your man saw we were harmless," He Who Sees says.

"And intervened." Suzanna smiles at Gerald. "It wasn't the last time he came between Enoch Jones and his baser instincts." She looks at the warrior, his muscular bare chest glinting in the firelight. "And now you have no need of intervention."

"Now I will soon have sons of my own to keep from harm." He Who Sees gestures proudly toward the dancing women. "That one in the white buckskin and the purple beads. She is mine. We are newly wed."

Suzanna studies the girl. "She is very pretty." The girl's head has the tilt of an attractive fifteen-year-old in love with life. The other women are starting to flag, but she looks as if she could dance until sunrise. She flashes her husband a brilliant smile as she turns.

Suzanna's eyes follow her, then move to the other side of the watching circle. Little Squirrel's eyes are also on the girl. But his gaze isn't the polite attention of a mere observer. The light in his eyes is more intense than is entirely appropriate for a young man watching a girl who's married to another man.

CHAPTER 39

Even though they don't speak each other's language, Suzanna finds herself looking for reasons to visit Sings Quietly's cooking fire, whether to offer garlic for the pot or to gesture a request for beading instruction. The older woman has a quiet strength that's somehow restful. And a mutual language isn't necessary to demonstrate knowledge about moccasin construction or beading designs.

Suzanna is moving through the camp from a mute conversation with Sings Quietly about decorative flower designs when she glimpses Little Squirrel, crouched behind a Sioux tepee. A flap in the hide cover has been pinned up to allow air to circulate into the lodge. The boy leans toward the opening, his head tilted beseechingly to one side. Suzanna pauses to watch him.

"Please come out," she hears him say. "I just want to talk with you."

A woman's voice answers. Suzanna leans forward, then catches herself. It's none of her business. She turns away and takes a step forward, right into He Who See's bare chest.

"Oh!" she says. "Excuse me! I didn't see—"

But he pays her no attention. His gaze is fixed on the lodge, where Little Squirrel is still crouched, oblivious to anything but the woman inside. "You there!" the Kiowa man barks.

The younger man jumps up, his face moving from startled to innocent by the time he's on his feet. "I was just looking for my knife." He looks at the ground and turns in a half-circle. "I dropped it last night."

He Who Sees' nostrils flare. "You were here last night? By my lodge?"

"No! Not here! Near here!" Little Squirrel waves a hand at the encampment in general. "I search wherever I go—" He stops, seeing the trap he's made for himself. Suzanna almost feels sorry for him.

He Who Sees scowls. "And you speak to the ground as you search?"

"No! I—"

The Kiowa moves forward, looming over the boy. "You keep away from my lodge and my woman."

Little Squirrel glances past him to Suzanna. His chin lifts. "I go where I please."

He Who Sees' hands clench, then loosen. "I will honor the peace of this fair because I have promised it. But if I see you near my lodge again before the market has ended, I will follow you as you return to the hills. It will be well to watch for my coming."

Little Squirrel puffs out his chest. "I will watch and we will see who is the stronger man."

Suzanna catches her breath but He Who Sees only smiles disdainfully. "You are a boy," he says as he turns away. "You know nothing."

He turns and brushes past Suzanna toward the front of the tepee, but Little Squirrel follows him. "It is you who know nothing!" he cries. He grabs the Kiowa's upper arm and Suzanna moves hurriedly out of the way. At the same moment, He Who Sees' young wife stoops out the teepee door and straightens. Her face is a curious mixture of fear and excitement.

Suzanna's lips tighten. The girl is a fool. She turns toward the men.

He Who Sees is staring into Little Squirrel's eyes, a combination of disgust and pity on his face. Then he pushes the boy's hand from his arm and moves away. Little Squirrel's head jerks back, his eye flashing. Then he throws himself onto the warrior's broad back. A knife blade glints in the sun.

"No!" Suzanna screams.

He Who Sees' shoulders twist once, then twice, and Little Squirrel is on the ground and the Kiowa is kneeling above him, one hand on the boy's chest, the other reaching for his own knife.

"No!" Suzanna screams again. Stands Alone materializes beside her and Gerald appears at the edge of the tepee behind He Who Sees.

As Gerald and Stands Alone move simultaneously toward the combatants, He Who Sees growls, "As you like," releases Little Squirrel, and bounces back onto his heels, moving into fighting position. His steel blade glitters in the sun.

The boy scrambles up to face him, his own knife at the ready.

"It is enough!" Stands Alone snaps.

As Little Squirrel glances at his father, He Who Sees lunges, taking advantage of the distraction. But then Gerald is there, thrusting his open palm under and up against the Kiowa's arm, throwing him off balance.

He Who Sees whirls, threatening Gerald with his blade.

Suzanna opens her mouth to scream again, but her throat is too dry to do more than croak a warning.

Gerald pulls away, straightens, and lifts his empty hands toward the Kiowa warrior, palms out. "I seek peace."

He Who Sees hesitates, nods, looks at Little Squirrel contemptuously, then sheaths his knife. "I also am for peace." He jerks his chin toward the boy. "That one seeks to disturb the peace of my lodge."

Suzanna glances at He Who Sees' wife, who's still beside the tent. Although her eyes are demurely on the ground, a smile plays on her lips.

Little Squirrel opens his mouth, but his father raises his hand. "My son is young," he says. "And foolish. We will speak again of this matter."

He Who Sees nods. He glances at the girl. "At the council fire tonight," he agrees. "And let there be restitution." He jerks his chin at Little Squirrel again. "Let him prove himself a man."

As the Kiowa turns abruptly away, Little Squirrel surges toward him, but Stands Alone clamps a hand on the boy's arm, restraining him.

Little Squirrel pulls away. "I am man enough!" he spits. But when his father moves toward the Ute encampment, the boy follows.

At the council fire that night, Suzanna sits with the other women outside the circle of men. She's helped serve the food and now waits beside Sings Quietly to learn how the altercation between the young Ute man and the Kiowa warrior will be addressed. The girl at the center of the dispute isn't present.

The men seem to have a specific smoking ritual for this type of dispute. Each man puffs solemnly, then moves it in some predetermined pattern she doesn't understand before passing it to the next man. The ritual seems to be more important than the conflict they're meeting to resolve. Suzanna moves impatiently. Her legs are beginning to cramp.

Then an intricately-carved speaking stick is passed around the circle until it reaches Gerald. He begins to speak, the piece of wood held lightly between his brown hands. He matter-of-factly describes the altercation outside the lodge without naming the young woman involved, then passes the speaking stick to Stands Alone.

Stands Alone tilts his head toward Little Squirrel, who sits beside him, but his eyes are on He Who Sees, on the opposite side of the fire. "My son has acted foolishly," the Ute leader says. "The horse he has raised from a colt is now that of He Who Sees."

He Who Sees grunts.

"And five bushels of corn."

There's a long silence, then He Who Sees grunts again.

"It is the act of a boy," Stands Alone says.

He Who Sees holds out his hand and the speaking stick is handed around the circle until it reaches him. "I accept this small offering because what has occurred is indeed the act of a boy," he says stiffly. Then his tone sharpens and his eyes glitter. "But if he approaches my lodging again, that will be the act of a man. And then there will be no peace. No recompense will be sufficient for such an insult."

Stands Alone gazes at him impassively for a long moment, then nods. "Let it be so."

Suzanna breaths a sigh of relief and the gathering disperses.

But conflict still haunts the fair.

Early the next evening, Suzanna is carrying a small basket of round green-and-white striped squash through the camp when she hears Stands Alone's voice bellow, "Enough!"

She stops in mid-step, then slips through the maze of hide-covered lodges toward the sound.

A cluster of Ute men stand around a fire. The sun is beginning to set and a slight chill has set in. The men are wrapped in Navajo blankets newly traded with the Taoseños.

Suzanna pauses in the shadow of one of the larger lodges. Another woman is already there. She turns toward Suzanna. It's Stands Alone's wife. Sings Quietly nods at Suzanna conspiratorially and cocks her head toward the men.

Suzanna edges closer. As the two women watch, Many Eagles adjusts his blanket. His thin face sharp as a hatchet in the firelight. "It is not right that an americano should speak for us to settle our quarrels," he says in Spanish. He scowls at Stands Alone. "He is not of our blood."

"He speaks with a clean heart."

"He is not of our blood."

Stands Alone's chin jerks toward the eastern mountains. "Those that are coming on this trail of the Santa Fe, they will listen to him."

"He takes our land."

"The land is not ours to give or be taken."

Many Eagles moves impatiently. "You speak as one who does not hear. The americanos are coming. They believe all is theirs for the taking. He is one of them."

"The americanos here are few," Stands Alone says. "It is los mexicanos who rule this land, as los españoles ruled it before them."

Someone else speaks up. "For now it is so. But in each season of travel more come from the land called Missouri in the country of Los Estados Unidos."

Stands Alone nods. "It is so. And as they come, our people will need those who can speak to them for us. Men of clean hearts."

"It is of no importance whether his heart is clean," Many Eagles says. "Men of unclean hearts come after him."

Stands Alone looks at him impassively.

"The man who attacked my sister, the daughter of Little Bear, is here in these mountains for this man of a clean heart," Many Eagles says bitterly. "The americanos bring more of themselves everywhere they go."

Suzanna shrinks back into the shadows. Yes, it was undoubtedly Jones who attacked the woman in Stands Alone's camp. Who else would it have been? But Jones is gone now, gone to Chihua-hua. She takes a step toward the men, to explain that Many Eagles' sister and the other women have little to fear. Jones is gone.

But as Suzanna moves forward, Sings Quietly touches her arm and shakes her head. Suzanna turns and gives her a quizzical look, but Sings Quietly only twists her mouth sympathetically and again shakes her head.

Suzanna nods reluctantly. These men won't appreciate a woman's interruption. And she has no way of knowing for certain that Jones is actually gone and won't return. Only Lieutenant Anaya's word.

But surely he's right. Why would Jones haunt this valley, above all others? Besides, he couldn't stay up here forever. He'd need to resupply and to find ways to pay for those supplies. Surely, even if he was up here, he's long ago given up haunting them. Surely what the lieutenant told them was based on more than mere rumor.

CHAPTER 40

But after the Sioux, Taoseños, and Utes have all left the valley, Suzanna has little time for dwelling on Jones' possible whereabouts. By mid-October, all she can think about is her growing physical discomfort. Her expanding belly seems to get in the way no matter what she's trying to do. Every move is awkward and tiring.

But she refuses to give up. Especially on the corn. Some of the smaller ears actually ripen in the lingering autumn warmth and Suzanna harvests them jubilantly. Then the nights turn frosty, and it's time to gather what remains, no matter how green it is. She grimaces and gets to work, snapping the ears off the drying brown stalks and dropping them with a thud into the wicker basket, which she drags after her down the dusty rows.

When the basket is filled, she bends to carry it to the house. But she can't lift it. It's too heavy and bulky to lift past her protruding belly. Suzanna straightens, put her hands on her hips, then shrugs. She'll just have to pull it and hope the corn piled on top doesn't spill out.

She tugs on the wicker handle. It lifts perhaps an inch. The corn is heavier than she expected. She yanks at the basket again and it lifts off the dirt, but when she tries to pull it down the row, it won't budge.

She huffs in disgust and drops the handle. The basket thuds as it hits the ground, then tilts to one side. Three ears of green corn roll out and the ones beneath them shift dangerously. As Suzanna grabs to stop them all from falling, Chaser runs up behind her. "Woof!" he barks happily.

Suzanna jerks in surprise and the basket tilts even farther. She reaches for the handle at the same moment the mastiff shoves his head under her arm. Suzanna, dog, basket, and corn all tumble into the dirt.

The ears of corn are scattered everywhere. Chaser extricates himself and backs away, big brown eyes anxious.

"You should be worried!" Suzanna snaps. She twists awkwardly to one side, flattens her palms on the ground, and leverages herself onto her knees. She kneels in the dirt, stretches to retrieve the spilled corn, and scowls at the dog. "And just how am I supposed to get back into a standing position with this belly in my way?" she demands.

The dog sits back on his haunches and barks happily at her again.

She gives him a dark look and reaches for more ears of corn. "First, they're green and now they're dirty." She turns an ear upside down and shakes it. Dirt scatters from the long green leaves that protect the kernels inside. Not that there's any way to tell if all the dirt has fallen out. This batch is going to have to be husked sooner than she's expected.

She glowers at Chaser, who's now watching her anxiously. As she returns the last of the corn to her basket, Ramón appears at the end of the row. Alma toddles behind him.

"I heard the dog," he says.

"He knocked me and the basket of corn over," Suzanna says. "I've picked up most of it." She peers between the stalks beside her. "There's a few in the next row, out of reach."

He moves into the row beyond, scoops up the scattered ears, and then comes around to drop them on top of the basket.

"The larger problem is that I'm not sure I can stand up by myself," Suzanna says.

Ramón looks at her in alarm.

"I'm not hurt." She gestures at her belly. "But my balance is off. I can't get up on my own."

He chuckles, holds out a weathered hand, and pulls her to her feet. He eyes the basket. "How did you carry this through the field?"

She laughs ruefully. "I dragged it by the handle. But now I can't lift it."

He bends and effortlessly lifts the corn to his right shoulder.

"You make it look so easy," Suzanna says.

He grins at her. "As easy as it is for a dog to bark."

She scowls at Chaser again. "His barking is what startled me and made me fall."

"But also what drew my attention."

"True," she says begrudgingly. She turns to Alma, whose tiny form is shadowed by the rustling stalks of corn, and holds out her hand. "Let's try to keep you away from the woofing dog. He's in a very mischievous mood today."

Chaser is feeling even more mischievous two weeks later, when Suzanna begins chopping down the dead cornstalks. They've dried rapidly in the cool weather and will make excellent kindling. And she needs the exercise.

Chaser, Dos, and Uno run happily over the downed woody stalks and grab gleefully at the rustling leaves of the plants that are still standing. In their excitement, they're oblivious to Suzanna and her machete. When they begin playing tug-of-war with a piece of stalk she's just cut, Suzanna chases them from the field. "Go!" she yells. "Get out of here!"

They dash off, crashing indiscriminately through the cornstalks and barking wildly.

Stupid animals. She rubs her chest with her left hand. Everything seems to ache these days. Or maybe it's just that the baby is riding so high and cutting off her ability to breathe deeply. She takes a careful breath, consciously slowing the process to force air farther into her lungs, and drops her hand to her protruding belly. The child sits so high and so forward. Does that mean it will be a girl or a boy? Encarnación would know.

Suzanna closes her eyes against the thought. How she misses Chonita, who would have either been out here chopping beside her, or bringing her hot tea and white rolls and telling her it could all wait until spring.

Suzanna turns, looking at what she's done so far and what's left. Actually, it probably can wait until spring. But, even though everything aches these days, the chopping actually feels good. A kind of mental release from thinking about what's ahead. She's in no hurry for the enforced lack of activity that winter will bring.

She swings the machete gently back and forth, testing the strength of her right arm and wrist. They aren't really tired. Though her back aches from bending forward. An ache she's never noticed in the past. Pregnancy certainly has its disadvantages.

She studies the field of half-cut stalks. She's chopped about a third of it. She glances toward the hay pasture, where the men are rushing to get one last round of bedding cut and barned before it snows. They certainly don't have time to help her chop the rest of the stalks or to do it for her.

Suzanna taps the tip of the machete blade against her boot. Does the patch truly need to be leveled? What she's done so far will supply a good deal of kindling. Besides, the cornstalks aren't critical to the coming winter fires. The men can always hatchet smaller pieces from the logs they've already split. In fact, they seem to like that sort of chore. It gives them something to do.

Yet she feels guilty about not finishing what she's begun. And the activity does feel good. In her shoulders, at least. Not the small of her back. She grimaces a little and rubs the sore spot at the base of her spine.

A raven settles noisily on the top of a stalk on the other side of the field and gives Suzanna a wary look, then turns its head. "Woof!" it says. It's a deep sound, clearly mimicking a mastiff's bark.

Suzanna's mouth opens in surprise, then she laughs in delight. "You've been listening to Chaser!"

The raven jerks his beak at her and lifts away from the corn, its wings rustling. When Suzanna laughs again, the baby kicks into her lower rib cage, cutting her amusement off sharply.

She gasps at the pain and waits it out, then raises the machete in a helpless gesture. "All right, I give up. I'll leave it. I'm sure it will all still be here come spring."

She turns and trudges up the hill, her body suddenly slack with exhaustion. But it's not a good kind of exhaustion. It's sheer discouragement. She might as well accept the fact that winter is coming, and that she'll be confined once again to the dim cabin and the limitations of late pregnancy. There's nothing to be done about any of it. As she moves up the path, her mouth twists bitterly at the thought of Ewing Young and the price of furs.

CHAPTER 41

Enoch Jones is on his belly pulling himself up the rocky foot-hill on the western edge of the valley, grunting as he goes. With the grass withering in the fall chill, the stones seem harder than usual.

Finally, he eases into position in the hollow spot just below the hilltop, props himself on his elbows, and pulls out the battered spyglass.

The bitch is alone again, this time in the cornfield. There's no shotgun in sight. He grins. And that machete sure ain't gonna save her.

He can just see her head and shoulders as she half-bends, then straightens and moves forward as another cornstalk drops behind her. "Choppin' stalks," he mutters. "Fool thing t' do. They're gonna rot just the same."

A raven lands on the far edge of the field and caws at the wom-an. Jones grunts in sympathy. "You tell her. Fool women are al-ways cleanin', instead of takin' care of their men." Then he grins. "But I'll teach her what to take care of."

Then she moves into an already-cleared section of the patch and he can see more than just her head. His grin drops from his face. "Big as one of those damn cows. Bigger." Bile rises into his throat. He lowers the spyglass, then raises it again and studies her belly. "Must be half a dozen brats in there. What's she gonna do, have two for each man?"

He snorts at his own humor. "Get her now, I could add a couple more and she'd burst at the seams when they all pop!" Then his lips curl. "Serves her right, the way she's been spreadin' her legs. That nigger and the greaser and then that Injun chief." He snorts. "Probably the Mex lieutenant too."

He moves the glass from his eye, pulls a dirty handkerchief from a pocket, and polishes the lens. She's big as a house. But she don't have the shotgun with her in that field. And a machete ain't a real weapon.

The dogs ain't around neither. Not that they're any damn use. 'Specially that big one. Over-grown pup.

He lifts the glass again and trains it on the men in the hay meadow. It's late to be bringing in grass. Stuff's nothing but seed by now. Even he can see that and he's never been weak-minded enough to try farmin'.

He remains in position an hour or more, watching the two men fork dry grass into the wagon, then hitch up the mules and move the hay to the barn. There's not gonna be any elk feed left in the valley by the time them two are done. That'll sure turn the Injuns against 'em.

He pictures red-painted warriors circling, the cabin burning, flames exploding in the barn as sparks find the hay, mules screaming in terror, the men running, spinning with the impact of Ute bullets in their backs. His tongue flicks across his lips. Redskins'll do his work for him.

And take the woman for themselves. A fist of anger burns in his chest. He saw the little bitch first. She'd of been his years ago if it weren't for that bastard she married.

He scowls and moves the spyglass back to the cornfield. She's still there, standing in the middle of the patch, machete in one hand, rubbing her back with the other, pushin' that belly out like she's proud of what she did to get like that.

A low growl rolls from his chest. Filthy bitch. He'll teach her to open her legs to anyone who comes along. Anyone but him.

Her head turns and she seems to be looking straight at the hilltop he's hidden behind. He flattens and drops down the slope. Then he rolls onto his back and stares unseeing at an eagle circling overhead. Gonna have to wait 'til spring now. There'll be no fun in takin' her when she's full of another man's spawn, even Locke's.

He slams his palm into the dirt, smashing the brittle grass into dust. He'd pulled back, thinking it'd give them all time to forget they might of seen him, get that damn Williams' stories and that Ute's tales out of their heads. Let the lieutenant's rumors do their work. Figured she'd be all relaxed-like by now. Ripe for the pickin', convinced he wasn't anywhere near.

He snorts in disgust. She's ripe all right. Riper in a way he doesn't even wanta think about. When he watched her scrubbing those clothes, he could see she'd gained a bit 'round the waist. Didn't figure she'd be fattenin' with a child though. Ain't she nursing the other brat? Don't she know anything? And now he'll have to wait 'til she's clear of this one.

His jaw tightens. When he finally gets hold of her, she's gonna be sorry she's put him to so much trouble, made him wait so long. By God, is she gonna be sorry.

CHAPTER 42

In spite of her increasing girth and therefore her inability to do much of anything, Suzanna feels remarkably cheerful as Christmas approaches. For one thing, it's been a relatively dry, though cold, winter. She's still able to get out and about without worrying about slipping on the ice.

And she has her father's visit to look forward to. He's sent word via a passing merchant that he'll arrive a few days before Christmas. Suzanna busies herself creating gifts and organizing the cabin to accommodate another person.

When he does ride in, Jeremiah slips easily into the valley routine, waking early from his pallet by the fireplace to help the men with the barn chores, then returning to the cabin to sit by the fire and read.

When Suzanna fumbles her bulky way down the ladder from the loft two mornings after he arrives, that's where she finds him. She smiles sleepily and crosses the room to kiss the top of his graying head. "It's like old times," she says. She frowns at the fire. "Is there enough light for you? You could have lit the lamp."

"I didn't want to wake you." He nods at her belly. "That one will keep you awake sufficiently, once it's been born."

She chuckles. "It's already keeping me awake." She waddles across the room, sinks into her chair, and pats the top of her belly. "If a large baby is a healthy one, then this will be a healthy child."

He smiles affectionately. "You look so maternal."

255

Ramón comes into the room, leading Alma by the hand. "There she is!" he says. "Go to mama!"

Suzanna turns her head. "Has she been in the way?"

"I helped!" Alma says proudly.

Suzanna raises an eyebrow. "She helped?"

"She cut out two biscuits and helped to wipe off the counter." Ramón gestures toward Alma's dress. "As you can see."

Suzanna looks at Alma. Her bodice and skirt are spotted with flour and damp. "I need to make you some pinafores," Suzanna says. "Go stand by the fire and dry yourself."

Alma gives her mother a brilliant smile, scampers to the fire, turns herself twice, then heads to her grandfather. She raises her arms beseechingly and tilts her head back. "I want up!"

Jeremiah Peabody laughs, puts his book aside, and pulls her into his lap.

Suzanna shakes her head and looks ruefully at Ramón. "Now you can see why I'm so spoiled," she says. "That's how I was also taught to obey."

Ramón grins. "I remember."

"I was stricter with you," Jeremiah tells Suzanna. He looks down at Alma. "However, grandfathers have a special dispensation."

"Play horsy?" Alma pleads.

He chuckles and begins jiggling her on his knee. A minute later, Gerald opens the outer door, bringing in the cold, and Jeremiah transfers Alma to his other knee, out of the draft.

"Now tell us all of the news from Don Fernando," Suzanna commands her father as Gerald takes off his wraps.

"Well, now," Jeremiah says. "Where shall I start? The merchants are all doing well, for the most part. Even with the lower prices for furs, there seems to be no shortage of money to spend. Like sensible men, Ceran St. Vrain and Charles Bent are catering to the women and have done nicely with the new calicos. Old Bill Williams is off to the South Platte this season, but you probably knew that." He looks at Gerald, who's moved to the fire, and the other man nods.

"And William Wolfskill's headed to your old stomping grounds to hunt beaver with a good thirty or more men," the older man continues. "Or at least that's where he said he was going. Rumor has it that he's actually headed to California."

"What in heaven's name is in California?" Suzanna asks.

Her father shrugs. "Horses, from what I understand. Horses and mules. There's also a market for woven goods. Some of the weavers in Taos and Chimayo are taking blankets there and returning with animals to sell here and in Missouri."

"New Mexico is becoming quite the international trade zone," Gerald says. He glances at Ramón. "We'll have to think about that."

"What other news?" Suzanna asks.

Jeremiah bounces Alma on his knee. "Hmmm. What else? St. Vrain's still talking about moving to Mora. He's steadily accumulating the silver he'll need to build himself the most stylish house in the valley." He shakes his head. "That man certainly likes his luxuries. He's been stockpiling glass windowpanes so the place will be bright and sunny year-round."

He glances down at Alma, who's suddenly twisting away from him. "Would you like to get down? There you go!" He lifts her off his knee and looks at Suzanna. "The Bents have devised a new system for bringing in the glass so it won't break. They're padding each pane with newspapers and then nesting them in sawdust or wood chips. That's a real benefit to me and Padre Martínez. There are now plenty of newspapers to choose from." He chuckles. "Although we're still required to pay for our news, even when the print's somewhat marred from rubbing against the freight it's been protecting."

"I hope Bent's giving you a discount to compensate you for the missing information," Gerald says.

Jeremiah chuckles. "He provides a slight reduction. I suspect he's making the Padre pay more than I do."

Ramón grins. "The Padre has the income. He can afford to pay."

Jeremiah nods. "That's quite true. Although it's an unusual way of doing business, this charging according to the customer's means."

A shadow crosses Ramón's face. "I don't believe Señor Bent weighs the means of his customers. His prices are based on other measures."

Suzanna frowns. "Do you mean that he charges as much as he can regardless of the customer's means? And doesn't care what the customer might have to do to come up with the funds?"

"So I have heard." Ramón shrugs and looks away. "But it may not be so."

"In that case, St. Vrain must be paying a pretty price for his glass windowpanes," Gerald says. He glances toward the squares of mica set into the wall beside the door. "He'll be driving up the price for the rest of us."

"Since he and Bent are partners, he's undoubtedly getting his glass at cost," Jeremiah points out.

"Undoubtedly," Suzanna says, not meeting her husband's eyes. The unborn baby kicks just then and she grimaces and rubs the top of her belly. She glances at the four pale squares of the window. Winter has barely begun and already the light can barely push its way through the wavy white layers.

She straightens her spine and looks at her father as Ramón turns and heads back to the kitchen. "And has there been news from the States?"

"Well now," he says. "Where shall I start? Are you aware that the Congress has passed what they're calling the Indian Removal Act? They're forcing the Cherokee Nation and other civilized tribes west, to this side of the Mississippi."

Suzanna frowns. "Isn't that going to push the tribes already on those lands farther this direction?"

"I doubt they'll get this far," Gerald says. He turns his head away from her, but she can still see concern crinkling the corners of his eyes. "Besides, the tribes here know us," he adds. "There's little danger."

"No more than if you were in Taos," her father agrees.

Suzanna's lips flatten. Now it's not just Gerald trying to placate her fears. Even her father is doing it. But there's no use in pointing this out. They'll continue to insist that there's nothing to be concerned about. Which will just make her more aggravated.

And she doesn't want to be irritated with them. After all, it's the Christmas season. And her father is here. She forces her face into calmer lines and looks at her father. "Have you heard or seen anything of Thomas Smith? How is he doing without a full set of legs?"

The two men look toward her, the relief on their faces palpable. "Smith has a wooden leg now and a new name. They're calling him Peg Leg Smith. That wound doesn't seem to have slowed him down much. He's still trapping, as far as I know."

There's no more talk of Indians or other dangerous topics, and their Christmas is pleasant, though uneventful. The following week, Jeremiah helps Gerald dismantle the bed in the attic and reassemble it in the main room. Suzanna tries to supervise the move calmly, but now that Christmas is over and preparations for

259

the new child have begun, her stomach seems to be in constant turmoil.

And she's so tired. She's not sure why. Is she tired because she's physically tired, or because she remembers so vividly how she felt that final month before Alma was born? She hates the thought of those last weeks of waiting, the perpetual discomfort, the dim room. The months afterward.

"It will all be over in a few more weeks," her father says as he steadies the rail Gerald is lashing into place. Alma leans against him, watching solemnly.

"If it's anything like last time, it'll be more than a few weeks," Suzanna says grimly. "And they'll be excruciatingly long. I believe I dread the waiting more than I do the birth."

Jeremiah raises an eyebrow at her.

"The birth is certainly uncomfortable," she says. "I haven't forgotten. But the waiting is so interminable!" She stops abruptly, hearing the self-pity in her voice. She lifts her chin and tries again. "Not knowing when it will end makes it difficult."

"Yes, I can understand that," her father says. "And the winters are always hard for you."

Gerald looks up in surprise.

"When she was a girl, I always doubled her reading assignments when winter began," Jeremiah tells him. "It kept her from noticing how short the days had become and how little there was to do in her garden plot."

Gerald looks at Suzanna. "So this impatience for spring isn't a new thing."

"I don't remember." She frowns at her father. "I don't remember that at all."

He smiles a little smugly. "Then the strategies I implemented proved to be quite effective."

Suzanna forces her voice to sound more amused than exasperated. "Unfortunately, I didn't learn to recognize what was happening and teach myself ways to deal with it."

"Reading is always a good approach."

Although reading requires sufficient light. She looks at the milky-white windowpanes and grimaces. But there's no point in having that discussion again. And it's as much her fault as anyone else's that there's no glass in those windows. Or the fault of the merchants in New York.

"The light from the lamp hurts my eyes," she says. She glances at Alma, who pushes herself away from her grandfather and toddles toward the head of the bed. "And candles seem dangerous with a child in the house."

"At any rate, candlelight is difficult to read by," her father acknowledges. "But there will be some sunny days. And surely you have sewing or spinning or knitting to do."

She nods, not wanting to point out that, even if she had more wool, all those activities also require enough light to see by. But it's not his fault she's dissatisfied and there's no point in making him anxious about leaving her. He needs to get back to Taos before the January snows start in earnest.

She certainly can't ask him to stay through her confinement. The cabin's simply too small. And she's too near her time to travel with him, even if he would agree to take her. He came by horseback this time and she can't ride in her present condition. Even in a wagon, jostling over the rough track to Taos would likely trigger her birth pangs before they were halfway there.

She shivers at the thought of giving birth in that long narrow canyon and lifts her hands helplessly. She has no options. She's going to be stuck here in bed, waiting, enduring the discomfort, the lack of privacy, the minimal light. It might only be a few weeks, but they're going to be long ones.

"This time, you'll have Alma to distract you," her father says, interrupting her thoughts. "You didn't have that while you waited for her."

Alma lifts her head. "Wait?" the child demands. "Why we wait?"

Suzanna grins in spite of herself. "I couldn't agree more, little one!"

CHAPTER 43

Three days after her father leaves, winter truly sets in. It's almost as if the clouds have waited until he left before they descended. Suzanna lies on the bed and watches the windowpanes change from a dim glow in the brief morning sunlight to the ominous gray they'll retain until full dark descends and they're so black they reflect the light in the fireplace.

She sighs and turns her head, then leans awkwardly across the bed to twitch the lamp slightly closer to the edge of the small table between the bed and the fire. She angles her book to get more light on the page, then closes her eyes. It's no use. She simply can't concentrate.

She half-shuts the book and looks at the spine. Caesar. In Latin. A Christmas gift from her father, to match the English translation she already owns. Suzanna chuckles and shakes her head. What a man. He just couldn't think of anything else she might want more than an edition of Caesar in Latin.

Then her eyes fill. The book drops onto the blankets as she leans her head back against the pillows. He is such a dear man. And so exasperating. To think how hard he worked all those years to protect her from the darkness that descends on her each winter. Shielded her so effectively that she didn't even realize the darkness was there.

She wipes at her wet cheeks with the back of her hand. His strategies don't work anymore. Especially here. In Don Fernando, there was more sunlight. And more people. That was a strategy he'd implemented without realizing it.

And there was Encarnación. Suzanna forces her thoughts away from the memory of that bright-eyed face.

Instead, she remembers Encarnación's domain. The bright kitchen, with its mixture of fire warmth and winter sunlight streaming through the open window. And the people she cooked and baked for. The trappers and merchants her father invited to the casa—

Her mind stops there, remembering the long handsome face of one particular merchant, the glow of self-satisfaction St. Vrain takes with him wherever he goes. But it's sheer foolishness to think about that now. She chose Gerald.

A smile glimmers on her lips. Dear Gerald. That broad brown forehead. That wavy black hair. Those patient, concerned grey eyes. So patient and good. So anxious that she not be sad, but so helpless to help her. St. Vrain wouldn't be so kind. And yet, she'd be in Don Fernando right now, if she had decided—

"Mama!" Alma exclaims from the kitchen door.

Suzanna opens her eyes and turns her head.

"Mama! I helped!"

Ramón appears behind the child. He gestures at her new pinafore, which is covered in flour. He gives Suzanna a rueful smile. "As you can see."

Suzanna purses her lips. "I hope you can get that out with a little rinsing. There'll be no laundry until the weather clears." She gestures toward her swollen belly. "And I can't reach past this to the washing trough."

"It will shake out," he says. "It didn't get wet."

"Miraculously."

Ramón laughs. "Sí, she is quite miraculous."

Suzanna's smile fades as she looks at the little girl, then the man. "What will we do with her when my time comes?"

Ramón nods soberly. "I have thought much on this. It is not well for a child to see how it arrived in the world."

"In Don Fernando, we'd take her to a neighbor's casa."

"But here that cannot be done."

"I should have sent her with my father." Suzanna turns her head to stare at the window. "I should have gone with him myself."

He looks at her in alarm. "It is too far for one in your condition."

She glances at him and makes an impatient gesture. "I know it. But I wish—" She closes her eyes. "Oh, never mind."

When she opens her eyes, he's bending to lift Alma, who reaches to tug playfully at his black hair. "We could send word to Stands Alone," he says. "He would happily bring his wife to attend you."

Suzanna shakes her head. "I like Sings Quietly very much," she says. "But having someone by me who I can't talk to would be very difficult. Besides, although I'm sure she has plenty of expertise in childbirth, her customs are not the same." She looks up at him. "I know it's a hardship for you, but I'd prefer that Gerald be with me and that you assist him. "

She frowns, realizing how selfish she's being. "I'm sorry. I'm asking too much of you. Surely you would prefer not to be here."

"I will do whatever is necessary for your comfort, señora. After all, you are my goddaughter."

Sudden tears rise in her throat. "Oh, Ramón. What would we do without you?"

He waves a hand, dismissing her words. "It is mí nita of whom we were speaking. What is to be done with her? Perhaps Stands Alone's wife—"

Suzanna shakes her head. "I doubt they're anywhere nearby. They'll have moved into winter camp somewhere east and probably south. To a place with less snow and wind."

He nods reluctantly.

"So we must find another means to provide for her."

He grimaces. "I can only suggest that she be shut into my room."

She considers this for a long moment. "It's too cold to leave her in the barn with the dogs."

"Although they would warm her."

The outer door opens and Gerald appears, a milk pail in each hand. "There isn't much milk now," he says. "The cows are drying up quickly." He chuckles. "I don't blame them. I wouldn't want to be milked in these conditions." As he unbuttons his coat, he looks from Suzanna to Ramón, then back again. "Why so serious?" He stops in mid-button and turns to Suzanna. "Are you all right?"

"I'm fine," she says. She twists her shoulders on the pillows. "Well, as fine as it's possible to be in this condition. We were just talking about what to do with Alma when the event occurs."

Gerald grimaces. "I've been thinking about that also." He turns to Ramón apologetically. "Except for the kitchen, your room is the only one with a door."

"I hate to lock her in there with no one to comfort her," Suzanna says fretfully. She looks at Gerald. "This is simply horrendous!"

He raises his hands helplessly, then bends to pick up the pails. "I don't know what else we can do," he says. "There are no other options. I'm certainly not leaving her in the kitchen by herself, or in the barn with the animals."

He crosses the room to the kitchen, Ramón and Alma close behind.

As Suzanna watches the door shut behind them, a wave of sheer fury sweeps over her. She lifts her book and throws it to the end of the bed, where it teeters precariously, then rolls off and hits the plank floor with a thud.

"No other options!" she hisses. "No other options than to be here in this hellhole!" She gives in to the tears then. It's safe enough to do so. The men know she's upset. They'll stay out of her way. She's not sure if the thought makes her more angry or more sad. She rolls awkwardly onto her belly and weeps into her pillow.

CHAPTER 44

Somehow, Suzanna endures the long wait. Outside, it snows, then clears, then snows again, eighteen inches at a time, turning the cabin into a fire-warmed, slightly stuffy, dimly lit cave. There isn't much wind, which means the snow falls straight down, burying the yard.

Suzanna is unbelievably tired, heavy with both child and boredom. Boredom tinged with fear. Weighted down like a rock at the bottom of a well. Even a trip to the outhouse is an endeavor. She doesn't argue when Gerald slips the chamber pot under the bed.

Ramón keeps Alma in the kitchen as much as he can, and the men dig a path from the back door to the barn, to minimize the amount of traffic through Suzanna's little den. She dozes, opens her eyes to stare at the fire, then sleeps again, rousing only enough to use the chamber pot, which Gerald empties as often as she fills it. Her back aches. Everything aches. Suzanna sinks back onto her pillows and dully accepts it.

When the contraction jolts her awake that late January afternoon, she doesn't realize at first what it is. She's been dreaming—something about an acequia ditch, wild turkeys, and Chonita. It's a peaceful dream, completely out of keeping with the searing pain that rips through her bowels and shocks her into consciousness.

Her head and shoulders jerk off the pillow. Then the pain grabs again. Suzanna gasps for breath and drops back onto the bed. She's suddenly shivering with cold. Her hands claw the blankets as she scrabbles for her shawl on the other side of the bed.

When the pain subsides, it's replaced with a ferocious urge to urinate. Suzanna rolls awkwardly to her side and leverages herself into a sitting position. The door to the kitchen is shut. She pushes off the bed and clings to the frame as she crouches down to pull out the chamber pot.

As she reaches for the pot, bile rises into her throat. She bites it back. One thing at a time. Bladder first, then nausea. She lifts her nightgown and clutches the bed with one hand as she shoves the pot into place. Ah, the relief.

Then she frowns, puzzled. She can't stop it. This isn't—. Oh, tarnation. This isn't urine. It's the watery flush that preceded Alma's birth.

So it's begun. A shudder runs down her spine. Well, at least the waiting is over. She steadies herself against the bed frame, cleans up as best she can, and scoots the chamber pot back into place.

Another twist of pain hits, but now that she realizes what it is, she's ready for it. She tries not to gasp for air as it moves over her. When the contraction has passed, she takes a deep breath, wraps her shawl more tightly around her shoulders, and moves gingerly toward the kitchen.

As she reaches the door, the pain hits again. Suzanna leans forward against the log wall until it passes.

When she opens the kitchen door, three startled faces turn toward her. Gerald slips Alma from his lap. "Are you all right?"

Suzanna shakes her head, closes her eyes, then nods. "It's time," she says grimly. Alma's eyes are wide with wonder and anxiety. "It's all right," Suzanna tells her as soothingly as she can. She turns to Gerald. "It's coming."

They both turn toward the little girl, but Ramón is already behind her, his hands on her small shoulders. "Go," he tells them. "I will care for la niña."

Another contraction stabs Suzanna's belly and she gasps as she bends toward it and grabs for Gerald's hand at the same time. When the pain has eased, she looks at Alma. The baby's eyes are even wider now, and wet with unshed tears. "It's all right, niña," Suzanna says. "You go with Ramón now and I'll see you in a while."

"Mama hurt?"

Suzanna chuckles in spite of pain. "Mama is hurting. But soon Mama will be well. You go with Ramón now and be a good girl."

"Come," Ramón says. The child takes his hand trustingly enough, but as they head toward the door to his sleeping area, her head turns toward her mother.

Suzanna smiles encouragingly, but then another pain grabs her. "Tarnation!" she exclaims. She buries her head in Gerald's shoulder.

He puts his arm around her waist. "Come. Let's get you back on the bed."

"Remember the hot water," she whispers. "And we'll need the old blanket."

He settles her onto the bed, kisses her forehead, and hurries to gather what's needed. Tarnation, she thinks irritably. He knew this was coming. And the supplies he would need. Why has he waited until now to collect it all?

But then he's back, moving her gently aside to slip an old blanket onto the bed and cover it with a clean sheet. She helps him as best she can, using her arms to leverage herself out of his way. She's more awake now than she's been in days. She watches him carry the filled kettle from the kitchen and position it near the fire. There's no point in actually heating the water just yet.

Then he brings in a large basin, clean cloths, twine, and the scissors. Suzanna smiles in spite of the next wave of pain. He's more organized than she thought.

Gerald carries a chair across the room and sets it beside the bed, but he doesn't sit down. "How are you?" he asks. She can see that he's working to remain calm.

She reaches for his hand. "At least this time I know what to expect." She glances toward the supplies he's brought in. "As do you."

He grimaces. "I can control that part, anyway." He strokes her fingers. "I'll be glad when this is over."

"So will I."

"You can scream if you need to. Ramón has cotton for Alma's ears."

"My poor baby."

He looks toward the fire. "It's part of life."

As he says it, another contraction squeezes Suzanna's belly. She grits her teeth. "Though, it's not your pain." She looks away from him, concentrating, then takes a deep breath. As she exhales, another pain hits, radiating from her groin. She grabs his hand. "Hell and tarnation! This seems so much stronger than it was last time."

Gerald's jaw tightens, then he makes a visible effort to relax. "Scream if you need to. Remember how it seemed to help last time?"

Suzanna shakes her head, her face tight with concentration, waiting for the pain to ebb. "Alma," she whispers. "I don't want her to hear."

She takes another deep breath and loosens her grip on Gerald's hand. He brings her a cup of water and wipes her forehead with a clean cloth.

"It's so difficult to watch you try not to cry out," he says. "I think it was better when you could let go of the pain with your voice, at least."

"I know," she gasps. "It's just—" The pain cuts across her belly again. "I swear!"

The mica-covered windows have grown dark by the time it's all over. Suzanna is exhausted, not just from pushing, but from forcing herself not to scream. Somehow, she's managed it. But the inside of her throat is raw and she can barely talk. A shudder of exhaustion runs through her as Gerald brings the swaddled infant boy to the bed.

"It's over," she whispers.

Gerald nods. "It is, thank God." He lays the blanketed bundle on the other side of the bed, moves to hoist Suzanna up and onto her pillows, then hands her the child.

"He's the most beautiful creamy brown," she says dreamily as she snuggles him. "And it matches his hair." She runs a finger down his cheek and his puckered mouth opens.

Gerald chuckles. "He's hungry already."

"He's not as large as I thought he would be. Especially given how big my belly was."

Gerald sobers and touches her hand. "The afterbirth—"

She looks up.

"There was another child." He turns his head away. "Or at least that's what it looked like."

She stares at him. "That's why it seemed so much more painful than before. And why my belly was so huge."

He nods without looking at her.

Her lips tremble. "I was carrying two children," she whispers. "And I didn't know it." She looks down at the baby. "That's why he seemed so active." She closes her eyes, her throat tight with pain. After a long while, she opens her eyes. "Boy or a girl?"

Gerald shakes his head. "I couldn't tell. It was— Not fully formed." His eyes are dark with pain. "I'm sorry," he says. "If there'd been a woman— If you'd had proper care and didn't have to work so hard—"

She shakes her head. "No. Don't blame yourself. There may have been something wrong. Doesn't that happen sometimes with the cows?"

He nods reluctantly and she turns her attention firmly to the infant in her arms. "And we have this one." She looks up at Gerald. "A baby boy. What have you decided to name him?"

He grins. "And what if you don't like the name I've chosen?"

Suzanna laughs. "Then we'll need to discuss it. But I chose Alma's, so it's only fair you should name this one."

"I thought perhaps Andrew," he says shyly. "It was my mother's father's name." He glances toward the kitchen door. "Andrew Ramón."

"I like it," Suzanna says. "Have you told Ramón?"

"Not until I had your agreement," he says. "In fact, I haven't even told Ramón that it's safe to bring Alma out of his room. They're still in there."

"He stayed with her the entire time? It's been hours!"

"Almost four."

There's a muffled knock on the other side of the kitchen door. "Come in!" Gerald calls.

Ramón opens the door just enough to peek through. "Is it all right for la niña?"

"Sí, gracias," Gerald says. As the door swings open, he rises and crosses the room to lift Alma into his arms. "Come and see your new baby brother." He looks at Ramón, then back at the little girl. "His name is Andrew Ramón Locke. Isn't that a nice sturdy name for a boy?"

CHAPTER 45

When the first new-baby euphoria has worn off and Suzanna's settled once again into motherhood, the exhaustion descends.

She remembers the bone-deep weariness after Alma's birth, so she isn't surprised that all she wants to do is stay in bed. Doesn't even want to twist her hair into its usual knot at the base of her neck. What does surprise her is the grief she feels. Every time she looks into Andrew's tiny face, a sense of desolation washes over her and the tears pour down her cheeks. There was another baby inside her, a face she'll never see. A child she didn't even have a chance to name.

She does her best to hide her grief, but eventually Gerald walks in and finds her cradling a sleeping Andrew and weeping silently in the dim cabin.

"I'm sorry about the lack of proper windows," he says. He gestures toward the table beside the bed. "Shall I light the lamp?"

She shakes her head and opens her mouth, but no words come out. Her throat is on fire with grief.

He takes her hand. "You were also sad after Alma was born. When spring came, you felt so much better."

She nods and lifts her free hand to wipe at her cheeks. Gerald pulls out his handkerchief and hands it to her. Andrew makes a smacking sound in his sleep, and she drops the handkerchief onto the blanket and positions him at her breast. He turns his head, eyes still closed, and latches on.

She gives Gerald a watery smile. "He certainly likes to eat. Just like his sister. But the way I feel isn't like it was after Alma was born. It's worse. It's more— I'm not quite sure." She closes her eyes. "More sad. Deeper. The way I felt after Chonita died."

"Grief for the twin?"

She nods wordlessly, her throat burning. Andrew pulls away from her breast and she lifts him to her shoulder and begins patting his back.

"But it was never born," Gerald says.

Suzanna shrugs helplessly. She can't explain the way she feels and if she tried, she would only begin weeping again. The baby lets out a long burp and she lays him facedown on her lap and begins rubbing his back, her hair drooping over her face.

"Is that possible?" Gerald asks. "To feel grief for someone you never knew?"

Irritation stabs her. "It's what I feel." She continues to rub Andrew's back.

Gerald moves in the chair, adjusting it slightly away from the bed. He leans toward her, his hand out, then pulls back. "I also wish it was otherwise."

"It's not a matter of wishing it was otherwise," she says wearily. "It happens sometimes, I know that. I just—." She shrugs and turns her head away. Her voice is suddenly thin and unsteady. "It's just how I feel."

"I wish I could do something to make you feel better."

The window blurs in front of Suzanna's eyes. "There's nothing anyone can do," she whispers. She bites her upper lip. There's no use in crying. It won't solve anything. But her throat feels like it's been scorched by fire. "Nothing," she whispers.

Gerald's chair scrapes against the plank flooring. Then he's leaning over her and Andrew's weight is shifting from her lap.

Suzanna continues to stare at the window as her husband carries the baby to the cradle.

In the kitchen, Alma squeals "Chaser!" and Ramón laughs.

Suzanna's head drops back onto her pillow. As Gerald leaves the room, she gropes blindly for his handkerchief and twists it between her fingers. It's as if all the pain she didn't express while she was giving birth is now forcing its way out through her eyes. Out of her soul. But still silently. The anguish will express itself no matter how much she tries to stem it.

And with the weeping, exhaustion. Even the mid-February thaw doesn't help. She's listlessly agreed to move the big bed back up to the loft, but scaling the ladder to it is almost more than she can endure. Especially at the beginning of the day, when she braces herself for the descent as if she's plunging into an ice-caked pond.

At the bottom, she clings to the side poles and gasps for air, forcing her lungs to open and close. When her heart stops pounding, she creeps into the kitchen and drinks the weak broom weed tea Ramón has decided will help her recover.

He seems unaware that this time is worse than before or that there's any reason for her to grieve. She hasn't asked Gerald if he told Ramón about the dead twin. She can't bring herself to speak of it. All she can do is smile weakly, drink the tea, then creep into the main room, lift Andrew from the cradle, and sink into her chair to feed him again.

This morning she sits next to the fire and watches the sunlight play through the milky-white windowpanes. Gerald has left the front door cracked open and a wisp of February warmth trickles in. It almost feels like spring.

Suzanna's head lifts. Then she remembers. It will all disappear in another week or so. And be followed by March rain and snow. And then April rain and snow. April, when tiny new leaves should be greening the trees and plants should be peaking from the ground. Blossoms on apricot trees. Lettuce sprouting beside adobe walls.

She closes her eyes and grief sweeps over her. For her lost child, for the garden in her father's courtyard, for Encarnación. Chonita would have known what to do for a mother's grief, for the despair and the dullness.

Suzanna opens her eyes and stares at the flames dancing in the fireplace and tries to feel grateful for the way Gerald and Ramón keep the fire going, for the piles of wood stacked behind the cabin. Andrew's mouth pulls at her nipple and she grimaces and looks down at him, steeling herself for the inevitable grief.

Then she steadies herself, forces all emotion away, and examines him as if he were a questionable ear of corn. He seems to be growing. There is also that to be thankful for.

In the kitchen, Alma squeals "Chaser!" and laughs with glee. Suzanna smiles wearily. She has two healthy children, a tender husband, and a friend who does more than his share in caring for her and her children. So much to be grateful for.

She leans her head back against the wooden chair and lets her sorrow close in again. She knows the weeping serves no purpose, that her swollen face will only give Gerald more grief he already feels. But she's helpless to stop the grief from showing.

A week later, she's still crying. She's a bottomless lake of pain, with no blue sky reflected in her dull surface. Gerald has stopped trying to comfort her, as if ignoring her pain will somehow dissipate it.

"Ignoring me," Suzanna mutters bitterly as she bends to place aired baby clothes in the storage chest near the fire. She notes grimly that, at least for the moment, her weeping has stopped. Anger at Gerald has replaced the grief.

She snorts in irritation. Then the tears well again. She swallows, forcing them back, narrowing her eyes, focusing on her aggravating husband. The anger feels good, a kind of relief from the endless weeping. But then her knees wobble under her skirt, and she's forced to close the chest lid and sit down on it, baby clothes still in her hands.

She looks down at the tiny garments. There should have been two infants to wear them. A boy and another boy. A boy and a girl. Another girl. A little sister for Alma. The tears well again and she wipes them away with the cotton shirts. Pain cuts through her belly, bending her forward to clutch the little clothes to her chest. "Oh, child!" she whispers. "Oh little one!"

The outer door opens and Gerald enters the cabin, a smile on his lips. When he sees Suzanna, his face falls. Then his jaw sets stubbornly and he turns to hang his hat on the pegs by the door. "It's really beautiful outside!" he says in a falsely cheerful voice. "You should see it!"

Suzanna's back straightens as if he's slapped her. "It'll start raining again soon enough," she says tartly.

He turns, his eyes still falsely bright. "More reason to enjoy the sun while it lasts."

She gives him a scornful look and turns her head toward the fire.

He crosses the room, places himself between Suzanna and the flames, and leans toward her. "You can't stay inside forever, wife," he says gently. "You love the sun." He holds out his hand. "Come outside and see it. It will make you feel better."

She gives him a withering look. "Do you really think that all I need is a little sunshine to make me feel better? That I weep because I haven't seen enough sunshine and blue sky?"

He drops his hand and straightens. "We can't grieve forever."

She glares up at him. "I can if I want to!" She stands to face him, hands on her hips, and the tiny shirts fall to the floor. "You say 'we,' as if your feelings are mine! As if you know every thought in my head! You have no idea how I feel!" She turns away and stalks toward the ladder to the loft. "Just leave me alone!"

As she scrambles upward, he says, "Well, at least you've got some energy back."

She turns, clinging to the ladder with one hand. "How dare you!"

He raises his hands helplessly. "Nothing else seems to work. Perhaps being angry with me is the best way to snap you out of this."

She leans toward him and lifts her hand from the ladder, then teeters and grabs the pole again. The indignity of her position adds to her fury. "How dare you!" Then she turns and scrambles into the loft.

In the room below, Andrew fusses in his cradle. Gerald's feet cross the room. The cradle creaks a little as he lifts the baby out. "It's all right," Gerald says soothingly. "Your mama is having a bad time of it, but she'll come around eventually. She just needs to do something besides take care of you."

Suzanna drops onto the side of the bed and glares at the fire-lit space below. What else will he say, knowing she can hear? As if his mere words can cure what ails her! Him and his unsolicited advice!

She reaches for a pillow and throws it to the other end of the bed, wishing for something harder, more breakable. How dare he! She balls her fist and slams it into the blankets, over and over again. As if he knows what ails her! As if a little sunlight will fix the pain balled in her stomach, the ache in her heart! As if February warmth will ease the perpetual burn in her throat!

279

The loss of Encarnación was bad enough, but it had been eased by Alma's birth. And Encarnación had a chance to live her life, cut off as it was. This child— This lost infant— It never even felt sunlight, felt the touch of spring air on its cheeks. It never—

She collapses into the pillow at the foot of the bed, her face in her hands. That she, The Woman Who Plants, could carry death in her all that time and never even dream it was there. That she could carry death and life at the same time. That Andrew, that tiny creamy-brown baby, could have existed alongside a decaying corpse.

Her stomach heaves and nausea floods her throat. She lunges upward and makes it to the chamber pot just in time. It's unbearable. She kneels beside the pot, stares at the poisonous remains of her morning meal, and gags again. It's all so unbearable.

She creeps back onto the bed and lays down again. And Gerald, who has no idea how she really feels, is convinced that all she needs is some sunlight. Revulsion mingles with the fury that sweeps over her.

Her anger and grief don't subside with the passing days. If anything, they grow stronger. Suzanna clings to her side of the bed. Andrew tends to be fussy at night and she uses this as an excuse to bring him into the bed between her and Gerald.

Gerald doesn't protest, just scoots a little farther toward his edge of the pallet, and strokes the baby's fuzzy brown head with his fingertips. Suzanna, pretending to sleep, tightens her shoulders against the lack of affection towards herself, but doesn't reach for Gerald's hand. When he approaches her during the day, she moves away from him almost unconsciously, looking down at her handwork or turning back to her dusting, which is taking more and more of her time.

"I can't help you, if you won't let me," Gerald says abruptly one day in mid-March when he finds her wiping down the bookshelf she'd cleaned the day before.

"I didn't ask for your help." She lifts the Latin copy of Caesar and studies the spine, which seems slightly skewed. "This looks like it's been dropped." She turns to Alma, who's sitting in front of the fire patting Chaser's broad forehead. "Have you been playing with my books?"

The little girl's head lifts. "No, mama."

"You leave them alone!"

Gerald sticks his hands in his pockets and studies the window as Suzanna turns back to the bookcase.

"I can do the housework well enough," Suzanna says over her shoulder.

"I wasn't talking about housework."

She sniffs and bends to the next shelf. "Dog hair everywhere," she mutters. "This cabin is too small for him to be in here all the time." She straightens. "Chaser! Out!"

The dog lifts his head and Alma frowns. "We playing."

"Out!" Suzanna marches to the door and opens it. She waves her hand at the mastiff, who stands and stretches lazily. "Now!" she commands. "Out!"

"I go too!" Alma hops up and runs to the door.

Suzanna scowls at her. "It's too cold for you to be out there." She peers into the yard. "It's raining again and everything's muddy."

Alma frowns, then brightens. "Boots!"

"No boots!" Suzanna says. The dog shuffles out the door and she shuts it behind him with a thud.

Alma pouts, then puts on her most beseeching smile. She spreads her hands, palms up. "Please boots?"

"You'll simply track mud in," Suzanna says. "Mud I'll have to clean." Andrew begins to fuss and she crosses the room to the cradle, picks him up, and begins jiggling him up and down. When she turns back to Alma, the child is still standing by the door. "I told you 'no,'" Suzanna says impatiently. "Go find something else to do."

Alma's shoulders rise, then fall. She trudges across the room toward the kitchen, her head down.

Gerald chuckles as she passes him and Suzanna's eyes snap. "I see nothing funny about a child who doesn't take 'no' for an answer."

Alma disappears through the kitchen door. Gerald shakes his head and gives Suzanna an amused look. "She did do what you told her," he points out. "Eventually."

Suzanna sniffs. Andrew's head turns toward her breast and his mouth opens and shuts like a little fish. "Are you hungry again?" Suzanna asks wearily. "All right. Just a minute." She crosses to the bookcase and reaches past Gerald to straighten the books and collect the dusting cloth.

As the baby begins to wail, Suzanna carries the dustcloth to its shelf in the kitchen and returns to the main room. Gerald is beside the bookcase with the Caesar in his hand, examining its spine. Suzanna settles herself in her chair, opens her bodice, and grimaces as Andrew latches onto her nipple.

Gerald returns the book to its shelf. "Is he hurting you when he feeds?" he asks.

Suzanna shrugs. "No more than usual." She bends her head and repositions Andrew to relieve the pressure on her arm.

The front door clicks shut. When she looks up, Gerald is gone. She leans her head back against the chair and closes her eyes as the baby nurses his fill. Until the next time he's hungry, of course.

CHAPTER 46

She's feeding Andrew yet again when Stands Alone and Sings Quietly ride into the yard a few days later. They've been in Taos, Stands Alone says, and are heading down the Cimarron Canyon to rejoin their extended family. "In the place of the shared elk," he tells Gerald with a glint of amusement as Alma toddles to his knee.

Gerald looks up from the fireplace, where he's just fed another piece of wood to the flames. "Ah, that broad spot in the canyon where we first met and shared the elk. What Old Bill calls Ute Park." He turns to Suzanna, who's now jiggling a fussing Andrew. "It's a beautiful spot. We should take some time this spring and go visit them there."

As Suzanna nods distractedly, Andrew pulls his knees toward his chest and begins screaming in pain. The men look at each other. Stands Alone swings Alma into his arms and rises. As he goes out the door, Gerald and Ramón follow him.

Suzanna scowls after them all, then raises her eyebrows at Stands Alone's wife and shakes her head. The other woman chuckles and lifts her hands, palms up in a hopeless gesture. Then she crosses to Suzanna's chair, stretches her hands toward the baby, and curls her fingers toward herself.

Suzanna hands her the wailing child. "He's just started doing this," she says.

The other woman nods as if she understands exactly what Suzanna has said, and carries the baby to the wooden storage chest by the fire. She lays him on his back, moves the bottom edge of his tiny shirt up onto his chest, and holds him in place with one hand while she gently probes his stomach and abdomen with the other.

"Aaah," she says. She begins moving her forefinger in gentle circles over his lower abdomen, barely touching the soft baby skin. Andrew's screams stop abruptly. He hiccups once, then stares into Sings Quietly's face. Suddenly, he pulls his knees toward his chest and a long whistle of gas bursts from his bottom.

"Oh my goodness!" Suzanna giggles. Then she suddenly finds herself crying helplessly.

Sings Quietly tugs Andrew's shirt back into position, lifts him from the chest, and snuggles him against her shoulder. She paces to the window and back as she rubs small circles over his shoulders and down his spine.

On the fourth turn, she stops in front of Suzanna's chair and says something in Ute.

Suzanna wipes her face with the back of her hands and looks up. "What?"

The older woman gazes at her, then frowns slightly and points to Suzanna's stomach. She holds up two fingers and raises her eyebrows in a questioning look.

Suzanna's eyes widen. She covers her belly with her hands. "Yes," she whispers. She nods. "There were two. One of them died." She bites her lip. How can she make the other woman understand? She points at her stomach and raises two fingers, then points at the baby and raises one.

"Ahhh," Sings Quietly says. She points at Suzanna's face, then her own, and traces her fingers down her cheeks.

Suzanna closes her eyes and nods.

The other woman clucks sympathetically. Just then, Ramón opens the outer door. Sings Quietly turns and says something to him in Ute. He gives her a puzzled look, then pulls back to the porch. "Your wife," he says. "She wishes to speak."

Stands Alone and Gerald enter cautiously, Alma holding her father's hand. Sings Quietly gives them all an impatient look, then places Andrew in Suzanna's lap and brushes past the others to the porch, gesturing to her husband to follow.

They're gone a long time. Ramón carries Alma off to the kitchen to help with the meal and Gerald turns to Suzanna. "What did you say to her?" he asks. "She seems upset."

"I didn't say anything." Suzanna rises and begins preparing a fresh cover for the baby's bottom. "We can't speak each other's language, remember? All we have are gestures and a screaming child." She places the squirming baby on the top of the storage chest and begins unfastening his diaper.

Alma trots in from the kitchen. "Time to eat!" she lisps.

Suzanna scowls at her. "I'm cleaning Andrew," she says. "And our guests are outside. It will have to wait."

Alma's brown eyes study her. "Sí, mama," she says solemnly. "I tell Amón." She turns back to the kitchen.

"She's just a child," Gerald says quietly. "And she's only repeating what she's been told to say."

"Well, she needs to learn some manners," Suzanna says, over the baby's gurgles. "Stay still, Andrew!" She glances at Gerald. "The rest of us don't have to jump just because she says so."

Gerald moves to the window. Silence fills the room. Suzanna finishes changing Andrew and returns him to his cradle.

When the outer door opens, Gerald turns toward it eagerly. "The meal is prepared," he tells Stands Alone and his wife. "If you would like to eat."

The Ute man looks from Gerald to Suzanna, then nods, and they all troop into the kitchen.

It's a silent meal, enlivened only by Alma's chatter and Gerald's care for the guests. Suzanna sits silently at the end of the table and crumbles a tortilla into small pieces. She isn't hungry. Just bone-weary.

Stands Alone's wife says something to him and he turns to Suzanna and opens his mouth, then seems to think better of it. Suzanna watches them watch her but can't find the energy to do more than drink the tea Ramón places before her.

After the meal, the Utes thank Ramón, then follow Gerald and Suzanna back into the main room. Alma trails behind them. Suzanna crosses the room to check on Andrew in his cradle.

Alma follows her. "Mama?" she asks.

Suzanna closes her eyes in aggravation, then turns, fighting to keep her voice even. "What is it?"

"I go outside play?" Alma's hands clasp and unclasp over her pinafore. "Chaser want me."

Suzanna raises an eyebrow. "The dog wants you? And how do you know that?" She waves an impatient hand. "Oh, never mind. Yes, go outside. It'll keep you out of the way."

When she turns back to the adults, Sings Quietly is frowning at Stands Alone and nodding emphatically. The Ute chief turns to Gerald. "Your children," he says.

Suzanna's eyes narrow. He sees her look and smiles. "They are good children. Blessed. But it is good sometimes for children to be away from their parents. They learn strength in a different way."

He turns to Gerald. "In our camp, there is always someone to watch, to give rest to the parents." Stands Alone looks around the room. "This is a good place, but you have no one to give you rest."

Suzanna snorts an agreement and drops into her chair. The others follow her lead, placing themselves on the cushion-covered benches.

Stands Alone keeps his eyes on Gerald's face. "My wife, she has no small children now," he says. "Little Squirrel thinks he does not need her care." He pauses and says something to his wife in Ute and she snorts and rolls her eyes.

"That one, he is too old now for a mother's advice or reprimand," Stands Alone continues. He chuckles and turns to Suzanna. "Also, there is a woman in our camp who has recently lost her nursing child. She can provide food for el niño and my wife will watch over him and la niña. It would be a comfort to the women, a gift to them. Perhaps until the new moon."

Suzanna stares at him, her throat clenched. How dare he presume to suggest that she can't care for her own children! Her fists ball in her lap. She glances at Gerald, who's looking thoughtfully from Stands Alone to Sings Quietly and back again. He's considering it. He truly is. And without consulting her.

Suzanna's breath tightens. Her fingers stretch toward him involuntarily, as if they'd like to reach across the room and slap him into sense. How can he even think of sending his infant son and toddler daughter into a strange Indian camp? Where Pawnee could strike at any moment?

She glares at him, but he is studiously avoiding her eyes. There's a long pause, then he nods.

Suzanna's eyes blaze at him, but Gerald is completely focused on Stands Alone and his wife. "We would be most grateful," he says. "And when the new moon arrives, we will come for them in the valley of the shared elk." He smiles warmly. "Alma will enjoy it very much." He glances at Suzanna, then away. "A rest will be quite welcome."

Suzanna is rigid with anger. But she has her price. She won't contradict her husband in front of the Ute and his wife. Her eyes narrow. He's going to be sorry he's done this.

CHAPTER 47

She's still angry three days later. She has to admit that there's a certain relief in not having Alma underfoot or Andrew demanding to be fed every hour of the day. But that doesn't reduce her fury. Gerald was wrong to make such a decision without her consent, and she isn't about to admit his choice might have been the right one or motivated by anything other than a desire to aggravate her.

And then Lieutenant Gabaldón de Anaya shows up again, this time with only two men in tow. When Gerald invites them inside, Anaya waves his men to the barn, but follows Gerald into the house. He accepts the offer of tea graciously, much to Suzanna's surprise. In fact, he seems to be trying to ingratiate himself with them, asking after their health and that of Ramón, who's in the barn with the lieutenant's men.

"And los niños?" he asks as he accepts a cup of tea from Suzanna's hands. He glances at her as if unsure how to proceed. Perhaps he has some manners, after all.

Gerald comes to the officer's rescue. "Yes, los niños," he says. "Another child born early this year. A boy, this time."

"A boy?" Anaya beams at Gerald. "I congratulate you!"

As if a boy is better than a girl, Suzanna thinks sourly, turning away. She pours out another cup of tea and hands it to Gerald.

The lieutenant looks around the room and smiles at Suzanna. "La casa is so quiet. I had not thought children and quietness were things that can be combined."

Before she can respond, Gerald chuckles. "It hasn't been terribly quiet," he says. "But we're enjoying a bit of a respite. Stands Alone and his wife have taken them for a bit and given us a small vacation. Alma was quite eager to sleep in a real Indian lodge."

The lieutenant lowers his tea cup. "You've left your children in the hands of savages? Alone?"

"They aren't alone," Gerald says. "They're with Stands Alone and his wife."

"Americanos," Anaya mutters. He turns to Suzanna. "You are of this country," he says. "Did you agree to this action?"

How dare he comment on how they raise their children, even if he's right? Suzanna compresses her lips at the lieutenant's impertinence and glances angrily at Gerald. She doesn't know who to be more irritated with, Anaya for being judgmental or Gerald for giving him something to judge.

Gerald, apparently misreading her face, leans forward. "They are my children, also," he says. "In America, just as in nuevomexico, the father has a say in the disposition of his children."

The lieutenant gives Suzanna a sympathetic look, then turns to Gerald. "Certainly, you may do as you wish in such a matter." He waves a hand. "But this is not the matter of which I came to speak. I have received information which concerns you."

Gerald straightens and takes a careful sip of tea.

The lieutenant studies him, waiting for a response. Gerald sips his tea.

Anaya nods abruptly and carefully places his cup on the table. When he looks up at Gerald again, his face is stiff. "My informant tells me furs are hidden in the hills of the Cimarron."

Gerald lifts an eyebrow.

"It is necessary that you come with me for these furs."

Gerald takes another sip of tea.

"The law demands that you be faced with the evidence."

"What evidence?"

"The evidence of your activities."

Gerald places his own cup on the table and leans backward. His hands tighten, then he seems to consciously relax his fingers. He lifts his hands and flattens his palms on his thighs. "And what activities would those be?"

"The activity of illegal trapping and selling of furs."

"It isn't illegal to trap and sell furs."

"Furs that are contraband," Anaya amends. "Plews hidden away and destined for Los Estados Unidos without payment to el fiscal."

Gerald's jaw tightens. "The last time you were here I showed you the only furs I have. They're still in the barn, waiting to be carried to Taos for sale to the merchants there. Whether those merchants pay the appropriate taxes before they transport them to Missouri is not my concern."

A note of contempt creeps into the other man's voice. "The furs you showed me were not of the best quality."

"No, they certainly weren't," Gerald agrees. "And they haven't improved in quality over the course of the winter, either. Nor have they increased substantially in number." He glances at Suzanna. "I was otherwise occupied this past season and didn't do much trapping. The beaver up here haven't returned in any strength and their plews aren't exceptional, either."

"Those plews that you've chosen to display, at any rate."

Gerald opens his mouth, then shuts it again. His hands tighten against his thighs, pressing into his trouser legs. "Please, lieutenant. If you will," he says. "Say what you have to say without preamble or evasion."

"It is you who are displaying evasion!" The lieutenant leans forward. "I have come here to reveal the truth of this matter.

There is a cache in the hills above the Cimarron and I have received detailed directions for locating it. When I do, you and your man Ramón Chávez will be present at its opening. We will see what resides there and whose mark is on the furs it contains!"

Gerald looks at Suzanna. "It will take some time to prepare for such a trip," he says. "To ensure my wife's comfort and the provision of the animals while we're gone."

The lieutenant rises. "There will be no time allowed to prepare." His voice is clipped, as if he can barely restrain his irritation, but there's also a note of triumph in it. "Such time would provide you opportunity to go to the cache before I reach it and spirit the plews to the eastern plains, where doubtlessly your associates await them."

"Since I don't have any idea where this supposed cache is, it would be difficult for me to open it and clean it out," Gerald says drily.

He turns to Suzanna, who stares back at him. Her anger at the two men has been replaced by an impassive weariness. She really doesn't care where furs are hidden in the hills along the Cimarron or who they belong to. Even in her exhaustion, she can see that the lieutenant isn't going to take 'no' for an answer. The thought of helping to hunt them makes her sick to her stomach. She has neither the energy nor the will to wander the rocky slopes to the east while these feuding men locate a cache which may or may not exist and excavate it.

She forces herself to speak. "The cows will still need to be milked and the chickens fed," she says. The bitterness creeps into her voice and she doesn't try to conceal it. "I'll stay here, as usual."

Gerald stares at her and Anaya's lips twitch, but she ignores him. Let him think what he will. He's already formed his opinion, anyway. She's an unnatural woman. A woman who allows her

292

children to be carried off to an Indian camp and any number of unknown dangers. Tears catch at her throat but she swallows them down. She lifts her chin and stares at her husband. A strange kind of fierce energy suddenly fills her. It feels good to make a decision that he doesn't like.

"I'll stay here," she says again.

"What about Jones?" Gerald asks quietly.

The lieutenant's eyes narrow. "That Enoch Jones? The one in Chihuahua?" He clearly thinks Gerald is looking for an excuse to remain in the valley.

But even if Jones isn't in Chihuahua as the lieutenant believes, Suzanna finds she doesn't really care. She looks at Gerald, her jaw set stubbornly.

He makes a helpless gesture. "I don't like it, but I suppose it's the only thing to do, since the lieutenant feels the need for both my presence and Ramón's." He turns to Anaya. "I hope this map of yours is accurate, because I certainly don't know where we're going. How long is this going to take?"

The lieutenant shrugs. "Two days. Perhaps three."

Gerald nods grimly. He turns back to Suzanna. "Please stay close to the house. And take the shotgun and the dogs with you wherever you go."

"I know what to do," she says impatiently. "I'll be perfectly fine."

He frowns, then nods. "We'll leave the cows in the pasture. Except for the milker. We'll put her in the corral, so you won't have to bring her in. That way, you can stay close to the house and barn." He nods, pleased with his plan, although he still looks worried.

Suzanna doesn't respond. She just wants them to go, even though she's now paradoxically furious that they're willing to do so.

A kind of cold heat fills her as she watches the men spend the next hour driving the milk cow into the corral, seeing to their gear, and saddling their horses. Ramón eyes her worriedly, but only points out the meat and tortillas he's leaving for her and wraps what the men will take with them in a clean cloth.

Even though they say they're concerned, both Gerald and Ramón move so quickly and efficiently that Suzanna begins to suspect that they're glad she's staying. They clearly feel any amount of risk to her is worth resolving the lieutenant's doubts once and for all.

She suppresses a disgusted snort. Not that this little expedition is likely to truly ease Anaya's suspicions. He's apt to never be fully satisfied. After all, if he doesn't have his suspicions, what will he have? Gerald should just refuse to go with the man. If he really cared about her safety, he would do just that.

For a moment, she wavers toward tears. Then the anger surges again. She forces her face into immobility when Gerald reaches to touch her cheek in farewell.

"Please be careful," he says.

The lieutenant, already mounted, is watching them. Is that sympathy in his eyes, or amusement? Suzanna nods stiffly. "I will." Chaser nudges her skirt and she shoves at him with her knee. "The dogs will be here, at any rate."

"You wanted—" Gerald says, but then he glances at the lieutenant, who's still watching. Gerald's mouth tightens and he turns away from Suzanna and swings into his saddle. Anaya wheels his horse and canters past the cabin and down the hill toward the marsh. It's still frozen. It'll be safe enough for them to enter the canyon that way and faster than going up and over the hill behind the house. Ramón clucks at his mount and follows the lieutenant.

Gerald follows, but slowly. At the far end of the cabin, he reins in and turns to give Suzanna a long look, somewhere between anxiety and irritation. She raises a hand in farewell and he mimics her gesture, then disappears down the slope.

She doesn't cross the yard to watch them into the canyon. The exhaustion has hit again. She moves to the porch and climbs wearily up the steps. She sinks onto a bench and stares into the valley. The cattle graze peacefully in the meadow beyond the cornfield. Its dead stalks are still standing in spite of the past winter's snow and wind.

Regardless of what Gerald decided, those cows really ought to be barned before sundown. What with mountain cats and other night-time predators, it's not worth the risk to leave them out overnight.

Suzanna grimaces. Her skirts will be soaked by the time she gets those contrary beasts out of that pasture. But the sun is making an effort to break through the clouds. Maybe the grass will dry a little.

She leans her head back against the cabin logs, letting the rough wood support her. Her shoulders loosen and she closes her eyes. It feels good to sit here knowing no one is secretly watching, trying to gauge whether she's angry or happy, smiling or weeping. Making judgments about her emotional state. "I just want to be left in peace," she mutters as the tears well again.

CHAPTER 48

Except for dragging herself out to milk the cow, Suzanna sleeps for the next forty-eight hours. Then suddenly she's awake and alert in an eerily silent house. She paces the floor, her mind churning. What if the men never return? What if the lieutenant, in a fit of stupidity and frustration, decides to eliminate his supposed contrabandistas once and for all?

And her children, still in the hands of the Utes. The lieutenant is right. Sending two children off to live with the Indians, even for a short time, is insane. What had she been thinking? But she hadn't been thinking, she reminds herself bitterly. It was Gerald's idea to agree to Stands Alone's proposal. Not hers.

Her jaw tightens. She pictures Gerald's stiff face as he told her to stay close to the cabin. As if she's a child, required to do whatever he says, follow his every instruction.

Her chin lifts and she heads toward the door. She's not a slave, chained to the house and yard, moving childishly back and forth between barn and cabin, no mind of her own. She needs something to do besides walk the floor. She lifts her coat from its peg then pauses, considering her options. The garden is still a half-icy mess. There's no point in trying to dig.

But the cornfield needs to be cleaned out. Most of last year's stalks are still standing. She'd been so big with the baby— She takes a deep breath. Her hands tighten on the wool coat. If she thinks about why she was so big, she'll start weeping again, and crying only makes her want to cry more. Activity is the only thing that's going to keep her sane.

Activity Gerald apparently thinks is only good for her when he's supervising. A part of her knows this is unfair, that he's concerned for her welfare. But a larger part of her wants to be angry with him. Anger is a relief compared to the despair that's been smothering her.

Besides, Jones is in Chihuahua. And how likely is it that a cougar will creep up on her in the middle of the cornfield?

She pulls on her coat and boots, and reaches for the shotgun. Then she pauses. It's only going to be in the way. She can't very well swing the machete with one hand and hold the gun with the other. Given the time of year, the corn patch will be a mass of icy mud. Anywhere she puts a weapon down there, it's going to get filthy. She turns and opens the door.

Gerald would disapprove of her decision. She shakes the thought away impatiently. The dogs will frighten off anything that's likely to get too close. She doesn't need a gun, she needs to chop. She heads to the barn to collect the machete and mastiff.

The mongrels look up at her from their nest of hay, then settle back to sleep. She doesn't want them anyway. They'll just romp through the field and be a nuisance.

At the edge of the field, Chaser ambles to a small patch of sodden brown grass beside it and settles onto it sleepily, muzzle on his paws.

Suzanna stands with her hands on her hips and studies the rows of dead and woody cornstalks. They've weathered a dirty gray. Their tops are broken off, and some of them tilt wildly, but they're still standing. Their long ranks run steadily toward the uninhabitable mountains, the ground between them thick with muddy ruts. It's all a symbol of her life. Ugly. In a valley not fit for habitation.

She sighs, lifts the machete, and swings it experimentally reacquainting her wrist and arm with the feel of it. Impulsively, she whips it toward the nearest cornstalk. The broad metal blade whistles in the cold morning air but doesn't hit the stalk straight-on. The woody stem splinters haphazardly, tearing up and down its length instead of breaking cleanly off.

Suzanna's lips tighten. The damn corn is just like Gerald, refusing to budge. Anger feeds her arm and she swings again, the blade biting well below the splintered section, into the stalk's base, slicing it clean with a snapping sound. The result is strangely satisfying. At least there's one thing in her life she can control. She straightens and moves steadily up the field, shearing as she goes.

She's breathing hard by the time she reaches the end of the row. She bends forward, catching her breath, then turns to glance toward the cabin. Her eye catches a flash of movement among the pines on the hill behind it, and she straightens and stares. Gerald? Stands Alone, with the children?

Nothing stirs. No one is there. No one is coming. She isn't worth the bother.

She turns back to the corn, steps across the frozen mud to the next row, and begins cutting again, automatically now, focused more on her thoughts than her work. She should just go back to Taos and leave the children with Gerald. He clearly knows better than she does what they need, she thinks bitterly. He and Ramón would manage between them. Besides, Sings Quietly would be happy to step in if they need her. They're all better parents than she is.

And she truly is a bad mother. She's impatient and wants only to get away from the constant demands of the nursing baby. He never seems to be satisfied.

None of them ever seem to be satisfied. Gerald. Sings Quietly. The lieutenant. They're all judging her and she doesn't measure up to anyone's standard. Suzanna drops the machete and covers her face with her hands.

A dog sniffs at her skirt. She kicks out at it. "Leave me alone!" she snaps. Then she opens her eyes. The mastiff is standing in the middle of the row, looking at her with sorrowful brown eyes. "Go away!" Suzanna says.

She turns to the corn and realizes that she's finished a second row. The work has warmed her. She pulls off her coat, tosses it onto the dead grass at the end of the patch, and loosens the top of her bodice. The cool air feels good on her throat. She picks up the machete and moves to the next row of corn.

Chaser maneuvers through the patch until he's ahead of her, then sits in the mud and watches her advance up the row.

"I said go away!" Suzanna waves the machete at him and the mastiff gives her a reproachful look, then rises and begins pushing through the stalks to the other side of the field. His massive shoulders ram into the dead corn, knocking the stalks that are already tilted closer to the ground.

Suzanna scowls. Stupid beast. The corn he's pushed aside will now be more difficult to cut down.

She finishes chopping the row she's working on, then immediately turns and begins felling the next one. As she starts down the fourth, she mutters, "I should just go back to Don Fernando. At least my father appreciates me. Sees me as more than just a baby-maker."

She stops suddenly, drops the machete blade to her side, and looks up at the western mountains, the green-black barrier between herself and her father's casa. Memories wash over her. The soft light on the parlor's white-washed walls, the neat shelves of books on either side of the fire, the always-welcoming smile in her father's eyes. He never looks at her with such disappointment. The way Gerald does.

The tears threaten then, but she irritably brushes them away. He certainly never made her cry like this. She turns and slashes the machete blade through the base of the next dead stalk of corn. He never took her to a place that refused to produce what she needs. She hacks blindly at the row of corn, the machete ruthlessly scattering woody gray stalks on the frozen mud behind her, refusing to acknowledge the wetness on her cheeks.

CHAPTER 49

Stupid bastards left her alone this time. Jones grins and raises the spyglass again. Not that he needs it this close to the cabin. He's on the hillside behind the house, in the fringe of pines below the barren snow-swept top. The cabin roof blocks his view of the yard, but he can see over it into the cornfield beyond.

His tongue flicks his lips. The glass lets him see her close up and it's quite a view. Bodice half open, bending slightly with each swipe of the machete. Her breasts creamy brown in the March sunlight.

All alone, too. Not even a squalling brat. He was watching from across the valley when the Utes went off with the papooses. And they ain't come back yet.

His eyes narrow, considering his options. If he gets rid of the bitch after he's done with her, he can move on to the Injun camp and collect the brats. They'll be worth somethin' in the Spanish settlements. Settlers are always buyin' Indian kids to raise. Turn 'em into slaves and make it sound righteous by sayin' they're raisin' 'em Catholic. Civilizing 'em. He snorts. Makin' 'em work for civilizin' they ain't asked for.

Then he shakes his head. But those two are too young. They'd be more trouble than they're worth. Better to just bash their heads in. He grins. That'd be a nice touch of revenge on that bastard Locke. Kill the girl and her spawn, too.

Then Suzanna stops moving. She's looking away from him, toward the mountains. Sure has got her figure back since that baby was born. The big dog snuffs at her feet. Her skirts flare when she kicks it away. She waves the machete and the dog crashes clumsily off across the field. Overgrown pup. If her men think that thing'll protect her, they're in for a shock.

The big man grins. They're in for a shock, all right. When they find him standin' over her, waitin' for them. The look on their faces will almost be better than takin' her. He chuckles and his groin stirs impatiently. Almost.

And now's the time. Finally. It's taken long enough. But everything's got itself arranged to his satisfaction. Men gone. Kids out of the way. He grins, then scowls. It's about time.

He moves carefully away from the pines and eases down the slope to the top of the gully between the hill and the cabin, then down the ice-slicked ravine to the edge of the marsh.

He glances up at the cabin and the woodshed, then slips around the base of the hill to where he can just see the corn patch. She's still there. Heading west, chopping stalks. Talkin' to herself, from the sound of it. Or the dog.

The remaining rows of dead corn are all that screen him from her view. He needs to move quickly, while she's still pointed at the mountains. He crouches and scuttles toward the field, taking the low spots wherever he can.

When he reaches the edge of the patch, he pauses, listening. Then he grins. Mad at her esposo, huh? Well, he'll give her somethin' more to be mad at him about. Locke left her here alone, didn't he? But then, maybe she's mad enough at him that she'll be wantin' to play with someone else for a change.

Jones chuckles, deep in his throat, where she can't hear, and moves forward, stalking his prey.

CHAPTER 50

Suzanna machetes her way to the top of another row. Six down, ten to go. She pauses and looks down the field. Chaser is lying on the grass at the edge of the patch, watching her.

"Lazy dog," Suzanna says, but she doesn't really mean it. Her forehead is beaded with sweat. She wipes at it with the back of her hand and takes a deep breath of the spring air. She's feeling better. This exercise is what she's needed. Even though Gerald seems to think she should be tied to that dark cabin, the only light the lamp and the fire.

The thought brings back her anger. She scowls and moves between the rows to tackle the next set of stalks. "Just can't see!" she mutters as the machete blade bites into the woody stems.

As she moves down the row, Chaser suddenly jumps to his feet and barks sharply. Suzanna glances toward him. Deer on the hillside? But the dog's teeth are bared and he's looking at the field behind her, not the hill above. She turns more fully to follow his gaze and her mouth opens in shock.

Enoch Jones grins at her. He's perhaps six feet away, his shoulders massive under a filthy wool shirt that might have once been bright red. "Can't see me, either, can you?" he sneers.

She takes a step back. Chaser moves toward her.

Jones barks in amusement. "That all you got to protect you? That overgrown pup?"

Suzanna shifts the machete in her hand.

"That dog and a big knife?" Jones jeers. He moves toward her. He's perhaps three feet away now, almost close enough to grab her. He grins lasciviously. "That man a yours just don't care anymore, does he?"

She glances toward the cabin.

Jones snorts. "I know there ain't no one up there. I seen 'em leave. Them and those Utes with the brats. There ain't even Injuns around t' protect you."

Suzanna swallows her fear and lifts her chin, forcing her voice steady. "What do you want?"

His hands open as he lifts them, palms up. "Just wanted to talk. Got somethin' you oughta know."

"You know nothing that I want to hear." She moves backward a single step. Chaser's shoulder brushes the back edge of her skirt.

Jones takes a step closer. "Somethin' about your man. Him and his lies."

She licks her dry lips and throws more intensity into her voice. "You have nothing to say that I want to hear!"

He chuckles. "Smart one, ain't ya?" His eyes run over her body and she takes another step back. Chaser's beside her now, his eyes fixed on the big man.

Jones matches Suzanna's movement, maintaining the distance between them. His fists open and close. "You always thought you were smarter'n the rest of us. Smarter'n me." Then he grins. "But you didn't even know I was in this valley, did ya? I was watchin' you all along, and you never knew I was here." He barks a laugh. "You and that Locke. You think you're so smart."

Suzanna moves again, sideways toward the edge of the field. Chaser skirts around her and positions himself between her and Jones.

"Good dog," Suzanna says. Her voice wobbles slightly and she tightens her grip on the machete.

Jones snorts derisively. "That dog ain't gonna keep you from hearin' what I got to say."

Suzanna braces herself. "Then say it and go."

Jones chuckles. "That what you really want?" He takes another step toward her and Chaser bares his teeth. A growl rumbles from the dog's broad chest.

Jones' eyes are fixed Suzanna's face, his big hands clenching and unclenching as if he's keeping himself under control by sheer willpower. As if he could break her in two.

She digs her heels into the mud. "Say it!"

"That man of yours ain't what you think."

"He's better than you!"

"That why you been so mad at him?"

Her eyes widen. "What are you talking about?"

"I seen you. Stompin' away. Refusin' his kisses."

She swallows against the sudden bile in her throat. "You really have been spying on us," she whispers.

He snorts. "I told you I was." Then he scowls. "You better start listenin' to me, bitch." He takes another step toward her. Chaser growls menacingly and edges closer to Suzanna.

Jones glances at him. "Useless pup," he says.

Chaser growls again.

Jones is so close now that Suzanna can smell the filth of him, a combination of dried sweat, blood, and something else. Fecal matter. "Get away from me," she croaks.

Then his left hand is on her right arm and the mastiff is springing, pushing Suzanna to one side. The dog has the big man's arm in his teeth, and Jones is staggering against Chaser's weight, his feet stumbling on the frozen ruts in the field. Suzanna, more accustomed to the rough surface, jumps to one side, out of the way.

"You bastard!" Jones howls at the dog. He raises his arm, trying to pull it away from the mastiff's grip, but Chaser's jaw simply tightens as the dog lifts onto his hind legs, growls rolling out of his chest.

Jones wrenches his arm higher, out of the dog's reach, and Chaser lets it go, steps back, and then springs for Jones' throat instead.

When the mastiff hits Jones' chest, the man topples and crashes sideways into the dead corn stalks. Chaser's growl is stronger now, not a warning but a promise. His teeth cut into the big man's throat. Jones shoves upward, trying to fend him off. Chaser doesn't budge. Then Jones' hands move underneath the mastiff's chest, shoving with the right, fumbling with the left.

Suzanna gasps as a long-bladed knife appears in Jones' left hand. The steel flashes in the sun as Jones bellows with rage and reaches up and around the dog, stabbing at his back.

Chaser leaps away, back into the frozen mud. Then he turns to face Jones head on, eyes mere slits of wolf-like light. He's silent now, completely focused on his opponent, ears flat against his massive head. He darts in, aiming again for the throat.

Jones is still on the ground, but he's kneeling now, and he's ready. He jabs the knife into the dog's chest. Chaser's forward momentum drives the blade deep into his heart. Chaser snarls and then drops, knocking Jones into the dirt as he falls and pinning him to the ground.

Something pulls at Suzanna's skirt. She looks down. Dos and Uno have appeared. They huddle against her and gaze at Jones and Chaser, tangled together in the mud.

Then Jones shoves the dead mastiff off his chest and heaves himself to his feet. He points his dagger-like blade at Suzanna. "See what happens when you get in my way?"

She opens her mouth but no words come out. The Ute dogs huddle closer. Jones snorts and waves his knife at them. "The two of you together ain't worth half of him. And see where he's at?"

Suzanna's hand still grips the machete. "What do you want?" she asks hoarsely.

Jones sticks his knife back into his belt, grins lasciviously, and moves toward her. "You know what I want. You want it, too. What that man a yours got in the way of, that time back in Taos."

So this actually has nothing to do with Gerald. It's simply Jones' desire, so crudely expressed that day so long ago, when he tried to kiss her and Gerald intervened.

"What that cook woman of your pappy's gave me 'fore she died," Jones says.

"So you did kill Chonita." There's anger in her yet. More than fear. She glares at him. "You bastard."

He chuckles. "That's the way." He moves closer, the stink of him smothering her. "Keep talkin' mean like that." He gestures to his groin. "That'll do it."

Her eyes go cold. "You filthy beast."

He chuckles and leans toward her. "I'll start with a kiss."

Suzanna steps backward, moving blindly toward the grass at the edge of the field. The dogs crowd her feet. Jones follows her, still grinning.

Then she realizes what she's doing and stops. Let him stay in the rutted frozen mud. Let it slow him down just a bit.

But he seems to sense what she's thinking. He lunges, shoving her away from the field and onto the grass, and grabs her free arm. The dogs yelp in panic and flee up the hill toward the cabin.

Suzanna jerks her arm, trying to pull away, but Jones' fingers only clamp tighter. "That's more like it," he says. "Keep goin' like that. I like a little fire in my woman."

The bastard! Her grip tightens on the machete and she swings at him wildly. The flat of the blade slaps against his backside.

He twists away, drops her arm, and grins at her with yellow teeth. "That's the way."

307

She springs back, feet braced on the grass, the machete in both hands, and raises the blade straight up in front of her, like a sword. "Get away from me!" she yells.

He snorts disparagingly and crouches into a fighting posture, hands ready to grapple, his eyes amused. "Gonna cut me, huh?" He moves to his right. "That's the way."

Suzanna turns slowly left, following him, her eyes on his leering face. She points the machete's tip straight toward him, keeping him away.

Behind her, a dog yips nervously and another one howls. Suzanna doesn't turn her head. Every muscle is fully alive, tense, preparing for what lies ahead. She loosens her left hand slightly, letting the right settle more firmly onto the machete's smooth cottonwood handle. "Get away from me!" she hisses.

Jones darts in then and she slashes downward, a good solid thrust that slices the sleeve on his lower left arm and draws blood. When he pulls back, he's no longer amused. "Little bitch!" he spits. "You whore!"

She lunges at him, but he dances away, onto the grass. He's quick on his feet for such a big man.

"Two men at a time!" he spits. "Got all sorts of seed in those kids of yours!"

She straightens in shock. "How dare you!"

He snorts and lunges toward her, and Suzanna realizes what he's doing. She swings the machete again and the blade flashes sideways and slaps his right side.

He dances away from the steel, back into the muddy field. "Two men at a time!" he taunts. He kicks aside a broken cornstalk, fumbles at his waistband, and pulls out his knife. He raises it at her in a kind of salute. "So, you wanta play now, do ya?"

He lunges toward her and she jerks back, staying on the grass.

Jones laughs. "That scare you? Didn't even draw blood." His eyes narrow. "You just wait'll I'm through with you, you little bitch. Then you'll know what it means to be scared."

Suzanna steadies her breath. He's saying these things to get her riled, distract her. Her stomach rises in her throat, then she glances at the dead mastiff. A fierce coldness seizes her.

Her chin lifts as she faces the mountain man. He may be a big man, but he's a sloppy one. Living wild has put an edge only on his rapacity. It hasn't made him any more intelligent. Two can play at this game.

"You're a bastard if ever I saw one," she spits. "Did your mother hate you so much that you have to take it out on every woman you happen across?"

"You bitch!" he roars. He lunges toward her, but this time she's ready. She steadies her breath, braces her feet, raises the machete waist-level, and waits.

When he's within striking distance, Suzanna swings her blade up and then sharply sideways and down. The machete cuts deep into his left thigh.

As she jerks the blade away, he howls, "You godforsaken whore!" and stumbles back into the muddy field. He bends over and grabs at his leg. His palm is bloody when he lifts it away and his eyes are mere slits. He moves toward her again, almost as quickly as before, in spite of the wound.

"Go away!" Suzanna screams. She swings again but this time, instead of pulling back Jones twists to one side and leans in. His big hand closes on the machete handle, just above her hands while his knife swings toward her right shoulder.

"No!" Suzanna screams. As his knife comes down, she twists away, but she doesn't let go of her weapon. Her fingers tighten on the smooth wood and she pulls desperately, fighting to break his hold. If she lets go of the machete, he'll use it against her. If she doesn't, he'll pull her into the cornfield with him. Into the mud. Mud now slick from Jones' big feet and his fall. Slick with Chaser's blood.

Suddenly, there's a fury of yipping and growling at Jones' feet. Dos and Uno dance around him, snapping at his ankles, darting backward, then flinging themselves forward again.

As Jones kicks out at them, his grip on the machete loosens slightly. Suzanna's hands tighten and her wrists twist and the handle slips from his grasp.

Jones growls wordlessly and leans toward her, knife slashing. The blade tip slices a thin line across her shoulder and she gasps in shock. Then the dogs are snarling and flinging themselves at Jones and Suzanna is leaping away.

Her hair has come undone and it's tumbled into her face, but her feet are steady on the grass, and she's swinging the machete wildly, despite the pain in her shoulder. A black fury fills her. There's a roaring in her ears and she hardly knows what she's doing. The machete and her arms move as one, as if they have a life of their own.

She wings again and yet again. Her blade slaps something soft and she hears Jones grunt. She slashes sideways and down, into something else, bone hard. Jones laughs and her arms surge with new strength. How dare he?

She slashes, moves sideways, and swings again, harder this time. She's standing in the muddy field now, but it doesn't matter. She's pulling back to swing again.

And then suddenly there's no more resistance. Her blade hits empty air. Suzanna staggers back, the momentum of the empty blow pushing her sideways. She blinks and shakes her head as the bloodlust lifts.

Jones is on the ground in front of her. Blood spurts from his wrist, above the knife still clenched in his fist. There's a long slit in his mud-covered shirt. Yellowish-white snake-like bowels ooze from beneath it, slick in the valley sun. The dirt is slick with blood.

The dogs lie in the mud beside him. Dos's throat is slit and his eyes are milky with death. The gash in Uno's belly seeps blood and bowels. As Suzanna bends toward her, the dog's muzzle twitches, then goes still.

As she straightens, Jones groans and turns his head. His mouth opens. Suzanna jerks back, her blade up, but he doesn't speak. His eyes are glazed.

Suzanna shudders and looks down at her machete. The blade and handle are smeared with red and dotted with mud. Her skirt is spotted with gore. Her hands are cold and sore, but her stiff fingers don't want to release the weapon from their grasp.

She looks again at Jones, then at the dogs. Nausea overwhelms her. She drops her machete into the mud and lurches to the edge of the field, where her knees collapse beneath her. She clutches her stomach, leans forward, and heaves until there's nothing left.

She takes a deep breath, pushes herself to her feet, and straightens wonderingly. She turns slowly, as if seeing the valley, the cabin, and the mountains beyond for the first time. And Gerald. Her babies. "I could have lost them all," she whispers. She covers her face with her hands.

Then there's a rustling sound from the dry cornstalks on the far side of the field. Suzanna leaps to her feet, dashes for her machete, and straightens, feet braced on the frozen mud, ready for whatever comes.

An arm shoves the stalks to one side and Gerald crashes toward her, Ramón at his heels, the lieutenant behind him.

Suzanna drops her weapon and runs into her husband's arms.

311

EPILOGUE

"The calabacitas are coming up nicely," Gerald says as he studies the garden and the green-and-white striped squash peaking from beneath their broad leaves.

"But, once again, the corn is not doing well at all," Suzanna says. She shakes her head. "I suppose I should just concentrate on squash and lettuce and beans and give up on trying to grow maíz. Our growing season is just too righteously short, as Old Bill would say."

She looks down at one-year-old Andrew, who's perched face-out in her arms, and swings him sideways. He crows with laughter. "We'll just have to grow children instead."

"Papa! Mama!" a breathless voice calls from behind them. Alma is running down the path from the cabin, her curly black hair and bonnet bouncing on her back.

"Tío Ramón says to say that the meal, it is ready," the little girl gasps as she slides to a halt beside her father. She tilts into his leg and he reaches to keep her from falling. She grabs at his arm and laughs up at him.

Suzanna chuckles. "Your hair is very disorderly," she says. "Don't you want to be a ladylike little girl?"

Alma's brow furrows. Then she grins. "Not 'specially." She tilts her head. "Eventually?"

Gerald laughs. "That's my girl!" He bends to swing her onto his shoulders.

Suzanna gives him a mock-frown. "You are making it absolutely impossible for me to train her properly. She is becoming quite willful."

He grins at her. "So she *is* learning from you!"

Suzanna shakes her head at him, then looks up at Alma. Her eyes narrow. "You should at least try to keep your bonnet on. The sun is making your skin splotchy."

"Spoch!" Andrew crows

Gerald laughs. "He certainly picks up the oddest words to repeat. He's quite the scholar!"

Suzanna grins. "It may be a little early to determine that." Then she nods at Alma. "Although I do think my winter project this year is going to be to try to get some learning into his sister. It's time she knows how to read."

The little girl looks down at her thoughtfully, then at the squash and corn beyond. "I'll read about plants!"

Gerald grins and tilts his head to give her a mischievous look. "Just like your mother?"

Alma nods vigorously. "With no bonnet!"

Suzanna chuckles and shakes her head. "I foresee trouble ahead," she says as Gerald turns and she follows him up the path to the cabin. "Trouble twice over!" she says to Andrew, who gurgles happily and waves his arms at the long valley and the gleaming pine-covered mountains.

THE END

NOTE TO READER

In most people's minds, the words "New Mexico" trigger visions of blue skies and sunshine. New Mexico does indeed have plenty of sunshine and an abundance of blue sky. But even in the Land of Enchantment, the weather varies from location to location. Other aspects of the landscape also change. New Mexico isn't entirely blooming cholla, the smell of creosote bush, and dry shades of red and brown.

The Sangre de Cristo mountains where *Not My Father's House* takes place are both greener and wetter than much of the rest of the State. The location where I imagine the Locke cabin (today's Eagle Nest area) averages 15.38 inches of rain a year. This is in sharp contrast to Las Cruces in southern New Mexico, which receives 6.28 inches, or even Albuquerque, in the center of the State, which averages 8.65 inches.

New Mexico's Sangre de Cristo range is pocketed with valleys like the one in this novel. Many contain villages that were established in the 1700s—locations such as Chimayó (1706), Quemado (before 1748), Truchas (1752), and Las Trampas (1751). The moisture these settlements receive and the rich soil that surrounds them provide opportunities for garden and cash crops that wouldn't survive in dryer climates.

But one of the downsides of living in the mountains is the way the peaks block the rising and setting sun and effectively shorten the available daylight hours. If you're used to the lingering sunsets of Albuquerque, Santa Fe, and Taos, the way the light is rapidly extinguished by the Moreno Valley's western peaks can be a bit of a shock. And when the winter rain and snow clouds descend, the days can seem very short indeed.

Nowadays, our response to short dark days is to flip a light switch. But this wasn't possible in the late 1820s and early 1830s, when *Not My Father's House* takes place. The only sources of indoor lighting available then were firelight, candles, and oil lamps.

On the eastern part of the continent, these light sources were supplemented during the day by the sun shining through glass windows. But glass windowpanes were a rare luxury in New Mexico until the railroads arrived in the 1880s. Though glass was available before then, it had to be transported in mule-drawn wagons over the roughly 800 mile Santa Fe Trail from Missouri or the 2,000 mile Camino Real from Mexico City via Chihuahua. This made it expensive.

Instead of using glass, windows in most 1830s New Mexico houses were open to the air and barred with carved wooden grills or thin sticks set into the adobe walls. At night or in foul weather, heavy wooden shutters were fastened over the openings to protect the occupants from the cold. During the winter, thin semi-transparent animal hides or waxed cloth might be tacked up to keep the cold and wet outside during the day while still allowing a little, albeit heavily-filtered, light inside.

In wealthier homes, sheets of selenite, or mica, were set into the window aperture. These milky-white, uneven panes could be as much as 10 inches wide and high and provided protection from the elements while allowing more light inside than did waxed cloth or scraped hide. But they weren't nearly as transparent as glass. In fact, they weren't really transparent at all. They allowed some light inside, but anyone inside couldn't see through them and the light was refracted by the veins and varying thickness of the panes. That's why Suzanna gets so frustrated when she's trying to distinguish between black and dark blue thread in the dim winter light from her cabin window. Even though the mica set into the frame is a luxury, it still doesn't provide the light she needs.

But then, Suzanna doesn't just need light in order to be able to sew. She suffers from what will be identified as Seasonal Affective Disorder, or SAD, in the mid-1980s, 150 years after this story's time frame.

According to the Mayo Clinic, symptoms of SAD include feeling depressed; low energy levels; changes in appetite or weight; feeling sluggish or agitated; difficulty concentrating; feeling hopeless, worthless, or guilty; and frequent thoughts of death or suicide.

Although SAD can occur any time of year, Suzanna's hits her in the wintertime and is exacerbated by postpartum depression. The depression, fatigue, and guilt she feels are characteristic of both conditions, while her mood swings and frequent crying bouts are classic symptoms of postpartum, as are her intense irritability and her difficulty bonding with her newborn.

I've imagined Suzanna as suffering from what most scientists today consider the second form of three identified postpartum conditions. The first, which is the most common and the least severe, is often called the "baby blues". Fifty to eighty percent of new mothers experience this type of postpartum, but they usually recover within a couple weeks.

The second form, postpartum depression, is more severe than the baby blues and affects eight to twelve percent of women after childbirth. Clinicians describe it as a middle-range clinical depression that isn't actually psychotic.

The third form of postpartum is a psychosis so strong that a mother might actually kill herself or her child. In *Not My Father's House,* Suzanna isn't depressed enough to do away with her baby or herself. But she is definitely depressed. As Old Bill Williams would probably put it, she's just righteously buffaloed and a little loco, too.

If Suzanna lived in the United States instead of New Mexico during the late 1820s and early 1830s, she might well have been placed under a doctor's care. It's probably just as well that she was in nuevomexico. At the time, typical East Coast treatments for postpartum included physical restraint and bloodletting. A more advanced physician might have also prescribed an early form of electroshock therapy.

Other options included water immersion, in which the patient was held underwater until they almost drowned, and spinning. Spinning involved whirling a new mother on a special stool designed to make her dizzy. The idea was that the dizziness would rearrange her brain contents into their correct positions.

Nowadays, treatment for postpartum depression is more likely to range from antidepressants to a less medicated approach. The strategies implemented today instead of medication are similar to those Gerald and Ramón make possible for Suzanna—plenty of rest, help from others, and physical activity. In Suzanna's case, physical activity means gardening. An additional benefit of this strategy is that it gets her outside and into the sunshine she so desperately needs to stave off her seasonal affective disorder.

Gardening may fight Suzanna's postpartum depression and SAD, but it also produces its own set of frustrations. Although she's raised corn, potatoes, lettuce, squash, and other produce in Taos, the Moreno Valley is 1,000 feet higher in altitude. The growing season is shorter and the daylight hours are reduced by the proximity of the mountains. Learning just what she can and can't grow in her new home is an ongoing experiment.

In my personal experience, cool weather plants such as peas, spinach, and chard can be grown successfully in the Moreno Valley. Experienced gardeners there tell me potatoes also do well, but trying to raise corn, chile, and other plants that need a long, warm growing season is simply an exercise in frustration. Of the three crops most often associated with New Mexico (chile, corn, and squash), only certain types of squash will grow at elevations of 8,000 feet and above. Even then, as Suzanna discovers, the season may not be long enough for a satisfactory yield.

While New Mexico's northern mountains are problematic for growing warm weather crops, in the early 1800s they were an excellent location for stashing goods and furs going to and from New Mexico. Although Lieutenant Gabaldón de Anaya is a fictional character, the attitudes and frustrations he expresses in this novel reflect those of New Mexico's government officials at the time.

The smuggling activities of americano merchants and trappers like Ceran St. Vrain, Ewing Young, and Old Bill Williams were a constant source of irritation to the officials responsible for assessing and collecting customs duties in New Mexico. During the time period covered by *Not My Father's House,* one of the government responses to this problem was to base a troop of soldiers in Taos. The troop's primary task was to monitor the smuggling activities of the trappers and merchants in the area, a task made more difficult by the ruggedness and sheer volume of the nearby mountains.

Goods were smuggled across the Sangre de Cristo (literally Blood of Christ) mountains in both directions. Furs cached there were moved east onto the plains to the wagon trains headed for Missouri. Wagons heading west could pause east of the mountains at Point of Rocks, load merchandise onto pack mules, and send them directly to Taos, thus avoiding the customs officials in Santa Fe. This kind of activity is described in *Not Just Any Man,* the prequel to *Not My Father's House.*

Once in Taos, the goods could be distributed surreptitiously to the various American merchants or sold directly to the public. At least one American-owned distillery in the area was constructed over subterranean spaces where merchandise could be stored until it could be safely brought out for sale.

Besides stationing soldiers in Taos, customs officials also dispatched soldiers onto the eastern plains to intercept traders before they had an opportunity to send their goods over the mountains. In the spring of 1830, General José Antonio Vizcarra and his men stopped at least one American caravan to investigate what it was carrying. That particular wagon train included Ceran St. Vrain and presumably carried some of his merchandise.

Of course, smuggling goods into the country without paying import fees on them was only profitable if there was a market for the items smuggled, customers who didn't care whether the goods for sale were legal or not. And there was definitely a market. In fact, some New Mexicans who bought merchandise tax-free may have actually felt they were making a political statement by doing so.

Taxes were something of a sore point in New Mexico. Under the Spanish, the region had not been required to pay taxes to the Crown, but when Mexico gained its independence from Spain, the new government needed more revenue. Assessments increased accordingly and so did discontent. In 1837, the threat of additional taxes became a rallying cry for revolt in the mountains of northern New Mexico.

That revolt is the framework for *No Secret Too Small* (2020), the next Old New Mexico novel, in which Gerald and Suzanna's marriage will be tested to the breaking point. I hope you will be as interested as I am to find out whether their relationship, after recovering from Suzanna's postpartum depression and Enoch Jones' attack, can survive yet more disruption.

Not only will revolt threaten their way of life, but Suzanna will discover that her upstanding husband has not been entirely forthcoming about his past. I'm sure she'll have something interesting to say about that. But will she forgive him?

HISTORICAL CHARACTERS
IN NOT MY FATHER'S HOUSE

Archuleta, Jesus Ruperto Valdez 'Pepe' (?-after 1911) Bill Williams' camp follower from 1830 to Williams' death in 1848. Archuleta and Williams met somewhere in the Taos area when Archuleta was quite young. The scene in this novel in which they meet at the Locke home is my invention. Archuleta accompanied Williams on trapping and horse-raiding trips to the Rockies, Idaho, Yellowstone, and California and was probably with Williams on the fateful 1848 John Fremont expedition that ultimately led to Williams' death. Archuleta eventually moved to the St. Louis area, where he was living in 1911 when he gave an interview about his adventures to the *St. Louis Globe-Democrat*.

Beaubien, Charles 'Carlos' (1800-1864) Quebec-born trapper of aristocratic French-Canadian descent who arrived in New Mexico in early 1824. Beaubien gave up trapping relatively early to become a merchant in Taos. He married María Paulita Lobato of Taos in 1827 and applied for Mexican citizenship two years later. In 1841 Beaubien was co-grantee, along with Provincial Secretary Guadalupe Miranda, of what would become the Maxwell Land Grant in Colfax County. Following the 1846 American invasion, Beaubien was named one of New Mexico's three Superior Court justices. His 14-year-old son Narciso was killed during the 1847 Taos Revolt.

Bent, Charles (1799-1847) Mountain man turned merchant whose first venture into the West was with General William Ashley's 1822 trapping excursion up the Missouri River. He moved from there to a more investment and sales-oriented strategy, as a partner in the Missouri Fur Company, as a subagent to the Iowa

Indians, and as a merchant with an 1829 caravan to Taos. Bent remained in New Mexico and joined Ceran St. Vrain in a mercantile venture that included a store on the south side of Taos plaza. In the early 1830s, he and his brothers also constructed a fort on the Arkansas River, just north of the U.S./Mexico border, a location which became a major rest point on the Santa Fe Trail. Following the U.S. invasion in the spring of 1846, Bent was appointed governor of New Mexico. He was killed the following January during the Taos revolt.

Carson, Christopher 'Kit' (1809-1868) Mountain man and trapper famous for guiding Colonel John Fremont to California in the 1840s and infamous for his part in forcing the Navajo from their lands and onto the Bosque Redondo reservation in the 1860s. Carson was a teenager when he arrived in New Mexico in late 1826, shortly before the beginning of this novel.

Martínez, Padre Antonio José (1793-1867) Member of a prominent Taos family and the Catholic priest there from 1826 to 1857. Padre Martínez also operated a printing press, a school, and a Catholic seminary in Taos. He played a leading role in New Mexico politics under both the Mexican and American governments.

Pratte, Sylvester (1799-1827) Trapper and investor who arrived in New Mexico in 1825. As the representative of the St. Louis-based Bernard Pratte & Co. fur trading firm, he led trapping parties and funded others' endeavors as well as his own. Pratte died in late 1827 in what is now Colorado during an expedition in which Old Bill Williams and others participated. The injury and subsequent amputation of Thomas L. Smith's left foot that Williams describes in this novel occurred on that trip.

Smith, Thomas Long 'Peg Leg' (1801-1866) Trapper who would become famous as the mountain man with the missing foot. Smith was in New Mexico by 1824. In 1829 he joined Sylvester

Pratte's trapping expedition to Colorado. During that hunt, Smith received a leg wound that required amputation of his left foot, the incident Old Bill Williams describes in this novel. Smith was known the rest of his life as Peg Leg Smith. He died in San Francisco in 1866, where he had been making a living retelling his adventures.

St. Vrain, Ceran (1802-1870) Taos-based trapper and trader who was a descendant of French nobility and was the nephew of the last Spanish lieutenant governor of Louisiana. St. Vrain grew up in St. Louis and arrived in Santa Fe in March 1825 with a William Becknell wagon train. He remained in New Mexico the rest of his life, working as a trapper, trader, and then building a grist mill in Mora. A big man who made friends easily, he had four children, each by a different woman, and is buried in Mora.

Sublette, Milton (1801?-1837) Kentucky-born descendent of French Huguenot refugees and one of five brothers who all participated in the Rocky Mountain fur trade. Milton and his oldest brother William went West with William Ashley's 1823 trapping expedition. Over six feet tall, Sublette had a reputation for audacity and recklessness that earned him the nickname 'Thunderbolt of the Rocky Mountains.' He assisted Thomas Smith in amputating Smith's foot.

Williams, William Sherley 'Old Bill' (1787-1849) Garrulous mountain man with a gift for languages who left his Missouri home at age sixteen to live among the Osage Indians. He hunted with the Osage in the Rocky Mountains and headed there permanently in the mid 1820s after his Osage wife's death. Based in Taos, the lean red-headed Williams had a taste for gambling and Taos Lightning, and a propensity for trapping on his own or with only a camp keeper as companion, a role filled by Pepe Archuleta after 1830. Williams was a self-confident man with strong opinions. After John C. Fremont hired him to guide an 1848 expedition across the Rockies, then didn't follow his advice, the party became trapped by harsh winter conditions. Twenty-one of the group's thirty-two men died in the subsequent attempt to escape. Williams himself died several months later as the result of an effort to retrieve the party's abandoned records and equipment.

Wolfskill, William (1798-1866) Kentucky-born merchant and trapper who arrived in New Mexico with William Becknell's 1822 train over the Santa Fe Trail. Wolfskill plays an important role in the previous novel, *Not Just Any Man*. In the late 1820s, he led a party of roughly twenty men across the Great Basin into southern California and settled there permanently. He and his brother and sons created an agricultural venture that introduced the Australian eucalyptus, the soft-shelled almond, the chestnut, and the persimmon to California.

Young, Ewing (1793?-1841) Farmer with carpenter's training who became a mountain man. In early 1822, Young sold his newly-acquired Missouri farm and joined William Becknell's second caravan to New Mexico. There, he and William Wolfskill engaged in mercantile trade and also led trapping expeditions, including the one to the Gila/Salt/Colorado River that Gerald Locke, Jr. and Enoch Jones are members of in *Not Just Any Man* and the hunt that Young invites Gerald to join in this novel. In 1830, Young led a party of trappers to California and stayed on the West Coast, eventually settling permanently in Oregon.

LIST OF SOURCES

Cobos, Rubén. *A Dictionary of New Mexico and Southern Colorado Spanish.* Santa Fe: Museum of New Mexico Press, 2003.

———. *Refranes, Southwestern Spanish Proverbs.* Santa Fe: Museum of New Mexico Press, 1985.

Dimino, Debora K. "Postpartum Depression: A Defense for Mothers Who Kill Their Infants." *Santa Clara Law Review* 231, No. 1 (1990): 230-264.

Etulain, Richard W., ed. *New Mexican Lives, profiles and historical stories.* Albuquerque: University of New Mexico Press, 2002.

Favour, Alpheus H. *Old Bill Williams, Mountain Man.* Norman: University of Oklahoma Press, 1936.

Hadley, Craig, ed. *A Nineteenth Century Slang Dictionary.* Accessed November 15, 2018. https://mess1.homestead. com/nineteenth_century_slang_dictionary.pdf.

Hafen, Leroy R., ed. *Fur Trappers and Traders of the Far Southwest.* Logan: Utah State University Press, 1972.

———. *The Mountain Men and the Fur Trade of the Far West.* Spokane: Arthur H. Clark, 1968.

Johnson, Michael G. *Encyclopedia of Native Tribes of North America.* Buffalo: Firefly Books, 2014.

Márquez, Rubén Sálaz. *New Mexico, a brief multi-history.* Albuquerque: Cosmic House, 1999.

Mayo Clinic. "Postpartum Depression." Accessed July 17, 2017. https://www.mayoclinic.org/diseases-conditions/ postpartum-depression/.

Mayo Clinic. "Seasonal Affective Disorder (SAD)." Accessed December 12, 2018. http://www.mayoclinic.org/diseases-conditions/seasonal-affective-disorder/.

Moore, Michael. *Medicinal Plants of the Desert and Canyon West*. Santa Fe: Museum of New Mexico Press, 1989.

Moreno Valley Writers Guild. *Lure, Lore, and Legends, a history of Northern New Mexico's Moreno Valley*. Angel Fire: Columbine Books, 1997.

Paterek, Josephine. *Encyclopedia of American Indian Costume*. New York: W.W. Norton, 1994.

Nemade, Rashmi. "Historical Understandings of Depression Continued." Gulf Bend Center. Accessed December 21, 2018. https://www.gulfbend.org/poc.

Rockwell, Wilson. *The Utes, a forgotten people*. Montrose: Western Reflections, 2006.

Simmons, Marc. *Coronado's Land, essays on daily life in Colonial New Mexico*. Albuquerque: University of New Mexico Press, 1991.

Weber, David J. *The Taos Trappers, the fur trade in the far southwest, 1540-1846*. Norman: University of Oklahoma Press, 1970.

Made in the USA
Middletown, DE
15 January 2022

58754787R00186